LASSOED Love

ANN EINERSON

Cover Character Art by @chelseakemp_art
Cover Design by @madicantstopreading
Dev Edited by @bryannareads
Edited by Britt Tayler, Jenny Sims Editing4Indies
Proofread by Virginia Carey
Formatted by Champagne Book Design

For the girls searching for their happily ever after, sometimes it's the possessive cowboy who's been pining after you for years. And to that, I say ruin the friendship.

PLAYLIST

You Look Like You Love Me—Ella Langley, Riley Green

What Ifs—Kane Brown (feat. Lauren Alaina)

Cowgirl—Parmalee

Drink Alone—Tucker Wetmore

Beautiful As You—Zack Hood

In Case You Didn't Know—Brett Young

Country House—Sam Hunt

Wranglers on the Floor—Kingery

What My World Spins Around—Jordan Davis

Sober—Hudson Westbrook

Country Boy's Dream Girl—Ella Langley

Worst Way—Riley Green

Friends Don't—Maddie & Tae

Man I Need—Olivia Dean

Wood—Taylor Swift

AUTHOR'S NOTE

Hey, Reader!

Thank you for picking up *Lassoed Love,* where spicy lessons turn into undeniable chemistry, blurred lines, and broken rules between a reformed cowboy Casanova and the girl he's secretly pined after for years in this steamy, friends-to-lovers, fake-dating, small-town romance.

The FMC's mom has young-onset Parkinson's disease. This depiction reflects one possible experience shaped by the story's unique circumstances. While informed by firsthand experiences, creative liberties were taken to support the characters' emotional journeys. This portrayal is not meant to reflect every person's experience with Parkinson's disease.

Lassoed Love contains explicit sexual content, profanity, and parental chronic illness.

Lastly, this is a work of fiction, and while I aim for accuracy, some details have been altered for storytelling purposes.

Reading is meant to be your happy place—choose yourself, your needs, and your happiness first!

Xoxo,
Ann Einerson

LASSOED *Love*

CHAPTER 1

Mugshots & Secret Obsessions

Walker

"**W**ELL, I'LL BE DAMNED IF IT ISN'T MY FAVORITE REPEAT offender," I drawl.

Birdie glares at me from the wooden bench inside the jail cell. Her pink overalls are rumpled, and the floral bandana she's wearing has shifted, letting loose strands fall around her flushed face.

She points a finger in my direction. "If you're responsible for this, I'm totally putting glitter in your body wash the next time I'm at the ranch, *Deputy*."

Damn, she's sexy as hell when she's riled up.

I stifle a laugh as I fold my arms across my chest. "You're awfully mouthy for someone behind bars."

Birdie stands and crosses the small space, tipping her chin to peer up at me through the metal bars separating us. Her head barely reaches my chest, but her glare is downright lethal.

"And you're awfully smelly for someone who just started their shift."

I frown and subtly sniff the collar of my shirt, instantly wrinkling my nose. I guess mucking stalls before coming in for my shift wasn't the best idea. But skipping it would've earned me a lecture from Heath, and after a busy week of filing disorderly conduct reports, chasing down old man Grady's runaway pigs again, and breaking up bar fights fueled by cheap whiskey, I've run out of patience to deal with my brother.

"So… you playing good or bad cop this morning?" Birdie chirps.

The corner of my mouth quirks up. "That depends. You have anything you want to confess?"

I had nothing to do with her ending up in here, and I fully intend to let her go—but it's one of the rare moments I get to be alone with her, and I'm not about to waste it.

"Nope," Birdie replies, popping the P. "Why don't you be a gentleman and break me out of this joint?" She lightly raps the lock with her knuckles.

I chuckle, adjusting the brim of my cowboy hat. "Now why would I do that when we're having so much fun together?"

She shrugs. "Because friendship comes with built-in jailbreak privileges."

Her use of the word "friendship" makes me wince.

"Even if they're guilty as sin?" I walk over to the desk in the corner and grab Birdie's file. "Trespassing and stealing farm animals aren't exactly minor offenses. Who's to say if I let you go that you wouldn't nab an unsuspecting goat on your way home?"

She rolls her eyes. "As deputy sheriff, you should know that Montana doesn't have many stray goats roaming the countryside. And for the record, it's rescuing, not stealing," she adds, raising a finger for emphasis. "Those animals were neglected, and someone had to step in before it was too late."

I arch a brow. "That sounded an awful lot like a confession."

One I'd reject even if she came clean, but Birdie's too clever to jeopardize the animal sanctuary she runs out of her house.

"*What?* N-no," she stammers. "I'm just saying that whoever did was probably trying to protect them. Everyone at the fair could see how miserable they looked. The baby cow had a limp, and the donkey had the saddest eyes I've ever seen... uh, at least that's what I heard," she corrects herself. "If that's the case, it would have been cruel to split them up at auction—or worse, to let someone send them to the slaughterhouse." She blows out a long breath, briefly closing her eyes.

Birdie's reaction isn't surprising. She's fiercely protective of vulnerable animals and has a reputation for going to great lengths to keep them safe. Even when it lands her in a cold jail cell overnight. Though since her dad's the sheriff, she normally gets off with a slap on the wrist.

Mason really screwed up bringing her in. It's only his second week on the job, and he should have known better. Lucky for him, Sheriff Matterson has been out of town all week—but unlucky for him, I'm just as protective of Birdie, and he'll quickly learn what happens when he treats her like a common criminal. My blood boils just thinking about him hauling her in here. If he had used cuffs, I'd be sitting in a cell of my own for teaching him a hard lesson about touching what's mine.

Okay, she's technically not mine *yet*, but anyone who crosses her will have to answer to me.

I pull Birdie's mugshot from her file, taken when Mason brought her in last night. She stands straight, facing the camera with an unapologetic smile like she's posing for a Christmas card instead of a booking photo. Even now, with fatigue dulling her eyes and loose strands of hair clinging to her cheeks, she's the kind of beautiful that makes my chest tighten.

I hold out the mugshot so Birdie can see it through the bars.

"This little gem is prime blackmail material, don't you think? I bet Charlie would give anything to get her hands on this."

Charlie is one of her best friends. She's a total firecracker and has a weakness for town gossip.

Birdie snorts. "Try it, and I'll tell everyone about the time you got spooked by a mouse in the tack room and screamed like a girl."

A smirk tugs at my lips as I fold the paper into fourths and tuck it into my shirt pocket. As fun as it is to tease her, I have no intention of letting anyone else see her mugshot.

"Can't do that if I keep you locked up."

I quickly shut down the intrusive thought, ignoring how tempting it would be to have unlimited access to her.

Birdie's eyes twinkle, holding me pinned in place. "We both know Briar would never forgive you if you kept me in here."

I scoff. "I'm not afraid of my sister."

Okay, maybe just a little. Behind Briar's brilliant smile is a force of nature when it comes to protecting her friends.

"Maybe. Maybe not." She grips the bars as she angles her face closer. "Still, I'd hate for you to have to explain to her and Charlie why I spent the night shivering and starving while you did nothing to intervene."

Birdie knows full well my shift only started an hour ago, but she isn't above using a little creative license to get a rise out of me—and she's succeeding brilliantly.

I should've figured this could happen with Mason left alone on duty. One of his many shortcomings is his inability to cover even the basics for someone in custody. There's not even a god-damn pillow or blanket in Birdie's cell, and it's a good thing I arrived when I did, or she might've been in far worse shape than just uncomfortable.

My hands twitch at my sides, fists tightening as guilt settles in my chest. I would've come sooner if I'd known, but I was caught up delivering a calf, and complications kept me busy until well past dawn.

I only work three shifts a week as a volunteer deputy. The rest of my time goes to running Silver Saddle Ranch with Heath. Still, I should've kept a closer eye on Birdie with Sheriff Matterson out of town. She's one of my sister's best friends and as sweet as they come, yet she somehow manages to cause more trouble than anyone I've ever met.

"Let me guess—you spent the night at Blue Moon Tavern, and had to drag yourself out of some woman's bed for this?" Birdie chimes in when I don't respond right away. "You do have a knack for getting yourself into questionable positions…" My lips twitch into a crooked grin, and when she looks at me, a rosy blush spreads across her cheeks. "Uh… I just mean that you're popular with the ladies."

She's so damn cute when she's flustered.

I take a step closer to her cell. "Are you jealous, Birdie?"

"Me? Jealous? That's absurd." She scoffs, the flush on her cheeks deepening.

Admittedly, I had more than my fair share of flings back in high school and my early twenties. In a town this small, gossip spreads like wildfire, and my past still precedes me. Sure, there were perks, like women bringing me homemade pie to the station and constantly approaching me at the bar, but the thrill quickly faded.

These days, I prefer my nights low-key, and yes, sometimes that means keeping tabs on the one woman who doesn't seem interested in anything more than friendship.

Birdie tips her head, rocking back on her heels. "So are you planning to bust me out of here, or am I calling this cell my home until my dad's back? If I'm staying, you're in charge of feeding my animals. That means stopping by three times a day—Nugget expects her midday snack of cheese and mealworms at two, and

Pickles won't touch her slop unless there are apple slices mixed in. Thin ones, not chunks. I made that mistake last month, and she flipped the trough. She held a grudge until I apologized with a peace offering of warm, molasses-soaked oats." Birdie dramatically wipes her brow and then seems to remember something, adding quickly, "Just don't go in the shed, okay?"

I eye her suspiciously. "Why not?"

She avoids my gaze, suddenly fascinated by the concrete floor. "No reason."

"Any chance I'd stumble across a limping cow or a donkey with sad eyes in there?"

She lets out a nervous giggle, waving me off. "No, nothing like that. It's just a mess. That's where I store all the animal supplies, and I can't organize to save my life."

"I see," I say, tone deliberately neutral.

Even if she weren't the worst liar in Bluebell, the surveillance footage Mason showed me earlier leaves no doubt that my little thief was behind the county fair animal heist everyone's been gossiping about for almost a year. Her face is obscured, but her signature pink overalls and the floral bandana tied at the top of her head might as well be a name tag—which is why that footage will never see the light of day.

My phone buzzes in my pocket, and I check to see that I have a text from my sister.

Briar: We're here. You finished with your power trip yet? I'd like my friend released now.

Walker: She'll be out soon.

When I found out Birdie was in custody, I called Briar so she and Charlie could come get her. Their loyalty runs deep, and they'd do anything for each other. On more than one occasion,

Birdie has roped them into her rescue missions, and they've jumped in to help her, no questions asked.

I grab the key from the desk and unlock the cell, the hinges groaning as the door swings open.

"You're free to go," I tell Birdie.

She doesn't move, like she's unsure if I'm serious.

"Seriously, all of that suspense just to let me loose?"

I shove my hands into my pockets, and rock back on my heels. "Would you rather I scheduled a drop-off at the county jail? They'd be happy to hold you until the sheriff gets back."

Her eyes widen a fraction before she saunters past, giving me a patronizing pat on the chest. "I take it back. Thanks for being so generous."

"Mason's on duty this weekend, so try not to stir up any more trouble unless you want a repeat performance of last night."

"Bummer, I was really looking forward to an encore," she quips, already halfway out the door.

"See you later, troublemaker."

"Bye, Walker," she calls over her shoulder in a singsong voice.

I should feel nothing but relief that she's out of the cell and safe, yet I can't deny I'm disappointed that our conversation was cut short. Most of the time, my sister or other people are around, or we cross paths when she visits her dad. But it's never enough.

With Birdie gone, I remind myself that I'm here to work, not brood. First order of business: take care of some damning evidence.

CHAPTER 2

Fresh Out Of The Slammer

Birdie

As soon as Walker lets me go, I bolt out of the sheriff's office, not taking any chances. I'm at the front entrance of the building, fingers poised on the door handle, when I realize I left my bag behind.

"That's just great," I huff.

I must have left it on the counter when Mason returned my personal belongings. I was so focused on checking my missed calls and messages I didn't look to see if I had everything. I drop my head and groan before forcing myself to trudge back the way I came, bracing for Walker's merciless teasing.

I'm glad it's a Friday and no one else is around this early to witness my second walk of shame this morning. Honestly, it'd be less humiliating if I were sneaking out of someone's apartment after a one-night stand—at least then I'd be exhausted for reasons I could actually brag about.

I've just turned the corner into the processing area when I spot Walker. He's standing by the row of filing cabinets in the corner, head buried in a file. I flatten myself against the wall and carefully peek around it, relieved to see he hasn't noticed me. He's scanning the page, fingers brushing the scruff along his jaw.

The charcoal-gray deputy's button-up is tucked into his Wranglers, and his favorite cowboy hat sits perched on his head. My eyes linger on the way his biceps tighten when he moves his arms. There's no question he's the hottest guy in Bluebell, and plenty have tried to rope him in—but he's also lived up to his reputation, leaving behind a trail of broken hearts.

Stop ogling your friend's brother, Birdie.

I may admire him from afar, but I'm fully aware he has a type, and I've never fooled myself into thinking I'm it. I've always just been his little sister's friend, someone he looks out for, and who, over the past few years, has become a good friend. I accepted long ago that's all I'd ever be, and I'm just glad he doesn't find me too awkward to hang out with like other guys have.

Before I can gather the courage to come out from my hiding spot, Mason storms out of the holding area across the room, his face beet red as he beelines for Walker.

"What the hell did you do with it, Halstead?" he growls.

Walker lifts his head slowly. "Do with what?"

"The video evidence from the fairgrounds. I left it on my desk, and now it's gone." Mason jabs an accusing finger at him. "I've looked everywhere, and it's not here. You're the only other person who's had access to this area, so don't bother lying."

"That's quite the imagination you've got there, kid," Walker drawls, setting his folder on top of the closest filing cabinet. "Shame you lost the tape. It was the only thing tying Birdie to the scene."

It's probably wrong to eavesdrop, but their conversation is about me, so I figure listening a little longer can't hurt.

Mason throws his hands in the air. "Oh, come on. I wasn't born yesterday. She's the sheriff's kid and one of your sister's closest friends. And don't think I didn't notice you two looking rather chummy earlier."

Walker's expression hardens. "Careful. If you're suggesting I'd tamper with evidence because of who the suspect is, you're walking a very fine line." He takes a step closer, looming over Mason. "I've been a deputy for six years without ever giving the sheriff a reason to doubt me. You, on the other hand, have only been here a couple of weeks and will definitely be on his shit list when he finds out you brought his *daughter* in without consulting him first."

My dad might not agree with my methods, but he raised me to stand up for what I believe in, even if it means bending a few rules along the way. But Walker's right—when my dad finds out Mason left me in a holding cell overnight, he'll have some choice words for his newest deputy.

Mason opens his mouth, hesitating, then closes it.

"Figures you wouldn't have a good comeback." Walker scoffs, his gaze returning to the file he'd been reviewing before he was interrupted.

I might've felt a twinge of sympathy for Mason if he hadn't called me stupid for risking my freedom to save Daisy and Peaches. Anyone who treats animals as disposable rather than worth protecting deserves exactly what the universe throws at them.

Deciding I've pushed my luck far enough, I duck around the corner, disappearing from sight. I'll get my bag later.

Besides, even if I asked Walker, he would deny helping me. Whatever he did was probably a favor for my dad or Briar, and he'd likely shrug it off if I tried to thank him. It's best to let him think I'm still in the dark and act surprised if it ever becomes public knowledge.

When I finally step outside, I squint against the sunlight and inhale the sweet scent of blooming flowers. Mason hauled me in right after my second shift at the feed store yesterday, so it was dark when I got here. He probably thought he'd be the hero bringing in the person he assumed was responsible for last year's theft at the county fair, not realizing he'd signed himself up for a world of trouble.

It's not the first time someone's accused me of stealing animals, but I usually walk away with a warning. I probably should have figured my luck would run out eventually, especially with Mason left alone overnight at the station, eager to prove himself.

I'd resigned myself to the possibility of being stuck in that holding cell until my dad got back from his work trip. What I didn't expect was Walker Halstead swooping in to rescue me.

A smile spreads across my face when I see Charlie and Briar waiting at the curb.

"Rough night?" Charlie calls out. "Thank god you weren't sent to county jail because those green uniforms would be unforgiving with your complexion."

I shake my head as I go down the stairs to join them.

"Glad your concern is for my wardrobe and not the fact I spent the night behind bars," I deadpan.

Charlie leans against the hood of her red SUV, grinning. "They took your mugshot, right? I have got to get my hands on it."

I shake my head. "Nope, they didn't," I lie.

Walker better have been kidding about handing it over to her, or I swear I'll make good on my own blackmail threat. Years of hanging out at the Halsteads' ranch means I have more than enough of his secrets stockpiled. Like the time he and Heath crashed their dad's brand-new Ford F-350 and lied, telling him a mule deer darted out of nowhere on the road into town.

As I reach the curb, Briar rushes to me, her hands gripping my shoulders as she scans me from head to toe. "Are you okay? I nearly had a heart attack when Walker called to have us come get you."

"I'm fine," I assure her. "Your brother had his fun teasing me, but don't worry, I got some jabs in too," I add with a small smile.

"You totally got off easy," Charlie interjects, muttering under her breath. "If that had been anyone else, they'd already have been shipped off to county."

I'm sure that was Mason's plan all along, and there's no telling how long I would've been stuck there. A chill runs down my spine just thinking about it.

Briar opens the passenger door of the SUV and grabs a paper bag with the Lasso & Latte logo on it. When she hands it to me, I find an oat milk latte with a dash of cinnamon on top and a blueberry muffin.

"We figured you could use some caffeine and a sweet treat after the morning you had," she says with a sympathetic smile. "It's probably a little cold now, sorry."

I pull the coffee from the bag, letting out a satisfied hum as I take my first sip. "This is perfect, thanks."

By this time most days I'm already three coffees in, so it tastes more like a lifeline than a treat.

"Did you guys get something too?"

Briar nods. "Yeah, we ate while we waited for you."

I turn to Charlie, who's still leaning against the hood of the car. "You got the sugar-free syrup in your drink, right?"

"Yes, *Mom*," she huffs, rolling her eyes. "You do remember I'm a year older than you, right?"

"Technically only by eleven months," I counter. "Yet somehow I'm the one always monitoring your blood sugar."

Charlie was diagnosed with diabetes at sixteen, and even though the owner of the coffee shop stocks her favorite sugar-free red velvet syrup, she prefers to order the regular syrup when I'm not there to stop her from turning her coffee into a sugar bomb. She's stubborn to the core and not even a serious medical diagnosis can compete with her sweet tooth.

Being the youngest in our friend group hasn't spared me from being teased for mothering everyone. Am I overly cautious? Absolutely. But after having to step up when my mama's health declined a few years ago, it's become second nature to take care of the people I care about, particularly when it involves medical issues that could easily take a turn for the worse.

"Why don't we save the bickering for later," Briar suggests, trying to lighten the mood. "Let's get our girl home to rest."

"Sounds great," I agree, my eyes stinging from the lack of sleep.

The wooden bench in the cell offered zero comfort, and Mason kept me awake most of the night with *The Great British Bake-Off* blaring from the other room. Not exactly the kind of show I'd imagine someone watching who likes to play the tough guy. Every underbaked cupcake and overwhipped batch of cream was met with him shouting at the TV, and by the time I finally drifted off, sunlight was starting to stream through the single window in the cell.

I slide into the back seat of Charlie's SUV, setting my coffee in the holder and sinking into the headrest as the fatigue finally catches up with me. To keep myself awake, I check my phone and find a string of worried texts from Wren, the latest sent a few minutes ago. Charlie and Briar must have looped her in when they found out what happened.

Wren: Please tell me you survived your stint in jail.

Birdie: Barely. It's a miracle I didn't come out with a tattoo and a nickname that Charlie would never let me live down.

Wren: Did she get a copy of your mugshot yet? I have to see it immediately.

I let out a theatrical sigh.

> Birdie: Ugh, not you too! You're supposed to be on my side.

Wren: One of my best friends ends up in a holding cell, and you expect me not to want to see the proof? Please.

> Birdie: Sorry. There was no mugshot.

This time, I feel zero guilt lying about it.

Wren: Such a tragedy.

"It's absolutely not," I mutter quietly.

Charlie throws a glance at me through the rearview mirror as she drives down Main Street. "What are you mumbling about back there? You should be celebrating now that you're a free woman, not sulking like someone stole your muffin."

I look up from my phone. "Just checking in with Wren."

The four of us have been friends since kindergarten and were inseparable through high school. I used to think we'd all stay in Bluebell forever until Wren dropped the bombshell that she was moving to Florida with Cole, her boyfriend. We've never been a fan of his, but after they had Lottie, we knew she wasn't coming back. At least our group chat keeps her in the loop on all the town gossip.

Charlie lets out an exaggerated gasp. "She's texting you outside the group chat. The audacity."

There's no way I'm telling her what Wren is pestering me for, or she'd probably flip a U-turn and march into the sheriff's office herself.

"Wren probably figured staying off the chat would keep you from being distracted and avoid getting pulled over again for texting while driving," Briar says from the passenger seat, smirking.

Charlie got lucky when Walker pulled her over and let her

off with a warning since it was her first offense this year. I'm not the only one with a knack for bending the rules—me for my unauthorized animal rescues, her for breaking traffic laws.

"Birdie was texting me while being chased by that angry goose she found on the roadside. How could I not reply and tell her to record it?" Charlie asks innocently.

It was terrifying in the moment, but I caved and got her the video. I nearly died tripping over a rock while trying to capture the raging goose that looked ready to eat me for an afternoon snack, but against all odds, I managed to walk away with only a scraped knee while still somehow rescuing the ungrateful bird in the process.

I open my mouth to reply, but my tongue refuses to form words as I struggle to stay awake, the rhythm of the car lulling me closer to sleep. As Charlie and Briar carry on about her questionable driving habits, my eyelids grow heavy and my phone slides from my hand onto my lap as I nod off.

"Birdie. It's time to wake up, babe. You're home."

I slowly blink my eyes open at Briar's soft voice, and I smile when I look out the window to see we're idling in front of my farmhouse. I take it in like I've been gone much longer than twenty four hours. Its pitched roof with twin gables and black shutters that match the railing along the wraparound porch. The fading white paint and the wood siding show years of weathering that only give it more character. Overall, the place is modest and a little run-down, but it's mine, and I wouldn't trade it for anything.

The breeze rustles the large oak out front and reminds me I need to pick up more sunflower seeds on my next shift. It houses a family of squirrels I've grown quite fond of, and they seem to like the kind we stock at Prairie Pines.

I shake my head and stretch my arms over my head, letting out a long yawn. "Thanks for bailing me out," I say to my friends.

"Technically, Walker did that. We just came by with coffee and a getaway car," Briar jokes, flashing me a cheeky grin from the front seat.

I chuckle. "You're right. Next time, you'd better bring a full marching band and confetti."

"Sorry, our budget only covers a kazoo player, but maybe we can squeeze in a few party poppers if we all pitch in," Briar says with a wink.

Charlie turns in her seat to face me. "Don't forget the oversized sunglasses to offset the visual trauma of you in a green jumpsuit."

"Glad that you've decided my future jail stint is inevitable. How considerate."

"What?" She shrugs, holding her hands up. "I'm just being realistic."

I can't argue with that. As long as there are animals out there being abandoned or mistreated, I'll keep saving them, legal consequences aside.

"Guess I'd better enjoy my freedom while it lasts, starting with a long nap after everyone gets their breakfast." I open the car door. "Seriously, though. Thanks for coming to get me."

"Always," Briar replies.

"Of course. We're your ride-or-dies, and you'll never find anyone better," Charlie adds with a cheeky grin.

"Love you both. I'll see you later."

I climb out of the SUV and wave goodbye as Charlie swings the car around and heads back down the long driveway.

Once they're out of sight, my shoulders slump, the weight of the night pressing down on me. As much as I want to go inside and crawl into bed, dozens of hungry mouths are waiting for breakfast. At least it's my day off. I'm not sure I'd survive dragging myself into work on so little sleep.

After retrieving a bucket of food scraps from the house, I swing by the shed out back. I'd planned to fix it up someday, but I'm not exactly handy, and with everything else on my plate, it got put on the back burner indefinitely. The roof is sagging, and several slats are missing on one side which is patched with plywood, but it's done the job so far. However, with its current occupants, I'll eventually have to come up with a better long-term solution.

Someday, I'd like to buy the fifty acres behind mine. It's been on the market for years because of the rough road access and its remote location—neither of which fazes me. There's even a big red barn on the property that's in functional condition and would be ideal for housing more rescues. The problem is, Mr. Grady refuses to sell it in pieces, and there's no way I could afford the current price, even if I worked at the feed store until I was old and gray. I've accepted that it's a pipe dream, but that's okay. I'll make do with what I have—I always find a way.

I leave the food scraps outside before slowly opening the shed door, the hinges groaning in protest, and poke my head around the corner to make sure no tails or hooves are in the danger zone as I fully open it.

Daisy is curled up in the far corner with her head resting on a pile of hay. She's a one-year-old Hereford cow with a shy demeanor, preferring to observe before she interacts with anyone. Her tiny, knobby horns are just starting to peek out from her fuzzy ears, and the patch of white on her forehead contrasts with her deep brown eyes.

"Good morning, sweet girl," I coo.

On the other side of the shed, Peaches the donkey has her eyes fixed on me like she's about to file a formal complaint with PETA. She's dappled in shades of gray and tan as if the sun faded her coat unevenly, and her mane juts up along her neck in a stubborn ridge no matter how often I brush her. She was skin and bones when I brought her home but has filled out nicely in the months since.

"Sorry I'm late," I murmur, resting my palm against her warm neck. "I was caught up in town, but don't worry, I'm here now, and no one is taking you away from me."

Her unimpressed gaze doesn't waver. Whatever happened to Peaches before I rescued her left her with trust issues and zero interest in reassurances that aren't backed up with food.

Once I've laid out fresh hay, water, and some homemade oat treats, I retrieve a bucket of scratch grain from the corner and head out to check on the other animals.

I've just closed the door when I hear a shrill voice coming from my driveway.

I glance up to find my neighbor Mrs. Bixby, striding across my lawn toward me. She's a spry woman in her seventies, with silver hair pulled into a loose bun, oversized glasses sliding down her nose, and a floral apron over her faded denim dress.

"Whoo-hoo," she calls out, waving.

I give the shed door an extra tug, making sure it's shut tight. The woman has a bad habit of dropping by unannounced and using her visits as an excuse to snoop around my property. She's been very vocal about her disapproval of my unofficial animal sanctuary within city limits. She won't rest until she has enough evidence to get it shut down, which would force me to remove the animals from my property.

I plaster on a faux smile, returning her wave. "Hi, Mrs. Bixby." I lift the bucket of food scraps with my free hand and start toward the pond, glancing back to make sure she's following, putting as much distance between us and the shed.

The ducks and geese come waddling toward me, eagerly honking and quacking as I toss them handfuls of scratch grain. Most of them are from rescues in surrounding towns that didn't have the capacity, and I couldn't deny giving them a better home. They live in a wooden coop I got on clearance at the feed store that's near the pond.

"You're not an easy woman to track down," Mrs. Bixby pants, pushing her glasses up her nose.

I toss another handful of grain before turning to her. "What can I do for you?"

"Came by to drop this off." She lifts a casserole dish. "I made you another one of my famous veggie lasagnas."

"That was very thoughtful of you."

"It's no trouble," she says, her eyes darting around my yard, clearly looking for something. "I know how much you like them."

Unfortunately, she's right. I wouldn't touch the food she brings based on principle alone if she weren't such a fantastic cook. Good vegetarian food is hard to come by in a small town where everyone seems to survive on meat and potatoes.

However, I'm aware that the woman doesn't do anything out of the goodness of her heart. She has an agenda, and my guess is she got word about my overnight stay at the sheriff's office and is looking for Peaches and Daisy. There's a reason I keep them in the shed during the day, only letting them venture outside to graze once she's asleep.

To make matters worse, she's convinced my dad being the sheriff earns me special treatment, which only fuels her resentment toward me. She's always poking around and wouldn't think twice about reporting me if she ever does find Daisy and Peaches.

Now that my theft accusations are public, I'll have to take extra precautions to keep them safe. I can only hope that Walker really did get rid of the evidence linking me to the auction animal heist like I think he did because otherwise I'm in big trouble.

Mrs. Bixby follows me to the pig pen, where Hammy and Peppa, my newest rescues, are wallowing in the mud. I found them at a run-down farm three towns over, where the owner's health was failing, and he could no longer care for them. Peppa is carrying piglets, her rounded belly swaying as she nudges Hammy with her snout. With the babies expected in the next few weeks, I'll be keeping a close eye on her.

I toss the food scraps into the trough in the corner of the pen and wipe my brow. "Is there something else you need, Mrs. Bixby? I had a long night, and I'd like to finish my chores so I can go inside and relax for a while."

She clicks her tongue. "I heard about your stint at the sheriff's office. Seems like you're courting trouble for the sake of a few silly animals."

I blow out a breath, not allowing her to get to me. "I'm not exactly sure what you heard, but my being held overnight was a misunderstanding. I have nothing to hide." It takes all my self-control not to glance toward the shed. "All the rescues here are better off than they were before, and they're well cared for, as you can see." I motion toward Hammy and Peppa, trotting over to the trough, letting out happy snorts.

Mrs. Bixby narrows her eyes at me. "Let's hope that's the case for your sake. The truth always has a way of catching up," she adds in warning, holding out the lasagna. "You'd better take this so I can go home and check on the stew I have on the stove."

I have to fight back a sigh of relief as I accept the dish. "Thanks again. Can't wait to try this one."

She wipes her hands on her apron as she heads in the direction of her place. "See you soon, Birdie."

I'm sure she'll be stopping by more often now that she thinks she's close to catching me in the act of harboring stolen animals.

To her credit, I'm sure being my neighbor isn't easy with all the constant commotion. I do take in several animals each month, but at least I'm able to find most of them homes pretty quickly to avoid my place being too overcrowded. It's kind of like being a used car salesman. I have to persuade people to adopt while making sure the animals are going to a better home than they were in before.

My rescue isn't officially registered as a business yet, and I don't ask for donations. I cover all the costs myself, which is the main reason I work at the feed store. The employee discount helps make stocking up on food and supplies more manageable, but it still adds up fast.

After finishing my rounds outside, I head back to the house, lasagna in hand. As I step through the door, I get a text I've been waiting for, and I balance the casserole in one hand to read it.

Tess: Good morning, sweet girl.

Birdie: Morning. How's Mama today?

Tess is one of my mama's nurses and checks in with me after every shift, so she must have worked overnight and is heading out for the day.

Tess: She slept well but woke up with leg pain.

Tess: I gave her a mild muscle relaxer and a berry smoothie for breakfast.

Birdie: Thanks for taking such good care of her. Planning to drop by this afternoon.

Tess: She'll be so happy to see you.

Going over to my parents' house to see Mama is the highlight of my week. I visit as often as possible, though weekends give me the most time with her. As an only child, we're especially close, sharing everything from small worries to my biggest milestones. When she got sick, our roles reversed, and I stepped up to help take care of her, making sure she made it through doctors' visits, managed her medications, and stayed on top of her physical therapy.

When I reach the kitchen, I find Nugget, my chicken, sitting on an orange in the fruit bowl.

"Miss me?" I ask, stepping closer to the table to stroke her back. "Hatch anything while I was gone?"

Nugget responds with a low trill, leaning into my hand as she fluffs her feathers, pretending she didn't hear my teasing accusation.

She hasn't laid a single egg since I brought her home from Mr. Grady's where the other hens were pecking on her, and she was about to be executed. My friends and I staged a covert chicken rescue, and Nugget and I have been inseparable ever since.

For the first few days, I kept her inside so she could regain her strength. When I tried moving her to the coop outside, she'd march up to the front porch every night and squawk at the top of her lungs until I let her back in. After several neighbors complained about the noise, I caved and installed a doggy door so she could have free rein of the house.

Unlike most chickens, she prefers sleeping in until noon before venturing outside. She spends her afternoons pecking around the yard and exploring, then sleeps inside on whatever inanimate object she's decided she's going to attempt hatching that night.

She's already dozed off again, and that's all the encouragement I need to follow her lead. I'm taking full advantage and grabbing some sleep while I can—before I'm hit with the full weight of my reality again.

CHAPTER 3

Stalking Your Crush: A Beginners Guide

Walker

I DROP THE LAST OF FIVE BAGS OF MEALWORMS INTO MY cart before pushing it to the end of the aisle, craning my neck to the front of Cattleman's Feed & Supply, where Birdie stands behind the register. She's wearing pink overalls with a white T-shirt underneath and the store's standard-issue navy-blue apron tied around her waist. Her hair is pulled into a ponytail, a strawberry-print bandana wrapped around her head. She gives the customer she's helping one of her trademark smiles as she scans and bags their items with practiced efficiency.

It's only been twenty-four hours since I saw her at the sheriff's office, but I couldn't wait any longer to see her again—no matter how much grief Heath will give me later for buying more feed when we're already well-stocked.

I scratch the stubble on my jaw as I watch her from a distance. God, she's so damn pretty it knocks the wind out of me.

A tight coil of impatience twists in my chest when I see three more people are still in line waiting to check out.

Dammit. This is taking too long.

I glance around, making sure no one has noticed me staring at Birdie before sidestepping to the nearest endcap loaded with livestock manuals. I grab one at random, skimming the pages as I flip through it, my eyes darting up every few seconds.

Normally, I avoid coming here during the midday rush, but I promised Heath I'd meet him in an hour to work through the second round of cattle for their vaccines. The ranch hands do most of the work, but he likes to have an extra set of eyes on them to make sure everything goes smoothly and that the animals are treated right. Even as a large cattle ranch, we do our best to handle them humanely.

Birdie's not exactly a fan of my family's ranch since we raise cattle for beef. When she was visiting a while back, one of the cows died during labor. She begged Heath not to raise the calf for meat, saying it was too tragic. When she started crying, he caved and agreed to keep it in the barn for a while. Fast-forward almost two years, and he has a full-grown cow named Petunia. Ever since, he's been more mindful about how we treat the animals, putting their welfare above convenience or profit.

"Having trouble with the ladies?" I snap my head up to find Ed, the feed store manager, standing beside me. He must have come from the back while I was busy watching Birdie.

"What? No." My gaze darts between him and the register. "Why would you think that?"

He tilts his head, nodding to the book in my hand. "Unless you're doing some light reading, it appears you're struggling to integrate a rooster into your flock."

I frown, flipping to the front cover: *Poultry Mating 101: So, Your Chickens are Getting Busy.*

"Uh, no." I scramble for an explanation. "Just being proactive. Figured it's best to brush up on rooster etiquette before introducing a new one to the flock."

"If you need advice, I have got plenty of tips to keep those hens of yours from staging a mutiny," Ed offers.

I nod absentmindedly, only half listening as my attention is still firmly on Birdie and not on how to negotiate peace among a flock of hormone-crazed hens.

When I don't answer, Ed eyes my overflowing cart with a furrowed brow. "Your brother told you we agreed to free delivery for the ranch, right?"

"He did," I answer curtly.

It took Heath a year to convince the store owner that the sheer quantity of orders we place merits it. I should be happy about the chance to make fewer trips to the store—but I'm not. Now I'm forced to find creative excuses every time I want to come in and steal a moment alone with Birdie without looking like a certified stalker.

Ed pulls out a pen and a pad of paper from his back pocket. "How about I take stock of everything you want and have it delivered with Heath's usual order tomorrow?"

"No thanks," I say, cutting him off. "It's already in my cart, so I'll grab it while I'm here."

"You sure? It's no trouble at all."

It'd be great if he could try to be less helpful right about now.

I pinch the bridge of my nose. "Positive."

I'm seconds away from losing my cool when I glance over at the register and find there's only one guy left in line, and the store appears otherwise empty of customers.

Finally.

"I've gotta run, Ed." I shove the manual into his hands. "Mind putting that back for me? Thanks."

I turn and push my cart to the front, slipping in behind the last person waiting to check out. I don't recognize him, which is unusual. He looks around my age, with shoulders like a quarterback and shaggy blonde hair that falls past his cowboy hat.

When Birdie calls him up to the register, a flush creeps into her cheeks. "I can check you out now, sir… I mean, I can ring you up," she stammers.

He steps forward, setting a wrench and a flannel jacket on the counter.

"Thanks for your patience," she says softly.

"No problem, sugar. I had a nice view while I waited," he replies, shooting her a wink.

Birdie bites her lower lip, a smile tugging at the corners of her mouth. She's so starry-eyed over the stranger that she doesn't even notice me standing behind him.

"Mine isn't so bad either," she murmurs as she scans the guy's items.

I'm surprised the cart handle hasn't cracked from how tightly my knuckles are gripping it. It's impossible to stop the visceral reaction that hits me as I watch her swoon over an out-of-towner who looks nothing like a real cowboy—crisp jeans and boots so shiny they might as well be props for a photo shoot. *What a tool.*

Birdie doesn't appear to share the same sentiment, sneaking glances at him while she rings up his things. When she presses the jacket's security tag into the magnetic detacher, she struggles to get it loose, grunting softly as she pushes harder until it finally pops free.

The guy flashes her an easy grin. "You've got a real talent for that."

I swallow hard, exhaling through my nose as I fight to keep my cool. He's clearly into Birdie, and I'd rather shove a hot poker into my brain than watch him ask her out. If miracles exist, now would be a hell of a time for one to intervene. I'd take a power outage, a spilled pallet of feed, or even a moose charging through the front window—I'm flexible as long as it puts a stop to this nauseating spectacle unfolding before my eyes.

"Thanks, I'm really good with my hands," Birdie replies as

she folds the flannel. "The secret is applying the right amount of pressure. I've had a lot of practice…" Color rises to her cheeks. "With removing security tags," she quickly adds.

I might hate that she's flirting with someone else, but her nervous little stumble and the way she tries to correct herself are ridiculously adorable.

The guy gives her a tentative smile. "Uh… right. Makes sense."

Birdie gives a nervous, high-pitched laugh. "Anyway. Flannel, huh?"

I shift uncomfortably as silence stretches between them, the conversation suddenly teetering toward awkwardness.

He rubs the back of his neck. "Yeah."

"Great choice. It's all the rage right now. Even Nugget, my house chicken, is a fan," Birdie says as she puts the jacket and wrench into a paper bag. "She claimed my favorite flannel shirt to nest in and totally lost it when I tried to move her after she pooped on it. It's nothing soap and water can't fix, though." Birdie's face pales when the guy visibly recoils at her suggestion. "Totally kidding. I'm never wearing that thing again. Rest in peace, flannel."

The guy's gaze drifts to the exit as he takes out his wallet. "How much do I owe you?"

It's obvious he's eager to cut their conversation short, and honestly? I don't blame him. Even from here, their exchange has been excruciating to witness.

It's no secret that Birdie gets nervous under pressure, and I can only imagine how unsettling it must be to go from a guy giving her googly eyes to one searching for an escape route in less than a minute. I *almost* regret wishing for that miracle, but it's his loss for not seeing what was right in front of him.

Birdie reads off the total, and he swipes his card. While she waits for him to go through the prompts on the keypad, she nudges the bag of items toward him. Her fingers fidget with the gold necklace at her throat, a nervous tell I've noticed. As soon as the receipt prints, she rips it from the machine, but in her hurry, she knocks over a wire cup of pens, sending them clattering across the counter and the receipt floating to the ground.

"I'm so sorry," she stammers, scrambling for the pens before they fall to the floor.

"No worries. I actually don't need a receipt." The guy takes his bag and heads straight for the exit.

"Oh… okay. Have a nice day," she calls after him, her tone half-hearted.

Once the guy is out of sight, Birdie buries her face in her hands. "Why do you always have to make things so awkward?" she mutters under her breath.

Not about to stand by and let her blame herself, I roll my cart to the register, gathering up the remaining pens that rolled out of her reach. "Why the long face, sweetheart?"

She startles at my voice, slowly lowering her hands and fixing me with a withering stare. "What are you doing here, Walker? Did you come looking for more blackmail material?" She glances around before dropping her voice to a whisper. "Isn't the mugshot enough?"

I frown at her response. Normally, she'd have a sarcastic retort, but her usual spark is nowhere to be found.

"I'm actually off-duty for blackmailing activities today," I tease, leaning over the counter and dropping the pens back in the cup. "Just a friend checking in to see how his favorite troublemaker's doing and stocking up on supplies."

Because friends stalking friends at work is totally normal behavior.

Birdie's eyes flicker discreetly around the store. "If I tell you what's bothering me, promise you won't judge?"

I nod. "Cross my heart."

She moves forward, resting her elbows on the counter.

"Pretty sure the guy ahead of you was flirting with me, and I totally botched it," she confesses in a whisper.

"*That* was your attempt at flirting?" I taunt playfully, raising a brow.

She playfully jabs my arm. "No judging, remember?"

"Right, sorry." I stand straight, shoving my hands in my pockets and trying to keep a straight face. "It wasn't all bad. You've got the sexual innuendos down. It's just your delivery that could use some finessing."

"You don't have to sugarcoat it, Walker. I told the man my chicken pooped on my flannel, and I was still planning to wear it," she grumbles. "He was a solid nine, and my brain just short-circuited."

I scoff, taking a step back like I'm personally offended. "Please. That wannabe cowboy was a six at best. Besides, we talk all the time, and you never have trouble speaking your mind."

"That's different," she says, waving me off. "We're friends. I'm not worried about impressing you so you'll ask me on a date."

I choke, immediately bringing my fist up to mask it with a cough. *If she only knew.*

"So…" I clear my throat and rock back on my heels. "What you're saying is I'm good-looking too, but it doesn't count because we're friends?"

Birdie gives me an exasperated sigh. "I may be socially awkward, but I'm not blind. You're obviously hot. Half the women in town wouldn't circle you like vultures if you weren't. Not that I'm one of them… I'm just lucky to have you as my friend." She fiddles with her name tag, looking anywhere but at me.

I'd be elated that she called me hot if she hadn't simultaneously cemented my status in the friend zone. To her, I'll always be Briar's older brother and the guy she hangs out with when she wants to confide in someone. To hide my disappointment at her inadvertent rejection, I resort to my usual tactic—humor.

"Only half the women in town, huh? Bummer. I was hoping I'd have a full fan club by now."

Birdie snorts. "Heaven forbid. Your ego does *not* need that kind of encouragement."

"Easy, there," I warn with a chuckle. "I brought you something, but I might have to reconsider if you keep sassing me."

Her eyes brighten, and she lifts on her toes to get a peek inside my cart. "What is it?"

She is almost always doing things for others, but when she's on the receiving end, the pure joy she radiates is priceless.

I hold out the paper bag I had in the fold-down seat of the cart. "I swung by the Prickly Pear on the way here and figured you probably hadn't eaten yet, so I grabbed your favorite."

Most places in town aren't vegetarian, but luckily, the diner has a mushroom burger she loves, so I usually bring her one of those and an order of sweet potato fries whenever I stop by.

Birdie gives me a soft smile. "I appreciate it, but what have I told you about bringing me lunch?"

"That I don't have to do it?"

She gives an exaggerated shrug. "Yet here we are."

"I think what you mean is 'thanks for the burger, Walker. You're my hero.'"

Her face softens as she takes the bag. "It was really kind. Thank you. I accidentally skipped breakfast this morning, so I'm starving."

I narrow my eyes. "How do you accidentally skip breakfast?"

"The geese staged a full-on revolt because the ducks were hogging the breadcrumbs again, so I had to step in before things got ugly," she explains, sliding the bag of food behind the counter. "Patrick, one of the male ducks, likes to chase me around the yard when he's in a mood, and I was not interested in dealing with one of his tantrums this morning. Then Nugget was upset because I forgot her favorite mixed berries and mealworms treat, and by the time I was finished, I was already running late."

"I brought something else that might cheer you up."

I grab her tote from the cart that she left at the sheriff's office yesterday. She must have been in such a rush that she forgot it. By the time I noticed it was still there, Mason had cornered me about the missing video footage, and when I finally stepped outside after he stormed off, Birdie was already gone.

"My bag," she exclaims, hugging it to her chest. "I was down to my last ten dollars in cash, and my favorite bandana is in there. Thanks so much for bringing it."

"Anytime."

When I pull up to the ranch house, Heath is leaning against one of the porch pillars with his thumbs in his pockets, waiting for me.

Technically, we live with our parents, though each of us has a loft apartment on opposite sides of the main house. Briar lives with her fiancé, Jensen and their son, Caleb, in the cottage on the other side of the ranch. They're in the process of building a home on the property, but it's taking longer than anticipated.

Even though our places have kitchens, Ma still expects Heath and me at dinner a couple of nights a week, and when she's off work on weekends, she goes all out for breakfast. It's the best of both worlds, though sometimes I wish my comings and goings didn't require a full debrief.

I hop out of the pickup and circle to the tailgate, lifting it to reveal the bed packed with supplies.

"What the hell is all this?" Heath grumbles as he trudges down the porch steps.

"I stopped by Prairie Pines while I was in town," I say, deliberately keeping my answer vague.

He arches a brow. "Don't you think we have enough chicken feed to last a lifetime?"

Fair point, considering I had to build a third shed last month to store the overflow.

I shoot him a sheepish look. "With the number of hens we've got, it's better to be overprepared, don't you think? You never know when an apocalypse might hit. Plus, the feed store could shut down for two weeks again." That happened last year after an electrical storm, and I ended up driving two hours one way just to grab enough feed to get us through until they reopened.

Heath drags a hand over his mustache as he scans the bags stacked in the back of my truck. "Right. So scratch grain and mealworms are part of this emergency stash too?"

"Whatever makes the ladies content," I say with a grin. "Happy hens mean more eggs. Simple as that."

"If you're so set on preparing for an apocalypse, why not make one big order and have it sent here? I went through all the trouble, and you haven't taken advantage of it once. Unless, of course, you're not actually going there for supplies." Heath fixes me with one of his *I'm on to you* stares.

I scratch my neck, trying to act casual. "I have no idea what you're talking about."

He crosses his arms, letting out a low hum. "See, I think all these trips are just convenient excuses to see a certain blue-eyed blonde."

"Who? Birdie? That's ridiculous." I scoff. "Why would I go out of my way to see Briar's friend?"

I'd rather that word didn't get back to Briar about my drop-ins, honestly. She'd get the wrong idea and tell me to back off. She's fully aware of my past and would probably worry I'd hurt Birdie if we ever got together.

"Birdie is your friend too," Heath reminds me. "Hell, I'd bet money you spend more time with her than Briar has lately."

Damn him for being so observant.

Although I shouldn't expect anything less. Nothing gets past Heath—he's perceptive to a fault. Maybe he wouldn't be so interested in my personal life if he had one of his own. As it stands, his sole focus is the ranch and turning it into one of the most successful cattle operations in the country. Since taking over from Dad, he's thrown himself into it completely, leaving no room for anything else.

"You're right. Birdie and I are friends, nothing more," I admit.

"My mistake. I forgot you don't do relationships. What did you use to say? No commitments, and no strings?" Heath says, lifting two bags from the truck bed and hoisting them over his shoulder. "Guess that means I can give my buddy the green light to ask her out."

Wait. What the hell did he just say?

Heath heads down the path toward the fenced-in coops, leaving me reeling from the bomb he just dropped. I grab a few bags and jog after him, determined to get answers.

"Hold up. What *buddy*?" I snap.

He isn't known for having a wide circle of friends. Outside of me, he only hangs out with a couple of guys he occasionally grabs beers with and a few other ranchers he networks with, but that's the extent of his social life.

"His name is Dylan. He moved to town with his brother. They're taking over Mr. McAlister's family practice," Heath calls over his shoulder. "He saw Birdie at the bar last weekend and asked if she was single."

Even if Birdie weren't off-limits and wanted more from me, I wouldn't stand a chance against a guy who saves lives. He probably rescues kittens and volunteers at the homeless shelter on the weekends, for fuck's sake. Birdie has devoted her life to saving animals from certain death while I'm out here running a damn cattle ranch. That's hardly a match made in heaven.

I can only hope that if this guy tries asking her out, Birdie's nervous energy keeps him at bay, distracting from her generous heart, quick wit, and infectious energy. Otherwise, I'm totally screwed.

"What did you tell him?" I ask, unable to hide my curiosity.

"You said you weren't interested in Birdie, so why does it matter?" Heath smirks, adjusting the bags on his shoulder as he opens the door to the nearest storage shed.

I huff in frustration and follow him inside. "That doesn't mean I'm okay with her dating some stranger. What if he's an asshole? She deserves someone who treats her right."

Heath tosses his feed onto an empty shelf before turning back to me. "Or what if he's the real deal? Would you be happy for Birdie then?"

He walks out before I can respond, and a sense of dread settles inside my chest.

At this rate, there's a good chance she'll end up with someone else before I get the chance to make her mine.

CHAPTER 4

Good Luck, Babe

Birdie

AFTER A LONG DAY AT WORK AND A VISIT WITH MY MAMA, I'm looking forward to a hot shower and curling up on the couch in my sweats.

"You're pretty quiet back there, Miss Birdie," Earl remarks from the front seat. "I reckon the past forty-eight hours have been a real doozy—going from a night in lockup to an eight-hour shift would leave anyone wiped."

It's no surprise the news has already spread like wildfire. Several customers were in the feed store parking lot when Mason hauled me off, and I have no doubt he's told anyone who'd listen about taking in the sheriff's daughter, bragging as if it were something to be proud of.

I straighten my seat. "Are you speaking from experience?"

"Let's just call it an educated guess, on account of some stories best being left in the past." Earl winks at me through the rearview mirror, the car veering off the road when he does.

My fingers instinctively curl around the door handle. "Come on. Don't leave me hanging."

"Not a chance, sunshine. I've seen how fast news travels to those chatty friends of yours. One slipup and the whole town'll be talking. Case in point: you."

I chuckle. "Touché."

If Bluebell's residents love one thing, it's juicy gossip, and the sheriff's daughter being brought in will have everyone buzzing over coffee and pie at the Prickly Pear for at least a month. I suppose I should be flattered that my rumored rescue missions are front-page news. Maybe folks will think twice before treating their animals inhumanely if they know I'm liable to intervene, no matter what the law says.

Earl jerks the wheel sharply around the next corner, and I lean into the turn, clutching my seat belt with my free hand.

As sweet as Earl is, driving isn't exactly his forte. He's been Bluebell's taxi driver for the past forty years, driving locals around town and shuttling visitors to and from Silver Saddle Ranch—the only tourist destination in town. They've got several cabins booked far in advance, keeping Earl busy year-round. The trouble is that he drives like he's racing a tornado and has advanced cataracts in his left eye.

Last year, the town council decided to look the other way when he ran over the mayor's prized rosebushes. Despite his tendency to confuse the gas pedal with the brake, he's a fixture in Bluebell, and there's no replacing him—for better or worse.

"You talk to your pops about Mason haulin' you in yet? I reckon he ain't too pleased with him," Earl remarks, switching the radio over to his favorite country station.

"Pretty sure he's more upset with me," I mutter.

He swivels to face me. "Can you say that again, Miss Birdie. My hearing ain't as good as it used to be."

"Oh, I said not yet." No reason to pull him into my family drama.

My dad's called several times since yesterday morning, but I've let them all go to voicemail. I'm certain someone at the sheriff's office has already filled him in, and I'm not ready to hear another lecture about how I prioritize my silly hobbies that only get me into trouble over Mama's care. Funny how he's the one always running off, while I'm left in Bluebell, juggling Mama's declining health and my animal sanctuary on my own. Sure, he's helping other towns that lack the resources to handle serious cases, but it doesn't make it any easier.

My attention snaps back to the road when Earl swerves sharply, almost taking out a mailbox. I tighten my grip on the door handle, but otherwise, I'm unfazed—his close calls are so frequent that it's routine at this point.

"By golly, I swear them mailboxes keep gettin' closer to the road." He laughs, shaking his head.

"All those decades of dodging potholes and raccoons have paid off," I reply, playing along.

I'll be the last person to ever tell him the truth about his driving. If that makes me an enabler, so be it.

He's been a lifesaver this past year, driving me around since a family of rabbits set up camp under my truck. Mama rabbit gave birth to her sixth litter of kits a month ago, and I'm pretty sure she's pregnant again. I figured they'd eventually move on, but I feed them diced carrots and fresh lettuce, keep their water bowls topped off, and add fresh hay to their nests. Why would they trade their corner of paradise for the outside world, where no one will look out for them? It might be inconvenient, but no way am I making them leave, which means I'll continue to rely on Earl to get me around for the foreseeable future.

I breathe a sigh of relief when we finally pull down the lane to my house. I may give the illusion that I'm a people person, but I'm an introvert at heart, and there's no place I'd rather be than home.

When the taxi comes to a stop, I dig out some cash and my punch card out of my bag and hand both to Earl. After my first few rides, he set up a system where every tenth ride is free. He calls it his token of appreciation.

He lets out a low whistle as he punches the card before handing it back to me. "Looks like your next ride is on the house."

"I am your favorite regular," I state proudly like it's a badge of honor, choosing to ignore Earl's track record of turning flowerbeds into mulch.

True to form, he gets out to open my door. I've told him it's not necessary, but he says it's the gentlemanly thing to do and to never settle for a man who doesn't do the same. Joke's on him, I'll probably be single forever if that awkward encounter with the cute guy at the feed store earlier is any indication.

I turn and give him a little wave when I reach my porch. "Thanks, Earl. Have a good night."

He tips his hat. "You're welcome, Miss Birdie. I'll see you in the morning."

I watch him hop into the driver's seat, his car rattling when he turns it on. As he peels away, he lives up to his reputation, running over my daisies on his way down the lane.

Once I've had a long, hot shower, I finally feel human again. I head to the kitchen to reheat a serving of Mrs. Bixby's veggie lasagna. I can't pass up the chance for a delicious meal I don't have to cook myself—even if it comes from a nosy neighbor who I wish would mind her own business.

When I reach the kitchen, Nugget is in the corner perched on one of my boots, somehow looking totally relaxed. She cracks one eye open when I take the container of leftovers from the fridge, clearly unamused by the disruption.

I plant my free hand on my hip. "There's a perfectly cozy chicken coop outside if these conditions aren't up to your standards." She shoots me a disdainful stare before fluffing her feathers and burying her head under her wing.

I let out a heavy sigh as I pop the dish into the microwave. "Suit yourself. Don't come complaining to me when your sleep is disrupted again when I walk around like I own the place… because I do." Although we both know that's up for debate.

Ever since I rescued Nugget and brought her home, she's ruled the roost, basking in being treated like a queen. Exhibit A: the doggie door. Exhibit B: her gourmet breakfast of scrambled eggs sprinkled with cheese. And no, it's not cannibalism when she doesn't know where eggs come from, plus they're packed with protein, vitamins, and healthy fats to keep her energized while bossing us all around.

Once my lasagna is reheated, I grab a fork from the drawer and turn off the kitchen light, tiptoeing to the living room so I don't disturb her again.

Just as I settle into the couch, placing my lasagna on the coffee table in front of me, my phone chimes with a new message.

Dad: You're ignoring my calls.

Birdie: I just got home from visiting Mama.

Dad: How is she doing?

Birdie: She misses you.

I instantly feel bad for trying to guilt-trip him and quickly send another message.

Birdie: We watched Gilmore Girls and she smiled every time Logan was on screen.

Dad: She's always in good spirits when she watches the seasons he's in. Her favorite is the episode where he gives Rory a Birkin bag.

Birdie: I mean, can you blame a girl?

Dad hearted your message

Dad: I'll have to take your word for it. Tell Tess I'll be back on Tuesday.

Birdie: I will. Love you, Dad.

Dad: Love you too, kiddo.

I've never questioned his devotion to Mama. It must be agonizing to watch the love of his life go from a vibrant school librarian to someone requiring round-the-clock care within a few years. I only wish he'd pull himself out of his grief long enough to remember that she's still here with us and that avoiding reality will only make the eventual loss harder.

Mama was diagnosed with young-onset Parkinson's on her fortieth birthday. What started as a small tremor in her hand gradually turned into a persistent stiffness that made even daily tasks like brushing her hair or putting on makeup a struggle. Her doctor ordered a series of tests when her symptoms didn't improve, which ultimately led to her diagnosis.

I was only fifteen at the time, and my parents made me promise not to tell anyone—not even my friends. It's common knowledge that my mama's declining health forced her to stop teaching, but only her doctor and the nurses my dad hired are aware of her specific diagnosis and understand it will eventually take her life. It's a heavy burden to carry alone, and I often wish I had someone I could lean on to make it easier.

Dad: Sorry I wasn't there on Friday.

Dad: Mason should never have kept you in that cell overnight.

Birdie: It's fine.

We both know it was warranted even though he never explicitly asks if I'm guilty. He doesn't have to—whenever I'm brought in, it's always for an animal rescue case. He knows full well I'll help any creature in need, no matter the risks. I think that's why he avoids coming to my house. He doesn't want to run into any of the rescues I've been accused of taking. It's easier for him to stay ignorant and look the other way.

Dad: We'll talk when I'm back in town. Think you can stay out of trouble until then?

Birdie: As long as there aren't any animals in need of rescuing.

Dad: This is serious, Birdie. I won't always be around to protect you.

I blow out a sardonic breath. It's not like he's done much of that lately. I cringe for even thinking about it. Dad has done his best, given the circumstances. He could have let the law catch up to me for any of the dozen times I've gotten in trouble—but he hasn't. He may not be around as much as I'd like, but he hasn't checked out completely when it comes to me, and I have to give him credit for that.

> Birdie: Don't worry, Dad. I'll behave myself.

Dad: Good. I love you, Birdie.

> Birdie: Love you too.

I pop a forkful of lasagna into my mouth, the herby flavor exploding on my tongue. It's easily one of the best vegetarian dishes I've ever had—rare in a small town devoted to steaks, burgers, and anything that once had a face.

When I was eight, I went on a school field trip to a local farm and learned how bacon was made. That day, I swore I'd never eat meat again, and I've kept my promise. I have made peace with the Halsteads' cattle ranch, though. Years ago, I decided I couldn't let my feelings about animal slaughter get in the way of my friendships. What I *can* do is advocate for the animals to be treated humanely and accept that it's enough to ease my conscience.

It reminds me that between work, Mama's failing health, and the rescue, I haven't had a moment to myself in forever. I'm constantly juggling scheduling conflicts, squeezing in a rescue before and after work, racing to emergency vet appointments, and making time for Mama whenever I can.

What I need is a night out on the town, free from the weight of responsibility, the constant ticking of my mental to-do list, and the pain of watching Dad struggle to cope with his grief.

Backroads & Bad Decisions Group Chat

> Birdie: Who's up for hitting the bar?

Wren: Wish I lived closer! Guess I'll have to settle for a relaxing bubble bath after Lottie goes to bed.

I don't think I'll ever get used to her living on the other side of the country, but I'm grateful our group chat keeps her in the loop—even if it's not the same as having her here in person.

> Briar: Can't tonight. Caleb's feeling under the weather, so we're staying in and watching the Lego Movie.

> Charlie: I'll be at the shop late restoring a set of midcentury tables.

She owns Timeless Threads, a vintage boutique in town where she gives secondhand clothes and home decor a new lease on life.

> Charlie: After that, I have a hot date with my vibrator.

> Birdie: We'd totally have more fun at the bar.

> Charlie: Clearly, you never took that gift we got you for Christmas for a spin.

I fidget with the gold necklace around my neck, wishing the ground would swallow me whole. I'm just grateful she's not here to see my reaction.

The girls gifted me a rabbit vibrator last year, and it's been tucked away in the back of my nightstand drawer ever since. I've been tempted to try it, but the handful of times I've used one in the past, I couldn't come and ended up far more frustrated than satisfied. Being a twenty-five-year-old virgin is embarrassing enough without having to ask my friends for advice on how to get off.

It's no secret that I'm inexperienced. I constantly stumble over my words whenever an attractive man is in the room and get flustered whenever the topic of sex comes up. I groan at the memory of my encounter with that cute guy at the feed store earlier. I still can't believe I talked about *poop*. Poop! I drop my head into my hands and resist the urge to scream.

My mind drifts to how, even though Walker teased me about the whole ordeal, he was quick to put me at ease. I can always let my guard down around him, and he makes me feel safe in a way no one else does—which makes it all the more mortifying that I told him I thought he was hot.

We have a good thing going. He lets me be my quirky self, tolerating it like a saint, and I make an effort not to let the drool escape down my chin when he shows up to my work in filthy Wranglers asking about fencing supplies.

Wren: Ignore Charlie. Her BOBs do all the heavy lifting.

Wren: Meanwhile, her hands-on experience is collecting dust.

Charlie: Not all of us have boyfriends standing by when the mood strikes.

Wren: I think you mean we can't all be Briar with the perfect fiancé helping build her dream nonprofit and giving her more orgasms than she can count.

Charlie: Peak fantasy right there.

Briar: Caleb fell asleep 5 minutes into the movie, and Jensen just got back from a business trip, so we're headed to bed. *wink face emoji

Her response makes it clear that getting a happy ending like hers with Jensen won't happen if I spend my Saturday nights hiding out in my house.

The feed store incident plays on a loop in my head. That guy probably would've asked for my number if I hadn't made such a spectacle. I have a habit of ruining things before they have a chance to go anywhere, and I'm exhausted by it. If I want anything more than a near miss, I have to be willing to take more risks and face my fears head-on.

It's only seven forty-five, which is early by bar standards. Normally, when the girls are busy, I stay in and rewatch whatever episodes of *Gilmore Girls* my mama watched that day so I'm caught up before our next visit. But tonight, though, feels like the perfect opportunity to do something wildly out of character—like put on a dress, go to the bar, and find a man to hook up with. Maybe with a little alcohol in my system, I won't overthink every detail like usual. It's as good a night as any to lose my virginity, and hopefully, with some experience under my belt, I can play it cool the next time someone shows interest in me.

With my mind made up, I finish off the rest of my lasagna, hop off the couch, and rush down the hall to my room, dialing Earl as I go—looks like I'll be cashing in on that free ride sooner than expected.

CHAPTER 5

Shots & Propositions

Walker

I STEP INTO BLUE MOON TAVERN, THE HEAVY DOOR swinging shut behind me. The place is dimly lit, filled with dark wood and worn leather. A long bar stretches the length of the room and mismatched tables are scattered around, their surfaces nicked and worn from decades of brawls and spilled whiskey. A fiddle-heavy country song blares from the jukebox, competing with the clink of glasses, loud laughter, and arguments that sound like one drink away from turning into a fist fight. Just an average Saturday night at the only bar in town.

"Well, I'll be damned. Our favorite deputy finally decided to grace us with his presence," Ryker calls from behind the bar. "Want your usual?"

"Just one." I take a seat, pulling off my hat and resting it on the counter beside me. "I have to drive back to the ranch later."

"There was a time you'd stay until close and leave with a pretty woman on your arm and still manage to show up here the next evening ready for round two." I wince, recalling a part of my past I'd rather forget.

Growing up, Heath was the reliable one, ready to take on whatever Pops sent his way, and Briar eagerly helped around the ranch, determined to do her part. As for me, I focused on finding ways to avoid my responsibilities, which inevitably got me into trouble, earning me far more lectures than praise as a teenager. I was reckless, forever chasing the next thrill and basking in every flirty glance from the beautiful women who crossed my path, never thinking about the consequences.

As I got older, I wanted more from life, and when Sheriff Matterson was searching for another volunteer deputy, I jumped at the opportunity. It was the chance I'd been waiting for to carve out a path for myself beyond the family business and prove that I could take on real responsibility.

What I hadn't expected was to catch feelings for Birdie in the process. Before I joined the sheriff's office, she'd just been Briar's friend. But she brought her dad lunch every day and started running her unsanctioned animal rescues shortly after I started at the sheriff's office, which regularly landed her in trouble. We started having long conversations while she waited for her dad to slap her on the wrist, and over time, falling for her became inevitable.

Ryker slides a chilled Coors Banquet in front of me, and I lean back as I take a long swig.

"Thanks, man."

He nods, watching me with an unreadable expression.

"What? You worried I'll bail without paying or something?" I tease.

He shakes his head as he pours a local IPA into pint glasses. "Just curious, are you here on official business or as a favor to Briar?"

I run a hand through my hair, confused by his question.

"Neither. I'd never drink on the job, and why would I be here for my sister?"

Briar occasionally drops by with her friends, but since she got together with Jensen, most of her weekends are spent at the cottage with him and Caleb. What started as a nanny gig last summer turned into her and Jensen falling in love, and the three of them becoming a family.

Ryker hands the pints to a nearby couple before coming back over to me.

"So Briar didn't call you?" he asks hesitantly.

"No. I was in town and decided to come by for a beer. Now stop being so cryptic and tell me what's going on." I scan the room, looking for something that doesn't belong.

At first glance, nothing seems out of place. There's the typical crowd of regulars enjoying a night of drinking, a lively pool game taking place, and a pair of cowboys bickering over a poker game at a nearby table. It's not until I glance at the other patrons at the bar that I spot the problem.

Birdie is here, sitting alone. There is no sign of Charlie or her other friends. She's perched on a stool at the short end of the bar, diagonally across from me, giving me a direct view. She's too absorbed in her drink to notice me, holding a cocktail with a pink umbrella, her lips puckering around the straw as she takes a sip. I imagine what it would feel like to have that mouth on mine as I run my hands along the curves of her hips.

Goddammit. Stay focused, Walker.

"When did she get here?" I tilt my head in Birdie's direction.

"Two hours ago." Ryker responds. "She asked for a shot of tequila and told me to keep them coming."

I count eight shot glasses in front of her, and slam down my beer, liquid sloshing over the rim. "What the hell? How many have you served her?"

"Take it easy," Ryker says as he wipes up the mess I made.

"She hasn't realized it, but she's been doing shots of ginger ale since her fourth, and that cocktail she's drinking?" He motions to the red liquid in Birdie's glass. "Is cranberry juice with sparkling water. She doesn't hold her liquor well, so I'd say a hangover is inevitable, but she's still coherent enough to carry on a conversation without slurring."

I grunt my appreciation. As much as I dislike that she came here alone, I'm relieved Ryker's watching out for her.

Unfortunately, my relief is short-lived when she scoots closer to the man sitting beside her. His name is Dalton Miller, and he's one of the ranch hands Heath recently hired. I don't know him well, but he's about to earn a top spot on my shit list if he lets Birdie get any closer.

My nostrils flare when she giggles at something he says, leaning in to run a hand along his tattooed bicep.

"Come on, Birdie, do something awkward. Anything," I mutter.

She's normally a whirlwind of flustered energy around men she's interested in, yet when there's another instance I need her to fumble, she's calm and collected. It seems a little liquid courage is all it takes to tame her nerves.

"You good?" Ryker questions as he mixes drinks for a group of women across the bar. "You look two seconds from decking someone, and I'd rather not deal with another brawl tonight."

"I'm fine," I grunt, taking a swig of beer.

My racing pulse says otherwise. With my shitty luck, I'm about to witness Birdie and Dalton share their first kiss, setting off a chain reaction that ends with wedding bells and a baby announcement.

"If you squeeze that bottle any tighter, it's going to shatter, and it'll be a pain in the ass to clean up." I blink at Ryker, his warning registering as I take a deep breath and loosen my grip. "Sure you're okay? I'm beginning to think you're the one who needs a ride home, and you've barely touched your beer."

"Yeah. It's just been a long day."

And it's only getting worse.

"I know exactly what you need."

"What's that?"

"To find a pretty lady to enjoy the evening with." He smirks.

It's been a while since I slept with someone—longer than I care to admit.

There was a time I would've agreed with Ryker without hesitation and shamelessly flirted with the first woman who caught my interest until she was begging me to take her home. I never took them to my place, which made it easy to stick to my no-strings rule. In hindsight, I'm not proud of how I used my charm to keep things casual and treated intimacy as a game, making a meaningful relationship impossible.

Now, years later, there's nothing I wouldn't give to be with a certain blonde, blue-eyed beauty who has me completely under her spell without even realizing it. If I were lucky enough to get a chance, it would end with her in *my* bed, where she belongs.

"I'm not interested in a casual hookup," I confess to Ryker.

He lets out a low whistle. "Don't tell me the infamous playboy is ready to settle down."

I bristle, but thankfully I'm spared from replying when I glance over at Birdie just in time to see her knock over several empty shot glasses. They topple behind the bar with a ringing crash, creating a scene similar to the one from just hours ago at the feed store. As she spins around to see the mess she made, her elbow connects with Dalton square in the nose.

He recoils, fumbling for napkins to stop the trickle of blood running down his face.

"Oh, cheese and biscuits," Birdie blurts loudly, her tone panicked. "I swear I'm not usually this clumsy."

Dalton just narrows his eyes at her and applies more pressure on his nose.

Birdie's next words are too soft to hear, but I watch her reach for another napkin to offer him. In her rush, though, she bumps his glass of whiskey hard enough that it tips over, sending amber liquid into his shirtsleeve. He's lucky there wasn't much left in the glass, or it would have spilled onto his pants and the floor.

"Why don't you stop moving before you make an even bigger mess?" Dalton snaps. He's pulled a few people's attention with his tone, and even Ryker pauses at the register and glances over.

The whole scene rubs me the wrong way. It was clearly an accident, and he damn well knows it.

Birdie's shoulders slump as she sinks into her seat, worrying her bottom lip to keep the tears at bay.

"I'd better go to the bathroom to handle this." Dalton sighs and gestures to his nose, then pulls out a couple of bills from his wallet with his free hand, dropping them to the counter. "I'm going to head out once the bleeding stops, so I'll see you around."

"Okay… I really am sorry," Birdie calls after him.

Turns out I was wrong. Tipsy Birdie is far more accident-prone than I expected. Now I feel like a jackass for hoping she'd stumble, though I can't deny I'm glad it happened—just wish she didn't have to pay the price in the process. I can only imagine how difficult it must be for her to be rejected yet again.

Ryker takes in the mess and rushes over with a towel, wiping down the counter where Birdie spilled the whiskey.

"I apologize for the mess," she says, lowering her head in shame. She's no longer speaking so softly, and I can't help the grin threatening to make an appearance.

He gives her arm a squeeze. "Don't worry. It's an occupational hazard. At least tonight I'm cleaning up after a polite regular instead of the usual burly cowboys who treat spilling drinks like a competitive sport."

If he didn't have a wife and kids waiting at home, I'd be itching to tell him to back off—but as it stands, I'm glad he's comforting her.

Once Ryker finishes cleaning down the bar top, he starts sweeping up the shattered glass on the floor. Luckily, it's all on his side of the bar, so he doesn't have to worry about drunken patrons stepping into it and adding to the mess.

When I glance back at Birdie her glum expression has me on my feet in an instant.

I put on my hat and make my way over, and it's then that I notice her lace-trimmed camisole dips low enough to tease a hint of cleavage. Her top is tucked into a leather miniskirt she's paired with black knee-high boots. She's fucking stunning. Even after the incident, guys are eyeing the open chair beside her, as if debating whether to risk joining her. There's no chance I'm letting that happen. She sways in her seat, squinting at her cocktail that miraculously made it out unscathed.

With my beer in hand, I drop onto the stool.

"Hey, troublemaker, what's with the sad face?"

She groans when she sees me. "Ugh. What are you doing here, Walker?"

"Good to see you too," I deadpan, taking a sip of my drink.

"Save the small talk." She props her elbow on the counter with her cheek pressed into her fist. "Don't pretend you didn't witness me ruin my last shot at getting laid tonight."

"Come again?" I almost choke on my beer.

"I was trying to find a guy to hook up with," Birdie states casually, as if she were ordering dessert rather than announcing she showed up at the bar to pick up someone.

Damn, she's got zero filter when she's had a few drinks. No wonder Briar and Charlie usually make her the designated driver when they go out.

"That was reckless." I point out the obvious. "What were you thinking?"

She downs the last of her cocktail in one gulp before jabbing a finger at me. "Oh, come on. You're the poster child for one-night stands, so you don't have any business judging me."

I lift my hands in defense. "Hey, no judgment here. I just don't want you getting hurt."

The truth is, picturing her in someone else's bed sends a sharp pang through my chest, and I rub at it instinctively. She might not be mine, but my body refuses to believe it.

Birdie snickers. "Please. I'm not some fragile thing you have to protect. And considering this is your usual hunting ground, it can't be that dangerous."

Touche. I don't bother correcting her that it's been a long time since I've picked up a woman. Even if I did, I doubt she'd believe me, especially if I explained why.

"Is it really so wrong that I wanted to be spontaneous for once?" she mutters, frowning at her empty glass. "I'm tired of being a virgin and am done sitting around waiting to do something about it."

My eyebrows shoot up, and I lean back, staring at her in disbelief. "I'm sorry. You're a *what*?"

"I'm a virgin," she repeats, loud enough to turn a few heads.

I shift closer, reaching out to brush a stray lock of hair from her face.

"Are you telling me no one has touched you?"

She shakes her head, eyes locked on mine. "I… well, no. That's why I figured I should just get it over with tonight."

My fingers trail down her cheek. "That's not something to check off like part of a to-do list. You should be cherished and adored your first time, and anyone worthy of you would know that."

Her lips part slightly, her breathing shallow as she takes in my remark.

I knew she was inexperienced, but I hadn't considered that she might be a virgin. I figured she's had at least one bad experience that left her wary of men and sex. It's not exactly a topic that comes up when I'm in the checkout line at the feed store or when we're at the ranch with my sister.

Birdie might think she wants a quick fuck, but I'm confident she'll regret it. And after the shit Dalton just pulled, something tells me he's not that guy.

"Is it really that big of a deal?" she asks, leaning forward in her chair, giving me a better view of the swells of her breasts. "Surely all men are the same in bed."

I drag my gaze back up to her face. "That's where you're mistaken." She's in for a rude awakening if that's her expectation. "Most guys only care about one thing—themselves. If I hadn't intervened, your little experiment tonight would've been a total letdown, and you'd have been left more on edge than you are now."

"Is that so?" She reaches over and plucks the beer from my hand and downs a generous swig. "Think you'd be any better, Deputy?"

She doesn't give me a chance to answer before she's out of her chair and sliding onto my lap, and I instinctively wind my arms around her waist to steady her.

"What are you doing, Birdie?" I keep my voice steady even though my pulse pounds in my ears.

The woman I've fantasized about for years is literally in my lap, enveloping me in her vanilla and orange scent. I want nothing more than to draw her close and nuzzle my nose in her neck, but I have to resist, no matter how fiercely every instinct is urging me to give in.

Birdie's lip quivers, and her downcast eyes lift to meet mine as she murmurs, "Are you going to reject me too?"

Her sadness hits me square in the chest, and I pull her closer, my hand settling on her hip. "No, I like you where you are—far more than I should."

The whole bar is watching, and I'm sure the rumors that'll have spread come morning will be far more scandalous than the reality. But even all the whispers won't stop me from savoring what could very well be the closest I'll ever get to Birdie Matterson.

She squints at me, blinking slowly. "You're only being nice because we're friends and because Briar would never forgive you if you weren't."

My hand frames her cheek, and I'm struck by how soft she is beneath my palm. "No. I'm here because you're important to me."

It's the most honest I've ever been with how I feel about her—partly because there's a good chance she won't remember in the morning, and partly because finally saying it aloud is like a weight lifted off my shoulders.

Birdie leans into my palm, her lashes fluttering before whispering, "Then I think you should be my first. I trust you."

It takes every ounce of willpower to ignore the fact that she just asked me to sleep with her. Naturally, it's my luck that I'm not only stuck in the friend zone but also the safe hypothetical she entertains after a few drinks. Fantastic.

I shake my head, moving my beer out of her reach. "I don't think that's a good idea."

She straightens in my lap, her eyes locking on mine like she's just had a revelation. "It's actually the perfect solution."

Good thing Ryker cut her off from more alcohol—she's clearly not thinking straight.

"What is?"

Birdie loops her arms around my neck. "I want you to teach me."

"Teach you what?" My voice is strained.

"Everything," she says breathlessly. "Like how to flirt… and, um, how to have sex." The last part comes out in a whisper.

My jaw drops as my grip around her waist loosens. "Whoa. Slow down a minute. You don't mean that."

Her playful smile fades, her expression growing earnest. "I'm serious, Walker. You're experienced and I feel safe with you."

I study her carefully. "As much as I wish I could take you up on the offer, I have a sneaking suspicion you'd never forgive me if I did."

She purses her lips. "You're wrong. I might be inexperienced, but I know what I want, and right now, I want you to fuck me." She leans in, running her nose against my collarbone. "Please, Walker. Fuck me."

Holy shit. Sober Birdie doesn't swear. Ever. Tipsy Birdie, on the other hand is a flirty little firecracker with a mouth like a trucker.

But as charming as she is, I'd never take advantage of her while she's intoxicated, and I'm certain that if she remembers this conversation come morning, she'll want to erase the memory entirely.

I take a deep breath, trying to keep my composure. There's only so much restraint one man can manage.

"It's time we got you home," I tell Birdie.

She huffs, tilting her head as she thinks over my suggestion. "Fine, but only if you come with me. And I want you to carry me."

I smile, brushing a piece of hair from her face. "Anything for you, troublemaker."

Content with my answer, she snuggles closer, her head settling on my shoulder.

I wish there existed a reality in which I could be her first, to show her how she should be worshipped and cherished. Birdie deserves the world, and I want nothing more than to be the one to give it to her. For tonight, though, all I can do is get her home safely, holding on to the hope that one day I'll be able to tell her the truth about how I feel.

CHAPTER 6

Hungover with a Heartthrob

Birdie

WAKE TO SUNLIGHT STREAMING THROUGH MY CURTAINS, my head pounding in protest. I cover my eyes, squinting as I attempt to sit up. I groan as the room tilts violently, then flop back onto the mattress. There's a reason I rarely drink, and I think my body is punishing me for believing I could toss back shots like water and not face the consequences—namely, the jackhammer rattling my skull.

Fun times.

My memory is hazy, but flashes of my misguided quest to lose my virginity play on a loop in my head. The elbow to the nose. The blood. The shattered glass and spilled whiskey… Gosh. And just when I thought my night couldn't get worse, Walker showed up. Why is he always around to witness my most embarrassing moments? Everything after that is still a blur, reduced to disjoined flashes refusing to line up.

I roll over to get more comfortable and notice my phone charging on the nightstand.

Huh, that's odd.

I figure I would've crashed hard when I got home and not have thought to plug it in. That's when I notice a glass of water and two white pills sitting beside it. Apparently, drunk me is far more responsible than I gave her credit for. I prop myself on one elbow, pick up the pills, and wash them down with a long sip of water.

My only complaint is that I didn't think to take my bra off before getting into bed. I'm wearing an oversized tee that reaches my thighs. Normally I'd just pair it with underwear and skip the bra. Hard to complain when I somehow managed to make it home in one piece without any recollection of how I got here.

I check my messages to see that I have multiple missed calls and dozens of unread messages. I open the group chat first, expecting updates on whatever the girls got up to last night while I was busy drinking myself into oblivion.

Backroads & Bad Decisions Group Chat

Charlie: Word on the street is Birdie left Blue Moon with Walker.

Briar: He was probably giving her a ride home.

Wren: It's no secret she's a lightweight.

Charlie: My source says they were getting pretty cozy.

Briar: I'm sure there's a perfectly reasonable explanation.

Charlie: The whole town has already shipped them as Balker.

I sit up in bed, fighting back the wave of nausea washing over me.

Briar: They're not even an item and have a couple name? So unfair.

Charlie: You and Jensen have one too.

Briar: How do I not know this? What is it?

Charlie: Brensen.

Briar: Aww. That's so cute!

Wren: Birdie, I have to come right out and ask...

Wren: Are you dating Walker?!

Briar: You two would make a cute couple.

I blink at my phone, convinced I've slipped into an alternate reality where my friends have turned into overzealous paparazzi.

Charlie: Have you forgotten your brother only has one-night stands?

Briar: You're right. Birdie is too good for him.

Wren: She's a virgin. There's no way she had a one-night stand.

I drag a hand down my face, letting out a long breath as I flop back onto the mattress. I'm mortified that while I was passed out, they were casually dissecting my nonexistent sex life. If last night had gone as planned, I would finally have some experience under my belt. Instead, I'm still a clueless virgin.

> Briar: I called Walker. It went straight to voicemail.

> Wren: Birdie didn't answer either.

> Charlie: Finally! It's about damn time she got some action.

> Briar: I don't need that image in my head.

> Charlie: What? We're all thinking it.

I'm halfway through replying when a muffled noise comes from the other side of the room. A few seconds later, I hear it again and set my phone down to investigate. What if an animal wandered in through the doggie door while I was asleep? I should've listened when Earl told me to bolt it shut at night.

I crawl to the other side of the bed, cautiously peering over the mattress, half expecting an opossum to be rummaging through my dirty laundry. Instead, I freeze when I find Walker stretched out on the floor with a blanket covering him, snoring softly as he shifts in his sleep.

Holy guacamole, Walker Halstead slept over at my house.

Amid the throbbing in my head, more fragments surface— Walker driving me home, me vomiting on his boots the minute we got in the house, him holding my hair back over the toilet as I babbled about how hot he was. And to make matters worse, I'm pretty sure I told him I'm a virgin and then begged him to be my first.

Oh my gosh. I drop my head in my hands and silently scream. He'll never look at me the same. Curse those darn tequila shots.

They gave me more liquid courage than I had any right to, and I swear I'm never touching alcohol again.

I decide the best course of action is to slip out of my room and hide out somewhere else until he wakes up and leaves. Avoiding him long-term could be a challenge since we see each other at least once a week, but that's a problem for future Birdie.

Maybe this is my sign to become a hermit. Earl could deliver my groceries and drive me to visit my mama. It's not a terrible plan, except Briar and Charlie would riot if I skipped our coffee dates. Plus, there are the animals… Ugh, I need a better solution, but for now, I have to get out of here before Walker wakes up.

I move to the far side of the bed and slide off, tiptoeing across the room, grimacing at every creak of the floorboards. The door is only a few feet from him, so I approach cautiously and crack it open slowly. I'm halfway across the threshold when his deep, gravelly voice stops me in my tracks.

"You sneaking out on me?" I spin around to find Walker awake and smirking at me.

"What did you expect when I woke up and found you in my bedroom uninvited?" I retort.

"Oh, you invited me all right. You were just busy multitasking while hurling into the rosebushes out front," he answers smugly. "Maybe next time you'll think twice before going on another solo drinking spree, huh?"

I lean against the doorway with my arms folded. "Honestly, I'm tempted to go for round two tonight. Eight shots, a cocktail, and half a beer and I'm still standing. That's impressive, don't you think?"

There's no way I'm admitting that I've officially sworn off drinking forever. He doesn't deserve the satisfaction.

Walker tilts his head. "Sorry to burst your bubble, sweetheart, but after your fourth shot you were drinking straight ginger ale. And that cocktail? Just cranberry juice with a splash of sparkling water."

I gasp, stunned. "How could Ryker do that to me? He was supposed to have my—" The rest of my thought catches in my throat when Walker pushes the blanket off him and stands.

Sweet mercy.

He's wearing nothing but dark-wash Wranglers. I can't seem to look away, completely caught off guard by the sight. The man is barefoot and shirtless, his frame rugged and his muscles honed. Heat rises to my cheeks as I take in every ripple and curvature of his bare chest, a light dusting of dark hair trailing over the firm planes of his torso.

"Lost for words?" he drawls.

I clear my throat. "Uh… what?"

When my eyes dart to his face, he's wearing a smug grin. "I'm flattered that you like the view."

"You're huge… I mean, your muscles are huge. Shoot, that came out wrong." I smooth my hair back. "You're practically naked. Staring is unavoidable." That sounded worse.

And this is why I should never open my mouth around attractive men, Walker included.

He strides toward me, his heated gaze trailing over me with molten intensity.

"You're not exactly winning a modesty contest either," he retorts.

I gasp when I notice the hem of my T-shirt has ridden up my thighs and tug it down the best I can.

"I'm assuming you helped me out of my skirt," I say, one hand pinned over the fabric to keep it in place.

"I did," he replies evenly. "Figured you'd be more comfortable and get a better night's sleep if you weren't in dirty clothes. Don't worry, I was on my best behavior," he adds with a smirk.

I swallow hard, my fingers curling tighter around the bottom of my T-shirt. A normal reaction would be embarrassment or even frustration toward Walker. Instead, disappointment washes over me. I can't believe I was drunk the first time a man undressed me.

My eye twitches at my unhinged reaction, eager to steer the conversation elsewhere. "Why did you stay over anyway? You could have easily dropped me off and asked Briar or Charlie to check on me this morning."

"I didn't want you to be alone in case you got sick again." He leans forward to brush a loose piece of hair from my face, causing goose bumps to rise along my arms. "Plus, someone had to make sure you survived the hangover you're pretending doesn't exist."

My stomach does a little flip knowing he gave up his own bed for my floor so he could keep an eye on me. He must be responsible for the pain meds and water too.

"That was very thoughtful. Thank you."

"You're welcome," he murmurs, meeting my gaze. "Why don't you get dressed and meet me downstairs. We need to get some food in you."

"Um, okay?" It comes out like a question.

Part of me is waiting to wake up and discover this was all a dream and that Walker isn't actually standing in my room, shirtless.

He takes my hand in his. "You're not dreaming, Birdie."

Did I say that out loud? That's just great. He has to leave before my brain fries out entirely.

"I'm not going anywhere until you've had a proper breakfast," he adds firmly.

"Crap, I did it again," I mumble.

Considering I'm talking to myself while sober, it's a miracle I didn't do more to embarrass myself at the bar.

Walker chuckles. "I'll be in the kitchen when you're ready. See you in a few minutes, beautiful." He gives my hand a squeeze before letting go, and I'm left staring after him as he leaves the room.

I catch my reflection in the mirror by the door. My hair's a tangled mess, there are mascara streaks under my eyes, and my pounding headache is a stark reminder that hangovers and I don't mix well.

There's no way Walker meant to call me beautiful after seeing me like this, right? That doesn't stop my heart from nearly beating out of my chest as my hand drifts to my cheek, still warm from his touch. Before I can read more into it, my phone buzzes on the nightstand.

Backroads & Bad Decisions Group Chat

Charlie: Birdie Mae Matterson, answer this text or I'm calling the sheriff's office, and we both know Mason would love any excuse to drag you back to that jail cell.

The last thing I need is for them to report me missing. That wouldn't go over well when they discover Walker spent the night—even though nothing happened between us.

Birdie: I'm okay, but I can't talk right now.

Wren: Oh thank god you're alive.

Briar: Where have you been?

Charlie: You're with Walker, aren't you??

Charlie: Girl, you better not leave us hanging.

I put my phone face down on the nightstand, choosing not to answer. They'll have to wait a little longer until I figure out the best way to respond. Right now, I'm going to get dressed and head downstairs to have breakfast with Walker, no matter how awkward it might be.

When I leave my room, a rich, buttery scent drifts from the kitchen. My idea of a home-cooked meal is limited to cereal or toast, so whatever Walker is making is already leagues beyond anything I'd attempt.

As a kid, I loved cooking with my mama. She'd stand beside me, teaching me how to measure and mix, laughing softly whenever I sent flour billowing into the air by stirring too hard or missed the bowl completely. She was always patient, reminding me that mistakes were half the fun. One of the first symptoms she experienced was loss of dexterity in her left hand, which made cooking difficult. Over the years, she had to stop completely, and I soon lost any interest in it too. It's a painful reminder of who she used to be and what's been taken from us because of an incurable disease.

I enter the kitchen and find Walker at the stove with his back to me. My throat goes dry, and I'm unable to look away from the curve of his shoulders and the way his muscles flex with each movement.

"You did have a shirt on when you got here last night, right?" I tease.

He spins around when he hears my voice, his eyes twinkling. "Checking me out *twice* before coffee? That hangover must be worse than I thought."

"I'm not checking you out," I insist as I move closer. "It's bad manners to roam around someone's house half-naked." Okay, I may have shamelessly stared, but it's hard not to when he looks like he stepped straight off the cover of a western romance novel.

"It's also not very polite to throw up on someone when they're trying to hold back your hair and you keep swatting at them for doing it wrong." He laughs as he sprinkles cheese on the eggs he's cooking before moving them off the hot burner.

My jaw drops in shock. "That's so humiliating! Why would you bring that up now?"

It's bad enough he saw me at my worst, but to be caught up in the middle of my drunken chaos is something else entirely. Then again, it's probably a good thing that part of the night is still fuzzy, or I might die of mortification reliving it.

"You were ridiculously cute, thinking you held your liquor well, and I didn't want to burst your bubble."

Walker is an enigma. Most guys bolt after my first accidental disaster or sign of awkwardness. Yet he remains unfazed, no matter how clumsy I am or how many times I trip over my words.

I reach across him to snag a piece of cheese that hasn't melted yet, popping it into my mouth. "How come I didn't know you could cook?"

He shrugs, taking two plates from the cabinet next to the stove. "I like taking care of the people who are important to me, and making them food is one way I do that."

My pulse spikes at the implication that I could be one of those people—and the alarming part is how much I want to be. Until last night, Walker was just Briar's brother and one of my friends. Even though I'm confident nothing physical happened, something has shifted between us. I'm all warm and fuzzy watching him take care of me. I can't stop staring.

"Want your coffee now too?" Walker asks.

"You made me coffee?" My voice comes out a little breathless.

He nods. "Everyone in Bluebell knows you can't leave the house without your full caffeine quota."

I'm stunned speechless as Walker crosses to the other side of the kitchen and retrieves a mug sitting in what looks like a hot water bath. He lifts it out, dries it with a towel, and hands it to me. "One oat milk latte with a dash of cinnamon—just the way you like it."

I'm left weak at the knees knowing he remembers my coffee

order down to the exact milk I prefer. Then again, I shouldn't be surprised, considering he's always showing up at the feed store with my favorite meals.

He motions to the table. "Take a seat, and I'll bring over your breakfast."

Still unable to find the words to answer, I do as he suggests.

My mouth waters when a minute later he sets a plate of avocado toast in front of me, complete with a drizzle of oil and a sprinkle of pepper flakes.

"This looks amazing," I manage to get out. "Your mom would definitely approve of the presentation."

Julie's cooking is legendary. It was always a treat when Briar invited me over for dinner at her place. My mama was a good cook, but Julie's culinary skills are on another level altogether.

"She should be," Walker says, chest puffed out with pride. "She spent countless hours drilling the basics into Heath and me, saying no son of hers would grow up without knowing his way around a kitchen."

I push back the sadness that creeps in, a reminder that he's lucky enough to still have his mom around in a way I'll never have mine again. To distract myself, I cut a piece of toast, add some egg on top, and take a bite—the flavors exploding on my tongue.

"It's so good," I exclaim.

Walker smiles as he takes the seat beside me. "Glad you like it."

I sip my coffee between bites, noting that it tastes far better than my usual attempts and even tops the one from Lasso & Latte. I've never had a man make me breakfast before, and as much as I wish we could enjoy the rest of our meal in peace, there's something important we have to discuss before he leaves.

"We might have a problem," I state reluctantly.

Walker leans back in his chair, resting a hand on his thigh. "And what would that be?"

"Word got out that we left the bar together last night, and now the whole town thinks we hooked up—including your sister." I stay perfectly still, holding my breath for his reply.

He runs a hand over his stubbled jawline, contemplating the information before giving a small shrug. "And?"

I let out an exasperated exhale, set my fork down, and turn to face him. "This is serious. I woke up to a bunch of messages in the group chat asking if we slept together, and I'm not sure how to respond."

"Let's get one thing straight." His eyes lock on mine. "If we'd actually done what everyone thinks, sleep would have been the last thing on our minds." I gulp, my heart hammering in my chest, unable to stop myself from picturing all the possibilities he's hinting at.

I shake my head, forcing those thoughts aside. "Your sister thinks we hooked up, and I doubt she'll believe me if I tell her otherwise when she finds out you spent the night."

I'm certain she or Charlie has already called Earl and confirmed he didn't bring me home. Plus, Mrs. Bixby will absolutely investigate when she spots the extra truck in my driveway. She doesn't miss the chance to stir up gossip, and soon everyone will know Walker was here.

Walker blows out a breath, raking a hand through his hair. "How much of what happened at the bar do you remember?"

I wish he'd tell me where he was going with this question so I could plan my response better. I'm tempted to claim it's all still a blur and hope he never brings it up again, but I can't bring myself to lie about this.

"I think most everything, why?"

He nods slowly. "Good. Do you recall asking me to teach you?"

I recall fragments of that conversation, including the part I assume he's referring to, but I'd rather not confirm it.

"Teach me what?" I ask, feigning innocence.

He scoots his chair closer, his gaze never leaving mine. "You asked me to take your virginity. To be your first, and to teach you how to flirt."

"I might recall," I say, my voice coming out hoarse.

"What would you think if I were to suggest we make that a reality?"

I blink rapidly. "Are you saying we should have sex?"

He clears his throat. "I'm proposing we give you what you want in a safe and controlled setting."

I instinctively lean forward, the draw to him magnetic. "And what is it you think I want, Walker?"

The question hangs in the air as he mirrors my posture, until our knees are touching and our faces are only inches apart. His warm breath grazes my cheek, and my pulse kicks into overdrive, heat pooling low in my stomach.

"To learn how to flirt and fuck. At least that's what you told me last night," he states bluntly. "If we pretend we're a couple, I don't see why we can't do both."

I stare at him, holding my hand up. "Wait… are you suggesting a fake relationship?" The words feel foreign on my tongue.

He gently grips my knee, sending a shiver down my spine. "Yes, I am. If you let me teach you, we'll be spending a lot of time together, so why not use the perfect alibi and pretend we're a couple? Seems like everyone already assumes we're heading in that direction anyway. Might as well kill two birds with one stone."

I'm too shell-shocked to scold him for using a metaphor that promotes poultry violence.

It's official—my brain has short-circuited because there's no chance Walker Halstead just suggested we pretend to date *and* sleep together. His type is women who are bold, sexy, and confident—everything I'm not.

"Two birds, one stone," I repeat softly, letting the concept sink in. "I thought you didn't date," I blurt out after a few seconds.

"There's a first time for everything. Makes it more believable that I'm so smitten you're the first woman to tie me down. You can even stage a big breakup when it's all over and publicly hurl insults at me."

As scandalized as I want to be by his proposal, it's no more reckless than walking into a bar prepared to go home with the first guy who showed me any interest. At least with Walker, I know he'd respect my boundaries and treat me right.

Truth be told, there's no one more qualified to teach me how to flirt and to practice being intimate. I'm both terrified and intrigued, unsure how I would survive his lessons without blushing myself into oblivion.

I straighten in my seat, meeting his gaze. "If I'm going to consider your offer, I have conditions."

"I love a woman who takes charge." He smirks. "Lay them on me."

My stomach flips as I give him a shaky smile.

Here goes nothing.

CHAPTER 7

Operation "Fake" Dating

Walker

BIRDIE TAPS A FINGER TO HER CHIN. "IF WE DO THIS, THE truth stays between us. Briar would be disappointed in us both, Wren would try to talk me out of it, and Charlie can't keep a secret to save her life."

I should put a stop to this immediately. Hell, I should've shut the door on our conversation last night instead of going along with the harebrained idea to pretend we're a couple.

The problem is that spending the night here has opened my mind to the possibility of having more with her, even if it's just a temporary facade of what could be. I can't shake the memory of her in my lap, how her body naturally molded to mine as if she'd always belonged there.

The reality is, if I don't step in, Birdie will eventually find someone else to experiment with, and there's no guarantee they'll treat her right. I'd never be able to live with myself if she got hurt when I had the chance to help her navigate her desires safely and show her that she's a treasure worth protecting. Someone who's deserving of love and respect.

"Can I tell Heath?" I ask.

Birdie shakes her head. "I'd prefer you don't. He'd judge me with that permanent scowl of his, and his grumpy attitude is intimidating enough as it is." She's got him pegged perfectly.

I snicker. "He's not so bad if you look past his grouchy exterior."

"You only say that because he's your brother. Putting up with each other is part of the gig." Birdie winks.

There's more truth to that statement than she realizes. Heath and I have always been close. We shared a bedroom growing up and have worked on the ranch together since we could walk. But that doesn't take away his frustrations with me for not fully embracing my responsibilities. Even now, I suspect he's still bitter that I took the deputy job instead of putting in more hours at the ranch, to help him expand it to its full potential.

Now that I think about it, he'd probably argue that faking a relationship with Birdie is a terrible idea, using my past mistakes to lecture me. Best to keep him in the dark for now.

"You're right. We shouldn't tell Heath," I agree.

I scoop up a generous portion of eggs, searching for anything to focus on besides Birdie's big blue eyes and the way they draw me in.

She shifts in her seat, twisting her hands together in her lap. "What about my dad?"

I stiffen, my gaze snapping to hers with my fork halfway to my mouth. *Holy shit.*

I forgot that if we go through with this, I'll have to tell the sheriff that I'm "dating" his daughter. He's the type to glare you into submission while packing a gun at his hip. It's no secret how protective he is of Birdie, and I'm betting he'll lose his shit. The worst part? I promised Birdie she could pin the breakup on me. I can only imagine how much her dad will hate me then. It would be equally bad if he found out it was all pretend. He'd probably accuse me of using Birdie, which couldn't be further from the truth.

"Maybe we should steer clear of your dad for a while," I suggest, giving Birdie a sideways glance.

"Oh sure, he's totally not going to ask questions if his best deputy goes off the grid," she says with a straight face.

The corner of my mouth quirks up. "I'm the best, huh?"

She rolls her eyes, holding her coffee mug against her chest. "It's not that impressive when there's not much competition. Eli falls asleep at his desk when he's supposed to be doing paperwork, Cole hides behind the diner eating donuts for hours instead of patrolling, and Mason's a total suck-up with no common sense."

Yeah, Sheriff Matterson's options are limited. That's probably why he was excited when I showed interest. The ranch is thriving under Heath's leadership, and with my share of the profits, money isn't a concern, making it possible to volunteer my time.

I put my fork down and push my plate away, deciding breakfast should wait until I've gotten an answer from Birdie.

"You'd better be prepared to have my mom invite you to family dinner more often. She's going to be over the moon when she finds out we're together… At least that she'll think we are," I stammer out quickly.

Suddenly, I'm the one tongue-tied, struggling to keep my cool, knowing that the future hinges on Birdie's decision.

"I'd never say no to one of your mom's home-cooked meals," she says, taking a sip of coffee. "My only other condition is that we keep our PDA to a minimum." She tugs her bottom lip between her teeth, watching me expectantly.

I shake my head. "Not a chance. The whole idea is teaching you how to interact with someone you're interested in, and that includes PDA. Besides, if we were really an item, I wouldn't be able to keep my hands off you." I take the mug from her hands, setting it on the table. "No one would buy our act if we looked uncomfortable whenever we got close to each other."

I take her hands in mine, brushing my thumbs along her palms, the soft hitch of her breath anchoring me. I'm beginning to think she's more affected by me than she lets on, sparking a glimmer of hope that this attraction might not be entirely one-sided.

Her throat bobs as she swallows, eyes darting between my face and the floor. "Fine, but I'm warning you—my friends will tease us mercilessly for every little public display. They've been waiting ages for me to have a boyfriend and won't miss a chance to make a fuss about it."

I bite back a grin. "You used the present tense. Does that mean you're in?" I hold her gaze, gauging every reaction. "If you don't want this, we stop now."

I'll walk away if that's what she wants, but that doesn't mean it won't hurt like hell.

Birdie studies me silently, her expression unreadable. The only noise is from the grandfather clock ticking in the hallway, each beat stretching the space between hope and disappointment.

When she finally speaks, my chest tightens with anticipation.

"It's a sweet gesture to offer me an out, but there's no need." She holds out her hand. "I'm in. Let's do this."

I take her hand, lifting it to my mouth, pressing a soft kiss to her knuckles. "Can't wait to start pretend dating you, troublemaker."

More than you know.

I'm eager to take her out and spoil her the way she deserves, but more than anything, I'm looking forward to the quiet moments when it'll be just the two of us—laughing, talking, and getting to know each other beyond friendship. I've spent so long imagining what it'd be like to call her mine, and now that I'm one step closer to making that a reality, I have to do everything in my power to get this right.

Birdie lets out a soft laugh. "Careful now. You might regret saying that."

"Never," I vow.

Birdie and I agreed she'd have her first official lesson after work tomorrow. In the meantime, she'll be busy fielding questions from her friends, and I wouldn't be surprised if Briar stopped by the ranch house later for an interrogation. She loves Birdie like a sister and wouldn't let anyone hurt her—including me.

Pulling up to the house now, I spot Ma on the front porch, knitting on her favorite rocking chair.

She's the principal at Willow Creek Elementary, and her weekends are her chance to decompress after a week full of staff meetings, wrangling kids, and dealing with parental demands—making her knitting all the more puzzling. She despises it, dismissing it as a tedious hobby. So the only reason she'd be out here with her needles on a Sunday morning instead of curled up with one of her romance novels is that she's waiting for someone—and judging by the gossip currently spreading like wildfire through Bluebell, that someone has to be me. Looks like Birdie won't be the only one busy fielding questions today.

I park and step out of the truck, tucking the keys in my back pocket. Sure enough, Ma comes down the porch to meet me.

"Where have you been? You never came home last night," she chides, stopping me with a stern look.

"Funny, I don't recall you fussing this much all the other times I've stayed out," I say, leaning against one of the porch columns.

That's only half true. Even with her kids grown, she still keeps tabs on us and isn't above using the town grapevine to stay informed of our whereabouts.

Which is why I'm proud that I've managed to keep a

particular semiweekly routine under wraps for so long. For now, it has to stay a secret, though it's tricky explaining why I'm coming home late or slipping away from the ranch after work without anyone knowing where I go.

Ma plants her hands on her hips. She may be a foot shorter, but her stance radiates authority.

"Enough with the games, Walker. Are you seeing Birdie Matterson or not?" Guess we're cutting right to the chase.

"Yeah, I am," I reply, not missing a beat.

This woman is a human lie detector, and if she catches even a hint of hesitation, she'll call me out. I'm not sure what I expected, but a broad smile immediately crossing her face wasn't it. I figured she'd start with a set of rapid-fire questions followed by a reprimand for keeping her in the dark.

"This is the best news," Ma exclaims.

"Glad you think so."

Her expression tightens, the corners of her mouth pulling into a frown. Looks like I was too quick to judge the situation.

"How could you keep something this important from your own mother? How do you think I felt when I went by the general store early this morning to drop off supplies for Ethel, and she asked me how I felt about my son dating the sheriff's daughter? I had no answers because you never tell me anything." She huffs in irritation.

Looks like she's kicking things off with a scolding, served with a side of guilt to make me squirm. Arguing now would be a losing game.

"I'm sorry, Ma." I stare down at the dirt, nudging a loose rock with my boot. "Birdie and I wanted to be certain before making things official. If it makes you feel better, everyone else will be equally as surprised when they hear the news."

Birdie and I made sure we had our story straight before I left her place. In a town where everyone talks, we didn't want anyone to catch any inconsistencies in our narrative.

"No, Walker, it doesn't." Ma sighs, a frown creasing her forehead. "You know how much I hate it when you keep secrets from me."

I push down the sting of guilt, knowing I'm doing exactly that right now, and it doesn't appear that she suspects a thing.

"What if I told you that you're the first person I've shared the news with?" I toss it out there, hoping it'll appease her.

Ma's eyes brighten, and I know I've struck a chord. "Am I?"

"You are."

Not that I intend to broadcast it later—everyone will know soon enough if they don't already. Heath will definitely give me shit about it, and Pops will act interested only because it's important to Ma. He's never been as invested in our love lives as she has.

I let out a grunt as Ma throws her arms around me, drawing me in for a hug. "I'm so proud of you. It was exhausting having a rake for a son." She steps back slightly, placing her hands firmly on my shoulders.

I chuckle. A *rake*? That must have come straight from one of her historical romances. I've read plenty of those lately, and it never fails to amuse me how much women swoon over a dashing lord with a reputation for scandal.

"You don't have to worry about that anymore," I tell her.

I have no interest in anyone but Birdie, and as long as our arrangement stands, she's off-limits to other men. I won't hesitate to make sure everyone gets the memo that she's taken.

Ma wipes her brow with exaggerated flair. "Thank the Lord. It's about time you settled down and gave me some grandbabies."

I lift a hand to stop her from going on about fictional children. "Whoa, you're jumping the gun, don't you think? Birdie and I just started seeing each other."

"Can't come soon enough," she counters with a mischievous grin.

My phone buzzes in my pocket, saving me from having to answer.

Looks like Heath texted.

Heath: You're late.

Shit. I was supposed to meet him in the south pasture half an hour ago, and he's not the type to be kept waiting.

Walker: Sorry. Be there soon.

Ma clicks her tongue in disapproval. "What's more important than talking with your mother?"

"It's Heath," I explain. "He's waiting for me, and I still need to shower and change." I'm still wearing my good jeans and a button-down—hardly practical for a day in the fields. "We'll finish our conversation later, I promise."

I turn to leave, but she catches my arm, stopping me short. "We most certainly will. And make sure Birdie is at the next family dinner. No arguments."

"She'll be there," I promise, thinking back to my conversation warning Birdie about this very thing.

She's been to more than a few, but this one will be different. This time, she'll be there as my girlfriend, not just Briar's friend.

Fuck, I love the sound of that. I'm already feeling territorial, even though our relationship is supposed to be pretend. Hard not to when I'm about to do everything I can to prove it's real.

"We should have Birdie's family over soon too," Ma says with a smile. "It's been ages since I've seen Elizabeth, and I'd love to catch up."

Birdie's mom taught at Willow Creek Elementary but retired early, nearly a decade ago. She never comes to town anymore and though Birdie talks about her often, she keeps details of her mom's life private.

All I know is that Birdie is going through a lot, and I wish I could help more. For now, all I can do is offer my support from a distance and hope that she eventually realizes she isn't alone. Fake relationship or not, I'll be there for her, even if it means helping her navigate complicated family dynamics. Every family has them, even if things look picture-perfect on the surface.

"We'll see. I'll have to run it by Birdie first."

Honestly, I'd rather skip dinner with her dad. Things could go sideways fast, and we'll already have plenty of awkwardness at work as is.

"Okay, but if Birdie has any concerns, I'll talk to her. I'm persuasive when I want to be," Ma says, clearly pleased with herself.

"Oh, trust me, I'm well aware," I tease, leaning in to press a kiss to her cheek.

She can get intense about things that matter to her, but it comes from a good place, and she'd do anything for our family. Too bad her excitement over my dating life won't last. I can already picture her disappointment when Birdie ends things. We haven't even started this pretend relationship, and I'm already dreading that part.

CHAPTER 8

Confessions In The Condom Aisle

Birdie

WALKER CLEANED MY KITCHEN BEFORE HE LEFT, AND once he was gone, the silence was deafening. I'm used to being on my own, but getting a glimpse of what it might be like to share my space with another person made the emptiness hit harder than usual. It had me second-guessing if I'd made the right decision. Until now, I haven't known anything other than being single. What happens when I finally experience what it's like on the other side, only to lose it when this charade ends? There's a real possibility that no one else would willingly step into the mess that is my life.

At least with Walker, I can hold on to pieces of the truth. A real relationship would put everything out in the open, exposing all my flaws and fears. For now, I'm choosing to live in the moment, taking in everything Walker is willing to teach me and dealing with the consequences later.

After feeding the animals, I'm anxious to get out of the house but not ready for Earl's barrage of questions, so I set off toward my parents' across town. It's a thirty-minute walk if I move fast enough to avoid any passersby who might try to strike up a conversation.

To pass the time, I muster the courage to message the girls back.

Backroads & Bad Decisions Group Chat

Birdie: Sorry for the short reply earlier. Walker made breakfast.

My thumb hovers over send, wincing when I press it. My text doesn't outright say he stayed over, but it's enough to gauge their reaction.

Charlie: Oh. My. God. I was right. You're totally fucking him.

Briar: Will you please refrain from referencing my brother and fucking in the same sentence?

Wren: Does this mean you're together?

Birdie: It does.

There's no turning back now.

Charlie: Did I mention I was right??

Briar: Repeatedly.

Wren: Birdie, I have to know what happened last night.

Charlie: Yes. We need all the details.

Briar: No. We really don't.

Birdie: Walker and I haven't slept together yet.

That's the truth.

Charlie: You're telling me Walker, Mr. Playboy Extraordinaire... what? Just crashed in your bed?

Birdie: Actually, he slept on the floor. I had too much to drink, and he wanted to keep an eye on me.

I'm glad we agreed to keep our story as close to reality as possible. It makes it easier to keep track of the details.

Wren: That's so sweet.

Briar: It's reassuring that my brother's not a total caveman.

Birdie: You're not mad?

Briar: At you? Never. Walker, on the other hand, is on thin ice. If he hurts you, he's a dead man.

After my chat with the girls, I'm feeling a lot better about my situation—at least the part where they seem to have accepted the story that Walker and I are together and are actually okay with it.

I'm out of breath by the time I reach my parents' house. It sits at the end of the block, surrounded by large trees in the front yard and a tall fence enclosing the ten acres at the back.

When Mama's health declined, the front yard became overgrown, and the house's exterior showed signs of wear and neglect—things she had once maintained before she got sick. Dad struggled to pick up the slack between work and Mama's care, so it all fell to the wayside.

However, recently I've noticed the rose bushes she loves so much have been pruned and are blooming beautifully. And the faded red door, which was peeling, has been painted robin blue. She used to paint it a new color every year, and seeing the tradition brought back makes the place feel like home again. It makes me a little less angry with Dad knowing he's finally making an effort to fix things around here, even if that means he's hired help. Either way, it shows he's trying, and that's what counts.

When I get inside, I kick off my sneakers by the front door and line them up on the shoe rack, keeping the hallway clear. I take the water bottle from my bag, grateful I'd had the foresight to bring it along before hanging the bag on the coatrack. My idea of exercise is chasing an injured pig around my yard, so the long walk here had my lungs screaming and my legs burning.

I find Tess in the living room, curled on the couch, reading. Dad prefers the nurses to stay by Mama's side, but she sees her alone time as her remaining independence. When he's out of town, the nurses respect her wishes rather than hover in her room down the hall.

Tess glances up, smiling warmly. "Hey, sweet girl. Earl take out any mailboxes on your way over?"

"Actually, I walked today. I needed the fresh air."

She closes her book, and sets it on the cushion. "Can't argue with that. It's lovely outside, and it's probably the safer choice."

One thing I appreciate about Tess is that she keeps to herself, steering clear of town gossip. That's why I like dropping by when she's on shift. After a rough day or a mishap while rescuing animals, it's nice to be here—a bubble away from the chaos. The only thing that would make it better is if Mama wasn't sick and Tess didn't have to be here at all.

I lean against the doorframe, taking a drink from my water bottle. "How's Mama doing today?"

"Good. She had a hearty bowl of cream of wheat topped with diced strawberries, and we followed it up with a stroll outside in the sunshine."

Tess pushes Mama along the backyard path in her wheelchair. Dad had it built when she was first diagnosed so she could enjoy fresh air in private as her condition advanced.

To this day, most folks are aware that my mama's health took a turn, though her diagnosis has been kept under wraps thanks to her doctor and nurses. I used to beg my parents to let me confide in my friends, wishing for their support, but they value their privacy and thought sharing the details would attract too much unwanted attention and pity.

Over the years, I've learned to shoulder the loss quietly, navigating the burden of keeping this part of my life a secret when all I want is to share it with someone else. But I respect my parents too much to go against their wishes.

"I'm glad her appetite's up. Any discomfort in her legs?"

"Thankfully not today," Tess says.

I let out a sigh of relief. "Is she watching *Gilmore Girls*?"

Tess nods. "Last I checked, she was on the episode where Rory reluctantly agrees to a date with a guy from school, and Lorelai needed a hand with a project, so she went over to Luke's garage."

At this point we could probably both recite most episodes from memory.

"Why don't you take a break for a couple of hours?" I suggest. "I plan to stay for a while."

I don't work on Sundays, so I can spend the afternoons here. It's the one day I'm not rushing around and can fully enjoy my time with Mama.

Tess gathers her bag from the coffee table, slipping her book inside. "All right. I'm heading into town, but if anything comes up don't hesitate to call me."

"I won't."

She stands, coming over to give me a hug. "You're a good daughter, Birdie. Your mama loves you very much."

I rest my head on her shoulder. Since Mama lost the strength to lift her arms, Tess makes a point of hugging me often. The nurses have become like family, and Dad and I couldn't manage without them.

"Thanks, Tess. For everything," I murmur.

"Always here for you, honey." She gives me one last squeeze before drawing back. "See you soon."

She moves to the entryway to get her shoes, and I head in the opposite direction.

My parents' room was originally upstairs, but my dad had the dining room and his home office on the main floor converted into a bedroom when the stairs became too challenging for Mama. A walk-in shower is connected, making it easier for the nurses to assist her. Lately she can barely stand for a few seconds at a time, so most of her days are spent in bed or in the reclining chair by the window, to preserve the little energy she has left.

I pause in the doorway of her room when I see she's sleeping. She's propped up in bed with a couple of pillows tucked behind her head, the TV on the nightstand playing softly in the background.

Wisps of silver-streaked blonde hair frame her face, the rest gathered into a loose braid over her shoulder, exposing hollowed cheeks. Her features are softened and slightly drawn in, a reflection of her reduced appetite and fading energy.

Her eyes flutter open, the blue of her irises the same shade as mine. She gives me a crooked smile, raising two fingers on her right hand to beckon me closer.

"Hi, s-sweet girl," she says slowly, a slight tremor in her voice.

Every word is a precious gift that I'll never take for granted.

"Hey, Mama." I cross the room and climb onto the bed beside her. "Watching without me again?" I motion toward the TV where Lorelai and Luke crouch shoulder to shoulder in his garage. Their hands accidentally graze, and they both freeze for a beat, looking into each other's eyes before breaking into amused smiles.

It reminds me of the tension simmering between Walker and me this morning, and how I couldn't stop staring at his chiseled abs or the way his mouth turned up at the corners when he smiled. As much as I wish I could talk about it with Mama, I don't want to cause her any undue stress—because finding out I'm dating Bluebell's resident playboy would definitely do that, especially when it will eventually end in a breakup.

"I c-couldn't wait. Season f-five is my favorite," Mama stutters slightly, tilting her head to get a better look at me.

I scoot closer, tucking a loose strand of hair behind her ear. "We both know it's because of Logan. Who wouldn't fall for a guy who gifts his girl a Birkin?" A small bubble of laughter escapes her, and it's music to my ears. "I'm here the rest of the day, so we should be able to get through the rest of this season."

"Good. I'm h-happy that you're here."

"Me too." I lean my head against her arm, turning toward the TV so she won't see the tears welling in my eyes. "I love you."

She presses a kiss to my head. "I love you too, sweet girl."

"I love you most," I whisper.

The doctor thinks we probably have a couple more years with her, but that knowledge doesn't make it any easier. I'd give anything to slow the clock and guarantee more moments like this.

Spending most of yesterday with my mama was exactly the reset I needed before the beginning of a chaotic week.

My nerves are shot thinking about my looming "lesson" with Walker, or whatever we're calling it. He sent a text saying he'll see me tonight, but he never specified whether that meant his place or mine. He does have his own apartment attached to the ranch house, but his family can easily watch me come and go—Briar included—so I'm desperately hoping he plans to come to my house.

The other thing bothering me is that I'm unsure if he's bringing condoms, or if that responsibility falls on me. I'm on birth control, but I don't know when Walker was last tested. I could ask him, but that would only pile on to my humiliation, and asking Charlie or Wren is out of the question. They'd never let me live it down, so being prepared is my only option.

Thankfully, I left for my shift at the feed store thirty minutes early this morning, giving myself time to pick up what I need before the day gets hectic.

I shift forward so Earl can hear me from the driver's seat. "Can we swing by Town & Country Drugs? I want to grab something before work."

He tips his cap with a nod. "Sure thing, Miss Birdie."

Before I can register what's happening, he swerves across the double-yellow lines, straight into the path of an oncoming SUV. Horns blare as I clutch the door handle, bracing for impact that never comes. We narrowly avoid a collision as the SUV screeches past, missing us by mere inches. I'm jolted in my seat as our tires scrape the curb, the front wheel riding up onto the sidewalk, where Earl parks us on the side of the road. In hindsight, I should have asked to stop at the drugstore before we were half a block away.

For a split second there, I thought I might die a virgin, only hours before I finally got to change that. The universe has a cruel sense of humor.

"We're here," Earl announces proudly, completely oblivious to the danger he just put us in. Bless his heart.

He hums his favorite Johnny Cash tune as he gets out and opens my car door.

"Thanks," I manage, slinging my bag over my shoulder as I climb out, my legs shaky with nerves. "I'll be quick."

"I'm coming with you. I'm spending the night at Ethel's, and she loves them fancy chocolates with the gold foil wrappers." He pretends to unwrap an invisible chocolate and pop it into his mouth with exaggerated gusto.

Earl and Ethel have been seeing each other on and off for decades. They don't bother with labels, but they seem content, so who am I to judge? I envy their ability to be unapologetically bold, not caring about what anyone thinks. Me? I'm diving headfirst into a fake relationship to learn how to be less awkward around men and sneaking around buying condoms.

"Oh no, really, let me get the chocolates. You can wait in the car," I chirp, my voice squeaking on the last word.

Earl gives me a dismissive wave. "That's mighty kind of you, but she's real particular about her chocolate. I'd better grab it myself to make sure I get the right one."

My shoulders slump as I give him a small nod. "Yeah. That makes sense."

I don't want to push further and raise suspicion. Looks like I'll just have to be extra stealthy inside, which obviously isn't my strong suit. I wish Walker were here—I could really use his advice.

I'm not even flirting with anyone yet and I'm already making a mess of things.

I tug my bag up higher onto my shoulder as I walk into the store, Earl trailing close behind. Fortunately, the only other person in sight is Clark, the clerk, who gives me a friendly wave as I pass.

"Good morning, Birdie. Can I help you find anything?"

"Just looking around, thanks," I say, then grab a basket.

Earl heads straight to the chocolate section, conveniently on the opposite side of the store from my target. To stay under the radar, I wander the aisles, feigning interest in a new pickle-flavored potato chip they recently got in, and then a lipstick display on an end cap near the aisle.

Once I notice Earl is distracted by a lively debate with Clark over milk versus dark chocolate, I make a beeline for the condoms. It won't take long, and on my way to the register, I'll toss a few extra items into my basket in case Earl decides to wait for me.

I'm confident about my plan—until I reach the condom aisle. Dozens of options span multiple shelves, and I scan them frantically like my life depends on it. Honestly, half of these labels might as well be in another language—*Extra Sensitive, Ribbed for Pleasure, Strawberry-Flavored, Glow-in-the-Dark, Extra Large, Jumbo, Latex-Free…* and the list goes on.

I pick up a purple box with a feather on it and read the description, wondering how I'm supposed to know if Walker has a sensitivity. Next, I reach for one labeled *Strawberry-Flavored* with a kiss stamped on the front. *Do people really give blow jobs when the recipient is wearing one of these?* The last one I reach for is a pack of jumbo condoms. *How am I supposed to know how big Walker is? Do guys measure themselves? What's the difference between Extra Large and Jumbo? Can a condom be too big?*

I'm sweating bullets, clutching the boxes to my chest, painfully aware of just how out of my depth I am. Just as I'm ready to buy one of everything, my gaze drifts to the other side of the aisle, stacked with row after row of lubricant, and another wave of panic hits me.

I'm moving that way when my tote bag bumps the shelves behind me, sending a cascade of condom boxes tumbling to the tiled floor. The racket is so loud you'd think I'd dropped a bag of bricks instead of a pile of small boxes.

Before I can react, Earl charges down the aisle, alarm etched on his face, brandishing his chocolates like a weapon, with Clark right on his heels.

"Miss Birdie, are you all right?" he asks, his voice tight with concern.

"I'm fine!" I reply, my voice shooting up an octave. "I got turned around looking for shaving cream and accidentally knocked over some merchandise with my bag. Just me being clumsy."

No chance they buy that pathetic excuse. I come here so often I could navigate the aisles blindfolded, and the layout hasn't changed in over a decade.

Earl's gaze sweeps over the boxes scattered at my feet before landing on the ones still clutched to my chest.

"I tried to catch some of the boxes before they hit the floor, but clearly, I failed spectacularly," I blurt out, letting out a squeaky laugh.

I shift from foot to foot, cheeks burning hotter than the fluorescent lights above. My mind races through every possible way to fix this disaster, but I come up empty. My only hope is that Earl and Clark agree to play along before anyone else walks in.

"It'd be amazing if we could pretend this never happened," I offer, silently pleading with my eyes.

I hold my breath, waiting for their response. If they don't go along with my suggestion, the entire town will soon learn about my public embarrassment in the condom aisle.

Clark sidesteps Earl, dodging the fallen boxes, and reaches for the ones in my hands. I hesitantly let them go and watch as he tucks them into his apron pockets.

"Earl, show Birdie where the shaving cream is? I'll clean all this up and meet you at the front when you're ready to check out."

My mouth hangs open in shock as Earl slips his arm through mine, steering me down the aisle. "Come on, Miss Birdie. Let's get what else you came for so you're not late for work." He glances around to make sure we're alone, then drops his voice to a whisper. "You done picked some good options back there. Ethel swears by the ribbed ones if you want a suggestion on what to try first." I could have gone my whole life without hearing that tidbit.

"Don't worry," Earl adds. "My lips are sealed tighter than a Mason jar." He mimics locking his mouth and tossing away the key.

Maybe I should be horrified that my taxi driver is doling out advice on my sex life, but instead I'm relieved to have someone in my corner. Somehow, I trust Earl to keep this between us, and I couldn't be more grateful.

The problem is, I can't even buy condoms without creating a full-blown disaster. How am I supposed to get through sex without screwing that up too? At least I gave Walker fair warning that he'd regret this arrangement, and I suspect it'll happen sooner than either of us expects.

CHAPTER 9

Man I Need

Walker

THE CLOCK ON THE DASH SHOWS I'M FIFTEEN MINUTES early to get Birdie. I called Earl earlier to give him a heads-up that I'd be the one picking her up from work for our date. He sounded oddly amused, then lectured me on being *responsible* and *safe*. Like he's one to talk; the whole town has dodged his vehicle at one point or another.

On the drive over, it occurred to me that I've never really done the whole dating thing. In the past, I'd meet someone at the bar and end up back at her place—easy, uncomplicated, and minimal effort required. With Birdie, I want to do this right and show her the kind of treatment she deserves. That's why I swung by the local florist and grabbed her favorite flowers. I may have earned several perplexed stares, but seeing her reaction will make it worth it.

I'm in the feed store parking lot, drumming my fingers on the steering wheel to the beat of "Something Like That" by Tim McGraw on the radio. While I wait, I figure I'll text Briar. I've been meaning to ask why Earl always drives Birdie around, and his comments earlier brought it to mind.

Walker: Why doesn't Birdie drive?

Briar: Well, hello to you too, big brother. It's so nice to hear from you.

Briar Halstead added Heath Halstead to the chat

Walker: Why did you add Heath to our conversation?

Briar: Because it's much more fun to tease you with backup.

Heath: I'd rather sit this one out.

Briar: Oh no, you don't. I'm your only sister, and that means you're obligated to participate.

Briar named the chat Group Therapy Halstead Siblings Edition

Walker: Can you answer my question? I don't have much time.

Briar: Until what? Midnight strikes and you turn into a pumpkin?

Walker: Birdie gets off work soon, and I'm taking her out.

Heath: So that's why you left the ranch early.

Walker: Is that a problem? I finished the fence repairs like you asked.

Heath: Would it matter if there was?

I grunt my irritation at his flat reply. Over text, he's impossible to read, and it's a constant guessing game to see if he's serious.

Briar: Nope. No arguing today. My former tramp of a brother is going on a proper date, and that's something worth celebrating.

Looks like Briar isn't taking any chances where Heath's mood is concerned.

Walker: Hold up. Did you just call me a tramp?

Briar: Former, if that's any consolation.

Walker: If I say yes, will you please tell me why Birdie doesn't drive?

Briar: Fine, but only because you said please.

Briar: A rabbit family is living under her truck, and she refuses to make them move.

Heath: If that's the case, she's never driving again. Those things multiply faster than weeds.

Briar: Charlie and I have been telling her that for ages.

> Heath: When did Charlie become an expert on population control?

> Walker: We've got to come up with a long-term solution. I'm not comfortable with Earl driving her around anymore with his deteriorating eyesight.

As nice as the man is, he can barely see past the end of the driveway, let alone navigate busy streets.

> Heath: Did you hear he nearly caused a wreck near the drugstore this morning?

> Walker: Was Birdie with him?

> Heath: Not sure. He almost got T-boned while cutting across traffic.

That only cements my decision. Until I figure out a long-term fix, I'll be Birdie's chauffeur.

I glance at the clock again—seven on the dot. Birdie should be coming out soon. She might like her job, but she's never one to stick around past her shift unless an animal needs rescuing, like the unsold chicken and ducks. She's been known to take them home rather than let them be abandoned or euthanized.

As predicted, less than a minute later, Birdie strolls out the front door in white shorts, a light blue V-neck, and her favorite sneakers. A floral bandana is wrapped around her head, and she's got a canvas tote with a matching print slung over her shoulder.

I get out of the truck, bouquet of wildflowers in hand. My chest aches to close the distance between Birdie and me, but I force myself to wait for her to come to me. I don't want to over-whelm her, though it's nearly impossible when she's so achingly beautiful, and I want nothing more than to wrap her in a hug.

Birdie lingers by the store entrance, scanning the parking lot.

She checks her phone before sliding it back into her tote, then shields her eyes from the sun and scans the area again, pausing when her gaze lands on me.

She heads in my direction, her arms crossed tightly over her chest, each step measured.

I tip my hat, flashing her a grin. "Hey, there. Ready for our date?"

"What are you doing here?" she asks, coming to a stop in front of me. "Earl's supposed to pick me up and should be here soon."

She glances toward the road, like she's expecting him to pull into the parking lot any second.

"Actually, he's not on his way," I tell her. "I canceled your ride."

Birdie blinks at me. "Oh… darn it. I was looking forward to another punch so I'd be one ride closer to another freebie," she teases, holding out a punch card.

The thing is roughly cut from cardstock, with *Birdie's Road to a Free Ride* scrawled in messy handwriting across the top, ten uneven boxes drawn in two lines, and a cartoon taxi doodled in the corner. Earl must have made it himself to reward Birdie for riding with him so often. It's a sweet gesture, but I still plan to take her where she needs to go from now on.

"How about you save your money, and I give you a free ride instead?" I wink, making her cheeks turn the prettiest shade of pink.

"Someone's in a giving mood tonight." She laughs, her eyes drifting to the flowers I'm holding. "Who are those for?"

I hold them out. "They're for you."

"Wildflowers are my favorite." She dips her head to inhale their sweet scent, tracing a fingertip over a bright red poppy. "They're beautiful. Thank you."

"You deserve to be swept off your feet," I say, mesmerized as her gaze meets mine. "Never settle for anything less."

She takes the bouquet, a soft smile curving her lips. If a simple floral arrangement makes her this happy, I'll bring her flowers after every shift.

"Why don't we continue this conversation in the cab?" I suggest, nodding to my truck.

Several onlookers linger in the parking lot, watching as I usher Birdie to the vehicle. Beneath her delight over the flowers, I can sense she's still worried about something, and I'd rather talk about it with her in private.

I open the passenger door and offer my hand. A spark of warmth ripples through me as she slips her hand into mine as I help her into the truck.

"Thanks," she murmurs, settling into the seat.

"You're welcome."

Her eyes lift to mine, something unspoken passing between us before she releases my hand and tucks hers into her lap. I wonder if I misread the situation or if she's just as nervous about our date as I am.

I shut the door and circle around to my side, satisfaction settling in my chest at the thought that I have the prettiest girl in town riding shotgun. When I climb inside the cab, Birdie stays silent, her eyes fixed straight ahead. She doesn't even glance my way when I start the engine and pull out of the parking lot. I'm hit with a twinge of unease—she hasn't asked where we're headed or tried to make small talk. Usually, she'd be peppering me with questions by now.

I replay our brief exchange before she got in the truck over and over in my head, trying to figure out what I could have said or done to offend her. Now that I think about it, she never responded to my text this morning about our first lesson tonight, so maybe that's part of why she's so distant. I'd give anything for a manual on how to play it cool while fake dating the woman I've wanted for years.

The silence is deafening, and after another minute, I can't take it anymore.

I look over at Birdie, who's staring at the passing scenery. "You're awfully quiet. Want to tell me what's on your mind?"

She shifts in her seat, fidgeting with the gold necklace at her throat. "It's nothing."

"You sure? It seems like something's bothering you."

She hesitates, then shakes her head. "Yeah… I'm fine."

I might believe her if she didn't look like she'd been struck by a live wire, nervous energy practically buzzing through her. She's as pale as a sheet, looking like she's plotting her escape from the moving vehicle.

"Birdie." I speak softly, coaxing her to meet my eyes. "We can't start our relationship by keeping things from each other. Please tell me what's wrong."

"It's nothing you should be bothered with… this is all just pretend anyway," she whispers, her voice barely audible.

My chest tightens at her words, and I can't bring myself to ignore her unease. I glance over my shoulder to make sure the road behind me is clear, then ease off the gas and pull onto the side of the road.

Birdie's eyes widen. "Why did we stop?"

I don't answer right away, shutting off the ignition and moving the flowers to the dash before sliding into the middle seat beside her.

"Let's get one thing straight. If we're doing this, we're a team." My knees bump against the dashboard as I shift to face her. "That means relying on each other when things get hard. From here on out, if you're in a bind or need someone to talk to, I'm your man."

As much as I hate this fake bullshit, I intend to treat it like an actual relationship. Do I have any clue what that looks like? Not even a little—but I'm committing to it regardless because Birdie is important to me.

"You've already gone out of your way for me, and I don't want to be more of a burden than I already am," she murmurs, barely above a whisper.

I exhale slowly, muttering a string of curses under my breath for messing this up again. Somehow, I've given the impression that I'm here out of duty, and it's on me to set the record straight.

"Lesson twenty-six: Never be afraid to take up space," I state.

She scrunches her nose as she studies me. "What happened to lessons two through twenty-five?"

"Never said I was going in order, now did I?" I wink. "A little unpredictability always keeps things interesting, don't you think?"

The corner of her mouth quirks up. "You going to tell me what the lesson means?"

"Your feelings are valid, and you deserve to share them with your partner without fear of judgment or worrying you're an inconvenience. Any man who can't see your worth in your most vulnerable moments isn't worth your time—period." I let my fingers trace over the knuckles of her hand resting on the bench between us. "Now let's try this again. What's on your mind, Birdie?"

I brace myself, half expecting her to clam up, but instead she clears her throat, meeting my gaze as she speaks. "Earlier, I panicked when you texted me about our plans. I wasn't sure if I was supposed to come to your place or if you were coming to mine," she explains, pushing a loose strand of hair from her face. "Then you showed up at the feed store, and every scenario I'd imagined went out the window, leaving me back at square one, trying to guess what would happen."

"If you had questions, why not text me back?"

"I didn't want to bother you," she confesses softly.

Unable to keep my hands to myself any longer, I scoot closer and cradle her face, gazing into her inquisitive blue eyes. "What did I just say? You're never a bother. Text me whenever you want."

I pause as an idea pops into my head. "In fact, let's make it a rule—you have to message me at least five times a day."

Her posture stiffens, a faint flush blooming along her neck. "I can't. That's way too much. You'll get tired of me."

Never.

"Fine, ten times a day it is. Sound good, or should I keep going?" I challenge.

She lets out an adorable huff of frustration, squaring her shoulders. "You're not playing fair, Walker."

"Never claimed I would," I counter. "I'm new to all of this too, so I get how overwhelming it can be."

She gives a dry laugh. "I don't see how you could possibly relate."

I sigh internally. If erasing my past would mean she saw me differently, I'd find a way to do it in a heartbeat.

Since I can't possibly tell her any of that, I settle for a particular truth that hides the full extent of how deep my obsession with her runs.

"I'm used to casual hookups, but I've never been on a real date. Not one with conversation, laughter, and a kiss at the end that leaves me counting the hours until I can see her again. The concept is terrifying, and I'm probably just as scared of screwing this up as you are." The confession isn't easy to share, but I hope she sees this isn't as easy for me as it might seem.

"Wait." I can see the wheels turning behind her eyes. "So… you were never planning on us having sex tonight?"

"No Birdie, baby." I like how the new nickname rolls off my tongue. "Tonight's about teaching you to expect to be wooed before you let a man take you to bed. That starts with flowers, holding open your door, and noticing the little things—like how you fidget with your necklace and bite your lip when you're nervous," I say, brushing my thumb across her mouth.

She smiles, pressing her cheek against my palm. "In that case, we'd better get started if you're going to woo me properly."

"Challenge accepted." I lean forward to brush a kiss across her forehead, and a contented sigh passes her lips.

Her reaction only strengthens my resolve to make this the best first date ever—one she'll never forget.

CHAPTER 10

Who Said Chivalry Was Dead?

Birdie

W E'VE BEEN DRIVING FOR NEARLY FORTY-FIVE MINUTES, and wherever Walker is taking me clearly isn't in Bluebell—which I can't deny is a relief. I love our charming town, but everyone constantly being in my business can be suffocating. Knowing our first official date will be away from prying eyes and whispered speculation makes it even better.

My cheek presses into the headrest as I watch the scenery pass by from the window. The sun dips low in the sky, bathing the rolling fields in deep gold, while cottonwoods dot the landscape with leaves that catch the warm evening light. The soft strains of "Tennessee Whiskey" drift from the radio, filling the silence that's settled between us since our roadside conversation.

I glance over at Walker, where he's focused on the road ahead, his cowboy hat tipped low and his black T-shirt stretched tight across his broad frame. Even dressed casually, he's sexy as all get-out, and the attraction burning inside me isn't staying dormant like it used to. No—it's blazing to life, flaring hotter than ever, refusing to be put out.

That fire explains the sparks that shoot through me whenever he takes my hand in his or the unexpected kiss on my forehead earlier. It was just as electrifying as if he'd pinned me to the bench seat and taken me for the first time on the roadside. The way he seems to know what I need before I do only intensifies my attraction, and his caring nature makes me want to open up to him.

I clear my throat before breaking the silence. "Earlier, when I assumed we'd jump straight into… sex," I whisper the last word. "I might have acted impulsive and done something silly instead of asking you for help." Though part of me wants to keep this to myself, I push past my nerves in the name of transparency.

Walker shoots me a glance. "Come on now. Don't leave me hanging."

"I had Earl take me to the drugstore before work this morning to pick up condoms. I wasn't sure who was responsible for getting them and didn't want to be caught unprepared. I have an IUD, but you can never be too prepared," I say softly, rubbing my palms against my thighs. "The problem was there were too many choices, and I got overwhelmed. How was I supposed to know what size to get or whether ribbed ones make a difference?"

I keep my eyes on the floorboards, too nervous to see Walker's reaction. "Of course, I didn't tell Earl the real reason I was there. But I guess that didn't matter—since I knocked over a shelf of condoms and he and Clark found me surrounded by them. I don't think my excuse of being in the wrong aisle was very convincing."

Oh fudge, I'm still rambling.

The truck veers slightly before Walker straightens it out, his hands gripping the wheel so tightly his knuckles turn white.

I gasp, holding the edge of my seat. "Everything okay?"

He nods, wiping his brow. "You can't go around talking about a man's dick size and not expect him to get distracted."

I shoot him a smirk. "No condom or cock-related commentary while you're operating heavy machinery. Got it."

Walker lets out a low groan and subtly shifts in his seat. "Birdie, I'm trying to be a gentleman tonight, but when I hear the word *cock* come from those pretty lips, it makes that damn near impossible."

I bite the inside of my cheek to keep from blurting something wildly inappropriate.

After a long beat of silence, Walker says, "I want you to know that I'd never put you in the position where you'd have to choose between protection and intimacy." He casts me another glance before focusing back on the road. "I apologize for not being clear from the start. You asked me to teach you, and I haven't been doing the best job."

"You're wrong," I say, undoing my seat belt and sliding into the middle seat, the urge to be closer to him impossible to ignore.

Walker's gaze hardens, bordering on frantic. "Woman, fasten your buckle right now, or I'm pulling over again."

I laugh softly. "All right, all right, don't give yourself a heart attack." I click myself into place, and Walker exhales in relief. "Satisfied?"

"Promise me you won't ever risk your safety like that again," he urges.

My lips twitch into a satisfied smile. It's obvious his concern for me is genuine and that alone makes me feel seen in a way I haven't in a long time.

I trace a cross over my chest with my finger. "Promise."

He grunts in approval. "Good. Now explain why it was so important for you to sit next to me while I'm doing sixty on the highway."

My hand drifts to his thigh, and he stiffens under my touch.

"I wanted to emphasize that I disagree with what you just said. In my opinion, you're the best teacher. You've been patient and kind and have already helped me in more ways than I can count. And I'm very grateful." I don't miss the subtle shift in his breathing when my fingers brush a little higher along his thigh.

"Dammit, woman. It's near impossible to concentrate with your hand on me." He swallows hard, jaw tightening. "I think you might be trying to kill me."

"Sorry," I murmur, but when I go to pull my hand away, he gently catches my wrist, holding me in place.

I grin and can't help but feel a surge of pride at the reaction I've elicited from him. Most guys are eager for any excuse to bail, not struggling to stay composed because a simple touch leaves them undone.

He keeps his hand on my wrist, rubbing circles along my skin. I settle in the peaceful silence, the gravel crunching beneath the tires as we leave the main highway and turn onto a narrow, overgrown lane. The sun sinks behind the distant hills, painting the sky in streaks of amber and violet. About half a mile down, Walker makes a right turn by a familiar looking, faded ice cream cone sign.

"Are we going to the drive-in?" I exclaim, clutching his arm with my free hand.

There's only one within a hundred miles of Bluebell, and it's been ages since I last came here.

"We are. That okay with you?" he asks, a hint of hesitation in his voice.

"Are you kidding? This was one of my favorite spots growing up."

"A rancher friend of mine owns the place. They normally only show movies Friday through Sunday, but he agreed to open on a weekday when I told him I wanted to take my girl on a proper date."

Did Walker just call me his girl?

"This is the best first fake date ever," I exclaim.

A frown flickers across his face but is quickly replaced with a twinkle in his eye. "I'm glad I've set the bar high so no other man will ever measure up."

Gosh, when he talks like that, I almost believe this is real, and that he's not just putting on a show.

Just then, we pull into the drive-in, joining a short line of cars. When we reach the front, Walker eases up to the ticket booth and rolls down his window, handing the attendant some cash in exchange for a ticket stub. At the far end of the lot is a massive screen flanked by rusted speakers. Rows of cracked asphalt fan out from the screen, each space marked with faded white paint and dotted with small tufts of grass sprouting through the gaps. A handful of antique light poles dot the perimeter, their amber bulbs flickering intermittently. The place might be run-down, but it has a charm that feels timeless—like stepping into a memory frozen in time.

Walker backs into a spot near the back that's angled toward the screen.

I crane my neck to look behind us. "Uh, how are we supposed to watch the movie if we're facing the wrong way?"

"Let me show you," he says before hopping out of the truck.

I open my door and swing my legs over the seat, about to climb down when Walker suddenly appears at my side.

"Lesson forty-eight: Always wait for me to open your door," he scolds with his arms folded.

"Really? Even though I can manage perfectly fine on my own?" I counter, brow raised.

"Yes. Now get back in the truck."

I tilt my head, lips quirking in amusement. "Excuse me?"

"You heard me, woman. We're doing this the right way," he states, leaving no room for debate.

I decide to play along, curious to see what he does next. Once I'm back inside, I settle into the seat, staring ahead and fighting the grin tugging at my lips. Aside from Earl, no one has ever made a fuss over opening my door—not that opportunities like this have come up often. It gives me hope that chivalry isn't entirely dead, at least not if I find a man who notices the little things, like Walker does.

When he finally opens my door, I'm expecting him to offer me his hand, but instead, he leans in and brushes his nose against my earlobe. "Good girl."

My breath hitches, and I nearly melt into the seat as goose bumps race down my spine. I'd let him open every door for me a hundred times over if it meant hearing it again.

"Thank you," I manage, doing my best to hide how two simple syllables have me nearly ready to combust. "So… you going to show me how to do this drive-in movie thing the right way, or what?" I ask, grasping for a distraction.

Walker hesitates, grazing his cheek against mine and sending my stomach into a whirlwind of flips. I'm seconds from begging him to keep going, to see where this leads when he finally pulls away, snapping me out of it.

He helps me down and leads me around back, removing the tarp covering the truck bed before popping open the tailgate to reveal a queen-size mattress layered with fluffy blankets, a mishmash of pillows, and several soft throws. A small speaker sits in one corner, ready to play the movie audio.

"Uh, Walker, are you absolutely sure we're *just* watching a movie tonight?" I ask, motioning toward the cozy fortress.

"Positive." He chuckles, propping his arm on the tailgate. "Never had the full drive-in experience, I take it?"

"I don't think so?" I say, sounding unsure even to my own ears.

Normally, the girls and I cram into Briar's Jeep with blankets and snacks. I've never experienced a setup like this—it looks like the movie-night version of luxury.

Walker lets out a low tut of disapproval. "I'm disappointed my sister never made sure you did it right. I thought I taught her better."

I rock back on my heels, smirking. "So are you going to show me, or just keep talking about it?"

He stands to his full height, tucking his hands into his pockets. "Step one: Secure the snacks." He motions toward a small trailer serving as the concession stand.

My stomach chooses that exact moment to remind me I skipped lunch. I was too nervous about our meetup, which somehow turned into a date, one that I'm relieved to discover includes food.

"Yup. We definitely need snacks first. I can't risk having a hangry Birdie on my hands."

I nudge his shoulder. "Oh, come on. I'm not that bad."

"I'm still recovering from the Prickly Pear Fiasco of last spring," he says, shivering dramatically.

He's totally exaggerating… or at least that's what I tell myself. A few of us had stopped in for food on the way to the rodeo, but they were out of veggie burgers, and the side salad I ordered did little to curb my hunger. By the time we reached the bull-riding portion at the rodeo, I was starving, cranky, and may have snapped at a man behind us who joked that bulls are dumb and can't feel pain like humans.

Walker had to physically restrain me before I could grab the idiot and shake some sense into him. Once I settled down, he walked twenty minutes to the nearest gas station and came back with a smoothie, a cheese stick, and a granola bar to tide me over until I got home.

Come to think of it, he's rescued me countless times, and I'm only now realizing how much of a presence he's been in my life the past few years.

"If you're so worried about my hangry side taking over, lead the way to the snacks," I say, nodding toward the concession trailer.

"I thought you'd never ask."

My mouth falls open when he threads his fingers through mine as we cross the lot. A thrill races through me like tiny sparks of electricity, sending a delicious heat blooming in my chest.

Several other moviegoers glance our way, but Walker appears completely at ease, letting our proximity speak for itself. If he hadn't admitted he'd never dated before, I might feel jealous that other women got to see this side of him. In all honesty, it's nice knowing this is new territory for him too.

Don't forget, Birdie—this is just pretend.

The reminder is sharp and sobering, but I won't let it ruin our evening. For all intents and purposes, this has to look real to anyone watching, so I'm going to enjoy being on the arm of the hottest cowboy in the county instead of dwelling on the truth. This facade comes with an expiration date, and there will be plenty of time to face that harsh reality later.

As we move forward in line, Walker glances down at my feet. "Your shoelace is untied. Let me get that for you."

I'm stunned when he drops to his knees in front of me, gathering the loose strings and carefully tying them into a bow, finishing with a double knot.

I could get used to seeing him on his knees for me.

Sweet Mercy. Get a grip, Birdie.

It's hard not to swoon when this feels like a scene from a romance novel where the hero's smallest act of thoughtfulness outshines any grand gesture.

Walker gazes up at me, smirking. "You're comparing me to a hero from a romance book, huh? Do you think I'd be the brooding, protective type or the hopelessly devoted golden retriever?" I'm pinned in place as he rises to his full height.

Oh, fudge—I did that thing where I talk to myself out loud

again, and I can't even blame a hangover this time. Thank goodness I didn't say the part out loud about him being on his knees.

He raises a brow. "What's that about me being on my knees?"

"Nothing," I reply, my voice higher than I intended. *I really need to stop thinking out loud.* "Wait… how do you know terms like brooding and golden retriever? Do you secretly read romance novels as a hobby or something?"

"Or *something*," he answers cryptically. "What I can tell you is that our first kiss will be far swoonier than any from a storybook."

The world around us fades, and my focus narrows to the delicious mix of longing and desire coiling low in my belly.

I rise on my toes, tipping my head so our lips are only inches apart. "I'm all ears, Deputy. Why don't you walk me through what it would be like."

He swallows hard, eyes flickering to my mouth. "I'd start slow and sweet, teasing the corners of your lips and giving you a taste but not fully claiming them right away." His other hand slides to the small of my back. "Drawing it out heightens every sensation, making the eventual kiss even more electrifying when it finally comes."

I let the silence stretch between us, waiting until the group ahead of us reaches the counter to order before responding.

"Does the same concept apply to foreplay and sex?" I murmur, my voice sultry.

Normally, I'd stumble over such an intimate question, but Walker's speech about not being afraid to take up space gives me the courage to be bolder and more playful.

"You ever heard of edging?" Walker's voice is so low I have to move in closer, our mouths nearly touching.

I shake my head. "No."

"It means bringing you to the brink of climax repeatedly, stretching the anticipation until you're trembling and begging for release." His warm breath brushes against my upper lip as he speaks. "And when you're finally given permission to let go, the pleasure will be beyond anything you've ever experienced."

I have a sinking suspicion he's spot-on, and the handful of times I've been close to bringing myself to orgasm pale in comparison to what he's describing. I'm clinging to his every word—suspended between restraint and surrender. Every nerve ending is alive at the thought of him holding my pleasure in his hands, controlling every touch, every tease.

Our gazes remain locked, and neither of us has moved, teetering on the edge of a scorching-hot kiss that, unfortunately, never comes.

Walker and I both startle when the concession worker shouts, "Next."

We step apart, and I notice we're the last ones left in line.

"You lovebirds planning to order, or are you too busy giving each other googly eyes?" he drawls, amusement edging his tone.

"We're experts at multitasking." Walker moves to the window and rests his elbow on the steel counter to get a better view of the menu. "We'll take an order of nachos and cheese, a soft pretzel, a side of fries, two bottled waters, and a bucket of popcorn. Toss in some mustard packets, will you?"

Normally, I'd bristle if a man ordered for me, but with Walker, it's kind of hot watching him take charge—especially when he chooses exactly what I would have, right down to adding mustard to dip my fries in. We've spent plenty of time together over the years, but I never expected him to notice such minute details like that.

The cashier jots down our selections on a small notepad. "Wanna add any candy to your order?"

"No thanks," Walker says, turning toward me. "Unless you want something. I know you love licorice, but they only have Twizzlers. Don't worry, though—I stopped by the grocery store earlier and grabbed Red Vines since they're your favorite."

"You remember my favorite candy?"

At this rate, I'm in real danger of melting into a puddle from all of his thoughtfulness.

"How could I forget? Last summer, I was buying my mom a hummingbird feeder, and when I got to the register, I found you doing a happy dance because they'd started stocking Red Vines."

"I could never resist the opportunity to celebrate my favorite candy," I answer with a wistful smile.

I remember that day vividly. My mama had taken a nasty fall the night before, leaving my dad and me shaken. Thankfully, she didn't break anything, but I was distracted at work. As ridiculous as it sounds, spotting our favorite candy on the shelf made me happy, reminding me that I'd still get to see her after my shift—and that she'd be as okay as possible given the circumstances.

What truly made that day so special was Walker buying me a pack, claiming he'd never seen anyone as passionate about anything as I was about Red Vines, and he wanted me to enjoy them. His sweet gesture was a bright spot in an otherwise rough week, and I've always wished I could thank him properly for turning an ordinary candy into a memory I got to share with my mama—one I'll never forget.

"That'll be twenty-seven dollars and fifty-two cents," the cashier says, pulling me out of my memories.

"I'll cover this one, since you got the tickets," I tell Walker, rifling through my tote for my wallet.

I pause and look up when he rests his hand over mine. "Not a chance, sweetheart. *Always* let the guy pay. If he ever suggests going Dutch or asks you to pick up the tab, run."

"Preach," the cashier chimes in, sounding as invested in our conversation as I am.

Walker takes out his wallet and hands the cashier a fifty-dollar bill.

"Keep the change, kid."

He blinks. "Seriously?"

"Consider it a thank-you for helping me teach my girl that a gentleman always pays," Walker says.

"Shame you're not a gentleman," I whisper so only he can hear.

"Definitely won't be one when our next lesson starts." He winks.

He slips his hand back into mine as we move aside to wait for our order, leaving me buzzing with anticipation for whatever lesson comes next.

CHAPTER 11

Just A Kiss (For Research)

Walker

"**I** DIDN'T PEG YOU AS THE ROM-COM TYPE," BIRDIE MUSES.

She studies me from her place beside me in the truck bed, propped up by several pillows and wrapped in a throw blanket.

The audio from *When Harry Met Sally,* playing on the big screen ahead of us, comes through the speaker I set up in the truck bed.

"I usually stick to explosions, car chases, and the occasional western showdown, but I figured *Die Hard* and *Tombstone* weren't first date material," I reply with a chuckle.

Birdie's eyes dance with amusement. "Drat, I was really looking forward to gunfights and a heroic rescue scene. This is such a downgrade."

The scene where Harry and Sally debate whether men and women can just be friends is playing out. I almost laugh at the irony—here I am with the girl I've been pining over for years, pretending to be her boyfriend so she can build her confidence to date other people.

"Harry is being so dramatic," Birdie observes, keeping her voice low. "Men and women can absolutely be friends—just look at us."

Fuck me. How the hell am I supposed to answer?

You're wrong, Birdie, baby. I've wanted you since the first time we had lunch together alone in your dad's office. You wore a blue floral dress that matched your eyes, and when you reached for a napkin and your fingers brushed mine, the spark from that small touch hit me like lightning.

"In case all those Red Vines put you in a sugar coma, let me remind you that what I plan to teach you isn't the kind of thing friends do," I tease.

Birdie lets out a burst of giggles, earning a sharp "shush" from the elderly couple two parking spots over. They got here shortly before the movie started and haven't been willing to tolerate any interruptions.

"Sorry!" Birdie whisper-shouts in return, flinching when she realizes how loud she'd been.

Damn, she's ridiculously cute when she's self-conscious about drawing attention to herself.

Unable to resist keeping my distance a second longer, I scoot closer and drape my arm around her shoulders.

She peeks over at me with a questioning look. "What are you doing?"

"This way we won't get any more noise complaints," I whisper, my mouth against her ear.

That's not the only reason.

Okay, fine. It's also a convenient excuse to have her close. I've held back since our concession run, craving the rush that ignites through my veins when we touch. The memory of her on her toes and my hand gripping her waist has left me powerless to resist her.

With all the damn foreplay, I'll probably have a permanent hard-on until I get that first taste of her mouth on mine. Hell, who am I kidding? The damn thing isn't going to be appeased until I have it buried inside her, and even then, it won't be placated for long if being inside her isn't a regular occurrence.

I'm glad Birdie is starting to loosen up compared to how tense she was when I picked her up at the feed store. We've been around each other so much in the past, I assumed we'd slip into our usual rhythm: me teasing her followed by her quirky come-backs, and the occasional playful jab. This time though, we don't have her friends or my family around to break the tension, leaving the two of us with all this unspoken anticipation hanging in the air.

I trail my thumb lightly over her skin. "You're tense. Want me to move back to my side of the mattress?"

She gives a small shake of her head. "No… I'm just too scared to move."

"Why's that?"

"Because I'm having a great time and don't want to risk elbowing you in the face or accidentally headbutting you and ruining our date… sorry—fake date." Her voice drops so low I barely catch the last part.

I grimace at her calling this fake. The warmth of her body pressed against mine is as real as the blood pounding in my veins, and I wonder if she can feel this connection too.

Birdie has spent far too long doubting herself, and it's up to me to show her that she's perfect the way she is—quirks and all. She just needs to get out of her head long enough to see herself the way I do: fierce, brave, and beautiful.

"Funny—at the bar the other night you seemed pretty confident when you were asking me to give you lessons, and earlier in the concessions line, you didn't hold back, did you?" I taunt playfully, my lips twitching into a grin.

She traces her fingers over the gold chain of her necklace. "I'd had a few drinks at the bar so that doesn't count. "

I tip her chin, meeting her gaze as her eyes glimmer in the flickering movie light like shards of sapphire. "Show me what you'd do if you weren't so worried about messing this up. It's only practice, so you can't get it wrong."

I wait patiently, letting her take the lead. Birdie exhales slowly, inching closer until our thighs touch, and her head rests on my shoulder. I brush a gentle kiss on her temple, anchoring us both in the moment, though her body is still locked up, one hand hesitating at her side.

"You're doing amazing," I say quietly, brushing her hair back. "Mind if I help make this even more comfortable for us both?"

Birdie looks up, a shy smile forming. "Please."

I reach over and take her hand, guiding it across my chest before letting it rest on my hip.

"This okay?" I ask.

She nods. "Perfect."

"Good," I murmur. "I love having your hands on me."

I'm struck by how perfectly she fits in my embrace, and I want to burn every detail into my memory so I never forget—from the softness of her hair to the way her body relaxes against mine, proof she's starting to let her guard down around me.

My heart skips a beat when she drapes her leg over mine and nestles further into my arms. I adjust my grip to keep her steady, enveloped by the warm, inviting scent of vanilla and oranges in the air.

"We're actually cuddling, and I haven't kneed you in the balls or anything," she declares triumphantly.

I stifle a laugh to avoid drawing our neighbor's attention. "I'm so damn proud of you."

God, I'd give anything to kiss her right now, but I promised to take this slow, and I won't risk spooking her just as she's starting

to relax. Instead, I settle for another kiss on her forehead as her gaze drifts back to the movie screen.

Birdie is curled up in the passenger seat, turned toward me, her eyes closed, and her mouth parted as she snores softly. Her hand remains outstretched across the bench seat from when she reached over to squeeze mine, telling me how much fun she had at the drive-in before promptly drifting off to sleep as we drove along the highway.

Guilt tugs at me for keeping her out so late. No doubt she'll be up at the crack of dawn tending to her animals. She has a steady stream of rescues coming through, and I have a sneaking suspicion that the old shed on her property is currently home to a couple of special guests—likely the reason behind her recent run-in with the law. But I'm not about to go digging into something I'd rather be in the dark about.

It's late when we finally pull up to Birdie's. I cut the engine, my gaze falling back on her sleeping form. The soft glow from the porchlight illuminates her features, highlighting just how stunning she is, and for all intents and purposes, she's mine.

I pull the keys from the ignition and step out of the truck. When I get to the passenger side, I open Birdie's door and retrieve her tote from the floor before scooping her into my arms. She nuzzles into my chest as I carry her across the lawn toward her house. Once I'm up the porch steps, I carry her to the porch swing and take a seat with her still in my lap.

She's so damn beautiful, and I'd give anything to carry her to her room and spend the night holding her close—but saying good night here will have to do.

"Birdie, wake up," I say softly.

She stirs, her eyelids flutter open, looking up at me with a drowsy smile.

"Hi," she murmurs.

"Hi, baby." I brush her hair from her face.

She sits up, rubbing the sleep from her eyes before glancing between me and the front door.

"Shoot, last time I checked, we were in your truck on the way home. Sorry—I guess I passed out mid-conversation, didn't I?"

"You did. Glad to know my voice doubles as a lullaby."

She lets out a melodic laugh. "Don't get ahead of yourself. Long car rides make me sleepy no matter who's behind the wheel."

"I'll stick with my theory that you were under my hypnotic charm." I wink.

She lazily drags a finger along my chest. "We'd better stick with your version of reality or your ego may never recover."

"You're extra sassy for someone who just woke up."

Birdie fiddles with her necklace, a sign she's nervous. I stay silent, letting her take the lead.

"Are you going to leave now?" she blurts out, wincing as soon as the words escape her mouth.

I lift a brow, tipping her chin so she meets my gaze, suspecting she's panicking.

"Is that what you want? For me to go?"

She tilts her head, shaking it. "No."

I exhale in relief. "What *do* you want?"

She swallows hard, her eyes flickering to mine. "I'm not sure."

My eyes shift to her lips. "Could it be that you were hoping for a good-night kiss?"

"Do first dates usually end that way?" Her tone is curious.

"Maybe not if you've just met the guy." I push down the jealousy brewing at the thought of her kissing someone else. "But since we're friends, and this is strictly for teaching purposes, I think we can make an exception."

I've spent countless nights fantasizing about kissing Birdie, wondering what it would feel like, what she might taste like. Now that I'm potentially seconds from finding out, my whole body buzzes with anticipation, and I'm suddenly the nervous one.

She winds her arm around my neck, giving me a sly smile. "I think you're on to something."

That's all the encouragement I need. I shift my hand to cup her cheek, my thumb brushing just beneath her ear, where I can practically feel her pulse racing under my touch.

"Walker," she whispers.

"Yeah, Birdie, baby?"

Her cheeks flush crimson. "Is now a bad time to mention I've never kissed anyone before?"

Holy shit.

I trace my finger along her lower lip. "In that case, we'd better make it a good one."

I can't believe I'm lucky enough to be the one she's going to share all her firsts with, even the ones that seem so small but feel monumental. On the outside, I manage to keep my expression neutral, but inside, my heart is pounding out of control, and I'm determined not to fuck this up.

Birdie's mouth parts slightly. "You'll show me how to do it, right?"

"Of course. Just follow my lead, okay?"

She nods as I lean in slowly, until our mouths are just shy of touching, leaving the remaining distance for her to bridge when she's ready. Her uneven breath grazes my cheek as she subtly shifts closer, her desire unmistakable.

Just when I think she might panic and withdraw, she surprises me by brushing her mouth against the corner of my lips. My grip tightens on her waist, holding her to me as she kisses me again in the same spot. This time, she lingers a second longer, as if she's testing the waters. I stay perfectly still, despite my cock already standing at attention. Tonight is all about Birdie and making sure her introduction to kissing is nothing short of perfect.

A third kiss lands squarely on my mouth, a gentle exploration that makes me release a soft groan. God, her lips are like velvet. She shifts back a fraction, eyes locking on mine. Fuck, the way she looks at me for reassurance winds my desire like a spring in my chest.

I move my other hand from her waist so both are framing her face. "That was very good… although I'm going to need a second demonstration to be sure it wasn't a fluke."

She licks her lips. "Practice makes perfect, right?"

"My thoughts exactly."

I tilt her head slightly and kiss her again, mirroring her curiosity earlier. She threads her fingers in my hair as she explores my mouth with determination. Birdie slips her tongue against mine, letting out a throaty moan. I respond in kind, tracing hers in a teasing rhythm. Her grip in my hair tightens as she molds her mouth to mine, her movements growing bolder with each pass.

As far as I'm concerned, every kiss I've had before this was erased out of existence the moment Birdie's lips touched mine.

When she finally pulls back, her lips are swollen, and a faint pink tints her cheeks. "Sorry. I might have gotten a little carried away."

I shake my head, stroking her cheek. "You were perfect."

A rosy flush spreads across her cheeks. "Really?"

I rest my forehead against hers, briefly closing my eyes as I breathe in her sweet scent. "That was by far the best damn kiss I've ever had."

If I thought I'd royally fucked up our friendship before, I'm certain of it now. Brief conversations with her at the feedstore and stolen glimpses when she's with her friends won't cut it anymore. Now that I've had her lips on mine and felt how hot the chemistry burns between us, I'm going to need that every damn day for as long as she'll have me. Hell, for as long as we both shall live would work too—but I'm getting ahead of myself. First, I have to help Birdie see that we belong together and no one will ever be capable of loving her the way I could if she'd let me.

"I better go to bed soon," she whispers against my lips. "Tomorrow's going to be a busy day."

I nod, reluctantly releasing my hold on her face. As much as I hate to let her go, I agree she deserves a good night's rest.

She stands up, and I follow her across the porch.

"I'll wait here until you're inside."

Birdie laughs softly as she opens the door and steps through, glancing back with a grin. "Satisfied?"

"Knowing you're safe in your house? Absolutely."

"Good night," she murmurs, her gaze glued to mine as she shuts the door behind her.

I stay where I am, ears straining, and let out a sigh when the click of the deadbolt never comes.

"Birdie," I call out.

"Hmm?" she answers almost instantly.

"I'm not leaving until you lock the door."

"Oh, right. I forgot." Her voice goes up an octave, followed by the sound of the locking mechanism.

When her footsteps fade from the entryway, I take it as my cue to leave. The only thing that eases the sting of walking away is the promise of more time with her later to explore our undeniable chemistry.

A sharp cluck startles me from my thoughts, and I spin around to see a chicken on the porch steps, staring at me. Could this be the infamous Nugget?

I crouch to her level. "You shouldn't be wandering around at night, little lady. You could become someone's midnight snack."

Considering all the creatures Birdie likely has roaming her property, I'm guessing at least one would see Nugget as a tasty treat, and I'd rather not have to explain to Birdie what happened if she goes missing tonight. The least I can do is get her to bed safely.

I extend my hand, letting out a soft whistle to coax Nugget over, but she refuses, pacing back and forth on the step, letting out a disgruntled cluck and fluffing her feathers as she sizes me up like she's debating if she can take me on.

I reach out to scoop her up, but at the last second, she flaps her wings and sails over my shoulder. Glancing back, I see her waddling toward the house and disappearing through the doggy door. I should've figured Birdie would let her sleep inside. I'll give credit where it's due—Nugget is gutsy, and I might've underestimated how she'd fare against a prowling fox or sneaky raccoon.

I shake my head, chuckling. "Good night, little lady," I call out after her as I head down the porch steps.

One thing is certain: life with Birdie is unpredictable, and I wouldn't trade a single chaotic second.

CHAPTER 12

Flirting 101

Birdie

T HE SMELL OF WORN LEATHER AND CEDAR CLINGS TO ME as I go about my day. I went straight to bed when Walker dropped me off, not ready to wash away his scent. I'm blaming it on my hormones going haywire and him being a thirst trap in Wranglers and cowboy boots, and definitely not on the fact that my lips are still tingling from our first kiss.

I'm not ready to confront those complicated feelings, so I'm keeping them under lock and key—happy to live in my delusional world, choosing to believe he's just showing me the ropes of dating, and that there's no way I'm developing any romantic attachments. The reality is, this can't mean anything more, or our entire arrangement goes up in flames, and our fragile balance will collapse.

It's still early, but I couldn't sleep. I've been up since sunrise, and after feeding the animals, I came to the kitchen to grab some coffee so I can return to being a semi-functioning human.

I take a sip of the oat milk latte I just made and scrunch my nose when the flavor lands on my tongue wrong. Even after adding an extra dash of cinnamon, it still isn't right. Ever since Walker made me one, I haven't found anything that compares.

It has me wondering how his morning is going. He's supposed to be working on the ranch today. Maybe I should check in—he did suggest I do just that. Before I can overanalyze my decision, I send him a message. After all, I agreed to text him an arguably unnecessary amount, and I can't very well go back on my word.

Birdie: Thanks for taking me to the drive-in.

Walker: Anytime, sweetheart. I had a damn good time.

Birdie: Me too.

I try another taste of my latte, still disappointed that it doesn't measure up to Walker's.

Birdie: Random question.

Walker: I'm listening.

Birdie: Did you put anything special in the oat milk latte you made me the other day?

Walker: No. Just espresso, steamed oat milk, foam, and a sprinkle of cinnamon.

Birdie: Well, in that case, I think my coffee machine is broken.

Walker: What makes you think that?

Birdie: Nothing I make tastes as good as yours.

Walker: That won't do. How can I help?

I should probably keep this conversation friendly, but after surviving our first kiss without a major catastrophe, I feel brave enough to try a little flirting. There's no harm in practicing, right?

Birdie: I think you owe me a new one, or you'll have to be my personal barista from now on.

Walker: Wait, am I being falsely accused and sentenced to unpaid coffee service? Do I need a lawyer? *wink face emoji

Birdie: Depends. Do I get damages plus interest?

Walker: If repayment means kissing you again, I'm definitely pleading guilty.

Walker: You tasted so damn sweet, I may never recover.

My fingers drift to my lips as I recall the way his mouth moved against mine, his hands molded to my waist, his erection pressed against my thigh.

Birdie: Careful, Deputy. You're making a very strong case for a repeat offense.

Birdie: Although I was hoping our next lesson might include some... advanced material.

I squeeze one eye shut as I hit send. Crossing off sharing a steamy kiss with a gorgeous man from my list of things I've secretly fantasized about was amazing, but it also left me wanting more. And for once, I'm feeling bold enough to ask for it.

Walker: That can be arranged.

Birdie: What did you have in mind?

Walker: Do you have any toys?

Birdie: Sex toys?

Walker: Yes.

Birdie: I have a vibrator.

Walker: Perfect. The next time you're in bed, I want you to use it.

Birdie: Are we talking about a live demonstration… over the phone?

The handful of times I've tried using a vibrator, I haven't been able to get off, which is the main reason I haven't touched the one the girls gave me.

Dirty talking is another thing I didn't expect I'd like to try, but the thought of Walker on the other end of the line, pushing me to the brink, is enough to send a rush of heat pooling in my belly.

Walker: I'd love nothing more than to watch, but first I want you to get comfortable doing it on your own and learn what you like so you can show me.

Walker: Think you can do that for me?

Birdie: I think so.

Walker: Good girl.

I swear, hearing those two little words again causes my brain to malfunction, leaving me thinking of all the possible ways I could please him next, just so I can hear them again.

I freeze when what sounds like a high-pitched meow drifts in from outside. I shake my head, certain I'm imagining it, until I hear it again, louder this time, and joined by others.

"What on earth is going on out there?" I mutter, rushing toward the front door to investigate.

When I reach the porch, I find a tattered cardboard box. As I peer inside my suspicions are confirmed: five little tabby kittens are inside. My heart sinks when I notice there's no sign of their mama. That doesn't mean they won't survive, but they'll need to be hand-fed and closely monitored if they're going to have a fighting chance.

To my surprise, Nugget is in the box too, with all the kittens nestled against her for warmth. When she sees me, she lets out a sharp cluck, as if complaining about their persistent mews—most likely from hunger and confusion at not being fed.

I raise my hands in mock surrender. "Don't look at me like that, Nugget. You've been a broody little thing lately, wanting babies—well, congratulations. Now you have a litter of hopefully healthy kittens to look after."

If only she could feed them herself. Instead, this unexpected responsibility lands squarely on me, and carving out time in my schedule will be a challenge. Still, whoever left these kittens knew I wouldn't let them down. This isn't the first time strays have ended up on my porch, and I'd take this any day over finding them abandoned on the roadside—or worse.

An hour later, I'm on the kitchen floor, elbows-deep in bottles as frantic little mouths scramble for their first meal in who knows how long. After checking over all the kittens, it looks like I have three spirited little ladies and two mischievous boys—all surprisingly healthy, considering they were taken from their mama too soon and abandoned on a doorstep. It's a good thing I keep the hallway closet packed with rescue supplies, or I'd be in real trouble with five starving kittens and no backup plan. Now, if only I had a few extra hands to feed them all at once.

Despite her initial reservations, Nugget has fully embraced her role as a surrogate mama and hasn't left the kittens' side since I brought them in. She's even let them burrow beneath her on a fuzzy blanket I grabbed from the living room to keep them warm.

"Look at you taking care of everyone," I coo.

She's definitely going to expect extra mealworms and shredded cheese after putting up with these tiny balls of fluff, and I'll happily give them to her for being such a trooper. I honestly thought she might bail after meeting them on the porch, but she's far more nurturing than I gave her credit for.

The kitten I'm feeding now has soft orange fur streaked with faint cream stripes, but despite his earlier cries of hunger, he seems more interested in battling the bottle than actually drinking.

I laugh as he swats at it with determination. "All right, little guy, let's settle down so we can eat."

I reposition him in my lap, keeping him snug against me, and exhale in relief when he finally latches on to the bottle.

"There you go," I murmur. "You're going to grow up big and strong, aren't you?"

As he greedily guzzles his milk, I decide now's as good a time as any to check in with my cousin Shep. He and his fiancée, Noelle, live in Pine Haven, Arizona, where he runs a world-famous honky tonk. He may be grumpy as all get-out, but I've been able to coerce him to adopt on occasion.

> Birdie: The most stubborn yet adorable kitten showed up on my doorstep this morning. I think he belongs to you.

I send a photo of the tiny menace in my lap, bottle clenched between his teeth, eyes narrowed like he's ready to throw paws if anyone tries to take his milk away.

> Shep: No.

> Birdie: But you're a match made in heaven. He's stubborn, has a permanent scowl, and pretends that he hates everyone—but secretly just wants cuddles.

> Shep: The answer is still no.

> Shep: We already have too many animals, thanks to you.

> Birdie: There's no such thing.

> Birdie: For the record, if I find another Highland cow, I'm keeping my promise to Noelle and sending it your way.

> Shep: I'd expect nothing less.

A while back, I called Shep, begging him to save Maple. At the time, she was a four-month-old miniature Highland cow found neglected in a backyard petting zoo a couple of hours from his place. At first, he refused to get her, but it wasn't long before his resolve crumbled.

Once he and Noelle got together, she was smitten with Maple too—and now she wants a friend for her.

A soft rap at the door draws my attention from my phone and

the kitten still in my lap. It's probably Mrs. Bixby, coming to investigate my latest rescues. I wouldn't be shocked if she'd seen them being dropped off and came to offer unsolicited advice. Another round of knocking shakes the door, louder and more persistent this time. When a third round rattles the doorframe, I sigh in defeat, accepting that whoever it is won't be ignored.

"Come in," I call out loudly, and the kitten flinches.

I'm not moving and interrupting his feeding now that he's settled. That would be asking for a tiny paw attack, and I'd rather stay scratch-free.

Whoever is here must have heard me because the door creaks open and footsteps echo down the hall.

"Birdie Mae Matterson, you'd better not be dead, or I'm switching to the full-sugar syrup at Latte & Lassoed. Your ghost will be stuck haunting me forever!" Charlie hollers, announcing her presence.

"We should've waited outside," Briar says in a mock-serious whisper. "What if my brother's here and he's not wearing any clothes? I can't handle that kind of trauma."

"That sounds like a *you* problem," Charlie quips. "He may not be my type, but I'm not above enjoying some eye candy while we're here."

I snort softly, adjusting the bottle as the kitten suckles, thankfully ignoring the commotion in the hallway.

"I'm in the kitchen!" I pipe up. "I'm alive, and unfortunately, Walker isn't here to wander around shirtless."

Not that I would mind if he were, though I'd rather not have witnesses when I see him naked for the first time because it could require resuscitation.

Seconds later, Charlie and Briar step into the kitchen.

Briar enters first, her long brown hair tied back in a ponytail, a few loose tendrils framing her face. Her tanned skin glows from countless hours in the sun, and her brown eyes are wary as she glances around, probably checking to make sure Walker isn't here.

Charlie follows, her red hair falling in loose curls. She's wearing an oversized T-shirt with the words *Raise Hell*, featuring a graphic of a cowgirl riding a tiger tucked into high-waisted jean shorts. As the style icon of the group, she tends to choose outfits that make a statement—usually in the form of vintage graphic tees.

She stops in her tracks when she spots me on the floor.

"Tell me I'm hallucinating and that you're not holding a cat. You know I'm allergic," she groans.

I shrug. "How was I supposed to know you'd show up an hour after someone left five kittens on my porch?"

She edges toward the table, treating the floor like lava, and drags a chair to the far side of the kitchen before plopping down in it.

"Sorry, you're on your own." She crosses one leg over the other and leans back. "If I get near those furballs, my eyes will puff up, and I'll look like a cartoon villain."

Briar rolls her eyes. "Don't sweat it, Birdie. I'm happy to help." She strides over to the box next to me and scoops out a black kitten with cream stripes and a white underbelly into her arms. "Does this one need to eat?"

I nod. "Yes, thanks."

She picks up one of my premade bottles from the counter and settles on the floor nearby, leaning back against the cabinets.

The kitten eagerly reaches for the bottle, whining softly as she guides it to its mouth.

"This one is absolutely adorable and has quite the appetite," Briar notes.

"Any chance you'd want to take her home?" I ask tentatively.

The hardest part of rescuing animals is finding them homes where they'll be safe and loved. Not everyone is willing to take in unexpected animals, but thankfully, Briar is one of the few who is.

"We both know she'll beg until you cave, so you might as well give in now," Charlie singsongs.

Briar chews on her bottom lip, glancing between the kitten and me. "Jensen and I have been thinking about getting a couple of cats to keep the mice out of the barn once it's done."

They're constructing one behind their new house for Ziggy, their fainting goat. I found him abandoned by the railroad tracks last year and rescued him—funny enough, I was in the middle of wrangling a lamb and another litter of kittens I had just saved when I begged Briar to foster Ziggy. It quickly turned into a permanent adoption.

"So does that mean you'll take three?" I question, giving her my best doe eyes.

I might be pushing my luck, but I'll do whatever it takes to get my animals into the best homes—even if it requires a little strategic persuasion.

"Okay, but the other two stay here," she warns, lifting a finger. "Jensen's already going to be frazzled when I break the news, and the only way I can justify keeping three is that it's one for each of us—him, me, and Caleb."

I scoot next to her and throw an arm around her shoulders. "You're a total lifesaver."

Taking care of two kittens instead of five is much more manageable—especially now that I've added lessons with Walker to my already frenzied schedule.

Maybe it's selfish to add that to my plate. My lack of sex isn't a life-and-death situation, but it's the one thing I'm doing solely for myself, and I'm not going to walk away now that I've finally begun to explore that part of me.

"So which one of you is going to tell me the real reason you showed up this morning?" I ask, looking between the girls. "I'm guessing it wasn't because you were hoping I'd have more animals for you to adopt."

Briar laughs, tilting her head back. "That definitely wasn't on my bingo card today."

"Think of our visit as an intervention," Charlie explains. "You drop the bomb about dating Walker, and then you only give us crumbs. Not cool."

I had hoped for more time before they confronted me. At the very least, I wanted them to wait until I'd slept with Walker, so I could give a full report without acting completely clueless or risk giving away what we're really doing. I can't shake the guilt of lying to my best friends about my dating life, and the less I have to talk about it, the better.

"I'm sorry," I whisper, ducking my head. "This is all new to me, and I'm learning as I go."

Briar reaches over and gives my arm a gentle squeeze. "We get it. We're just curious how this came about. You two have been close for a while, but I never got the sense you were interested in him as more than a friend."

I shrug, unable to meet her gaze. "I've always thought he was good-looking—then again, who hasn't? It's more that I never imagined he'd be interested in me, and since you're one of my best friends, he was firmly off-limits in my mind."

All of that's true. Beyond the occasional lustful thought, I never planned on acting on anything. Being with Walker remained safely in the realm of fantasy. And after our kiss last night, I'm starting to believe Harry was right when he told Sally that attraction has a way of dismantling even the best intentions.

I thought it would be easy for Walker and me to pretend we were dating while keeping things strictly physical, with no strings and no consequences. But the undeniable chemistry brewing between us isn't following the rules, and it's obvious things have shifted irreversibly.

My concern is that this illusion won't just convince everyone else it's real—there's a good chance it could fool me too, leaving me hurt and yearning for someone who will always be just out of reach.

"So what changed?" Briar asks, pulling me back to the moment.

"I was literally wondering the same thing," Charlie chimes in.

She's dragged her chair out in the hallway. Apparently, the distance across the room wasn't far enough to separate her from the kittens.

"The more time I spent with Walker, the more it became clear I misjudged him. He's generous, thoughtful, respectful… Everything I could want in a guy." My kitten has finished his bottle and is getting restless, so I set him on the ground to play. "When I learned he wanted me, I decided to give him a chance and see where this goes."

Everything I said about Walker is true—he's patient, kind, and attentive. Even though he seems genuinely invested in us, I can't help wondering if it's all just an incredible act. After all, we agreed to a fake relationship, so I have no right to expect more. Still, I've always longed for someone who genuinely wants me, and part of me can't help but wish that someone is Walker, even though our kiss could just be a part of an inconsequential lesson.

Briar nods slowly, weighing my explanation before responding. "How long have you and Walker been a thing?"

"Not long."

Less than twenty-four hours.

That's definitely one tidbit of information I'm keeping to myself. I'm pretty sure the girls would have me committed for agreeing to fake date a guy just so he could teach me how to flirt with men and have sex.

When you put it that way, it does sound worse than it is. I prefer to think of it as broadening my education with hands-on practice so I don't wind up single and outnumbered by cats. Then again, that's bound to happen with or without a man in my life—but more like a myriad of animals that would rival Noah's Ark, minus the reptiles. I draw the line at snakes and lizards.

"Honestly, I'm just offended that your sex life is about to become better than mine," Charlie complains, letting out a dramatic sigh.

She pulls her feet up onto the chair, shifting in her seat whenever the kitten I put down ventures close to her.

"Maybe it's my turn to buy you a vibrator then," I tease.

I'm grateful Charlie and Briar can laugh about this whole situation. It could've gone so differently, and it reminds me just how incredible my friends are. All that's missing is Wren.

CHAPTER 13

But Daddy I Want Him

Walker

"KEEP LETTING THE CATTLE SPREAD OUT LIKE THAT, AND we'll lose that one," Heath shouts, motioning to a calf who's slipping past my side of the herd and is darting toward a gap in the fence.

"They move easier when they've got space to roam," I call out. "But hey, if you think you can handle it better, be my guest."

He narrows his eyes, tugging on the brim of his hat. "It's fine. Just grab that little one before it sets off a stampede."

I spur Ranger, my bay quarter horse, forward with a sharp "giddyup," shifting the reins to one hand as we surge forward. Veering toward the fence, I grab my lasso from the saddle and swing it overhead, looping it clean around the calf's neck, leaving just enough slack to slow it down without hurting it.

"Easy, there," I say, easing the calf toward the herd with careful pressure on the rope.

Of all the chores on the ranch, nothing compares to being on horseback, riding alongside the cattle. It's the best part of the job and makes the days more manageable when I can break them up with a ride through the pastures, taking in the natural beauty of the land.

Once the calf is back with the herd, I ease the slack on the rope and, with a practiced flick of my wrist, slip the loop over its head, keeping the rope clear of its legs. I coil the lasso on the saddle horn, tucking the end under so it won't drag, and give Ranger a pat on the neck for a job well done.

"Still think letting the cattle spread out was a good idea?" Heath hollers, riding up beside me.

"It would've been fine if the fence was intact," I mutter defensively.

We're in the process of mending the fences in this field, but it's been slow going with the entire crew focused on tending to our ever-growing operation.

The late afternoon sun beats down without mercy, and I peel off my gloves and grab my canteen from my saddleback, taking a long swig of water to quench my parched throat.

We've spent the better part of the day finishing up the cattle vaccinations and are just now wrapping up herding them to the south pasture to graze.

By this point, tempers are frayed, and it's clear both Heath and I are itching for a break. We work best when we tackle separate projects. The minute we team up, he wants to take control. As the oldest, he's convinced he should call the shots, afraid I'd somehow screw up if left to my own devices—even though I've been doing this almost as long as he has.

He pulls a handkerchief from his pocket, wiping his neck as he shoots me a wary glance. "We going to keep ignoring this thing with you and Birdie?"

Other than the group chat I've shared with him and Briar the past couple of days, we haven't really talked about it—and honestly, I'm good with that.

I take another drink of water before responding. "There's not much to talk about."

He fixes me with a level stare. "That mean you're sticking to the story that you've been secretly seeing each other and only went public after getting caught at the bar?"

"That's what happened," I say, keeping my voice even. "I'm not sure what else you want me to tell you."

"Uh-huh," Heath replies, stroking his mustache and keeping a tight grip on the reins with his other hand. "So all those weekly trips to the feed store were only about stealing a few minutes with her—in public, surrounded by her coworkers and customers?"

I sigh, putting my canteen back in the saddlebag. "Can you stop picking apart my relationship and just be happy I found someone I care about, instead of sleeping around?"

Heath scoffs. "Walker, I'm not an idiot. You haven't done that in years, despite what everyone else thinks."

Seriously, why does he have to be so damn perceptive? We might not always get along, but he knows me better than anyone and has a knack for seeing straight through my bullshit.

I nudge my horse forward with my heel to guide another straying cow back to the main group.

"Everything changed the moment I realized I had feelings for Birdie. She's the only woman I've ever wanted a relationship with, and I knew I had become someone worthy of her." There's a sense of freedom in confessing part of the truth out loud.

Still, the very reputation I've been trying to outrun is the same one that made Birdie turn to me for help. Despite cleaning up my act and trying to become a better man, she still sees me as the charmer who's left a trail of broken hearts, and I worry she'll never recognize that she's the only person I can see a future with.

Heath glances my way. "You're too hard on yourself. Birdie's lucky to have you."

I snicker under my breath. "Says the guy who finds something to criticize no matter what I do."

He hesitates, worry creasing his brow. "That's never my intention. I'm grateful for everything you do around the ranch. This operation wouldn't be possible without you, Brother."

"Thanks. That means a lot coming from you."

He seldom gives praise, and when he does, it comes off stiff. So even though this doesn't erase the underlying tension between us, I consider it a small step toward him seeing that I'm fully committed to the ranch's success.

I guide Ranger to a slow stop at the pasture where the cows will graze for the evening. My phone buzzes in my shirt pocket, and I shift the reins to my other hand to fish it out.

Sheriff Matterson: I'm back in town.

Sheriff Matterson: Can you come to the station? We need to talk.

Shit.

I wipe the sweat from my brow, my eyes glued to the screen. There's only one thing he could want to talk about, and I'm not ready to face him about dating his daughter. Not only did I not ask for his permission, but we also made it official while he was out of town. There's no chance he'll let that slide.

"Why do you look like you just spotted a rattlesnake?" Heath asks.

"Sheriff Matterson wants me to come down to the station," I mutter.

He chuckles, shaking his head. "Oh, this is going to be great. Mind if I tag along?"

Of course the smug bastard finds it hilarious that I'm about to get my ass handed to me by a man twice my age.

"No, you're not coming."

My phone buzzes again.

Heath eases his horse closer, leaning carefully to catch a glimpse of my screen, and gives me a clap on the back. "You'd better get to the station, or things are only going to get worse for you."

I give him a sharp look. "Aren't you the one constantly complaining about me not pitching in enough around the ranch? Yet you're telling me to leave when I'm here working?"

He shrugs. "We were just about finished anyway."

"You're no help," I huff, running a hand over my jaw.

The way I see it, there's no avoiding this. Resigned to my fate, I type out a quick response and hit send before I change my mind.

If this were for anyone else, I'd bail on our arrangement to avoid this impending talk. But I'd do just about anything for Birdie—even face down her dad, who very well might shoot me.

Heading into the sheriff's office feels like I'm walking into my own funeral. The place is buzzing with activity—from the office clerk typing up a report to the receptionist fielding calls. Every head turns as I pass, probably all wishing they could sit in on judgment day.

Mason flashes me a smug grin, donut powder clinging to his lips. "Well, well, Halstead. Guess you overestimated your standing with the sheriff."

I narrow my eyes in his direction. "We'll see."

Unwilling to waste another second with him, I stride toward

Sheriff Matterson's office. The door swings open as I approach, and Birdie steps out.

She's wearing a blue sundress paired with cowgirl boots. Her hair is pulled into a high ponytail, leaving her neck exposed, and it makes me want to lean in and kiss the column until she's left breathless.

"Howdy, sweetheart," I drawl.

A smile tugs at her lips when she sees me. "Walker, what are you doing here? I thought you were working on the ranch today?"

"Your dad asked to talk to me, so I came straight from there," I explain.

Her gaze shifts to my dusty Wranglers and sweat-stained shirt. "Oh, I'm sorry he did that. He should have waited until you were on shift."

I can't help but chuckle as I wave her off. "Don't worry about it. I don't think that man has ever waited for anything in his life."

Birdie shakes her head, laughing softly. "You're right about that."

I open my mouth to respond when Sheriff Matterson's booming voice thunders from his office.

"Halstead! Stop flirting with my daughter and get your ass in here."

I can't see him from the doorway, but the sharp edge in his voice makes it obvious he's in one of his moods.

"Guess I'll see you on the other side," I deadpan.

"Cheer up, Deputy." She leans in, her lips brushing against my ear. "Survive this, and I promise I'll make it worth your while."

She's fucking sexy when her bold side shows, and I love that she's beginning to trust me enough to let it out more often. It makes it damn near impossible to focus on anything but her, and I'd give anything to be able to pin her against the nearest wall and kiss her senseless.

And that's how I end up walking into my boss's office with a raging hard-on—all thanks to his daughter, who's under the illusion she's too awkward to charm a man, but whose pouty mouth says otherwise.

"Shut the door behind you, Halstead." He nods to the chair in front of his desk. "Take a seat."

Even leaning casually in his seat, the man radiates power. His peppered hair is neatly trimmed, and a permanent crease between his brows hints at years of scowling. His polished pistol is on his desk within easy reach, a silent reminder of the authority he wields. Until now, I'd managed to avoid getting on his bad side, but I should have known that luck wouldn't last forever.

"What did you want to talk about, sir?" I ask, breaking the momentary silence.

Sheriff Matterson clears his throat, straightening in his chair. "You have something you want to tell me, son?"

He calls all the deputies "son," but right now that makes being reprimanded even more uncomfortable. Like I'm back in high school, being lectured by my dad for cow tipping in the middle of the night.

"I'm dating your daughter," I say, refusing to let my nerves show.

I figure it's better to rip off the Band-Aid and get this over with, proving I have nothing to hide—even if his impending reaction makes me uneasy.

He strokes his jaw as he studies me. "Is that so? What gives you the right to sneak around with *my* daughter behind my back?"

I shift in my seat, resting my hand on my knee. "With all due respect sir, Birdie's an adult." He sends me a glare, but I press on. "She wanted to take things slow and wait before we told anyone, and I honored her request."

"Even if it meant pissing me off? Your boss," he retorts.

"Birdie comes first. Always." I say it with my full chest.

He leans forward, his brow tightening as he watches me. "Is

that why you destroyed the video footage of Birdie at the county fair—to protect her?"

"I'm not sure what you mean."

"Mason claims he had proof she snuck onto the fairgrounds and stole that donkey and cow last summer—and somehow the evidence disappeared after you clocked in the morning after he brought her in." His jaw tightens when he mentions Birdie, no doubt picturing her in a jail cell.

"Like I told Mason, I've been a deputy here for six years and have never once given you a reason to doubt me. If you'd rather take the word of a man who made your only kid spend a night in lockup, be my guest." I lean back in my chair, arms draped over the armrests. "Far as I'm concerned, he never had proof to begin with—he just saw an opportunity to revive a year-old case and score some brownie points."

I'll take the truth to my grave. Protecting Birdie was the right call, and I'd do it again in a heartbeat. Wherever those animals are now, they're far better off than being auctioned at that fair, which makes it easy to sleep at night.

Sheriff Matterson doesn't respond right away. He reaches for the pen on his desk and rolls it slowly between his fingers. Every few seconds his gaze flickers to his pistol and back to me. It's intimidating as fuck, but I won't give him the satisfaction of seeing me rattled.

When he finally does speak, his voice is measured and calm. "I guess thanks are in order."

I tilt my head, frowning. "Sir?"

"You looked after Birdie in my absence, and I owe you for that. If not for you, Mason probably would have sent her to county without even speaking with me first."

My grip tightens on the armrests as images of what could've happened flash through my mind. "He's damn lucky he didn't."

"Don't worry. I'll have a word with him," Sheriff Matterson informs me.

"Good," I reply. "So… does this mean I'm off the hook for dating Birdie?" I ask.

His expression hardens, making me instantly wish I'd kept my mouth shut. "What do you think, Halstead? You might be a good deputy, but that doesn't make you good enough for my daughter."

"Never said it did. Believe me I know I'm damn lucky she's interested in me at all."

Sheriff Matterson sets his pen aside. "I've learned the hard way that telling Birdie what to do is like pushing a boulder uphill and expecting it to listen. She's chosen you, and whether I like it or not, that's something I'll have to accept." He leans forward, finger stabbing the air between us. "So you take care of my little girl. Because if you don't, you'll have to answer to me—and I won't be nearly as understanding the second time around. Are we clear?"

I swallow the lump in my throat, knowing that sooner or later Birdie will end our arrangement, and I'll be back in this chair, facing Sheriff Matterson—painted as the villain. In reality, I'll probably be the one left with a broken heart, forced to watch Birdie move on to someone she actually wants, after I've helped her build her confidence and shown her what she deserves in a partner.

Despite knowing what the future holds, I plaster on a mask of confidence. "I'd never hurt Birdie. Not intentionally. Not ever." I've never been so sure of anything in my life.

Sheriff Matterson's eyes soften just a fraction. "Good. You'd better hang on to that certainty."

"I will," I vow.

He clears his throat and stands, holstering his gun, signaling that our conversation is officially over. "I have some business to handle at town hall before they close, so you're dismissed."

Sheriff Matterson doesn't have to tell me twice. I put my

hat back on and stand. I'm halfway out the door when his voice stops me.

"That other thing you've been helping me with—I expect it to stay between us. It's not something I want Birdie to worry about right now. She's already got so much going on without adding more stress," Sheriff Matterson says.

I nod. "Understood."

As much as I hate keeping things from Birdie, I agree with her dad. If she finds out, she'll want to get involved and end up taking on more than she can handle.

CHAPTER 14

Please Please Please

Walker

BIRDIE'S ALREADY GONE BY THE TIME I FINISH TALKING with her dad. I figured she wouldn't wait around—most likely panicking over how the conversation played out and wanted to avoid the aftermath if it went south.

Since the diner is only a few blocks away, I decide to grab dinner there rather than chance running into Heath or Mom on the ranch on my way back to my loft, knowing they'd no doubt pepper me with questions.

On my walk over, I check in with Birdie.

Walker: That talk with your dad was interesting...

Walker: Felt like I was being sent to the principal's office, except your dad is scarier and carries a gun.

Birdie: Walker Halstead, don't you dare leave me hanging. What happened?

Walker: Want the good or bad news first?

Birdie: Good. Let's start on a high note.

Walker: Good news: He didn't kill me.

Walker: Bad news: No chance he lets me survive our breakup.

Birdie: What a shame. I'd hate to lose my favorite teacher. *wink face emoji

Walker: You did promise you'd make it worth my while if I got through that conversation so at least I have got that to look forward to.

Birdie: Lucky for you, I'm in a hands-on mood.

Walker: You're getting dangerously good at flirting over text.

Birdie: Perks of having an excellent teacher.

God, I'd give anything to be with her right now and put into practice everything our kiss last night promised would follow.

Walker: Got any plans tonight?

Birdie: Just visiting my mom, then a low-key night at home with Nugget and the kittens.

> Walker: Kittens?

> Birdie: Someone dropped off a litter of five on my doorstep this morning. Briar was kind enough to take three, leaving me with two adorable tyrants who won't negotiate when it's bottle time.

I'm momentarily distracted when I reach the Prickly Pear, holding the door open for an elderly couple before stepping to the side of the waiting area.

> Walker: Sounds like you've got your hands full.

> Birdie: Oh, if only you knew.

My thumb hovers over the screen, itching to ask if I can come over later, but I think better of it. If she wanted me there, she'd say so. Not willing to risk pushing her boundaries, I play this one safe.

> Walker: If you need backup, I'm only a text away.

> Birdie: I should be able to manage for now, but I'll keep you on standby. Never know when I might need a cowboy with a six-pack to come to my rescue.

> Walker: So you were checking me out when I had my shirt off the other morning.

> Birdie: Uh... Mama wants to watch our show. Gotta go.

> Walker: Don't think that deflection will save you the next time we're together, pretty girl.

> **Birdie: Talk to you later!**

I laugh at her Herculean effort to dodge the question. That's fine—there will be plenty of opportunities later to get the truth out of her. For now, I'm just glad she's enjoying her time with her mom.

After a quick bite, I head back to the ranch. Pulling through the entrance, I notice my parents' truck parked in front of Briar and Jensen's cottage. Whenever we have family dinners, Ma hosts at the ranch house, which means they must be babysitting Caleb.

The one time Heath and I watched him when Jensen and Briar first started dating, he stayed up well past his bedtime watching *Shrek* and eating way too many cookies—which was one hundred percent Heath's fault. Needless to say, our babysitting privileges were promptly revoked. That's okay—I've still got my favorite-uncle status covered with gifts, including books like *Dragons Love Farts: They're More Fun Than Tacos!* and *The Day My Butt Went Psycho,* because every kid could use a good laugh before bed.

When I pull up to the ranch house, I beeline it to my loft to dodge running into Heath. After a quick shower, I kick back on the couch with my feet on the coffee table, watching an old western with a cold beer in hand.

The sun has long since set, and I'm halfway through another movie when I decide to call it a night. I have an early morning ahead with feeding the horses and cattle before heading into my shift at the sheriff's office.

No sooner had I turned off the TV than Birdie texted me.

> **Birdie: I have a kitten emergency. Think you could come over?**

I'm on my feet before I even finish reading her message.

> Walker: Absolutely. You okay?

> Birdie: Got a new crate and the door won't latch.

> Walker: Did you try wiggling it while pressing down?

> Birdie: Yep, but no luck. I don't want them to escape in the middle of the night so I could really use some backup.

I'm no kitten expert, but a simple wedge against the door should keep them in if the latch is faulty. Then it hits me—Birdie's an animal rescue pro, so she's got several crates and carries on hand for emergencies like this.

Could this be an excuse to get me to come over for something else?

Frankly, I don't give a damn. If she wants me there, I'm going—no questions asked.

It's well past ten when I get to her place. The porch light is on, and the door is slightly ajar. I let out a low grunt of disapproval. Even if she was expecting me, she shouldn't have left the door open.

Against my better judgment, I decide that's a discussion for another day. She called me for help, and I won't risk making her regret it by picking a fight the second I get here.

I knock a few times, and when there's no response, I stick my head through the doorway.

"Hello? Birdie, I'm here," I holler, only to be met with continued silence.

I figure she's probably preoccupied with the kittens, but I

can't ignore my protective instincts, so I slowly open the door and go inside to make sure she's all right.

To my surprise, I find Nugget standing in the middle of the hallway, like she's guarding the place. A chicken roaming around the house would be alarming anywhere else, but at Birdie's, it's par for the course.

Nugget goes still when she spots me, fixing me with a skeptical stare.

Out of the corner of my eye, I catch Birdie peeking her head out from the kitchen doorway, but I pretend not to notice.

Instead, I tip my hat at Nugget and say, "Evening, ma'am. I'm looking for your pretty owner. She's got beautiful blue eyes and dimples for days. Any chance you know where I can find her?"

Nugget blinks and lets out a series of clucks before waddling toward the kitchen, where Birdie is now standing in the doorway, covering her mouth to stifle a laugh.

Birdie bends down and scoops Nugget up, cradling her in her arms.

"Did you bring me a visitor?" she coos, leaning in as if Nugget is answering. "He really said all those nice things about me? I'm flattered." Birdie glances at me, eyes sparkling with amusement. "I think we should let him stay—what do you think?"

Nugget squawks softly and ruffles her wings, which I'm taking as her stamp of approval.

"So what's the verdict?" I ask Birdie. "Do I get to stick around?"

She lets out a dramatic sigh. "I suppose since you're here now, you might as well be useful."

"Consider me at your service."

I follow her into the kitchen, my eyes immediately landing on a crate in the corner, covered with a blanket.

"That the one you wanted me to fix?"

Birdie's eyes widen and dart around the room. "Oh... uh...

no. The kittens were getting sleepy, and I found a spare one in the storage closet that I forgot I had, so I put them in there."

I tilt my head. "Oh? And where's the crate you said needs fixing?"

She nods toward the kitchen table, where a smaller one sits. "Right there."

Birdie sets Nugget down, and the chicken darts across the floor. When she reaches the large crate holding the kittens, she flaps her wings and launches herself onto the top, perching in the middle as if it's a giant egg.

"Nugget is convinced the kittens are hers," Birdie explains, reading my perplexed expression. "She got upset when Briar took three of them home, and now she's guarding the others like a hawk."

I inspect the crate on the table, flipping the latch open and shut a few times with ease. The hinge isn't bent or loose, and the door swings smoothly. I even check the corners for weak spots, but everything looks solid.

"I'm not seeing anything wrong with this," I tell Birdie. "Can you show me what was giving you trouble?" I step aside to give her space, but she doesn't budge. "Birdie?" I ask again.

She lets out a nervous laugh, twisting her necklace between her fingers. "If you say it's fine, I'm sure you're right. I must have been too scatterbrained between prepping the kittens' bottles and setting it up to open the latch properly. Sorry for making you come all the way out here for nothing."

I move closer, and she lifts her chin to meet my eyes, her chest rising and falling with quick, shallow breaths. The low-cut tank top accentuates the curves of her breasts, and her pajama shorts showcase her sun-kissed legs. She's all kinds of tempting, and my restraint is wearing thin.

"The crate never needed to be fixed, did it?"

A blush rises to her cheeks as she nibbles her lower lip. "Why would you think that?"

I close the last few steps between us, and Birdie lets out a soft gasp as I wrap my arm around her waist, drawing her against me.

"We agreed to be honest with each other, remember?" I murmur against her mouth.

She looks up at me, her eyes wide and vulnerable. "Will you leave if I admit that's not why I asked you to come?"

I tuck a strand of hair behind her ear, my fingers grazing her cheek. "No, Birdie, baby. I'm not going anywhere," I promise, holding her gaze. "Now—why don't you tell me the real reason you texted me."

CHAPTER 15

Toys As Teammates

Birdie

THIS IS THE PART WHERE I'D LIKE TO CRAWL INTO A HOLE and disappear. Somehow, I've managed to be both painfully awkward and completely incapable of fabricating a believable lie to get Walker to come to my place. Now I'm standing here while he waits for an explanation, my brain scrambling for any alternative that isn't the truth: that my libido is defective and I'm doomed to die a virgin.

Am I being dramatic? Without question. Is it warranted, given my impressive history of overthinking that leads to panic? Also yes.

"I got frustrated trying to follow your terrible advice," I mutter quickly.

Good thinking blaming the man trying to help you. Stellar strategy, Birdie.

Walker arches a brow. "And what advice was that?"

I let out a nervous laugh, rubbing my palms against my shorts.

"You told me using a vibrator would help me learn what I like, but it was a total bust…"

This would be a really great time for a fire alarm, an earthquake—honestly, I'd take Mrs. Bixby popping over rather than have this conversation. Especially if she brought a pan of her lasagna, I could drown my mortification in layers of cheese and pasta.

"Wait. You tried that tonight?" Walker's hands flex against my waist, and his eyes dart to the crate Nugget is sitting on. "Are there actually kittens in there, or…" He trails off, waiting for an explanation.

"I'd never lie about animals in need of rescue… just the part about a broken crate."

He nods slowly, a soft smile on his handsome face. "I'm curious, what made your little adventure unsuccessful?"

"I couldn't… come," I mumble under my breath.

It's humiliating to admit I can't get off with a stupid vibrator. I've grown more comfortable opening up to Walker over the past few days, but what he thinks matters to me and I'm not sure if I'm ready to lay all my insecurities at his feet just yet.

He tilts his head closer. "Sorry, what was that? You were so quiet I could barely hear you."

I sigh, dragging a hand down my face. "It doesn't work, okay? Simple as that."

Please let that be the end of it. I could've saved myself the embarrassment by not inviting him over and just telling him I'd used a vibrator and had a mind-blowing orgasm. Instead, I went and exposed my deep-rooted insecurities to a man who's practically a sex god—someone who could never possibly understand my dilemma.

"It probably just needs to be charged," Walker offers. "Where is it? I'll take a look."

I shake my head. "No, that's all right. It's late—you should head home, and we can revisit this later."

Better yet, we could pretend this conversation never happened.

"Or I could stick around and give you a hand," he says, a lazy smirk playing on his lips. "It'd be a shame to come all this way and not make myself useful."

Translation: he's not leaving until I've told him the truth.

"The vibrator isn't broken," I explain with a defeated sigh. "I just… I can't get off using one. I've tried in the past, but it's never worked for me."

Walker's gaze snaps to mine, his eyes darkening. "Birdie, are you telling me you've never had an orgasm before?"

I slowly nod, my voice barely above a whisper. "No, I haven't."

I'm half expecting him to laugh at the absurdity of the situation, but he surprises me by taking my hand and brushing his lips against my skin, sending butterflies dancing in my stomach at the tenderness of his touch.

"There's nothing to be ashamed of. The whole point of our arrangement is to help you explore your sexuality and build confidence, but I can't do that if you shut me out every time you hit a roadblock." He traces my palm with his thumb in soothing circles. "The problem is you're overthinking it. There's no formula for discovering what you like. It's all about trial and error, and that's part of the fun."

His analysis is spot-on: The second I start to feel any pleasure, whether with a vibrator or my own fingers, I get stuck in my head, and it all falls apart before I can climax.

"It's not your responsibility to solve all my problems in bed." I glance at the floor. "I don't want to sound like a broken record, but I'm worried you'll start to think I'm taking advantage of you."

My breath hitches as Walker drops to his knees before me.

"Wh-what are you doing?" I stammer, lifting my foot to step back, but his hands settle on my hips, keeping me in place.

"I want you to," he states, a dark edge to his tone.

I swallow hard. "Want me to what?"

"Use me—for your pleasure, to live out your every fantasy, to chase the rush of your first orgasm. All. Of. It." Walker's hand slides along my hip bone, tugging my tank top up just enough to reveal the curve of my abdomen. "All you have to do is ask, and I'm here to serve you."

He peppers kisses along my stomach, and I clutch his shoulders to stay upright.

A ripple of fire spreads through my veins as his eyes lift to meet mine, seeming to pierce straight through every defense I've built.

He nudges my tank higher, his mouth trailing along my skin, and a soft moan escapes me as he drags his tongue up my torso, leaving goose bumps in its wake. I'm lost in a haze of lust and can barely form a coherent thought as he teases me with the promise of what's to come if I allow him to take control, and trust that he'll take care of me.

I'm hit with the harsh reality that if I don't fully embrace this, I'll never get the results I want from these lessons—and in the process, I could risk pushing Walker away, which terrifies me. I've grown more attached to him than I ever thought possible, and I can't bear the thought of losing the open line of communication that we didn't have before. Especially now that I've felt his hands all over me and know how his touch can make me ache in ways I've never experienced. It's time to stop sending mixed signals, be brave, and quit holding back.

He peppers several kisses just below my bra, careful not to go any higher, his hands still firm on my hips.

"Walker?" I rasp.

He glances up at me. "Yeah, Birdie, baby?"

"Don't stop touching me."

He smirks. "You'll have to be more specific."

"I want you to help me come for the first time... please."

His warm breath teases my skin. "Does that mean you're done hiding from me?"

I nod.

"I need to hear you say it, pretty girl."

"No more hiding," I say as I hold his gaze.

The declaration feels more significant than it should, like crossing into dangerous territory, where our no-strings arrangement could transform into something real, beyond keeping up a charade for the sake of appearances and mutual convenience.

He brushes a final kiss to my breastbone before tugging my tank down and rising to his feet, forcing me to stifle a frustrated moan in the absence of his touch.

"Where's your vibrator?"

"Uh, in the trash bin… in my room."

Walker motions in that direction. "Will you show me?"

His words are measured, gauging whether I'm truly ready to take this to the next step.

I am.

I study him closely, noting the way his chest heaves and the hunger burning in his eyes. Every muscle taut, his restraint hanging by a thread, and it's clear he wants this as much as I do.

"Yeah, I will," I say.

Before I lose my courage, I motion for him to follow me down the hall, not bothering to look back—confident that he will. I move on autopilot, heat pooling low in my belly, and intensifying with each step, until even breathing feels like an impossible task. Before I know it, I'm standing next to the trash can by my bed, staring down at the vibrator I tossed earlier.

When I look up, Walker is in the doorway, his hands flexing at his sides, his gaze fixed on me.

"Nervous about going into a girl's bedroom? Don't worry, I'll hold your hand if that'll make it less scary," I tease, holding mine out to him.

Walker chuckles, shaking his head. "It's best if I stay put. If I'm close enough to touch you, I'll be tempted to do a whole lot more than watch—and I'm trying to be good tonight."

My lips round into an O.

"What if I don't want you to be good?" I ask tentatively.

His jaw tightens, hands flexing at his sides. "You're making it very difficult for me to act like a gentleman right now."

I'm on the verge of pleading with him to forget about that and skip a few steps to get to the lesson we're both eager for. But then I remember I'm about to get completely naked in front of him as he guides me toward what I hope will be my first-ever climax. I'm slowly building my confidence, but diving in fully overnight isn't realistic—no matter how loudly my impulsive, lust-driven side argues otherwise.

"Why don't you show me that vibrator of yours," Walker suggests.

I blink. "Oh, right."

Before I can overthink it, I pluck the infamous pink device from the bin, holding it out like radioactive waste. Just being near the thing is poisoning my optimism that tonight's outcome will be any different than in the past.

Walker studies it from across the room, scrutinizing every angle. "Is that the only one you've got?"

I cast him a sidelong glance, running my fingers through my hair. "I have another one, but I've never used it, and I'm sure it's just as useless."

"Why don't you show it to me anyway?"

I sigh, knowing there's no point in arguing. I rummage through my nightstand drawer until I find my blue rabbit vibrator. When I first got it, I took it out of the box, but after one look at the little attached arm, I got overwhelmed and shoved it in the drawer, where it's stayed out of sight until now.

A smile curves at the corners of Walker's mouth. "That'll do."

I tilt my head. "Care to elaborate?"

"You should use that one." He motions to the vibrator in my hand. "That is… if you're still up for this."

My grip tightens on the device as I glance between it and Walker. The choice is all mine, and I know that if I asked him to leave, he would—but I don't want that. Instead, I'm determined to pull a reaction from him, to prove that I affect him just as much as he affects me. The thought fuels my confidence, giving me the courage to speak my mind without restraint.

"Oh, I'm still game. The question is, can you keep up this little discipline act of yours while I'm sprawled naked on the bed, playing with my vibrator?"

Flirting with Walker makes my heart race, and when I'm not overthinking, it feels effortless—like we're drawn together by gravity, every glance and every touch pulling us closer.

He raises an eyebrow. "That's one dirty mouth for someone who claims to be so innocent."

I shrug. "What can I say? All those flirting lessons are doing wonders for my confidence."

"Look at you, putting what you've learned into practice." He takes a step toward me but stops himself at the last second. "Why don't you show me by taking off your clothes. I want to look at you," he says, his chocolate-brown eyes pinning me in place. "*All* of you."

There's no denying him when he uses that low, commanding tone that sends a shiver down my spine. I set the device on the bed, my hands slightly shaking as I lift my tank top over my head, revealing my plain white bra. I mentally scold myself for not wearing something sexier, fully aware there was a chance I'd end up here tonight.

I'm jolted out of my self-conscious spiral by Walker's firm tone. "Birdie, look at me."

I slowly meet his heated gaze. "Yeah?"

"You're so beautiful." His voice comes out rough.

I can't stop the smile from tugging at my lips, his words giving me the reassurance I need to slide down my shorts and panties, leaving only my bra.

When I glance back at Walker, I find his hand gripping the doorframe. The air between us crackles with tension, heat shooting through me and settling low in my belly.

"Take your bra off," he orders.

I inhale deeply as I reach around to unfasten the clasp. The straps fall from my shoulders, cool air brushing against my nipples as I toss my bra to the floor along with the rest of my clothes.

Walker gazes at me with reverence and want written all over his face. "Fuck, you really are perfect."

The lingering nerves that had been clawing at me a few minutes ago have dissolved into burning arousal, leaving my body taut and ready to snap under the weight of anticipation.

"Now what?" I ask softly, reveling in this little game of cat and mouse where he takes the lead and I follow, all the while pushing the limits of his self-control.

"Lie on the bed facing me and spread your legs so I can see you," Walker says, his throat bobbing with a hard swallow.

I let out a shaky whimper, his reply sending an electric current racing down my spine.

I climb on the bed and lie down on my back. The old me would be trembling with embarrassment, but seeing Walker leaning against the doorway, looking at me as he adjusts his hard-on, sparks a newfound sense of confidence. Even now, a simmering heat spreads through my core, whereas usually I'd barely feel a flicker of desire.

"You ready?" he asks, reinforcing that this is my call to make.

"Yes," I state, grabbing the vibrator from the mattress beside me.

Walker clenches his free hand at his side, his jaw tightening.

"Good. I want you to push the tip inside and get it nice and wet for me."

A shiver snakes down my spine, as I draw in a shaky breath. The second the device slips inside, pleasure blooms at the intrusion, and I imagine it's his cock. It's one of the only parts I haven't seen of him, but judging by the giant bulge in his Wranglers, it's safe to say he's packing.

Focus, Birdie.

After a moment to calm my nerves, I ask, "What comes next?"

"Turn on the vibrator."

Walker's voice anchors me as a soft hum buzzes through the air. The pulse courses through me, and I moan softly as the vibrations tease my entrance. Usually, this is when the frustration sets in because the stimulation is never enough to fully satisfy. However, it's different this time, and my skin is exquisitely sensitive to every flicker of sensation rippling through my core. Searching for more friction, I move the device in a steady motion, my gaze wandering to Walker.

"You're a damn vision, Birdie," he groans, his fingers digging into the doorframe.

His words are an aphrodisiac, making me pick up my pace, each stroke fueled by his praise.

"Oh, Walker," I gasp.

I wish more than anything it was his cock thrusting inside me, drawing me closer to a release I've only ever dreamed of until now.

"Angle the toy so the small arm is on your clit," he instructs, his voice catching slightly.

When the narrow arm finds my clit it sends a rush through me that knocks the air from my lungs. My free hand fists the comforter while I roll my hips in circles and drag the tip over the nub until I'm lightheaded. The rush of euphoria leaves me dizzy, but it's still not enough to push me over the edge.

I lift my head to see the corners of Walker's mouth quirking up, his grip on the doorframe so tight his knuckles have gone white.

"I need you," I whimper. "Please."

My vision swims as I struggle to focus long enough to push the main shaft farther inside, a moan tearing from my throat as the device continues to pulsate.

"God, you're so hot when you beg." His ghost of a smile deepens to a smirk. "You need me to help get you off, baby? Is that what you've been missing?"

I bob my head, propping myself up on one elbow to get a better look at him. His white T-shirt clings to his biceps, flexing with every movement, and I look down to the outline in his Wranglers, swelling against the fabric.

He unfastens his jeans and reaches beneath the waistband of his boxers, pulling his cock out. His jeans hang low on his hips, showcasing the delicious V-line and the hard planes of his abs. He's unbelievably huge, and though part of me wonders how it could ever possibly fit, another part is fantasizing about us jumping straight to *that* particular lesson tonight.

I remind myself to slow down and drink in every shared glance, every groan, every unspoken reassurance that passes between us. This moment will be fleeting and someday when I'm lying on this very bed alone without him here, I'll call on it to push me past the brink.

I'm mesmerized as Walker spits in his hand before stroking his shaft, starting at the bottom and reaching the tip, smearing the drop of pre-cum over the crown.

"Look what you fucking do to me." He glances down at his erect cock as he moves his hand faster up and down.

He looks untamed and uninhabited, jaw tight and nostrils flaring, and right now, he's all mine.

Witnessing his unfiltered reaction firsthand only fuels my

own hunger, and I bite my lip as my free hand moves to my left breast, cupping it firmly as I flick my nipple. The extra stimulation sends a ripple straight to my core, and my lids flutter closed as I'm lost in a rush of bliss.

"Eyes on me." The authority in Walker's voice demands obedience. "When you come, you'll look at the man who made you lose control."

I obey, snapping them open, wanting him to witness every tremor that claims me as I chase my first release. It's all because of him, and my body's surrender is a silent confession.

"Turn up the speed of the vibrator and roll your hips until you find your G-spot." His gaze remains locked on me as he moves toward the bed.

I do as he instructs, the stronger pulse sending a wave of heat through me as I tentatively explore, adjusting the device in search of the sweet spot I've only ever heard about. Just when I begin to think that it might not exist, the main shaft brushes against a sensitive area, sending a rush through me that knocks the air from my lungs.

"Now use the little arm of the vibrator to put more pressure on your clit," he growls.

I lick my lips as I push down on my nub again, the vein in Walker's neck pulsing sharply with every moan that escapes me. I'm immersed in a haze of desire, a swirling inferno of heat in my core pushing me to the brink. With him so close, I'm desperate for a tangible connection that'll be etched into my memory, and leave no doubt about how much I want this.

I meet Walker's gaze, panting. "I want to watch you come."

The muscles in his hand tighten around his cock, a low, guttural sound escaping his throat.

He tugs his shirt over his head with his free hand and holds it out in front of him, picking up speed as he strokes himself. He never takes his eyes off me, calling my name as he finds his release.

I'm mesmerized as ropes of cum land on his shirt, the musky scent filling the air as he coaxes out every last drop.

It sends me spiraling over the edge, my back bowing off the bed as I fall apart. I pull the vibrator from me, turning it off and dropping it beside me. My body is burning with a lustful haze, and I feel like I'm floating, suspended on a cloud of bliss. My head collapses on the pillow as I catch my breath. I glance over to see Walker wiping himself clean and tucking himself back inside his pants before tossing his shirt into the waste bin in the corner.

"Better not get pulled over tonight," I tease with a grin. "Then again, I'd love to hear the excuse you'd give one of the other deputies for driving home without a shirt."

"I'm sure they'd come to a conclusion close to the truth, but who could blame me for not being able to resist my *girlfriend,* who's also the prettiest girl in town?" He bends down and presses a gentle kiss to my temple. "I'm so fucking grateful I got to experience this with you."

I give him a sleepy smile. "Thank *you.*"

I'm lightheaded, grateful for Walker's patience, and his praise brought me to heights I thought were out of my reach. I barely notice when he slips from the room, coming back a minute later with a warm washcloth and gently wiping between my legs.

Once he's dried me off with a towel, he retrieves a clean oversized tee from my dresser. I slip it over my head and lay back in bed, letting him tuck the covers around me.

"Is there anything else you need, sweetheart?" he murmurs.

I'm flooded with conflicting emotions. The thought of him leaving after what we just shared twists my stomach into knots. I want nothing more than to beg him to stay, but I swallow it back. No matter how badly I long to be wrapped up with him all night, the butterflies swirling in my belly after he just called me his girlfriend has me worried that any hope of keeping my feelings in check where he's concerned is already lost.

"No, but thank you," I say, propping up on my elbow to kiss him. "Tonight was beyond anything I could have imagined."

"Just you wait until our next lesson."

"I'm looking forward to it," I whisper.

More than I probably should for someone in a no-strings-attached, fake-dating situation, but since I just had my first climax, I'm going to chalk it up to being temporarily delusional and thoroughly satisfied.

CHAPTER 16

Backroads And BJs

Walker

AFTER A LONG DAY IN THE FIELDS AND A QUICK STOP AT the loft to clean up, I'm parked at the feed store waiting for Birdie to get off work. Leaving her alone at her place last night was straight-up torture, and it took all my willpower not to throw caution to the wind and ask to stay the night.

I'll never be able to erase the image of that damn vibrator sliding into her drenched pussy as she moaned my name. Birdie's unintentionally burrowed so deep under my skin that she's become a permanent part of me—and I have every intention of keeping it that way. Now the challenge is showing her that a life with me could bring her true joy and that this isn't just a game of make-believe while she waits for someone better to come along. That begins with more thoughtful surprises and more time spent together, hoping she craves my company as much as I crave hers.

I'm leaning back against the headrest, tapping my fingers against the steering wheel to a country song on the radio, when I get a text.

Group Therapy Halstead Siblings Edition

Briar: How are my favorite brothers doing?

Heath: We're your only brothers.

Walker: Yeah. And we can't both be your favorite.

Briar: Guess I have to pick one, huh?

Walker: Yup. Who's the front-runner?

Briar: Right now? You.

Heath: I don't recall him bringing you lunch the other day when Caleb was sick and Jensen was out of town.

Briar: No, but I've never seen Birdie this happy, and that's because of Walker, so by default, he wins.

I can't decide whether I should be flattered or insulted by her backhanded compliment. Either way, it leaves me questioning whether Birdie's putting on a show for her friends or if being with me genuinely makes her happy. It's probably wishful thinking on my part, but the way her eyes locked on me as she climaxed for the first time last night proves our electric chemistry is mutual—and has me convinced a part of her is drawn to me beyond our agreed-upon arrangement.

Heath: Are you saying I'd have to date one of your friends to be the favorite?

Walker: I hear Charlie's on the market if you're looking for a fix.

Heath: Only if hell freezes over first.

Charlie and Heath have never gotten along, and the tension between them has only escalated over the years. Whenever they're in the room together their silent stares speak volume, each glance loaded with barely concealed irritation.

Walker: Sounds like you're in denial.

Briar: Don't think I haven't seen the way you look at her when you think I'm not paying attention.

Walker added Jensen Harding to the chat.

Jensen: Why do I have a feeling being added to this thread is a setup?

Walker: Couldn't let you miss the opportunity to give Heath a hard time for pretending he wouldn't go out with Charlie if her disdain for him wasn't so obvious.

Jensen: He'd totally jump at the chance if he could.

Heath: Please. I'd rather break in a wild mustang before agreeing to that.

Briar: Stop being a cranky sourpuss. You'd be lucky to have Charlie.

Walker: I thought you didn't want your friends dating your brothers.

Briar: That ship sailed once you and Birdie made your relationship official.

Jensen: As entertaining as this is, I'm still not sure why I'm here.

Walker: Because you're one of us now.

Briar: Not legally. We're not married yet.

Jensen: And whose fault is that? I'd marry you today if you'd let me, sugar.

Walker: He has a point, sis.

Briar: We all know Mama Julie and Charlie would have a fit if we didn't throw a big wedding, and I want to wait to have it in the community center once it's finished.

On top of building their dream house, they're constructing a nonprofit where Briar can provide a safe, healing space for kids, including those with emotional scars. She's hosted a few pop-up events at Silver Saddle Ranch but is planning to offer seasonal camps and year-round therapeutic horseback riding. As someone who suffered trauma when she was younger, she's always wanted to create a place where every child could experience the kind of unconditional acceptance and healing she longed for growing up.

Briar was adopted by Ma and Pops when she was fifteen. Her biological mom was a bartender at Blue Moon Tavern and was always chasing her next high—whether it came from pills or the fleeting attention of whichever man happened to be around—and she never met her biological dad.

Ma had been her elementary school teacher and took Briar

under her wing when she realized her home life wasn't stable. She spent her evenings at our place, and even before she was officially adopted, Heath and I saw her as the sister we'd always wanted.

I look up just in time to see Birdie jogging across the parking lot, her tote slung over her shoulder as she waves at me with a bright smile on her face. My heart slams against my ribs at how different her reaction is from the first time I picked her up. It gives me hope that my plan to make her fall for me might already be working.

Walker: Once you set a date, let me know, lovebirds. I have somewhere to be.

Briar: Tell Birdie I say hi.

I set my phone on the dash and hop out of the truck, tipping my hat. "Howdy there, sweetheart."

Birdie's smile widens as she gets closer. "You came."

"Told you I would, and I never break a promise."

I blink in surprise when she loops her arms around my neck and kisses my cheek, but I quickly recover, pulling her into a hug and breathing in her familiar, sweet scent.

"I could get used to that kind of welcome," I say with a sly grin.

She tips her head back, a rosy blush spreading across her face. "Sorry, I got a little carried away. I was just excited to see you. I hope that's all right."

"It's more than all right."

I lean forward, capturing her lips in a slow, teasing kiss. Birdie responds tentatively at first, then grows bolder, letting her tongue slip past mine, her hand moving up my chest as she kisses me. My troublemaker is quickly mastering the art of a make-out session, and I'm lucky enough to be her practice partner. I'm hard as steel just from her taking more than my intended peck, and it's all I can do to resist lifting her into my arms, being in public be damned.

Birdie is breathless by the time she breaks away, reaching out to touch her swollen lips like she can't quite believe what just happened.

"I'm not sure what's gotten into me," she admits, glancing at the ground.

"It's not a crime to explore what makes you feel good." I tuck a strand of hair behind her ear, letting my fingers linger on her cheek. "I'm just the lucky guy who gets to share this with you."

She lets out a throaty laugh. "You say that to all your girls, Walker?"

I shake my head. "Just you." *If only she knew that she already has all of me.* "Wanna get out of here?"

She hikes her tote higher up her shoulder. "Yeah. You going to tell me where we're going this time?"

"Figured we'd stop by the diner to grab a bite to eat."

"Sounds great," she replies. "I've been craving a veggie burger and sweet potato fries."

As I open the truck door, she slips her hand into mine, letting me help her into the passenger seat.

I walk around and hop into the driver's seat, grinning when I see she's slid into the middle seat.

"All set?" I ask.

She nods as she buckles up.

I set my hat on the dash, then take Birdie's hand in mine, resting it on my thigh. I'm expecting her to move away, but she just relaxes into my side as we pull out of the feed store parking lot. It's on the outskirts of town, and about a ten-minute drive to Main Street. We head down the county road in silence, the radio playing softly in the background. I take it all in—the warmth of Birdie's hand, having her this close. I'm determined to make the most of every second while it lasts.

My breath catches when Birdie's fingertips skim my thigh. At first, I assume it's unintentional until she does it again, and again.

When I look over, the smug curve of her lips confirms my suspicion that she's up to something.

She lets go of my hand and slides hers toward the crotch of my pants.

"Birdie, what are you doing?" My voice is hoarse.

"I want to touch you," she whispers, letting her fingers drift along my inner thigh. "Can I?"

"Always," I rasp out.

She hums as she grazes over the bulge pressing against my jeans. My grip tightens on the steering wheel as I try to focus on the road.

A low groan slips from my throat when she adds pressure, circling the outline. Even with the material between her hand and me, I'm fucking hard as a damn rock, and controlling my physical reaction is a losing battle.

"I've never given a blow job before. I've always wondered what it would feel like to have a cock in my mouth." *Fucking hell. I think she's trying to kill me.* "Will you teach me?" she asks sweetly, her fingers tracing up and down the outline of my shaft.

I clear my throat. "Now?"

She nods, unbuttoning my Wranglers. "No better time than the present, right?"

I force my eyes to stay on the road, resting my hand over hers as I shoot her a quick glance.

"You don't have to do this."

"I want to," she breathes, nipping at my earlobe. "It's my turn to make you feel good, Walker."

Her words strike a match to my veins, and the way she says my name while she looks at me with hunger in her eyes steals a shaky breath from me, leaving me powerless to deny her.

My vision tunnels when she unbuckles her seat belt and shifts onto all fours on the bench seat beside me. Any other time, I'd scold her for putting her safety at risk—but right now I'm too far gone. Thankfully, there aren't any other vehicles in sight as I slow down and flip on my blinker, turning onto the next dirt road and guiding the truck behind a row of pine trees, their long shadows keeping us hidden from view. I turn off my headlights once we've come to a stop, engulfing us in darkness. The only light is the soft flicker of fireflies outside, blinking like tiny stars scattered across the landscape.

The faint chirp of crickets is all I can hear over the shallow, ragged rhythm of my own breathing as Birdie tugs down my zipper. I lift up so she can tug down my boxers enough to take out my now fully erect cock. She saw it last night, but this is the first time she's touching me, and I never want this to end.

My hand clamps around the door handle, fighting to keep even a shred of composure as she traces my shaft with a feather-light touch, her fingers slowly curling around me, and gives a gentle squeeze. Pre-cum leaks from the tip and without prompting, she leans down, flicking her tongue across the crown to lick it off.

"Oh fuck."

Birdie lifts her gaze to mine, a smile curving her mouth. "Show me how you like it, Walker… please."

It's the *please* that does me in.

Every hot breath against my cock burns through sense and reason, and even if all she did was lick me, it'd be enough to make me come. I remind myself that this thing started because she asked me to teach her, and with her so eager to learn, how can I possibly say no?

I wind my fingers through Birdie's hair and push the tip of my cock against her mouth.

"Wrap your lips around the crown," I instruct.

She eagerly obliges, her tongue darting out to explore the texture of the head. I very slowly guide my cock down her throat and when she gets about halfway her gag reflex kicks in, a trickle of drool running down her chin.

I stroke the column of her neck with my free hand. "Focus on breathing through your nose so you can open your throat and take more of me."

She rests her hands on my thighs as she pushes up on her knees, her ass sticking in the air as she angles herself to accommodate my size, slowly taking me deeper in her mouth. The sight has me biting my bottom lip as I let out a growling moan.

"That's it, baby. Take as much as you can while I fuck that perfect mouth of yours."

A soft hum of approval rumbles from her chest, the sound reverberating around my dick. I instinctively rock my hips forward, and she takes a sharp inhale through her nose. Determined to drive me wild, she hollows her cheeks, swallowing hard around me.

My shaft pulses forward and when she's got me halfway inside her mouth, the rush crashes over me like a tidal wave, consuming every part of me.

"Damn, Birdie, you feel so good," I praise, stroking her hair.

Her gaze lifts to mine as she moves her hand back to the base of my shaft, holding me steady as she runs her tongue up, this time applying pressure to the veins. Every one of my muscles strains to maintain control, but Birdie has other plans as she swirls her tongue around the crown and back down my length. She may look innocent, but right now I'm utterly at her mercy—every motion an entrancing mix of mischief and unbridled temptation. It's enough to push me right to the edge.

I gently tug on her hair to pull her off. "I'm going to come."

She ignores me, leaning forward and pushing the head back down her throat.

"Fuck, Birdie, if you don't want me coming down your throat you have to stop," I grunt.

She shakes her head, tears gathering at the corner of her eyes. Her swollen lips bob up and down as she tentatively wraps her free hand around my balls. I let out a guttural groan when she gives them a light squeeze.

"Jesus Fucking Christ." My voice is strained as I tip my head back. "If you're going to finish me off, you better swallow every drop."

She nods the best she can as I spill my load down her throat. My cock jerks in her hand from aftershocks, and my eyes widen as she flicks her tongue along the shaft like it's a damn popsicle. I've never seen something so damn hot in my life.

When she's finished cleaning me off, she releases my cock from her mouth with a loud *pop*. She sits back on her heels, lifting her gaze to meet mine. A bead of cum drips from her bottom lip and without taking her eyes off me, she slowly licks it off, letting out a soft moan of satisfaction.

"Such a good girl," I croon.

"*Your* good girl," she corrects me with a smirk.

My eyes flare with possession. "That's right. *Mine.*"

She probably thinks this is just playful banter, unaware of how serious I am.

To reclaim a sense of control, I take a deep breath, tucking my semi-hard cock inside my boxers and zipping up my pants.

"Fuck, baby," I say, groaning. "I had every intention of taking you on a nice date, and now all I can think about is taking you back to my place and making you come with my mouth."

She flashes me a grin. "Don't tempt me with a good—" She's cut off when my phone rings.

"Dammit. I'm sorry—let me check to make sure it's not urgent." I pull out my phone and sigh, holding a finger to my lips before answering. "Hi, Sheriff Matterson."

Birdie's eyes grow wide, but she stays silent.

"I need you at the Blue Moon Tavern. There was a bar fight, and at least one patron is headed to the hospital," he starts, and I can hear someone cussing up a storm in the background. "It's going to be all hands on deck taking statements and potentially making an arrest. It'll probably take all night."

I have far more important things to do like take his daughter back to my place and feast on her pussy. But if I don't show up at the bar to help make sure things are done right, mistakes will get made, and it'll be a damn headache to fix later.

I rake a hand through my hair, glance over at Bridie, and mouth the words, "I'm sorry."

"I'll be there in thirty minutes," I grumble to the sheriff.

"I knew I could count on you, Halstead. See you soon," he replies before ending the call.

"Guess duty calls, huh?" Birdie says, trying not to sound disappointed.

I set my phone on the dash, and cup her face with my hands. "Lesson seventy-two: Never let a man leave you wanting," I say, letting out a resigned sigh. "And now I'm the jackass asking you to make an exception." I rest my forehead against hers.

"I'll accept your rain check on one condition," Birdie says, a smirk playing on her lips.

I draw back, raising a brow. "What's that?"

"You bring a veggie burger and sweet potato fries when you make it up to me."

"I'll do you one better and have Earl bring one to your house within the hour," I reply, capturing her mouth in a kiss.

The least I can do for cutting our night short is to show her how much she means to me and make sure she gets the meal she's been craving.

CHAPTER 17

Afternoon Delight

Birdie

S HORTLY AFTER WALKER RECEIVED AN EMERGENCY CALL from my dad, I got one from him too. Mama's night nurse couldn't make it because she came down with the flu, and he was tied up with the same public disturbance at the bar he'd called Walker about, which promised to keep them busy well into the morning.

Once I made sure the animals were settled in, the kittens and I spent the night at my parents'. Since they have to be bottle-fed, it was easier to bring them along than to worry about going back and forth. I could have asked someone to watch them, but that would've raised questions about why I had to stay with my mama.

Earl, of course, wouldn't stop grilling me when he showed up to drive me. He still had lipstick on his neck and was wearing his shirt backward—what I assumed had been a late-night rendezvous with Ethel. Somehow, though, he still managed to pick up the veggie burger and sweet potato fries that Walker had asked him to grab from Prickly Pear Diner before coming to get me.

I fell asleep in Mama's bed, wanting to stay close in case she needed me. Each rise and fall of her chest was a comforting reminder that she's still here with me.

When I wake up, I find her watching me, a weary smile on her lips.

"Good m-morning, honey," she says, voice a little shaky.

"Morning, Mama," I whisper.

I'm relieved she seems to be doing well this morning, a small bright spot in what's become increasingly difficult days.

The kittens are nestled between us. Mama helped me finally choose their names—Logan and Rory, named after her favorite *Gilmore Girls* characters.

Logan is batting at the tassels on the blanket draped over our legs. He has endless energy and refuses to sit still for even a moment, while his sister, Rory, is as mellow as can be, curled up on Mama's lap, purring softly as she cracks open an eye before closing it again. She's clearly not ready to start the day—and honestly, I can't blame her. It was a long night.

"Can I get you anything?" I ask Mama.

She gives a small shake of her head. "No... just s-stay with me."

I squeeze her hand gently. "I'm not going anywhere."

I was scheduled for a shift today, but I called my manager, Ed, last night to tell him I couldn't make it. Thankfully, he was understanding and didn't make a fuss.

Mama lets out a relieved sigh. "Good. Now t-tell me, how is Nugget doing? I w-wish you'd have brought her too."

She's always encouraged my love for animals. When I was little and rescued a stray puppy from an alley, she persuaded my dad to let me keep it. Years later, in middle school, I brought home a pig that was being sent to slaughter, and she helped me find him a good home since our backyard wasn't big enough to keep him.

Running the sanctuary is my way of honoring our shared

love of animals, even though she can't participate alongside me. During my visits, I always give her updates and bring along my rescues whenever I can. Nugget is a regular visitor and loves curling up on Mama's legs. We recently discovered she has a particular fascination with Kirk from *Gilmore Girls*, and anytime he's on the screen, she fluffs up and emits a series of contented clucks.

"Nugget thinks she's the kittens' mama." I pull up a picture on my phone of her snuggled up with Logan and Rory, their heads poking out from under her wing.

"I s-suppose that means you have to keep them, then?" she questions, letting out a small laugh that wavers with effort.

"You're right." I scoop up Logan, who swats playfully at my fingers with his tiny paws. "They're officially part of the family. I couldn't bear to separate them."

I'm not just keeping them for Nugget's sake—but for mine too. I get attached far too easily, and each goodbye to a rescued animal hurts more than the last. I'm constantly coming up with excuses to keep them even though I'm running out of space and time to care for them all.

Mama rests her hand over mine. "I'm so proud of you, sweet girl."

I swallow the lump in my throat, determined not to cry before breakfast. Every touch, every shared moment is precious—especially ones like this, when she reaches out on her own, even knowing it might be painful.

"You made me who I am," I murmur.

"Not true. Your courage and b-bravery come from right here." She slowly lifts her hand to my heart. "You're a r-remarkable woman and have accomplished so much despite everything life has thrown at you."

"I'm not sure Dad would agree," I mumble.

I haven't told her about my night in jail or how disappointed he is that I can't stay out of trouble. It would only ruin the fragile peace we've managed to hold on to.

"Oh, honey, of course he would. Your f-father loves you more than you know." She reaches out with a trembling hand, brushing my cheek. "He just h-has trouble showing it sometimes, especially when his personal life and c-career pull him in different directions."

I set Logan down on the bed and rest my head against her shoulder. "I miss the way things used to be."

Life before she got sick was ordinary in the best way. Sundays meant brunch at the diner, and Tuesdays were for Mama's homemade pizza and a movie. At night, she and Dad would take walks around the neighborhood while I sat on the porch reading a book. They held hands and gazed into each other's eyes, their love obvious in every glance. It breaks my heart that the carefree family we once were is now nothing more than a distant memory.

"Look a-at me," Mama whispers.

I find a solemn expression on her face when I do.

"What is it?" I ask.

"You h-had to grow up far too quickly because of my diagnosis, and I r-refuse to let you put your life on pause for me any longer."

"What do you mean? I haven't–"

She raises a brow, stopping me mid-thought. "Birdie, y-you spend all your free time in this house, and I know how lonely it's been not having anyone to s-share what you're going through, aside from your father and me."

"I *want* to spend time with you," I argue.

There's no guarantee how much longer we'll have together.

"Yes, b-but I don't want you to let life slip by in the process. Wren's off with her family in Florida, Briar's e-engaged with a son of her own, and Charlie will eventually meet her match—bless that poor soul," Mama jokes. "It's y-your turn to find happiness now, and I don't want you putting that on hold because of me."

I stay quiet, letting her words sink in. Looking back, I see now that whenever I had a chance to go out with friends or on a date, I chose to stay home if Dad wasn't around. It wasn't really a choice—it was a necessity. Even after he hired nurses to cover around-the-clock shifts, I let fear and guilt dictate my priorities, building a self-imposed cage I hadn't realized I'd constructed.

I suppose that's why I never pursued anything romantic before now. Compared with the responsibilities of caring for Mama, it all seemed trivial, and my lack of experience made me clumsy and self-conscious around guys whenever I did try to show interest.

"I'm actually seeing someone," I whisper.

A smile lights up Mama's face. "You are? When were you p-planning on introducing me to this mystery man?"

I don't tell her she's already met him. She and Julie used to work together at the elementary school before Mama had to quit, and she often stopped by the Halsteads when picking me up or dropping me off to play with Briar, so she knows Heath and Walker well. Even if she has met the guy I'm seeing, Dad would never allow him near Mama without first being certain he could be trusted to keep her health under wraps. One more reason dating has always been complicated.

I sit up and turn to face her, clearing my throat. "It's still really new so we're taking things slow. I just wanted you to know so you don't have to worry about me anymore."

I would have preferred to keep this to myself, but if it can give her a little peace of mind, even if it's not entirely the truth, it's worth it.

Mama chuckles softly. "Honey, I'm your mother. I'm always g-going to worry about you."

"Well, hopefully this at least eases your mind a bit," I tease with a smile. "Are you hungry? How about I make you a berry smoothie and some soup?"

"That s-sounds delicious." If she catches my attempt to redirect the conversation, she lets it slide. "I think I'll t-take a short nap in the meantime."

"Of course. Get some rest," I murmur, pressing a kiss to her cheek.

She settles back against her pillows, her eyes drifting closed. Logan has joined his sister on Mama's lap, and both are now dozing too, so I leave them where they are. No doubt when I get back, they'll be awake and ready for breakfast too.

I climb off the bed and circle around to her side to adjust the comforter. A new paperback catches my eye on her nightstand— this one is a trending MM hockey romance. Lately, there's been a book there every few days, and I'm not sure why, since the severe tremor in her hands makes holding a book or using an e-reader impossible.

Some of the nurses have offered to read to her, but she's always turned them down. She prefers a deep male voice when listening to romance novels. So she's either had a change of heart or maybe one of the nurses keeps their book here to read while Mama rests.

I head to the kitchen to begin breakfast, starting by turning on the coffee maker. I'm going to need all the caffeine I can get today. While it brews, I check my phone, and a smile crosses my lips when I see a new text message.

Walker: How's your day going?

I snap a selfie of me preparing the kittens' bottles.

Birdie: Playing hooky at Mama's.

Walker: Sounds like the perfect excuse to skip work. Wish I could have tagged along.

Me too.

I have the unexpected urge to tell him about Mama's Parkinson's. I shake my head, pushing the thought aside. I've already shared so much with him, and I'm not sure it surfaced only because he's been so patient and supportive about everything else—or because I'm just drained and desperate for a little comfort.

Walker: Have I mentioned how pretty you are?

Birdie: Once or twice, but I wouldn't mind a refresher.

Walker: Then let me remind you. You're stunning, and I'm counting down the minutes until I can see you again.

Birdie: Any idea when that might be?

I try to act nonchalant even though anticipation is bubbling beneath the surface.

Walker: How about tomorrow? I want to take you out again, and we can go back to my place if you're up for it.

Birdie: Oh... so I'm not seeing you tonight, then?

The disappointment hits harder than I expect when I realize I might have to wait a whole day to see him again. It's not just about wanting him physically. I miss Walker when he's not around, and that mix of longing and excitement is both exhilarating and terrifying. It's another thing I'm not prepared to unpack right now.

Walker: After I finish at the sheriff's office, I'm off to the ranch to help Heath mend fences. Probably won't be done until late.

Birdie: ~~You sure? I could~~'ve sworn your whole day was reserved for giving me orgasms.

Walker: Sounds like a position only I'm qualified for.

Birdie: Shame you're unavailable.

Walker: Guess I'll have to get creative, finding a way to make it worth your wait.

Birdie: Oh? And how do you plan on doing that?

Walker: For one, using rope in a future lesson.

Birdie: Use it how?

Walker: I'd love nothing more than to bind your hands above your head and put my mouth on that sweet pussy of yours.

Good grief. I press my legs together as heat spreads through my lower belly, imagining what it would feel like to have him between my thighs, making me come while my hands are bound above my head.

I never anticipated bondage to make it on my list of fantasies, yet now all I can think about is Walker's big hands winding rope around my wrists and securing me to the headboard, edging me with his tongue. I find I rather like the idea of submitting to him and giving him complete control.

Birdie: I think I'm going to need a demonstration.

I smirk at the phone as I hit send. Until recently, the idea of sending a flirty text would have left me paralyzed with panic—but now I'm sexting with ease, without batting an eyelash.

Now that I've had my first orgasm, it's as if a dam has burst, and every nerve in my body begs for another release—a stark contrast to before, when pleasure always seemed distant and out of reach. There's only one explanation for the change: Walker Halstead.

Walker: That can be arranged.

Walker: Your dad just called everyone into his office. I'd better go.

Birdie: Okay. Talk to you later!

Walker: Bye, beautiful. Looking forward to our next lesson.

Birdie: Me too.

More than anything.

I tuck the phone under my chin, staring at the floor with a dreamy smile. There's something magical about being called beautiful by a rugged cowboy who can turn a simple goodbye into a moment that lingers in my mind all day.

Walker has a way of showing up for me, even when he doesn't realize I need him, and it makes me want to do the same for him. It gets me thinking about how he hasn't slept a wink, and he has a full day ahead in the fields. It's going to be exhausting, and I'm certain he'll be wiped by the evening. It makes me think of my long shifts at the feedstore—and how the bearable ones are always the days he shows up with my favorite meal from the diner, and a warm hello.

The thought of returning some of the kindness he's shown

me sparks an idea. Why not surprise him with lunch at the ranch this afternoon? Briar or her mom usually drops something off for the guys and the ranch hands when they're out in the fields, but I'm sure they wouldn't mind if I did this time.

The problem is that, aside from our scheduled lessons and dates, Walker and I haven't really talked about what unplanned time together looks like when we're pretending to be a couple. My idea could easily backfire, and he might not appreciate it the way I hope—but I'm done playing it safe and avoiding things out of fear. It's time to stop holding back. I need to be confident enough to take a risk, no matter the outcome.

My dad gets back to the house around noon to take over Mama's care. Briar picked the kittens and me up, then stopped by my place so I could change and check on the other animals before taking us to her cottage. Jensen is out mending fences too, so she suggested we make lunch to take out to the guys, which solves my earlier panic. I helped her and Caleb make ham-and-cheese subs and trail mix, and now we're headed out to the field to deliver it. I decide not to tell Walker that I'm coming, keeping it a surprise.

Briar has the windows rolled down and is tuned into a local country radio station. Caleb's a big fan, bobbing his head to the music, one hand stretched out the back window, fingers catching in the breeze as we cruise through the ranch.

"Thanks for letting me tag along," I say to Briar.

She glances over and smiles. "No problem. I'm glad for the help. Heath doubled the number of ranch hands this year so there's a lot more mouths to feed. With Mama Julie busy helping with the summer program at the elementary school, I've been bringing food out to guys in the afternoons."

"Sure, it's not just an excuse to see Jensen?" I tease, waggling my brows.

She tips her head back, laughing. "As if you're not looking for an excuse to see Walker."

Touche.

Jensen splits his time between working on the ranch and helping Briar with her nonprofit, and since they can't stand being apart for more than a few hours, they're always finding excuses to be in the same place during the workday.

Gravel crunches beneath the Jeep tires as Briar pulls up beside the field where everyone is hard at work. Heath holds a new post steady while Jensen shovels dirt back in the hole, packing it tight around the base. Down the line, Walker and the ranch hands work in pairs, repeating the same process along a stretch of fence that Briar told me had seen better days.

My gaze drifts to Walker, his sleeves rolled up and dirt streaked across his forearm. His white shirt is soaked with sweat, clinging to his back as his muscles flex with each movement while he lifts another post into place. He's downright sexy, and I remember exactly what those hands are capable of—gripping my face, his mouth on mine, rough and urgent. I exhale, forcing myself to rein in my fantasy. Now isn't the time or place to have lusty thoughts.

Jensen notices us first and claps Heath on the back, pointing in our direction.

"Come on, little man," Briar calls over her shoulder to Caleb. "They look like they could use a break, and your dad sure seems excited to see you." Her gaze shifts to me. "And judging by that look on your face, you're eager for a reunion of your own." Her tone is teasing as she nods toward Walker, whose brow furrows when he squints in our direction and spots us.

I don't bother denying it as I climb out of the vehicle and wave to Walker. When he spots me, his expression shifts, a grin spreading across his face as he lifts a hand in return. Relief washes over me, the tight knot in my chest loosening.

I help Briar and Caleb lay out the ham subs, fruit and nut packs, and water so the guys can grab a bite when they're ready.

Heath and Jensen are the first to head over. Caleb runs straight into Jensen's arms, giggling as Jensen lifts him and spins him in a circle.

"Appreciate you stopping by, sis," Heath says, grabbing a bottle of water from the cooler and drinking it down in seconds. "Howdy, Birdie. Didn't expect to see you here."

My shoulders square on instinct. "Figured Briar could use some backup preparing lunch so you guys could get a break from this heat."

He slowly nods. "It's a scorcher today, that's for damn sure."

"Y'all making good progress?" Briar asks.

"We always do with Heath in charge. He's a tough taskmaster," Jensen interjects, moving to stand beside her, slipping an arm around her shoulder, and planting a kiss on her temple.

The ranch hands come over, and I'm caught off guard when I spot Dalton—the guy from the bar I accidentally elbowed in the nose. I didn't know he worked for the Halsteads. He stops in his tracks when he sees me, as if I'm capable of inflicting another injury from ten feet away.

I'm spared from an awkward interaction when Walker steps out from the front of the Jeep. His gaze flickers between Dalton and me as he comes to stand beside me.

His possessive gaze drops to my mouth as his fingers graze my hip. "You're here."

"I am," I say, smiling softly. "You've had a long day, so I wanted to bring you lunch. I hope that's okay."

"Okay? You just made my whole damn day, Birdie, baby."

He tips my chin and captures my lips in a slow, lingering kiss that feels a lot like he's staking his claim.

"Guess we're kissing in public now?" I murmur against his lips.

"Damn right. Gotta make it clear who you belong to." He shoots a warning glance at Dalton before leaning in to kiss me again.

Heaven help me, but I like this possessive side of Walker, and for a fleeting moment, our relationship feels dangerously real.

CHAPTER 18

A Little Birdie Told Me

Birdie

THE GUYS POLISHED OFF LUNCH IN FIFTEEN MINUTES flat, and Walker asked if I'd be around after he finished for the day. There's no chance I could say no while he trailed kisses down my neck as he asked—it was pure extortion, and I happily volunteered as tribute to guarantee a few more seconds of his mouth on me.

To pass the time, I spent the afternoon at the cottage with Briar and Caleb. We fed the kittens and played with Ziggy, Caleb's fainting goat. He also roped me into losing several rounds of Candy Land. The kid is a pro. He even had the audacity to laugh when I got stuck in the gumdrop forest for the third time in a row. I'm seriously considering drafting a formal complaint with Candy Land HQ for the emotional torment the game has inflicted.

As the afternoon eases into early evening, Walker texts me.

Walker: Where are you, pretty girl?

Birdie: At Briar's. Please tell me you're coming to my rescue. Caleb beat me at Candy Land five times straight, and my ego can't take another loss.

Okay, maybe I stretched the truth a little for dramatic effect. Briar actually sent Caleb upstairs ten minutes ago for his bath, but I couldn't pass up the chance to use my wounded pride as leverage if it means getting him here sooner.

Walker: We just finished. See you in a bit.

Birdie: Looking forward to it <3

I head out front to wait for him, settling into one of the rocking chairs on the porch. Briar went to put Ziggy away for the night before checking on Caleb, so it's just me and my thoughts out here.

Keeping my head in the sand has run its course, and I'm forced to face the cold, hard truth: I have feelings for Walker Halstead. The line between what's real and fake was obliterated the second we kissed, and the intimacy of our first shared orgasm only cemented that. I was just too naive to recognize the significance of those moments until it was too late.

The way I see it, I have two options: end things now before they escalate further, or continue our charade, fully aware there's a good chance I'll be heartbroken once this is over.

My first instinct is to break things off with Walker before things get messy. But I'm tired of running. Like Mama said, it's time I start living my life—which means living in the moment and not letting fear hold me back.

While I wait for Walker, a message pops up in the group chat.

Backroads & Bad Decisions Group Chat

Charlie: Careful, Briar. At this rate, Birdie and Walker are going to beat you and Jensen down the aisle. Shotgun wedding, anyone?

Birdie: Care to enlighten us on how you cooked up this wild theory of yours?

Seriously, she loves gossip more than a sugar-laced red velvet latte. It doesn't help that her boutique serves as a breeding ground for chatty women who can sniff out rumors faster than a bloodhound.

Briar: Oh boy. Here we go.

Charlie: A little birdie told me you brought Walker lunch today.

Briar: Just to be clear I am not said birdie.

Wren: Things must be getting serious if you're taking him lunch at work.

Birdie: It's not a big deal.

Briar: I don't know… you seemed awfully into him when he was nuzzling his face in your neck.

Birdie: Not said birdie, huh??

Charlie: Don't hold back now Briar. Proud of you.

Briar: I didn't even mention how he got all possessive…

> Wren: Facetime me later! I need all the details.

> Charlie: Count me in, too!

Trying to stop them would be useless. When Briar and Jensen got together, Wren, Charlie, and I spent hours on late-night calls, gossiping about it, so I can't blame them for doing the same to me. That's the price of public displays of affection—though I have zero regrets, especially after Walker staked his claim with that possessive kiss still living rent-free in my mind.

The crunch of gravel pulls me from the group chat, and I look up to see a blue pickup with Heath at the wheel and Walker and Jensen riding along.

Walker is the first to climb out, pulling off his hat and wiping the sweat from his forehead.

I push out of the rocking chair and rush down the porch steps to greet him.

"How'd it go?" I ask.

"Pretty boy put those new ranch hands to shame." He nods to Jensen, getting out of the back seat. "A year on the ranch and we've finally made a real cowboy out of him."

Jensen rolls his eyes. "Give me a break. I've been running circles around the whole crew since I got here."

"Uh-huh. We all know city life went to your head, but I'm just glad you're finally cured." Walker winks.

Jensen used to live in New York and was CEO of DataLock Systems, a major cybersecurity firm. When he discovered Caleb was his son and had lost his mom to cancer, they moved to Bluebell, where Jensen grew up, to have the support of the Halsteads. He and Heath have been best friends their whole lives and Jensen spent most of his childhood at their place. Not long after moving back, he fell madly in love with Briar, and the rest is history.

"I'm going inside to find Briar and Caleb," Jensen says, heading for the house.

Heath rolls down the window, lips pressed into a thin line, and hands wrapped tightly around the steering wheel. "I'm going to the ranch house," he grunts. "You two coming?"

Someone's extra grumpy after a rough day in the fields, not that I'm about to call him out on it.

Walker shakes his head. "Nah. We've got to decide what we're doing first. If we go there, I'll borrow Briar's Jeep."

"Okay, I'm headed back then," Heath says, rolling up the window and driving away.

I beam at Walker when he turns his attention to me. "You must be exhausted."

"Between hauling posts into holes and standing in the heat, I think I've aged ten years."

"Oh, you poor thing." I pat his chest with exaggerated sympathy, my lips curling into a playful grin.

"I definitely could use some comforting." He draws me into his arms, nuzzling my neck, and I giggle when his scruff tickles my skin. "I'm really glad you came by the field earlier," he murmurs, his tone softening.

"Me too."

I nearly let it slip that I miss him when we're not together, but I bite my tongue—deciding some thoughts are better kept to myself.

I'm saved from saying something I might regret when Walker's phone buzzes in his pocket. He takes it out, raising a brow as he scans the screen.

"Dammit," he mutters, rubbing the back of his neck.

I frown. "What's wrong?"

"Ma found out you're here and wants to have you over for family dinner." He sighs, dragging a hand along his jawline. "Nothing slips past that woman."

My guess is that Ethel told her I was around. She's the housekeeper for the Silver Saddle Ranch cabins and runs the general store in the afternoons after she's finished cleaning. She was on the porch sweeping when Briar and I passed by on our way to the fields earlier.

"And what's so bad about her asking me to join?"

Walker dips his head, nipping my earlobe. "Because I wanted you all to myself tonight."

I let out a giggle. "Is that so? Weren't you the one who suggested we wait until tomorrow to see each other? Surely you can survive a few more hours to have me alone."

I pull back to meet his gaze, his eyes dancing with mischief.

"Better idea. Let's sneak into my loft. Ma will be too distracted preparing dinner to notice."

I roll my eyes, chuckling. "Your mom's sixth sense is legendary. She always knew when Briar was running late for her curfew and would be waiting with the porch light on every time. I wouldn't be surprised if she's waiting outside now in case you try any funny business."

Walker exhales with a resigned sigh. "You're probably right. But if we do this, it means you're coming to my place after." He cups my chin, kissing me. "I'll need extra alone time to recover from having to share you."

How could I possibly say no to an offer like that?

Walker and I rode over to the Halsteads' with Briar's family. The second we arrived, Caleb disappeared to the craft room, clearly uninterested in hanging out with the adults.

"You came," Julie exclaims, glancing up from the counter where she's cutting watermelon into thick wedges.

The kitchen has wide-plank wood floors, a vaulted ceiling

accented by exposed beams, and a butcher block island at its center. A picture window above the farmhouse sink looks over the garden and the orchard beyond. The space is stunning, but it's the Halsteads' generosity and kindness that makes their home feel so welcoming.

"Thanks for having me," I say with a small wave. "Had I known about dinner sooner, I would've brought something."

Julie never does anything halfway, and I hate showing up empty-handed without at least a bouquet of fresh flowers or a bottle of wine from town.

"If she had brought something, it totally would have been from the diner," Briar quips.

"Says the woman whose macaroni salad is always the consistency of soup," Walker retorts.

"I've said it once and I'll say it again—soup salad is Briar's claim to fame." Jensen chuckles as he steps behind her, wrapping an arm around her waist.

"I'm just glad to have you all here," Julie says, wiping her hands on a hand towel before coming over to greet us.

I'm not expecting her to come to me first and draw me in for a hug. I've been over for dinner plenty, and while she's naturally warm, she usually reserves this level of affection for her family. I'm certain it's because she's over the moon that Walker and I are dating.

A pang of unease twists in my stomach, wondering if I'll still be welcome when her son and I eventually go our separate ways. I hope so. The Halstead ranch house is like a home away from home, and I've always seen Julie as another mother figure—a guiding light in my life, even though she doesn't know all the struggles I carry or realize how much her comfort means to me.

Just then Caleb comes darting down the hall with a broad smile lighting up his face.

"Mama Briar, look what I found!" he squeals with excitement.

He proudly holds out a children's book. The cover shows a lizard perched on a log, scowling straight at the reader with a white splatter on its head.

I cover my mouth to stifle a laugh when I see the title: *Who Pooped on Me.*

Julie shoots Walker a glare, resting her hands on her hips. "Walker Bartholomew Halstead, did you sneak another one of your books into the craft room? I thought we agreed those stay at Briar's and the craft room is for educational books only."

He rocks back on his heels, shrugging. "Sorry, Ma. I saw it in the toy store window the other day and couldn't resist adding it to the collection."

Briar filled me and the girls in a while back on Walker's on-going tug-of-war over children's books. He's given Caleb a few silly ones, and as a lifelong teacher, Julie doesn't think they're appropriate reading material. She doesn't mind him giving them to Caleb to keep at his house but doesn't want them here. Lately, though, Walker's been sneaking new ones into the craft room to get a reaction out of her.

Caleb comes over to Julie, whispering loudly. "Grandma Julie, can we read this one together like we did *Something's Wrong! A Bear, a Hare, and Some Underwear?*"

Walker clutches his chest with a mock gasp. "Ma, have you been giving me grief about my book selections while secretly reading them with Caleb?"

Julie huffs, pushing a strand of hair from her face, but doesn't answer.

"She does the funniest voices, like when the bear yells 'Who left my underwear in the fridge?'" Caleb chirps, giggling, before his eyes go wide. "Uh-oh… I was supposed to keep that a secret. Sorry, Grandma Julie."

She chuckles, giving his hand a reassuring squeeze. "It's all right, sweetie."

"Someone's got you wrapped around his little finger." Walker tuts.

"Who could say no to that cute face?" Julie says, nodding toward Caleb's beaming smile. "Now make yourself useful and take the meat out to your father and brother." She marches over to the counter and retrieves a dish of barbecue chicken that she thrusts into Walker's hands. "They're still wrestling with that new grill your father brought home last week and are struggling to make heads or tails of all the extra gadgets that came with it."

"Yes, ma'am," he replies, wisely not arguing.

"Jensen, you grab the pineapple skewers," Julie adds, passing him a tray full of them.

He nods. "Sure thing."

"What about me?" Caleb pipes up, puffing out his chest. "I want to help too."

"Of course you do." Julie bends down, giving his cheek a gentle pinch. "You've got the most important job."

His eyes light up. "What's that?"

She brings over a bowl covered in plastic wrap. "To make sure Gramps cooks the tofu and vegetables so Birdie can eat with us."

I'm touched that she goes out of her way to make vegetarian dishes when I come over. One time in high school, I brought my own meal, and after that, she always made sure there were plenty of options I could eat—never once making me feel like a burden.

"How come you don't like barbecue chicken? It's my favorite," Caleb exclaims.

"I'm a vegetarian," I say.

He blinks at me before turning to Briar. "Mama Briar. What's a veggie-tor-ian?"

Everyone bursts out laughing at his adorable attempt at the word.

"It's someone who doesn't eat meat. Birdie sticks mostly to fruits and vegetables," she explains.

"Oh." He frowns like he still might not fully understand. "Does that mean she doesn't eat the meat Uncle Walker makes?"

A cheeky smirk crosses Julie's face, and Briar and Jensen exchange amused glances. When I look over at Walker, he's chuckling, clearly entertained by a six-year-old calling him out on his career choice.

Admittedly, it used to bother me, but I've come to accept that society will never cut back on their meat consumption, and the Halsteads treat their cattle better than any other operation in the country—I know because I've done my research.

Besides, they've taken in more than their fair share of my rescues, and Heath even kept a calf named Petunia two years ago after her mom didn't survive her delivery—she's totally his pet now, even if he tries to deny it. Still, watching everyone's reactions to Caleb's innocent question thinking I might be offended is hilarious.

I crouch next to Caleb so we're eye to eye. "I don't eat the meat Walker makes but I've heard it's tasty. Those cows are lucky to have him and your Uncle Heath taking such good care of them."

"One day, I'm going to be a cowboy too," he declares with a toothy grin.

"You'll make a mighty fine one," I agree, giving his cowboy hat a playful tap.

"Come on, Caleb," Briar says, waving him over. "We better get this food out to Uncle Heath and Gramps so we can eat soon."

"Okay." He clutches the bowl he's holding tight, tiptoeing as if it were full of fine china, his tongue peeking out in concentration as he follows Briar and Jensen to the back door.

The little boy who I met last year and who he is now is night and day. When Jensen and Caleb first moved to Bluebell, Caleb didn't speak. His mom had just died, and he'd retreated into himself. Now he's a little chatterbox and we're all constantly entertained by him.

Walker shifts the tray of chicken to one hand and laces his fingers through mine as he heads toward the back door. "You defended me. I figured you'd take the chance to throw me under the bus," he says, winking at me.

"I've learned there are far worse things happening to animals that I can actually do something about, so as long as you and Heath keep treating your cattle with the respect and care they deserve I'll let it slide." I meet his gaze with a teasing smirk. "Besides, you're rather useful to me right now, so I'd better stay on your good side."

He chuckles. "Is that so?"

"Mh-hmm," I whisper, rising on my toes to kiss him.

Our lips have barely touched when Caleb's voice rings out from the back porch. "Eww. Kissing is gross."

I pull back just enough to glance up at Walker, his eyes twinkling with amusement, and we both break into laughter at Caleb's comment.

My chest swells with happiness, and I wish this moment could last forever, with Walker gazing at me like I'm his world and being surrounded by the lighthearted chaos of his family. It's confirmation that I'm exactly where I'm meant to be.

CHAPTER 19

Do You Want The House Tour?

Birdie

MY CHEEKS HURT FROM LAUGHING SO MUCH. WE SPENT several hours with Walker's family. It was loud, boisterous, and positively perfect. The Halstead siblings teased each other nonstop, but that doesn't diminish the close bond they share. They're fortunate to have such a strong support system.

I've been over for dinner many times over the years, but being there as Walker's girlfriend gave me a different perspective I've never had before. As an only child I'm used to the quiet, but spending the evening with the Halsteads reminded me how comforting the chaos can be.

When Briar, Jensen, and Caleb said they were heading back to the cottage for the night, Walker took it as his cue to excuse us as well. Briar agreed to watch Logan and Rory tonight, another reason she's such an amazing friend.

As we climb the stairs to Walker's studio apartment above the ranch house, a knot tightens in my stomach. I've spent so long imagining what sex would be like, cataloging every possible thing that could go wrong. Now I could be minutes from finally experiencing it, and my nervous anticipation twists into fear that I'll ruin the moment and fall short of making my first time worth remembering.

Even though this whole thing started with Walker agreeing to teach me to have sex under the guise of dating, I want this to be memorable for him too.

Briar gave me a tour when the Halsteads added on the two loft apartments, but I haven't been in this one since Walker moved in.

I take in the open floor plan, exposed brick walls, and the beam running across the ceiling, imagining the large windows along the side of the house must flood the space with sunlight during the day, though the blinds are drawn now. The reclaimed wood floors cause my footsteps to echo softly as I look around the loft.

The living room and kitchenette are on one end of the space. A well-worn leather couch faces a TV on a stand, and next to it is a bookshelf full of Westerns and action movies. In the kitchen area, there's a brown card table with a single chair, a compact stove and oven set against the counter with a microwave mounted above, and a small fridge tucked in the corner.

On the other side of the space, a queen-sized bed is centered against the wall with a black nightstand and lamp beside it, and a matching dresser sits against the opposite wall. And an open door leads to the bathroom.

The place might have minimal furniture and decor, but it's still a warm, welcoming space that reflects Walker's personality.

"Sorry, it's not much," he says, turning on the rest of the lights.

"It's really nice, but to be honest, I don't care about how your place looks." I close the distance between us, my hand brushing against his arm.

I've been waiting to be alone with him too, and not just so we could have a conversation.

Walker exhales sharply, and before I can react, he lifts me into his arms, my hands finding their way around his neck. He walks us backward until I'm pressed against the nearest wall, holding me steady with one arm while his other hand cups my face, his thumb and forefinger gently cradling my chin.

"I swear my family dragged out dinner on purpose," he complains.

He doesn't have to worry—I'm not leaving this loft until he's kissed me senseless, among *other things.*

"Now that you have me alone, what are you going to do about it?" I whisper.

He slowly runs his thumb across my mouth. "Ever since you had these pouty lips wrapped around my dick, all I've been able to think about is getting a taste of that sweet pussy of yours."

"Well? What are you waiting for?" I ask, drawing his thumb between my lips and swirling my tongue around the tip.

"Fuck me," he growls, a hunger sparking behind his eyes. "First, we've got to get you out of these clothes." He lowers me to the floor. "Turn around and put your hands on the wall."

I can't stop the whimper that escapes me as I do as he asks, placing my palms against the exposed brick. Every cell in my body is on fire as he pushes my hair over my shoulder, the cool air grazing against my skin.

He places one hand firmly on my hip and uses the other to slowly drag down the zipper of my dress. The suspense is unbearable. I exhale sharply as he grinds his rigid cock against my ass.

I'm grateful that he doesn't treat me like glass or give me a chance to get lost in my head. Instead, he makes me feel desired in a way I never have, as if every curve and contour of my body has him completely captivated. The way he knows just what I need to keep my nerves in check sends red-hot arousal racing through me.

"You wore this dress to torment me, didn't you?" he murmurs in my ear.

"I would never," I say as I press my backside further against him, grinning when he inhales sharply.

Was it impractical to spend a day on the ranch in a sundress? Definitely. But every heated glance I've gotten from Walker has made it well worth it.

"Want to hear a confession?" he rasps, tipping my head so I glance over my shoulder at him.

I answer with a quiet hum, nodding.

He leans in, grazing his mouth over mine as he speaks. "I've been thinking about this moment all day. I *need* to be inside you. Watching you come with that vibrator was incredible but now you're going to come on *my* cock like the good girl I know you are."

My eyes grow wide as I squeeze my thighs together, his crass remark giving me the courage to answer with the truth.

"I'm very much on board with that idea. In fact, it just shot to the top of my to-do list, so we should get on that immediately."

"I like your way of thinking, sweetheart."

Walker takes my invitation to heart, brushing my dress off my shoulders. I feel his breath against my skin seconds before he presses kisses down my neck. He unclasps my bra, freeing my aching breasts. He slides the straps down my arms, letting it fall to the ground before he reaches around to brush my nipples with his fingertip in teasing strokes. I whimper when he gently rolls them, the sensation nothing like when I do it to myself, and I'm dizzy from craving his touch.

"God, I love how damn responsive you are," he groans.

I whine in protest when he releases my nipples.

He pulls my dress down the rest of the way, letting it pool at my feet, before spinning me around to face him.

"Hold on tight," he urges, scooping me up.

I loop my arms around his neck as he carries me to his bed. He lays me on top of the comforter, in the middle of the mattress.

He takes off my boots, and I lift my hips as he bends down to grab the top of my panties, sending a shiver snaking down my spine. My breath hitches when he places tender kisses along the inside of my thighs as he slowly drags my underwear down my legs. He tosses them aside, and gazes at me, eyes roaming over every inch.

I instinctively cover my breasts, suddenly aware of how exposed I am. It's one thing to have Walker watching while I get off with a vibrator, but it's entirely different lying here on the verge of losing my virginity, terrified I won't live up to his expectations.

To distract from my nerves I watch as Walker slowly undresses. His shirt strains against his shoulders before he pulls it off, throwing it to the floor. The flex of his abs as he moves is enough to steal the air from my lungs. It should be a crime how hot he is, and I lick my lips as he drags down his pants and boxers, revealing his thick cock, the veins pulsing.

He pushes aside his discarded clothes, gazing at me like he's ready to devour me.

"Look what you do to me, Birdie," he says, stroking his erection from base to tip. "Don't ever question how much I want you."

It's a good thing I'm lying down because my knees would've given out if I were still standing.

Walker joins me on the bed, kneeling at my feet, settling at the end of the mattress, his palms gliding slowly up my calves. I gasp when his lips brush my knee, but he doesn't stop, moving higher, his stubble dragging along my bare skin.

His lips explore the curve of my hips, then he shifts to using his tongue, teasing along my stomach, and when he reaches my breasts, he moves my hands, setting them at my sides as he drinks in the sight of my naked body.

"Thank you for trusting me," he rasps. "I'm going to make this feel so good and worship every inch of you."

My eyes stay glued to him as he leans down to wrap his mouth around my nipple, gliding his tongue across the pink bud.

"Walker." His name passes my lips like a prayer.

He lets out a low groan as he alternates between flicking my nipple with his tongue and sucking on it. As he lavishes my breast with kisses his hand glides down my stomach, leaving a path of goose bumps behind.

My legs fall open in invitation as he settles his hand on my bare thigh. He slowly makes his way to my core, running his fingers through my wetness. I gasp when he slides a finger inside me, drawing him deeper into my heat.

"You're so fucking tight," he growls.

Words fail me as I quiver beneath him, grinding against his palm as he pushes his finger in and out in steady strokes, getting me used to the sensation. He moves his mouth to my other breast, suckling my nipple as he pushes a second finger into me. I wind my arms around his neck, welcoming the added intrusion as a strained moan escapes me, colliding with the ragged tempo of our intermingled breaths.

"That's it. Ride my hand and show me what a good girl you are."

His praise sweeps over me like a tidal wave, and I circle my hips as I chase the rush of euphoria surging through me.

"More, *please*. I need your mouth," I beg.

Walker shifts down my body, positioning himself between the apex of my thighs, grazing his teeth along my inner thigh.

"I've waited long enough for a taste of *my* pussy," he growls.

Before I can fully process his words, he inhales my scent and runs his tongue along my seam. My body moves on instinct, searching for more as I lift my legs over his shoulders to draw him closer, lost to the magnetic pull drawing us together. He grips my waist as I cross my ankles, rolling my hips and grind against his face. A strangled cry falls from my lips as his warm, wet tongue laps at my clit.

Walker pauses, lifting his head. "One taste and you've totally wrecked my self-control, baby."

How wasn't it wrecked already? Mine was shot the second I saw him naked. Every ripple and curvature of his well-defined abs on display, and his hard cock glistening with pre-cum as he climbed on top of me and told me how much he wanted me. The man is a hazard to my health, and I may never recover if every lead-up to a climax is this intense.

He returns his tongue to my clit, teasing the aching bud mercilessly. His movements alternate between quick, sharp flicks and slow, languid caresses. Each change in tempo leaves me gasping, edging me ever closer to climax.

Walker runs his fingers along my seam, circling my opening before pushing two back inside me. My back arches off the bed, sweat beading on my forehead as the pressure builds from within. He draws out my wetness with his finger and brings it back to my clit, applying just the right amount of pressure.

He moves his mouth back to my core, and as I lift my head and catch sight of him buried between my legs, it pushes me over the edge. I grind harder against his face, my vision blurring as the pleasure crests, sending me into a dizzying spiral.

My head falls back on the pillow, my chest heaving in shallow pants as the tremors fade. When I meet Walker's gaze, he's watching me with a heat that threatens to unravel me completely.

"I'll never get enough of watching you come."

A smirk flickers on his lips before he runs his tongue across my overly sensitive clit, a strangled whimper catching in my throat.

My whole body jerks. "What are you doing?" I mewl.

He doesn't ease up as he replies. "Making sure you're nice and ready for me."

Electricity tears through my senses, sharp and consuming as I thread my fingers through his hair. He groans against me, lapping at my pussy like he's starved for it, the slick evidence of my orgasm coating his chin. The sight is wickedly provocative, making my toes curl.

Walker's fingers circle my aching clit, sparking a second orgasm to ripple through me. I cling to him as my body shudders uncontrollably, my breaths coming out uneven and shallow. All preconceived notions about lessons, rules, and expectations have gone out the window. All that's left is a primal, insatiable desire coursing through my veins, and it's directed entirely at Walker.

"I need you inside me. Now," I cry out.

"Good because I need that too, baby."

He leans over and grabs a condom from the nightstand drawer, ripping the package open with his teeth before rolling the condom on.

"Remember, we're going to take this nice and slow," he says as he lowers himself back over me.

He grabs his shaft, lining himself up with my entrance and sliding it along my slit to coat himself in my arousal.

I nod eagerly, my body quivering with impatient excitement. Any thought of potential discomfort fades beneath the fierce anticipation, and I can't stop thinking how grateful I am to share this with Walker.

He presses the tip of his cock against my entrance, easing his way in, slowly stretching me.

"You're so big," I moan, digging my fingers into the comforter.

He leans forward, kissing me. "Breathe, sweetheart." He coaches me as he caresses the curve of my hip.

He sinks in farther, small thrusts at a time. The world shrinks to my ragged breaths, heat clawing through me as he makes his way inside—inch by torturous inch, my muscles coiling with the rigid intrusion.

Walker cups my cheek, deepening our kiss as he pushes until he's fully seated, and a painful stinging courses through my core. I breathe hard through my nose as I adjust to his size.

He lifts his head, looking at me as if I'm the most precious thing in the world.

"Are you all right?" he asks, his voice is strained.

I can feel him holding back while he waits for my answer.

"I'm okay." The initial unease is giving way to a rising tide of pulsing need, causing me to writhe beneath him, dizzy with the sensation of being stuffed with his cock. "Move. Walker. I want you to move," I demand.

He laces our fingers together, guiding my arms above me as he draws his hips back, driving forward again. The position immediately brings to mind when he told me he wanted to tie me up with his favorite rope, leaving me at his mercy as I screamed his name and begged to come. I have a feeling this won't be far off—rope excluded. Although I'm rather intrigued by the concept.

Walker rocks into me in steady strokes, my flesh stretching around him. With every moan that leaves me his pace increases as if my reaction is tearing at his control. His grip tightens on my hands as urgency takes the reins.

"I can feel you clenching around my cock," he pants out.

I can only whimper in reply as he shifts the angle of his cock, pushing deeper and pressing against my G-spot. I gasp for air as he drives into me with unrelenting force. He's lost total control, and the buildup between us bursts like a dam breaking, leaving me drenched, and lost in a haze of insatiable desire. His hips grind into mine—harder, faster—with each thrust. The sound of our labored breathing permeates the air, and each stroke grows more urgent than the last.

"We're going to come together," Walker states, the vein in his neck pulsing hard.

He reaches between my legs, rolling my clit between his

thumb and forefinger. The added pressure rushes through me with a force so fierce it steals the air from my lungs. A broken cry rips from my throat as his name falls from my mouth. He tenses above me, his own climax tearing through him as he lets out a gravelly groan.

Walker's still catching his breath as he smooths my hair from my face. "How are you feeling?"

I shake my head, running a finger along the rough edges of his five-o'clock shadow. "Perfect."

My core is tender from his cock thrusting into me and my hips are tight from his maneuvering, but I wouldn't trade this contentment for anything.

Walker kisses my temple as he slowly pulls out. "Let's get you cleaned up."

He climbs off the bed, discarding the used condom in the trash before slipping on his boxers. He turns off the lights in the loft, except for the bedside lamp, before disappearing into the bathroom. As I wait for him, my gaze drifts to the nightstand, where a stack of romance novels catches my eye. Several of the titles are familiar, though I can't quite place where I've seen them before.

I don't have much time to dwell on it before Walker returns with a warm washcloth to wipe me clean and I fight every instinct to close my legs.

There's a rare vulnerability in letting someone care for me like this, yet with Walker I'm at ease. I get the sense he's being attentive because he wants to be, not out of obligation, and that speaks volumes. Even so, my mind races, unable to stop wondering if I'm supposed to leave now or what happens next, since we've never discussed this part of our arrangement.

Walker tosses the washcloth into a hamper by the dresser, then moves to the bed and lifts the covers on the empty side, motioning me under. I don't overthink it, crawling beneath the warm blankets. I watch as he slides in beside me, drawing me against him so we're face-to-face.

He brushes a kiss against my forehead as I settle my hand on his chest.

"Stay the night."

I glance up at him, nibbling my lip. "Are you sure? Is that normal in this situation?"

"I wouldn't know," Walker admits, sincerity shining in his eyes. "I've never brought another woman to my place before, let alone asked her to spend the night."

"Oh." That's not the answer I was expecting. "Did you have me get into bed before asking so I'd be less likely to say no?" I tease, swatting his chest.

"Maybe." He smirks. "Is it working?"

I meet his gaze and press a soft peck to his lips, draping my leg over his torso, settling in against him.

"Yeah, it is," I murmur.

This suddenly feels like another turning point in our relationship—another step on a path that could change everything for better or worse. As my hand drifts absently over Walker's chest, I'm struck by the realization that even with my limited experience, no man will ever measure up to Walker Halstead.

"Thank you for trusting me to be your first," he murmurs into my hair.

As I lie curled up against him, a wishful thought slips into my mind: what if there's a chance he could be my one and only too?

CHAPTER 20

Head Over Boots

Walker

I STIR AS GOLDEN SUNLIGHT SPILLS THROUGH THE BLINDS, casting a soft glow across my bedroom ceiling. Part of me is afraid to get up, convinced last night was too good to be real and must have been a dream. The familiar scent of vanilla drifts through my senses, giving me the courage to crack an eye open, and I sigh in relief when I find Birdie curled beside me, her blonde hair a tangled mess on the pillow. One arm is draped across my chest, the other tucked beneath her chin.

She responded to my every touch last night as if she were made for me, each movement drawing another low moan or gasp until she was begging for release. I half expected her to shy away afterward, but she surprised me by lacing her fingers in mine and murmuring her thanks as she drifted off to sleep.

I'm the one who should be thanking her for showing me what true happiness feels like. I was blinded for so long thinking fleeting connections were enough, when all along nothing could compare to the way it felt being inside her for the first time, claiming her just as fiercely as she claimed me.

Birdie's chest rises and falls in a steady rhythm, a faint smile playing on her lips. I lean in, pressing a soft kiss on her forehead.

"I think I'm falling in love with you, Birdie, baby," I whisper.

There's a sense of peace in saying those words out loud and admitting the truth—even if only to myself.

Birdie Matterson is my endgame. I may have been her first, but I fully intend to be her last.

I've lived a life without her in it, where she was just a friend, and now that I've experienced what it's like to call her mine, there's no going back. I'll wait as long as it takes to convince her that what we share isn't temporary. We belong together, and I intend to fight for our future and earn my place in her heart. I can only hope she understands that everything I've done for her reflects how much she means to me—including looking after the people who matter most to her.

I brush a loose strand of hair from Birdie's face, taking in every detail—from the way the sunlight dances along the curve of her cheek to the birthmark I discovered earlier on the top of her left shoulder. I'm still not sure how I got so damn lucky to be the one she trusted enough to spend the night with, but I'm not taking a single second for granted.

After several minutes, her lashes finally flutter open, and she blinks up at me with a soft smile.

"Hi," she whispers.

"Good morning." I shift to hover over her, brushing a kiss across her lips. "How did you sleep? Are you sore?"

"A little, but in a good way," she admits, a flush coloring her cheeks.

"Don't get shy on me now, sweetheart," I say, trailing a finger along her jawline. "There's no shame in admitting you enjoyed all the things we did last night."

She playfully swats my arm, letting out an exasperated sigh. "You're too smug for my liking." My lips trail along her collarbone as my hand slides over her hip. "Walker, what are you doing?"

"Just making sure you remember how much you loved my charming side last night." I press slow kisses along the swells of her breasts, my eyes locked on her. "Is it working?"

She tilts her head, letting out a throaty moan. "You're incorrigible."

"It's not my fault you're so irresistible," I murmur, moving back up to capture her mouth in another kiss.

She leans back, her gaze searching mine. "Is this usually how the morning after goes? You know… after sex…" She trails off.

I wince, not wanting the reminder that for her, this might have been just another lesson—when for me it was a religious experience, and I'd declare my love for her on my knees if I thought she'd have me.

"*This*"—I motion between us—"is unlike anything I've ever experienced, and if we didn't have to work today, I'd bury my face between your thighs again and make you come until you couldn't think straight."

Birdie groans. "Now you're just being a tease."

"Don't worry, we'll have plenty more time for *that* later." *Every damn night for the rest of our lives if I can manage it.* "For now, I'm going to cook you breakfast and then get you to work on time."

It's the closest I'll get to seeing her all day with my shift at the sheriff's office—unless, of course, someone reports suspicious behavior at the feed store, like haphazardly stacked hay bales that could be a danger to pedestrians or a bag of chicken feed mysteriously left in the middle of the aisle.

Birdie sits up, eyes bright. "Does this breakfast of yours include an oat milk latte? Preferably two."

"Sure does." I grin.

I'd stocked up on all the supplies to make her coffee

order, including an espresso machine the day she agreed to our arrangement.

I give her one last kiss before I climb out of bed, heading straight for the kitchen. I measure and tamp down the espresso grounds, place a mug under the nozzle, and pull the shot to start Birdie's coffee.

"You're working at the sheriff's office today, right?" she asks from her spot on the bed.

"Yeah. I'm working a double and I have a mountain of paperwork to catch up on." I pull the oat milk from the fridge and set it on the counter. "Not the most exciting part of the job, but it's unavoidable."

"I've been meaning to ask—do you like splitting your time between there and the ranch? Or do you find it challenging to balance the two?"

Makes sense she'd ask, since I rarely discuss it with anyone— not even my family. Heath and my parents had questions when I first took the deputy role, but I never gave them a chance to press for more details. Over time, they stopped asking and eventually adjusted to the change in my schedule—mainly Heath.

I'm momentarily distracted as I watch Birdie slip out of bed, her creamy skin on full display. She casually picks up my T-shirt from the floor and slips it over her head. The shirt hangs from her frame, the hem hitting mid-thigh, and my cock stirs, growing hard from just the sight of her in my clothes. Each sway of her hips as she saunters toward me is a battle to keep my hands to myself and resist the urge to claim her again.

"You going to answer my question?" She hops up onto the counter next to the espresso machine, shooting me a smirk. "Or are you too busy staring?"

I settle between her thighs, bracing my hands on either side of her. "You're mighty distracting this morning." I lean closer, our lips barely an inch apart. "But I did promise I'd behave myself."

She lets out a huff of disappointment when I step back and move to the machine. The espresso shot is finished, steam rising from the cup. "To answer your question, it's a challenge juggling being a deputy and helping Heath run the ranch, especially on days like yesterday when an emergency had me pulling double duty."

Birdie leans back on her hands. "I can imagine. Dad has mentioned he wishes he could have you around full-time."

To distract myself from the way my shirt rides up her thighs, I pour oat milk into the frothing pitcher and heat it, the liquid swirling until it's hot and foamy.

"If the sheriff were ever serious, he'd have to take that up with Heath," I reply with a dry chuckle. "Though, he's already convinced I'm not invested in the ranch's success as much as I should be, so I'm not sure he'd even be surprised if I wanted to step back more than I already have."

I've never given it much thought. Sure, the sheriff has mentioned it in passing, but it's never been a serious offer.

"Think you'd ever consider it?"

"Truthfully? I have no idea." I pause to pour the steamed milk over the espresso shot, then add the foam on top. "Heath might doubt my commitment, but I could never leave him high and dry after all he's done to turn the ranch into a success. I'm really lucky to be a part of it, it's just that it's not..."

"Your dream?" Birdie finishes for me.

"Right." I sigh, glancing at the ground then back at her. "There's nothing I love more than riding out on the pastures and tending to the cattle. Still, I sometimes struggle with the idea of spending my entire life solely devoted to ranch work. It's a solitary existence, and I thrive on the energy of social interactions and being part of a community. Being a deputy has given me a balance that eases that pressure, and I'm grateful for it."

I'm a people person through and through. The best days on the ranch are when the entire crew is together, rounding up the cattle or mending fences, trading stories and joking around. But most days aren't like that—everyone sticks to their own tasks, the energy more subdued and the sense of isolation suffocating at times.

Birdie studies me carefully, her voice barely at a whisper when she speaks. "Have you ever told Heath how you feel?"

I shake my head. "He wouldn't understand."

I've always wanted to do my part to carry on the family legacy, but it's never been my true calling—it's Heath's. He's known what he's wanted since the age of five. He's built for the endurance, determination, and endless grind it takes to run a large cattle ranch, and he has devoted every ounce of himself to it, no matter the personal cost—not caring that his social life is practically nonexistent.

"He might be a one-man thundercloud, and a little intimidating, but he's your brother," Birdie reminds me. "I think you're underestimating how much he cares about your happiness."

I sprinkle some cinnamon on her latte and hand it to her. "Maybe."

"You'll never know if you don't talk to him about it," she points out before taking a long sip of her drink.

I've always let Heath make his own assumptions about my intentions and figured that dealing with his grumpy moods was inevitable. But Birdie might be onto something. Heath is a hard-ass, but he's not heartless or unreasonable. If I explained that my decision to become a deputy was about striking a balance between prioritizing my interests and my responsibilities, maybe he'd finally cut me some slack.

I arch a brow. "Never thought you'd end up as my therapist, did you?"

"It's a perfectly fair trade for mind-blowing sex and world-class coffee." She takes another drink from her mug, letting out a pleased sigh. "Seriously, you make the best lattes."

"Glad you think so." I grin. "Be sure to leave a Yelp review before you leave."

She bites her lip. "You sure you want my honest rating? I won't sugarcoat it."

I come to stand in front of her again, resting my hands on her knees. "Lay it on me, pretty girl."

She tilts her head to the side, thinking it over with a playful frown. "Last night's performance was four stars at best. Three orgasms was a solid start, but I know you weren't giving it your all." She smirks over the rim of her mug. "But this morning's excellent coffee and stellar service? That definitely bumps you up to four and a half stars."

I click my tongue as I drop to my knees. "That won't do."

"Walker." Birdie swallows hard as I move my hands to her thighs and spread them apart. "What are you doing?"

I hike up her T-shirt, giving me a clear view of her pussy. "I can't send you home unsatisfied, now can I?"

CHAPTER 21

Eavesdropping & Espionage

Walker

One Week Later

I F I HAD IT MY WAY, I'D HAVE SPENT THE LAST FEW DAYS holed up in my loft with Birdie. Instead, we've had to make do with frequent texts and late evenings together—me cooking for her, followed by hours of exploring every inch of her body and discovering what pleasures her most. I'm addicted to the sweet sound of her moans spilling from her lips when I'm inside her, and the way she gazes up at me—eyes heavy-lidded, mouth slightly parted—every time she gives herself over completely, crying out my name.

Unfortunately, I have to wait until later than usual to see her tonight. She's working at the feed store and I'm pulling a double shift at the sheriff's office stuck doing paperwork which is painfully boring. Sheriff Matterson visited a neighboring town training a group of new deputies today and there haven't been any calls that require attention.

My second shift overlapped with Mason's by a couple of hours but luckily, aside from the occasional clipped question or sideways glance, he's stayed out of my way. Now that he knows Birdie and I are together, he's learned not to test me where she's concerned—and he's been smart not to bring up the missing video footage again or my impromptu chat with the sheriff the other day.

When the deputies are in the office, we sit in an area that has four desks arranged in two rows. Today, I'm seated in the back row on the left. Mason got here an hour after me and sat at the desk farthest from me. It's a wise choice to keep his distance, though the space is small enough that it doesn't offer much privacy.

"Deputies," Margret, our night shift dispatcher, shouts from her desk at the front of the room. "I've got a lady on line two who's looking to report some suspicious activity. I offered to take down her information, but she won't hang up until she speaks to one of you."

"I'll handle it," Mason rushes out. "Put her through to me."

I shake my head, chuckling under my breath. Everything's a competition with him. Glad he's dealing with the call. It's probably old man Grady reporting that his pigs have run away again. I'd pay good money to watch Mason chase them across the muddy pasture as they squeal in his ear.

"This is Deputy Thatcher speaking. Who am I speaking with?" Mason asks as he rummages through his desk drawer, pulling out a pen and paper. "Mrs. Bixby, it's good to hear from you. What can I help you with today?"

My attention snaps from the document I'm reviewing when I realize he's speaking with Birdie's neighbor. The woman is a constant nuisance for the sheriff's department, always calling to complain about trivial things like dogs barking at night and tractors driving too fast down her road. Mrs. Bixby has even reported Birdie on multiple occasions for running what she calls an "unsanctioned animal circus." That's one battle she's never going to win as long as Sheriff Matterson's running the place.

Mason adjusts the phone against his ear and straightens in his chair. "Hold on—did you say Birdie Matterson?"

I stiffen at the sound of her name, instantly on edge.

He glances around, and I duck my head, pretending to be too absorbed in my paperback to pay attention to his conversation.

Mason angles his body away from me, cupping the phone and makes a half-hearted attempt to whisper. "I heard you, ma'am. You think she's keeping a donkey and cow in her shed." He jots something down on his notepad. "Yes, the sheriff is out of the office today but will be back tomorrow. We can stop by first thing in the morning to investigate if you'd like."

My hands curl into fists as I shoot daggers at Mason, but luckily, he's too immersed in his scheme to go after Birdie to notice. Either Birdie's neighbor was snooping around her property when she wasn't home, or she's just speculating after hearing rumors about her recent run-in with the law. Either way, I'm not taking any chances.

"Looking forward to seeing you too, ma'am," Mason says before hanging up the phone.

He pulls his cell phone from the desk drawer and leaves the room. No doubt he's calling to leave a voicemail for the sheriff, knowing he goes to bed early, especially after a long day out of town. He typically checks on any urgent matters first thing in the morning. He does have a second phone for emergencies, but Mason isn't foolish enough to use it for something like this.

Sheriff Matterson takes every complaint of suspicious activity seriously, which will leave him no choice but to show up at Birdie's place on his way to the station tomorrow. Luckily, that still gives me time to fix this and keep Birdie out of trouble—although destroying video evidence is one thing… Moving smuggled animals without being seen is a whole different challenge. If I'm going to pull this off, I'll need reinforcements.

Group Therapy Halstead Siblings Edition

Walker: We've got a problem.

Briar: Oh, look who finally came to the group chat for backup.

Jensen: Ignore her. She's just excited that you initiated for once.

Heath: Looks like Briar and Jensen have you covered.

Briar: Nope. Whatever is going on, we're ALL supporting our brother.

Heath: Can't it wait? I've got a cow that's ready to drop a calf any minute.

Briar: Pops told me we've got at least a week before that calf comes.

Walker: Guys, this is serious.

Briar: What is it?

Walker: Someone reported Birdie for keeping a donkey and cow in her shed. I think Mason is going to ask the sheriff to go with him to check it out first thing in the morning.

Briar: Oh shit. I'll loop in the girls.

Heath: Wait she actually took them? I figured that was town gossip.

Jensen: Nope. That woman has no sense of self-preservation.

Walker: For starters, she RESCUED those animals.

I still have no idea if they're actually on Birdie's property, but based on the video evidence, there's no disputing that she did take them from the fairgrounds.

Walker: Second, her courage and compassion are what make her so damn special.

Briar: Aww, look at you defending your woman. How romantic.

Walker: Briar focus.

Briar: Right. I'll text the girls and get back to you shortly.

Jensen: We'll be ready when you need us.

Walker: Thanks.

Briar: Heath???

Heath: Fine... I'll get one of the ranch hands to take over cow duty so I can be there.

I can picture him grumbling and wearing a scowl while he

texts his reply. Even still, I appreciate him dropping what he's doing to help.

Briar: That's the spirit!

I breathe easier, knowing Birdie has both me and her friends in her corner, and we'd all move mountains for her. Two things I know for certain: she's not going to jail, and I'm about to wipe that smug grin off Mason's face once and for all.

CHAPTER 22

Chaos & Cucumbers

Birdie

I**S IT CLICHÉ TO SAY I FEEL DIFFERENT NOW THAT I'M NO** longer a virgin? I thought I might be disappointed, since I'd hyped up this moment in my mind far more than I should have, but it exceeded all expectations—and that's because of Walker. He was patient and respectful yet commanded the situation in a way that left me hanging on his every word. The pain only lasted for a fleeting second, giving way to a surge of heat that rippled through me from head to toe. Even now, after a week has passed, I ache for his touch and fear I may already be hooked on him.

Work has dragged on today, made worse by the fact that Walker couldn't stop by since he's pulling a double shift at the sheriff's office. I didn't realize how much I'd come to look forward to his visits until recently, and now his absence hits me harder than expected.

It's only thirty minutes until closing, and there aren't any customers in the store, so I'm stocking the front shelves when I get a text.

Backroads & Bad Decisions Group Chat

Briar: SOS

Charlie: Isn't that Birdie's code for an emergency animal rescue mission?

Briar: Bingo. And this one is going to be a race against time.

Wren: Ugh! I wish I could be there.

I scrunch my nose as I reread the thread. I'm the one who usually gets notified when animals need rescuing, and as of a minute ago, I haven't received any messages or emails about this one.

Birdie: Briar, what's going on?

Briar: That nosy neighbor of yours called the sheriff's office claiming you're stashing the donkey and cow from the fair in your shed.

Briar: Mason told her that he and your dad will check it out in the morning.

My pulse spikes and my palms grow clammy. I haven't been home much these past few days, but that doesn't mean Mrs. Bixby hasn't been snooping. Could she have gotten into the shed? There's a padlock, but with the right tools, it wouldn't take much to break or force it open.

The problem is I've been keeping this particular secret for nearly a year, and even now, I can't quite bring myself to tell them the truth.

Birdie: Mrs. Bixby is mistaken.

Briar: Birdie, I'd bet my life savings that those animals are at your place. It's not much but that's besides the point!

Wren: There's no one else devoted enough to pull off a solo heist.

Charlie: If we don't come up with a plan, you're looking at a one-way trip to the county jail, and they have limited vegetarian options.

Charlie: At least you won't spend the rest of your life in jail as a virgin… right?

Briar: Don't answer that!

Charlie: Ignore her.

Birdie: I've spent every night with Walker this past week…

That's about as close as I'll ever come to admitting outright to Briar that I slept with her brother.

Charlie: Start at the beginning and don't leave a single detail out! BRB, making popcorn.

Briar: Don't we have a donkey and a cow to save?

They've got me trapped in a corner. If I don't admit I took the animals, I'll be left handling this on my own—but if I do, I'm confessing to breaking the law… again.

Birdie: You're right. Daisy and Peaches do need our help.

Charlie: So what I'm hearing is that you did commit animal theft. I'm so proud.

Birdie: Thanks?

Wren: Look at you out here building a criminal empire one farm animal at a time.

Briar: Guys, focus! I have a plan and will loop you in on our way over to Birdie's place.

Charlie: Fine. But I'm driving.

Wren: Good luck! I expect at least one incriminating selfie!

Charlie: I'll add a blur filter for plausible deniability.

Wren: Perfect. I'll have your bail money ready just in case. *wink face emoji

Panic creeps in as I realize there's a good chance we'll get caught moving Peaches and Daisy, and that they'll be taken away. I don't care about getting in trouble for rescuing them. All that matters is making sure they're not sent somewhere they'll be neglected or mistreated.

My hands shake as I stock a shelf with grooming supplies. I pause, gripping the edge of the counter while my heart pounds in my ears. I can barely focus on anything beyond the dread settling in my stomach. It's a good thing my shift is almost over. Otherwise, I'd be scrambling to make an excuse to leave early.

In the midst of my spiraling thoughts, my phone goes off.

Walker: I know you're worried, but we'll come up with a plan. I promise.

Birdie: You told Briar about Mrs. Bixby's complaint.

It's a statement, not a question.

Walker: Yeah. I overheard her filing a complaint with Mason.

Birdie: You do know that as a deputy fraternizing with criminals is frowned upon, right?

Walker: No one messes with my girl.

My heart nearly beats out of my chest when I realize that he's willing to put everything on the line for me. At this moment, whatever is happening between us feels as tangible as every breath I draw.

I glance down when my phone buzzes again, and what I see solidifies my confidence that no matter what comes next, things will work out as long as Walker is by my side.

Walker: See you soon, troublemaker.

"We should wait for the guys to get here," Briar whispers.

She's standing near the shed door, angling a lamp hooked to the handle while Charlie and I attempt to coax Peaches and Daisy out. It's important that we stay quiet and avoid drawing attention. My neighbors are far enough away that any noise shouldn't travel, and the light shouldn't alert them, but I wouldn't put it past Mrs. Bixby to pull an all-nighter just to keep an eye on my place. Thankfully, when we got here, every light in her house was already off, so I'm hoping she stuck to her early bedtime—our whole plan depends on it. To play it safe, Charlie parked her SUV out of sight from the road.

She and Briar picked me up from work, and we came straight to my place. Walker met Heath and Jensen at the ranch, and they should be here soon. Caleb's having a sleepover at the ranch house with Julie and Samuel, and they think we're all going out for drinks, which is a lot easier than explaining that we're relocating stolen animals to keep me out of jail. I can't imagine they'd be thrilled about their son dating a convicted criminal, even if my reasons were justified.

Your relationship isn't real, remember?

It's a sobering realization, one I'm struggling to process. What began as an agreement to pretend to date Walker—which I once thought was a brilliant idea (I blame the tequila shots)— has turned into me picturing what it would be like if this were real. I've resigned myself to the fact that eventually we'll have to talk about it, and I'll either have to confess my feelings or risk watching him move on. The thought makes my stomach turn.

Charlie scoffs. "Not sure why you roped the guys into this. We've handled countless rescues on our own and have never needed a man's help—let alone three."

"We've never had to move a three-hundred-pound donkey with an attitude problem before," Briar says, nodding to Peaches, whose gaze is fixed on Charlie as she holds a loose lead rope around her neck.

"Oh please. I've survived you and Birdie both hangry on a road trip with only a handful of granola bars and no gas stations within a fifty-mile radius." She adjusts the rope in her hand as she rolls up her sleeves. "I've got this."

Tonight, she's rocking a pair of black leather tights with a long-sleeve graphic tee that reads *Free Spirit* in vintage lettering above a minimalist line drawing of flying birds scattered in front of a silhouette of rolling hills and meadows. She's completed the look with platform Dr. Martens—clearly not letting our last heist, where she nearly tripped in heels while running across a field, get in the way of her fashion choices.

Charlie gently tugs on the rope, clicking her tongue. Peaches glares back, refusing to budge from where she's standing in the corner, utterly unimpressed, looking like she's drafting her next PETA complaint for being woken up and dragged out of her warm bed.

"Come on, Peaches," Charlie whines. "Work with me here. I can't have Heath stroll in and roast me for losing a standoff with a farm animal."

She lost it when Briar mentioned Heath would be tagging along. I had to remind her that he's bringing one of his trailers, so we need his help.

The plan is to get Daisy and Peaches to Mr. Grady's old property behind mine, where the guys will have the trailer waiting. The place has been abandoned for over a decade, and with open pastures on every side except the back, there's no chance anyone will spot us at this hour.

Walker and Heath have graciously offered to keep the animals in one of the storage sheds at Silver Saddle Ranch. It's one only they have access to, so the animals will be safe until I can figure out a long-term solution. There's no way I'll be able to bring them back here as long as Mrs. Bixby is snooping around.

"Try giving Peaches a cucumber slice," I suggest.

I focus back on Daisy, running my hand along her neck to guide her while holding a cucumber in front of her with my other hand. She limps along, stopping every few steps to nibble on her snack before hobbling forward again.

"There you go," I coo when we finally reach the exit.

Charlie sighs as she plucks a cucumber slice from the bag I gave her earlier. Peaches has a habit of trying to eat fruits and vegetables whole, so I have to cut them up to prevent her from choking.

Peaches takes a cautious sniff of the cucumber, letting out a disgruntled snort and tossing her head, rejecting the offending vegetable with all the drama of a diva.

"You've got to be kidding me," Charlie huffs, narrowing her eyes at me. "You couldn't have brought better treats to bribe her with? No sane animal would move an inch for a sad little cucumber." She waves the bag of slices in the air for emphasis.

"She didn't mean that," I tell Daisy, patting her on the head. "Enjoying a healthy snack is nothing to be ashamed of." As if in agreement, she sneaks another bite of her favorite treat.

At least one of the animals is cooperating.

Charlie drops the lead rope and sidles up to Peaches's backside, giving her a light tap. When she doesn't budge, Charlie presses both hands on her hindquarters and nudges again, but Peaches stays put.

"Oh, for crying out loud," Charlie exclaims. "Can't you see we're trying to save your ass?"

I let out a mock gasp. "Stop insulting Peaches. She's sensitive to being called names."

Charlie stands straight, throwing her hands in the air. "You do realize she's a literal ass, right?"

Briar chuckles from the doorway beside Daisy, shrugging when I shoot her a pointed look. "What? She's not wrong." She reaches her hand out for the half-eaten cucumber in my hand. "Why don't I take Daisy and start walking over to Mr. Grady's property while you two work on getting Peaches out?"

"That's a good idea," I agree, handing it over.

She pulls a flashlight from her pocket and clicks it on, slowly making her way to the back of my lot with Daisy trailing behind, her emotional support cucumber dangling in sight.

Unfortunately, when I return to the shed, Charlie hasn't made any headway with Peaches. At this rate, we'll still be here when my dad rolls in tomorrow morning, and he'll have no choice but to take them away. All the effort that I put into saving them will have been for nothing. But before I can spiral further, Charlie moves in front of Peaches and kneels on the ground.

I furrow my brow. "Uh, Charlie… what are you doing?"

"Peaches and I are going to have a little chat, woman to woman, so she understands the severity of her situation," Charlie replies, cupping the sides of Peaches's face. "Here's the deal, buttercup. If you don't let us get you out of here, the sheriff will have to take you away, and who knows where you'll end up. You love your warm blankets, head scratches, and all the treats you could ever want, right?" She pauses like she expects Peaches to respond. "Okay, so the treats are subpar, but we have to cut Birdie some slack. She's a vegetarian, so she's not exactly a culinary connoisseur," she adds in a conspiratorial whisper.

"Hey, I heard that," I interject.

Charlie glances over her shoulder, grinning. "I'm just being honest. She deserves to know what she's signing up for if she stays long-term."

"She's been here a year. If that's not long-term, I don't know what is."

"Peaches still reserves the right to change her—"

She's cut off by Heath's deep voice rumbling as he enters the shed and moves past me to stand behind her. "If you were that keen to get on your knees for me, all you had to do was ask, Charlie." His gaze is dark and unyielding.

"Of course you couldn't cooperate before *he* got here," she mutters, motioning accusingly at Peaches as she stands to brush off her tights.

I step out of Heath's way, not wanting to be caught in the middle of whatever is going on between him and Charlie.

"Even if I was on my knees, you'd be the one begging, cowboy," Charlie quips.

Heath draws in a sharp breath before smoothing his features with practiced control.

"Care to explain why the donkey is still in the shed when the whole point is to get her out of here?" he grunts, ignoring Charlie's jab.

"As shocking as it is, Peaches's stubborn streak puts yours to shame," she retorts.

Heath drags his thumb along his mustache, eyes fixed on her. "Or maybe you just don't have what it takes to get her to comply."

Charlie puts her hands on her hips. "Let me guess, you'd solve that with brute force?"

Heath smirks, taking a step toward her. "Wrong. It's all about patience, paying attention to her nonverbal cues, and drawing her in until she can't resist following my lead."

I swear Charlie shifts forward, a flicker of interest in her eyes—but it's gone as quickly as it appeared. "By all means, I dare you to do better. All you've got to work with are these soggy things." She tosses him the bag of cucumber slices, and Heath catches them with one hand.

He tucks the bag into his shirt pocket before side-stepping around Charlie. "Hey there, Peaches. How are you doing tonight?" He slowly reaches out, stroking her muzzle, and Peaches closes her eyes briefly at the touch. "We really need to get you out of here, but I promise I have a nice cozy spot waiting for you at the ranch."

Peaches stays put despite Heath's persuasive pep talk, but that doesn't deter him. This time, he rubs behind her ears, and her nostrils twitch.

"Oh, you like that, sweet girl, don't you?" Heath croons as he gives her a good scratch.

Charlie and I both stare at him in shock, and I'm convinced we're witnessing a glitch in the Matrix. This isn't the broody cowboy I'm familiar with. Apparently, all it takes is a stubborn donkey in trouble to bring out the soft side hiding beneath his grumpy exterior.

He withdraws his hands from Peaches and steps back toward the door. Her ears perk forward, tail swishing, and she trots after him, nudging his arm with her nose in search of more attention.

"Unbelievable," Charlie mutters.

Heath smirks. "See? All she needed was some gentle persuasion and a firm hand."

"I'll show you a firm hand," Charlie says under her breath as she follows Heath.

She may be irritated by the turn of events, but I'm just relieved that backup is here. Maybe we'll actually manage to clear the shed without getting caught.

Butterflies take flight in my stomach the second Walker steps across the threshold, all rugged charm in his charcoal-gray deputy's button-up tucked into his dark-wash Wranglers, and a rope slung over his shoulder. How I wish he'd toss me over his shoulder, carry me to my bedroom, and fuck me until I'm screaming his name. I only lost my virginity a week ago, and I'm already addicted to sex... More specifically, sex with Walker.

When he spots me, his face breaks into a wide grin. "Howdy, sweetheart."

"Hi," I breathe.

He crosses the distance between us, pulling me into a hug that nearly turns me into a melted puddle at his feet. I loop my hands around his neck, fingers clutching the hair at the nape of his neck, basking in the safety of being in his arms.

Walker leans back, tipping my chin. "Are you okay?"

"I am now," I murmur, meeting his gaze.

In the past, I've handled most rescue missions alone or with the girls, and Charlie's right—we've always managed without incident. Yet having Walker here brings a sense of peace I've never experienced before. It's a silent promise that I don't have to carry this burden alone, and the reassurance that he won't let anything go wrong.

When I step back, I notice Charlie, Heath, and Peaches are no longer in the shed, which means they finally got her out—thank goodness.

I'm about to follow, stopping when I glance back at Walker, my eyes landing on the rope draped over his shoulder.

"How come you brought that?" I ask, pointing at it.

"Figured it might come in handy with the animals, but since you and the girls have that handled, I'll save it for another night." He smirks with a glint in his eye. "I do recall I owe you a lesson involving rope."

I inhale sharply, tugging my bottom lip between my teeth. "That you do, Deputy."

I've fantasized about him tying me up countless times, and the promise that it could happen soon has my heart pounding in my chest.

"Birdie, Walker, are you coming?" Charlie calls from outside, her voice raised just enough to carry.

"Yes," we answer in unison, both stepping toward the exit.

As we head into the dark yard, I grab the lantern from the door, holding it ahead so everyone can see where we're going. Briar's flashlight is bobbing far ahead, already in the middle of Mr. Grady's property, so Jensen must have found her and helped move Daisy along despite her limp.

Walker closes the shed behind us and takes my hand in his. We make for the back of my lot where there's a large gap in the fence. Charlie and Heath stay ahead of us, bickering in hushed tones the whole way about who gets to pet Peaches and where she likes it best.

Walker leans in and whispers, "Those two argue like it's foreplay."

I chuckle softly. "Don't tell Briar that. She might have come to terms with us dating, but I can't imagine she'd react well if those two got together." I nod toward Charlie and Heath, who are now locked in a tense stare off ahead of us. "I know our relationship isn't exactly permanent, so maybe she'd be fine with them seeing each other."

Walker's hand stiffens in mine, and when I look over, his jaw is clenched.

"Are you okay?" I ask.

"I'm fine," he says a bit too quickly.

I check that Heath and Charlie are far enough ahead of us before I reply. "You sure? I just figured eventually you'll get tired of teaching me. Plus, I'll be ready to date without accidentally elbowing a guy in the nose—hopefully." The last part comes out in a whisper.

Honestly, the idea of going out with anyone else has my stomach in knots.

Walker doesn't laugh like I thought he might. In fact, he doesn't even blink. He just stares at me, his expression unreadable.

I can't help wishing he'd shown even a flicker of jealousy when I mentioned dating other men, but instead, I'm left guessing what he's thinking. There's no denying that I'm falling for him, and I can only hope he feels the same—but sneaking across a pasture in the middle of the night with a donkey isn't exactly the right time to ask.

We're halfway across Mr. Grady's property when Mrs. Bixby's backyard floodlights turn on.

"Fuck," Walker mutters under his breath.

I drop his hand, fumbling to turn off the lantern to avoid being seen from her second-story windows, which overlook Mr. Grady's property.

"We'd better make a run for it," Heath hisses, and we all bolt forward. Peaches is now fully on board, trotting behind him as he steers her with the lead rope.

It's not like Mrs. Bixby could catch us even if she tried, but she could certainly call the sheriff's office again, and with Mason on duty, he'd drop everything to investigate reports of movement on Mr. Grady's supposedly vacant property. So it's critical that we get out of here as quickly as possible.

We don't stop until we reach the abandoned barn at the front of the property. Its paint is chipped and faded, and the doors hang crooked on their hinges. Still, it has a certain charm, and with some work, it could make an amazing space for my animals. I push down the longing that rises as I imagine transforming the place, accepting that I'll likely never be able to afford it and that eventually I'll have to watch someone else turn it into their own vision.

Heath's truck and trailer are parked by the barn, and Briar is pressed against the trailer, her hair tousled, Jensen stands in front of her with his hands caging her in, and it's obvious they'd been making out while waiting for us to catch up.

When they notice us, Jensen turns around. "What took you guys so long?"

"*Someone* kept trying to take over guiding Peaches, and it slowed us down," Heath says, glaring at Charlie.

"Excuse me?" she pants, trying to catch her breath. "You're the one with a hero complex and wouldn't let me help even when your hand was cramping from petting her at an awkward angle."

Jensen smirks, his gaze darting between them. "Why don't we get her inside the trailer with Daisy so we can get the hell out of here?"

"Great idea," Briar adds, coming up to give Peaches a good scratch behind the ear so she'll follow her.

"It's a good thing this place is vacant, or we'd have been spotted by now," Walker says in a hushed tone. "I've always found it strange that old man Grady never sold it after moving across town."

"It's not for a lack of offers," Charlie chimes. "Even Birdie has made several, but he'll only accept cash. Too bad—it would have been the perfect animal sanctuary." She hops into the front of the truck, scooting to the middle seat, no doubt planning to antagonize Heath on the drive to the ranch.

I start to follow, but Walker gently grips my wrist, stopping me.

"Is that true?" he asks.

"Yeah. Having the extra space would have been amazing. I could've torn down the rest of the fence and turned it into one big property, finally making my sanctuary official and running a full-fledged operation without having to turn animals away," I explain wistfully.

It's exhausting having to find homes for every creature I encounter that I can't take in myself, knowing that if I fail, their lives could be at stake.

Walker studies me for a moment. "You've put a lot of thought into this, haven't you?"

"Sure, but I came to terms a long time ago that it was just a silly pipe dream, and that's all right. I'll manage with the space I have, like always," I add with a smile.

Walker frowns, clearly not satisfied with my answer, but before he can push further, Briar calls out to us.

"Walker, Birdie, let's go," she whisper-shouts from the truck.

That's when I look around and see that everyone else is already inside, waiting for us.

The rest of my life might be imploding, but at least I have the best friends a girl could ask for, the kind who don't think twice about showing up, no matter the risk.

CHAPTER 23

You Belong With Me

Walker

"**T**HANK GOODNESS YOU'RE HERE," MRS. BIXBY EXCLAIMS to Sheriff Matterson as she marches down Birdie's drive. "That daughter of yours is hiding that donkey and cow in her shed, and it's the last straw. I already have to deal with being neighbors to dozens of wayward animals." She gestures toward the group of rabbits huddled under Birdie's truck.

"Now, just a minute, Mrs. Bixby. While I appreciate you bringing this to our attention, let's hold off on accusations until we investigate further, all right?" he replies, tugging on his collar like it's too tight.

I don't envy the position he's in—caught between doing his job as sheriff and being a father.

He sent me a message early this morning, saying Mason left him a voicemail about Mrs. Bixby's complaint and that he'd be stopping by Birdie's to check it out—asking if I'd be there. I figured it was his subtle way of warning her through me while keeping it on the down low. Not sure what he expected we could do about it on such short notice, but regardless, we've got this handled.

I made a point to show up dressed in a casual gray T-shirt and Wranglers, making it clear I'm here strictly as Birdie's boyfriend and not in any official capacity. She deserves someone whose only focus is on her, free from outside distractions or agendas.

Mason came straight from his shift at the sheriff's office, insisting on being here since he took the call. He's got that damn smug grin plastered on his face, making my blood boil. The only silver lining was the shock on his face when he showed up and found me standing on the porch. He clearly wasn't expecting me to be here, which makes what's about to happen all the more satisfying.

Birdie steps outside, smiling as she straightens the floral bandana on her head. It's only been a few hours since I saw her, but it feels like a lifetime. We didn't get to spend the night together because I had to get Peaches and Daisy settled into their temporary home and check on them again before heading over this morning. I'm running on fumes, but seeing her makes it completely worth it.

"Morning, everyone," she says with a cheerful wave. "I wasn't expecting any visitors. Is everything all right?"

"Good morning, kiddo. Sorry to come by unannounced." Her dad apologizes with a tip of his hat. "Mrs. Bixby reported seeing that missing donkey and cow in your shed. Mind if we take a look?"

"Is that right?" She turns to Mrs. Bixby with a polite smile. "I wish you'd asked me directly. It's always a pleasure when you stop by, especially when you bring one of your delicious lasagnas."

She is calm and composed, not a trace of nervousness in sight. Even knowing that things will go in her favor, the old Birdie would have been fidgety and unsure. Seeing how much her confidence has grown fills me with pride.

"You haven't been around much lately," Mrs. Bixby says,

shooting a glance between Birdie and me. "And when I spotted the stolen animals, I couldn't just stay quiet if it might help the authorities close the case."

"I understand. I know my dad… I mean, Sheriff Matterson, appreciates the tip," Birdie replies.

The sheriff opens his mouth to add his two cents when suddenly Nugget bursts through the doggie door, clucking as she hops down the porch to where we're standing, weaving between Birdie's legs. She squawks loudly in Mrs. Bixby's direction before waddling over to Mason and giving his shoe a sharp peck. I laugh as he yelps, stumbling backward like he's being attacked by a feral predator instead of a tiny, curious chicken.

Unimpressed by Mason's reaction to her inspection, Nugget flaps her wings before shooting across the yard toward the pond where the ducks and geese are enjoying their morning swim.

"See what I have to put up with? There's something seriously wrong with that thing," Mrs. Bixby says, gesturing toward Nugget, who's settled onto a rock and fluffed up like she intends to hatch it.

"It's just a chicken, ma'am. We have them all over Bluebell," Sheriff Matterson explains.

She shakes her head. "Ones that live in the house and come running out of a doggie door? I don't think so."

Even before I showed up this morning, I was convinced that Birdie needs a better setup for her animals. After getting a first-hand glimpse of what she deals with from Mrs. Bixby, I'm now more determined to come up with a plan that allows her to rescue and keep as many animals as she wants without landing herself in trouble again.

So what if some of the animals are different? That's what makes them special—just like the woman who saves them. Birdie also deserves a haven of her own. I admire how she's opened her home and yard to every creature in need, but she's sacrificed so much of her personal space and deserves more than living on the margins of her own home.

"Why don't we get on with what we came here for?" Sheriff Matterson suggests, motioning toward the shed in the backyard.

"Fine by me," Mrs. Bixby says, leading the way.

Mason is right behind her with a bounce in his step, while Sheriff Matterson follows reluctantly, glancing back at Birdie every few seconds. She offers him a small smile, and I hate that he can't comfort her the way a father should. It's one of the unfortunate consequences of being sheriff—sometimes the law has to come before everything else.

I weave my fingers through hers and brush my thumb over her palm in soothing strokes, silently assuring her that everything is going to be okay.

When we get to the shed, Mason steps past Mrs. Bixby.

"Allow me, ma'am," he says with a gleam in his eye.

He opens the shed door, and even though Birdie knows what he'll find, she still tightens her grip on my hand.

I press a kiss to her temple and whisper in her ear. "Everything's going to be fine, remember?"

"Thank you," she murmurs. "For everything."

"Always here for you."

We both watch with bated breath as Mason sticks his head inside the shed.

"What the hell?" he mutters.

"What is it?" Mrs. Bixby pushes her way past him to get a look. "This isn't possible. Where are the animals?"

The rest of us shuffle in behind them. The faint smell of hay and straw hangs in the air, and a mixture of both is scattered across the floor. Several blankets are strewn about, some chewed at the edges, and an empty water trough and food bowl sit in the corner. It's obvious animals had been living here until recently, though there's no concrete evidence without them here.

Sheriff Matterson lets out a low whistle. "Well, would you look at that. No donkey or cow in sight."

Mrs. Bixby scowls. "I'm positive they were in here just yesterday. I saw them myself!"

He lifts a brow. "Huh. And were you by chance looking around my daughter's property without her permission when you spotted them?"

Birdie's long driveway and a line of trees divide their yards, which would have made it impossible for Mrs. Bixby to see Peaches and Daisy from her house.

She scoffs, waving Sheriff Matterson off. "Don't be silly. I was bringing by a loaf of my famous banana bread but got distracted when I heard a strange noise coming from the backyard. I wanted to make sure no one was hurt."

"It was probably just Daffy, one of the ducks," Birdie chirps. "He has terrible indigestion and has a habit of making a racket when he's eating, the poor guy."

I bite the inside of my cheek to keep from laughing. Coming from anyone else, it would be a ridiculous excuse—but with Birdie, it's totally plausible.

Sheriff Matterson removes his hat and wipes his brow. "Well, there you have it. False alarm."

Mason steps forward. "But, boss, don't you want to—"

"Son, I appreciate your concern for the animals and your dedication to the badge, but as you can see, there's no proof of any wrongdoing." He motions around the empty shed. "We've got bigger crimes to solve than chasing down livestock that disappeared last year, don't you think?"

Mason shoves his hands into his pockets, grumbling, "Yes, sir."

Thank god Peaches and Daisy are safe and sound at the ranch, and we can finally put this all behind us. Wiping that smug-ass grin off Mason's face was just a bonus.

After the search, I took Birdie to see Daisy and Peaches. When we got to the ranch, Heath and Jensen had already set up a makeshift perimeter so the animals could explore the field next to the shed where they're being kept. It's a step up from being cooped inside all day, and Birdie was relieved to see they'd settled in nicely.

Heath even brought his cow Petunia over to spend the day with Daisy and Peaches, and within minutes, they were following her every step. I didn't miss Birdie's subtle observations about how well they got along, and I wouldn't be surprised if Heath ends up with two more four-legged companions.

Afterward, I took her to Silver Ridge Lake. Nestled at the back of the ranch, it's surrounded by trees, with mountains rising on one side. It's reserved for my family and guests staying at the cabins. Guests usually rent canoes and fishing gear at the general store, but I made sure that Birdie and I were the only ones here today.

"You've got to stop spoiling me like this," she murmurs, leaning back against me as she takes in the view.

"Where's the fun in that?" I tease, tracing her bare shoulder as I admire her yellow sundress that shows off her sun-kissed legs— tempting me straight into trouble.

With Briar's help, I put together a date on the dock, complete with a flannel blanket and throw pillows, an umbrella shielding us from the afternoon sun, and a wicker basket loaded with fresh veggie wraps, caprese skewers, berries, a bottle of sparkling water, and an oat milk latte in a thermos. Afternoon coffee is nonnegotiable for Birdie, and I wasn't about to make her skip it.

"I think I could stay here forever. It's so calm and peaceful." She sighs softly.

I rest my head on her shoulder. "That's why it's one of my favorite spots on the ranch. My dad used to bring Heath and me here in the summers to fish, and I like to come whenever I need to clear my head."

She tilts her head to look back at me. "Have you talked to Heath about your work on the ranch yet?"

"No, but I've been thinking about what you said. The cattle operation is growing faster than expected, and he could use more ranch hands—hell, what he really needs is to hire a foreman to keep everything running. So yeah, I think it's time we talked."

Lately, the sheriff's been asking me to pick up more shifts, and that call to help with the aftermath of the bar fight wasn't the first time I've worked straight through the night, taking statements and filing reports.

I've always known that juggling both responsibilities wouldn't be sustainable forever, but nothing had ever been important enough to make me rethink my priorities—until now. Having gotten a glimpse of what it's like being with Birdie, I'm ready to do whatever it takes to make it permanent, and I know that something else will eventually have to give. I just don't know what that is yet, which is why I need to talk to Heath before making any decisions.

Birdie eases out of my arms and turns to face me, folding her legs beneath her. "That makes me happy to hear."

"What about you?" I ask. "Still planning to run the sanctuary out of your house?"

She nods, twisting her necklace between her fingers. "For now. Mr. Grady's place might be off the table, but I'm not giving up on finding another property. It'll probably take a few years, though—everything I make at the feed store goes toward bills and the animals, so there's not much left over to save for land," she explains as she picks a strawberry from the picnic basket and pops it into her mouth.

I grimace at my own oversight, not realizing until now that Birdie's been footing all the expenses for her rescues. I should've known, given it's not an official operation, but I figured since she's so damn good at convincing people to take in animals, she'd have already been collecting donations too.

"Have you thought about turning the sanctuary into a nonprofit?" I suggest, leaning back on my hands. "I'm guessing it'd be easier to get donations and apply for grants."

"I've looked into it. I'd need special permits, licenses, and routine inspections. Zoning alone could get me shut down for operating on a residential property. So for now, I'm just doing what I can on my own," she says, forcing a smile that doesn't quite reach her eyes.

An idea floats through my mind of how to solve the problem, but I hold my tongue. Right now, Birdie needs someone to listen and validate what she's going through—not try to fix things. There will be plenty of time for problem-solving later.

"You're amazing, Birdie, just don't forget you're not in this alone. You've got me, my family, and your friends." I reach over to give her leg a gentle squeeze. "Briar's had to navigate starting her nonprofit, so I'm sure she'll want to share everything she's learned with you when you're ready."

"Thanks. I appreciate that." Birdie pauses, looking out over the lake. "She really does know the process better than anyone. I have no idea how she finds the time to run the foundation, help manage the house construction, and take care of Caleb."

"She's amazing and a damn good mom," I state.

I never expected Briar to be the first of us to have kids, yet she's taken it all in stride.

Birdie nibbles on another strawberry, chewing thoughtfully before speaking.

"Do you want kids someday?" she asks.

With you? More than anything.

I clear my throat, sitting up straight. "I do."

"How many?"

"I might be biased, but three seems like a good number. And if I had a daughter, I'd want her to be the youngest, so she'd have two older brothers looking out for her," I say, grinning as I picture a little girl who's the spitting image of Birdie.

When my parents adopted Briar, it was like the last puzzle piece finally slid into place for our family. Not only did she bring Ma the immeasurable joy of having the daughter she'd always wished for, but she also gave Heath and me the chance to grow closer as siblings, united in our goal to love and protect her.

"Three sounds perfect," Birdie says around another berry, and I let myself imagine she means *our* future children. "Being an only child can be lonely, and I like to think things might have been easier to get through with siblings." The last part is barely audible, meant more for herself than me.

When she doesn't elaborate, I don't press. I know more about what she's been through than she realizes, and I can't imagine carrying those burdens without anyone to lean on. At the very least, she should've had her dad there to offer her the guidance and strength she deserved. Instead, he's buried himself in work when he should have been fully present for his family. He may believe his reasons are justified, but that doesn't excuse leaving Birdie to navigate years of hardship on her own.

"Is the infamous Walker Halstead thinking about settling down and starting a family?" Birdie muses.

I move closer and bracket her with my legs, setting my hand on her thigh.

"Birdie," I say softly.

She studies me, curiosity shining in her eyes. "Yeah?"

"I might have played the field when I was younger, but I left that part of my past behind shortly after I became a deputy." *And realized you were the only one for me.*

She frowns slightly, a crease forming between her brows. "You did? How come you never said anything?"

I shrug, glancing at the lake, the sunlight sparkling across the water. "Everyone assumed I hadn't changed, and I never bothered correcting them. I'm not proud of who I used to be, but I don't regret it—not when it led me to this moment with you."

Birdie tilts her head. "What do you mean?"

"We agreed to pretend to date as a ruse so I could teach you, and the only reason you asked me for *lessons* was because of my experience," I remind her as I trace circles across her thigh with my thumb. "Without it, I doubt you would've suggested the arrangement in the first place."

"That's true," she admits, tension visibly easing from her shoulders. "But I said yes because I trusted you and knew you were the only one who would understand without judging me."

I give her thigh a light squeeze. "Never. You're always safe with me."

Birdie leans in, resting her hand on my cheek. I melt into her touch, letting the warmth settle through me. She meets my gaze, and it's as if time itself has stopped, leaving only the two of us suspended in the moment.

"Walker, what are we doing?" she whispers, her eyes searching mine, a thousand questions lingering there.

"We're enjoying a date at the lake," I murmur, leaning into her hand.

Birdie subtly shakes her head. "No, I mean, what's happening with us? This was supposed to be a no-strings arrangement, but it feels like it's become more than that." She looks down at the blanket, drawing in a slow breath before continuing. "I miss you when we're not together, and my heart skips a beat whenever you walk into a room. Sometimes I think you might feel it too, but other times, I wonder if it's all in my head and this is still just an arrangement to you like it was always meant to be." Her voice trembles, unguarded emotion spilling out.

I blink at her in disbelief, trying to process the reality that she just confessed her feelings for me. It's not something I thought would ever happen in this lifetime, and as much as I wish I could lay my heart bare, I know it's better to take things slow and avoid scaring her off. She's still sorting out what's real versus pretend, and I don't want to push too hard and risk the fragile trust we've built.

That trust will be tested soon enough when the truth about what I've done for her family comes out. I'm not naive enough to think it'll stay a secret forever, and there's a chance she'll be upset that I kept it from her—but we'll cross that bridge when it comes.

For now, I'm going to treasure her admission and make the most of our time alone, leaving no doubt in her mind about how much she means to me.

I capture her lips in a soft kiss. "You're not imagining a thing, Birdie, baby. This is as real as it gets."

CHAPTER 24

Save A Horse, Ride The Cowboy

Birdie

I MELT INTO THE KISS, LOST IN A BLISSFUL HAZE UNTIL Walker's words finally register.

"Wait—you *do* feel the same way?" I ask.

He nods, grinning. "I do, sweetheart. Nothing about this relationship has been fake for me."

"So then, what do we do now?" I say, matching his grin.

Walker peppers kisses along the corner of my mouth. "Whatever you want, Birdie. I want a future with you—not just for today or tomorrow but forever if you'll have me. I'll wait as long as it takes for you to decide whether you want that too, because you're worth it."

My heart practically leaps from my chest at his declaration, realizing the man I've been falling for yearns for me as much as I do him, which makes falling for him all the more effortless. There has never been any pressure or expectations—only the need to make me feel cherished and protected.

My hands curl into his shirt as I gaze up at him. "I want that too."

He exhales, his shoulders relaxing. "You have no idea how happy that makes me. I was ready to pull out all the stops to convince you."

I raise a brow, intrigued. "Oh, really? And how exactly would you have done that?"

A smirk crosses his lips as he trails a finger along my jaw. "I think it's best I show you… if you're up for it, that is."

My pulse spikes at his tantalizing offer. The future may still be uncertain, but knowing it will include Walker is enough.

For now, the tension hums between us like a live wire, sparking with every glance, every touch, and I long to surrender to the wanton desire burning through me.

"I do love a man who takes initiative," I retort, playfully nipping at his finger.

"If that's true, strip for me," he says, his voice coming out husky. "So I can make sure you understand just how much I want you."

My breath shudders as I glance around the lake. I know we're the only ones here, but his request still sends a flutter of nerves through me. Even so, I refuse to let them get the better of me. Walker would never put me in a position where I wasn't safe, and I want nothing more than to prove how much I trust him.

He stays seated, resting back on his hands, and watches as I shimmy out of my yellow sundress and take off my bra and underwear. When I'm standing naked in front of him, he shifts forward, brushing a kiss across the top of my hand.

"You're so goddamn pretty," he says reverently, tapping my thigh to signal for me to step out of the clothes pooled around my feet. "Now lie back on the blanket."

I scramble to obey, crawling to the middle and rolling onto my back. My palms are sweaty, and I'm restless, unsure of what's coming next. Through my eyelashes I peek at Walker, flashing him a sultry smile. Silently daring him to make his move.

I trace his movements closely as he reaches for the wicker

basket and digs through it, a slow grin spreading across his face when he pulls out two pieces of rope and holds them up.

"What are you planning to do with those?" I ask, heart hammering in my chest.

I think I have a pretty good idea.

"Lesson ninety-two: rope play." Walker winks, winding one of the ropes around his wrist in demonstration. "If memory serves, you were intrigued by the prospect of being restrained. If you're still interested, we'll start simple by tying your hands above your head while I eat your pussy."

I squeeze my legs together, wetness pooling between my thighs. When Walker brought up rope play before, it was a distant fantasy used to spark curiosity. Now that it's a real possibility, I'm eager to feel the rush firsthand.

"What do you say? Can I restrain your hands while we play?" he asks, his voice low.

Walker tosses his hat to the side, and stands so he can take off his T-shirt, giving me an unobstructed view of his sculpted abs and the smattering of hair leading down to his V-line.

I lick my lips, shamelessly drinking in the sight of him. "Yes. I want that. Very much."

He pulls his pants and boxers down, leaving him naked, his cock stiff and gleaming with pre-cum.

He kneels before me. "Hold out your hands."

"Yes, sir," I reply cheekily.

His response is a sharp exhale, his nostrils flaring.

"Do you like it when I call you that, *sir*?" I tease as I sit up and hold out my hands.

"Fuck. You know I do." He loops the rope around my wrists three times before finishing with a knot, leaving just enough slack so it won't dig into my skin. "How is that? Too tight?"

I shake my head. "No, it feels… good."

There's a thrill in being bound and in surrendering completely to Walker's control.

His darkened gaze follows the trail of his finger along the coils, admiring his handiwork.

"Good. Now, I want you to lie down," he orders.

He helps ease me onto my back on the blanket, gently guiding my arms above my head.

I watch as he retrieves the other length of rope, winding it around his hand with a few inches left loose before hovering over me. I gasp as he grazes the frayed ends of the rope over my breast, each coarse fiber sending a shock wave through me. He drags it across my skin until it reaches my nipple, teasing it back and forth with slow, tantalizing strokes. My hands curl into balls, the tips of my nails digging into my palms.

Next, Walker brushes the rope across my other breast, letting the strands glide over the curve. His brow tightens in concentration as he guides it down past my navel.

"Spread your legs, and show me how wet you are, baby," he croons.

They fall open of their own accord as he lowers himself, his hot breath whispering across my upper thigh as he trails the rope over my pussy and lightly across my slit. My back arches, a whimper slipping free as electric sparks flare from the delicious caress along my core. When he pulls the rope away, it glistens with my arousal.

"As much as I'd love to play with you for hours—until you're writhing beneath me and begging—I have to taste you now," he groans, tossing the rope aside.

His stubble rubs against me as he moves up my thigh, inch by torturous inch. My legs quake with anticipation as he reaches my apex and inhales deeply. He slowly licks along the seam of my pussy before plunging his tongue inside me. I buck my hips, shamelessly grinding against his face as he eagerly explores, alternating between licking and sucking. When he eases two thick fingers inside me, a shiver courses through my veins, and I gasp as heat ripples through me.

"Walker," I rasp out. "I want to come while I'm riding you. Please."

His gaze locks on mine, pinning me in place. "I don't have a condom."

"I'm on birth control, and I don't want anything between us."

He freezes. "Are you sure? I've been tested. I haven't been with anyone in years, and I've always used a condom. But if you're not ready for this, we can wait."

I'm left speechless by his admission. He's implied that he hasn't been with other women in a while, but hearing it outright stirs something deep inside me. The thought of being his first without protection, and of him wanting to share such an intimate moment with me as much as I want to share it with him, fills me with a quiet certainty that this is right.

I give him a warm smile. "I want this, Walker. I want to *feel* you inside me. *All* of you."

"I want that too," he murmurs.

What started as a temporary arrangement shifted along the way, leading us to cross a line, and what we share now goes far beyond him teaching me how to flirt, building confidence, or exploring intimacy. I want to show him just how much he means to me without any barriers between us.

Walker licks my pussy one last time before he pulls away, and I feel the absence of his touch like a brand. I don't have long to overthink it as we switch spots. He lowers himself to the blanket, pulling me down to straddle him. I loop my bound wrists over his head and rest my hands on his shoulders as I sink onto his cock, my pussy clenching around him. Our mingled moans drift through the stillness around us.

Walker grips my hips as he guides me to rock against him in smooth, controlled movements.

"I'm your first and last, baby."

"First and last," I echo.

I sense that his declaration carries a deeper meaning, but I'm distracted as he shifts his hold to my ass, guiding me as I slide along his shaft. My back arches with every thrust, and I rake my nails over his heated skin as we push toward our shared climax.

"I'm so close, Walker." I moan as small tremors wrack my body.

He reaches between us and circles his thumb over my clit—a move that leaves me gasping for air. My hips shift in time with his fingers, every motion edging me toward release.

"Come for me," he commands.

As I clench around him, on the verge of letting go, he gently pinches my clit, sending me careening over the edge. I toss my head back, pulsing around him as a broken cry escapes me. And within seconds Walker reaches his peak, grunting as he comes inside me, the feel of us joined together with nothing separating us leaving me lightheaded.

In the moment, a single thought crosses my mind. *What if Walker really could be my one and only?*

I stir to the sound of buzzing, and nuzzle further into Walker's chest, determined to ignore it. After our date at the lake, we came back to my place to feed the kittens and check on the other animals. Somehow, we ended tangled up in bed for round two, staying awake far too late.

Walker rubs my back, pressing a kiss to my forehead. "Sweetheart, your phone is ringing. Want me to see who it is?"

I groan. "That's alright. I'll get it."

My phone goes quiet for a beat before the buzzing starts up again. I squint at the clock—it's 4:37 a.m. It's most likely an animal rescue call or someone trying to reach me about Mama. My stomach drops when I see it's Tess, and I steel myself for the worst before answering.

"Hi Tess, is everything okay?" I blurt, unable to hide my urgency.

She exhales shakily over the line. "Thank god I reached you. Your mom's been admitted to the hospital, and I wanted you to hear it from me. The ambulance woke the whole neighborhood, so the news will spread fast, even at this hour."

I bolt upright, tossing the comforter aside as I scramble out of bed. "Wait—Mama's in the hospital? What happened? Is she okay?" I bite back my next string of questions, realizing I'm firing them off without giving Tess a chance to respond.

"She was congested yesterday and woke up around midnight short of breath and disoriented. The doctor thinks it's pneumonia," Tess explains, a muffled announcement crackling from an intercom in the background.

I frown, pulling a T-shirt and shorts from my dresser. "Pneumonia? Are you sure?"

"It's not as common this time of year, but it can happen, and it's especially serious for someone medically fragile, like your mom," she replies.

"Does the doctor think she'll be okay?" I choke out.

"They're optimistic," Tess assures me. "They'll keep her in the hospital to treat her with antibiotics and monitor her oxygen levels. If all goes well, she should go home in a few days. For now, she's in good hands—I promise."

Tears well in my eyes as I step into my shorts, trying to steady my hands. "Where's my dad?"

He should be in town, but with his demanding work schedule, he still has a nurse stay overnight to watch over Mama—just in case something goes wrong, as it did tonight.

"He's with your mom. She dozed off shortly after the doctor left, and he didn't want to leave her side, so he asked me to call you."

The weight of guilt pins me in place, making it hard to breathe.

I wasn't there when Mama needed me, and it hurts in ways I can't fully describe. Rationally, I know being there sooner wouldn't have changed anything, but the helplessness still presses heavily on my chest.

I let out a sigh of relief. "Alright, I'm on my way."

"See you soon, sweetie," Tess says before hanging up.

I stand frozen, my phone and T-shirt still clutched in my hands. My mind races through the tasks ahead.

Just as the dread threatens to crush me, I glance up and see Walker striding toward me. In an instant, he's holding me close, murmuring words of comfort as I wrap my arms around his waist and bury my face in his chest, inhaling his familiar scent of leather and cedar. He may not know the details, but he heard enough of my side of the conversation to figure out my mom is in the hospital. It means everything that his first instinct was to comfort me when I needed him most.

He draws back, wiping a tear from my face. "Everything will be okay, sweetheart. I promise." He releases the shirt still gripped in my hand and gently pulls it over my head, guiding my arms through.

As I stare into his earnest brown eyes, I'm struck with the realization that he's become my safe haven—an anchor in a storm, the one I can cling to when my world is unraveling, trusting he'll keep us both afloat until I'm able to stand on my own again.

"Let's get you to the hospital so you can see your mom, okay?"

I nod. "Thank you, Walker."

"Always," he states.

There's no question in my mind that he means it.

CHAPTER 25

Good Intentions Paved With Secrets

Birdie

B Y THE TIME WE PULL UP TO BIG SKY MEDICAL CENTER, my stomach is in knots. Walker finds a spot near the entrance, and we rush inside, nodding at the security guard manning the front desk. Walker keeps his fingers laced through mine as we walk down the hall, his steady presence grounding me.

As we turn the corner leading to the medical wing, I spot my dad standing outside what must be Mama's room. He's holding a cup of coffee, finishing a conversation with a nurse who hands him a blanket before walking away.

"Dad," I call out, waving when he turns.

He gives me a feeble smile, and I take in his wrinkled shirt and the dark circles under his eyes.

"Hi, kiddo. I'm so glad you're here." He tucks the blanket under his arm, freeing a hand to pull me in for a hug.

"Are there any updates on Mama?" I ask.

He shakes his head. "No. The attending physician will check on her during his rounds this afternoon. Otherwise, they're just monitoring her oxygen levels and vital signs. She'll be so glad to see you. Tess got her set up with a show before I sent her home to get some rest. I figured the two of us could manage on our own while we're here." He glances at Walker standing beside me. "I'm assuming you're staying too?"

"Yes, sir. I'm not going anywhere as long as Birdie needs me," Walker replies, and my heart swells with gratitude.

"Birdie, can you take this blanket to your mother?" Dad asks, handing it to me. "I need to speak with Walker alone."

I assume he wants help sorting out coverage at the sheriff's office since he won't be in today, and Walker can't fill in.

"Of course. I'll see you in a minute." I squeeze Walker's arm lightly before stepping around them into Mama's room.

She's sitting reclined in the hospital bed, her hair braided over one shoulder and a blanket tucked around her legs. An overbed tray stretches across her lap, where she's propped an iPad playing an episode of *Gilmore Girls*. Thank god for Tess, who must have thought ahead to bring a little comfort from home to help Mama feel more at ease.

When she looks up and spots me, the corners of her lips lift.

"Mama!" I exclaim, rushing to her bedside and bending down to hug her.

"Hi, honey," she says, then gives a weak cough.

"I'm sorry I wasn't here earlier." I drape the second blanket over her legs and settle on the edge of the bed. "How are you doing?"

Another cough rattles through her thin frame, but she still manages to broaden her smile. "I'm b-better, now that you're here."

"Good," I answer, kissing her cheek. "Because I'm not going anywhere until you're discharged."

I texted my boss, Ed, on the way here, giving him a heads-up that I won't be in to work for a few days. Having lost his mom last year, I know he'll understand why I need to be here.

"I'm l-looking forward to it, my sweet girl," Mama says.

My eyes sting with tears. "You really had me worried."

She reaches out a trembling hand and squeezes mine. "Don't w-worry. I intend to be around for a while yet."

Her reassurance eases the tightness in my chest. Despite all the challenges we've faced since her diagnosis, we're extremely lucky she's with us—able to speak, laugh, and do the things she loves, even if in a modified way.

She glances toward the door with a furrowed brow. "Where's your father?"

"He's speaking with Walker, but they should be in soon."

"Walker H-Halstead?"

"Yeah, he's who drove me here. We're kind of dating," I blurt, the words tumbling out before I can stop them. "It's a little complicated, which is why I didn't mention it sooner. But I promise, once you're feeling better, I'll tell you everything."

Mama opens her mouth to speak, but stops, as if reconsidering.

If she has questions or reservations about Walker and me, I have no doubt she'll voice them when she's ready. The truth is, I don't have any answers right now anyway. Walker and I only confessed our feelings yesterday. There hasn't been time to talk about the future or what any of this means. All I know is that we want to be together, and right now, that's more than enough.

I get off the bed and tug the blankets tighter around Mama. "I'm going to check and see what's taking the guys so long. I'll be right back."

"Okay," she says, biting her lip.

I glance into the hallway, frowning when I don't see Dad or Walker. I head to the waiting area at the end of the wing, and when I turn the corner, I find them standing next to the snack station beside a row of chairs. They're alone—Dad's brow is drawn tight, and Walker's stare is unwavering. They're so absorbed in their discussion that they don't seem to notice me.

Curiosity prickles as I drift closer, trying to eavesdrop without giving myself away.

"I'm not hiding this from Birdie anymore," Walker insists, irritation edging his voice. "She deserves the truth, and I'm done keeping secrets from her."

Dad takes off his cowboy hat and rakes a hand through his hair. "She might not take it well."

"You won't know unless you give her the chance," Walker counters. "She has my full support—and her friends' too—but they can't be there for her if they don't understand everything she's been through, and that includes coping with her mom's Parkinson's."

How does he...?

Alarm bells ring in my head as I recall his earlier comment about not wanting any more secrets between us—implying he's kept something from me. Unwilling to endure the suspense any longer, I step forward, determined to get to the bottom of this.

I move to stand between Walker and my dad. "How do you know about my mom's diagnosis?"

They both freeze like deer caught in headlights.

Walker recovers first, clearing his throat before turning to my dad. "Sheriff Matterson, could I have a minute alone with Birdie?"

My dad hesitates before nodding. "Yeah, I think it's best if you two talk first." He turns to me with a somber expression. "Just remember, every decision I've made has been out of love for you and your mother, and I've done my best, given our situation."

I hesitate, taking him in. His eyes plead silently for me to keep an open mind, yet all I feel is confusion.

"I know, Dad, and I love you too," I whisper.

He leans in and presses a kiss to my temple before walking away. As he rounds the corner and disappears from view, Walker looks at me, his shoulders slouched and lips pressed into a thin line, guilt written across his face.

He gestures to a nearby bench. "Mind if we sit?"

I wring my hands. "Sure."

We take a seat, Walker settling in next to me. He takes my hand and rests it in his lap, holding it tight as if I might disappear if he lets go.

I shift to face him. "Could you please tell me what's going on?"

He inhales deeply. "About two years ago, your dad called me into his office and told me about your mom's diagnosis. He had been traveling more than usual and asked if I could help out with the yard and house maintenance."

My hand stiffens beneath his, heat creeping up my neck as I realize how oblivious I've been. I should have asked Dad who was doing the yard work when I first noticed the change. I assumed he was handling it himself or had hired a professional. It never occurred to me that he'd ask Walker. Then again, I should have known he wouldn't let just anyone around the house, not with how adamant he's been about keeping things under wraps.

"Why didn't you tell me?" I ask, unable to mask the pain in my voice.

I talk about Mama often, yet Walker never hinted that he was aware anything was wrong. He had countless chances to come clean, especially over the past few weeks.

"Your dad asked me not to tell anyone—including you," he confesses. "I couldn't risk breaking his trust and losing the chance to help your family. He'd been avoiding the situation, and I wasn't about to let you take on more than you already had."

"Did Mama know?"

I'm assuming that if she did, Dad had asked her to keep it from me too. That could explain why she hesitated after I told her Walker and I were dating.

"Not until a few months ago. She saw me shoveling the driveway from the living room window and asked her nurse to invite me in for hot chocolate. When I spotted a historical romance on the coffee table, I mentioned that my ma loves them too." He smiles wistfully. "Your mom looked sad when she explained that she couldn't read anymore because holding a book had become too difficult. So I offered to read to her. I've stopped by twice a week ever since—usually on nights you're working late or out with the girls."

I blink at him, unsure how to process his latest confession. Mama's always been particular about audiobooks and narrators, which is why she rarely listens to them. But Walker's voice is smooth, steady, with just a hint of huskiness, so it's no wonder she enjoys listening to him read aloud.

My thoughts drift back to our conversation at the drive-in, when I asked if he read romances. This must be what he meant when he responded with *or something*. It also explains the stack of books at his place and why they felt familiar. They're some of the same ones I've noticed on Mama's bedside table in recent months.

Even though I have every reason to be upset at him for hiding this from me, the newest revelation makes it nearly impossible. The man helps run a ranch and is a sheriff's deputy, yet somehow found the time to read to Mama—the woman who means more to me than life itself—and for that, I'm sincerely appreciative.

What I can't figure out is why he did it. I understand him agreeing to handle the yard work, but spending several extra hours each week at my parents' house doesn't make sense without a good reason.

"Has my dad been paying you?" I question, wincing.

It's the only plausible explanation, as much as it pains me to consider the possibility.

Walker leans back, eyebrows shooting up. "Never. Even if he'd offered, I would have declined."

"Okay, so why do it then?" I pause, glancing at the floor. "My dad may be your boss, but he wouldn't have held it against you if you'd turned down an unpaid assignment outside your duties as deputy."

Walker tips my chin, forcing me to meet his chocolate-brown eyes. "I'd hoped you'd have figured that out by now."

I tilt my head, searching his face for answers. "You're going to have to spell it out for me."

I'm suddenly left wondering whether I completely misread the situation and somehow missed the signs that were right in front of me all along.

"It was all for you, Birdie," Walker says reverently.

"How? We've only been together for a few weeks. We were friends before that, sure, but it's not like you really noticed me until we started pretending to date… right?"

"Sweetheart, I was never pretending." Walker trails his knuckles along my cheek, the weight of his gaze holding me in place. "I've wanted you since I started at the sheriff's office. You strolled in wearing a floral sundress with your hair framing your face in loose curls, going on about a gaggle of geese you'd found abandoned on the side of the road and ready to demand your dad track down the person responsible." He chuckles, the corners of his eyes crinkling. "From that moment on, I was starved for your attention, chasing every glimpse of your signature smile and willing to take whatever scraps of your time you'd spare."

My breath hitches, and I'm momentarily speechless. My mind flashes through every time he showed up at the feed store for supplies—conveniently when it was just the two of us so we could chat. How he went out of his way to bring me lunch most days he stopped by, and how he somehow always ended up by my side whenever we were with his family or our friends. I'd chalked it up to him being nice, definitely not that he wanted more than friendship.

I bite back a laugh at the irony, knowing I'd been attracted to him for ages, yet certain he'd never see me that way. Funny how wrong assumptions can be.

"Why didn't you tell me the truth instead of agreeing to our fake dating scheme?" I whisper, tracing the chain of my necklace with shaky fingers.

He leans forward, resting his forehead against mine. "Partly because you friend-zoned me," he says with a quiet laugh. "So when the opportunity to be together came up—even if it was supposed to be pretend—I took it, in case it was my only chance to call you mine."

My cheeks grow warm as I remember how I acted early on. I definitely didn't give Walker any indication that I was interested in him. I'd been naive, letting my assumptions keep me from seeing that the man I'm falling for has wanted me all along.

If I hadn't taken the risk of asking him to give me lessons, we might never have gotten together—and that's a frightening thought. For too long, I've let life guide me when I should have grabbed the reins and called my own shots, unafraid to chase what I want. One thing is for sure: I won't make that mistake again. I'm done sitting on the sidelines of my own story.

Walker's voice breaks through my thoughts, and I lift my eyes to meet him.

"I won't apologize for helping your parents. I never regretted it for a second. However, I am sorry for keeping things from you." He cradles my face between his hands. "I should have been honest about my feelings—and about knowing the truth. What I'm most sorry for is that you had to go through so much on your own, but I promise you'll never have to carry that kind of burden alone again."

"There's nothing to be sorry for, Walker," I murmur, leaning in to brush my lips against his. "You were there for my family when it wasn't your responsibility, and I'll never forget it."

He never should've been responsible for my parents' yard—or any other maintenance on their house, for that matter. Still, I'm endlessly grateful that he stepped up—not for recognition, but because he saw a need and quietly made life easier for us. My dad was wrong to ask him to keep it from me, though I understand why Walker respected his wishes. And knowing that Walker has been keeping Mama company on nights I couldn't erases any lingering frustration over the secrecy.

"Everything I've done was because I wanted to, and I'll continue to be here for whatever you and your mom need." Walker tucks a piece of stray hair behind my ear, his lips curving into a grin.

"You're my endgame, Birdie Mae Matterson. Like I said at the lake I'm in this for the long haul. I'll wait as long as it takes for you to see that I'm all in—today, tomorrow, and always."

The future, once hazy and uncertain, sharpens into focus—one shared with someone generous, kindhearted, and who makes me laugh.

My eyes sting with tears. "I'm speechless… but in the best way possible."

"That's all right, sweetheart. There's no need to rush any decisions. Right now, your focus should be on spending time with your mom and helping her heal," he says, gently wiping a stray tear from my cheek.

I swallow hard, my voice barely audible. "She's never going to get better…"

Yes, the doctors have said the pneumonia should clear up, but the prognosis is inevitable and will continue to take its toll until her body can't fight it anymore.

Walker draws me into his lap and wraps his arms around me. "That doesn't mean there isn't time to make plenty of new memories you can cherish forever." He leans back just enough to meet my gaze.

My lips curve into a faint smile. "You're right about that."

I've been so caught up in the thought of losing Mama someday that I forgot to appreciate the time we still have together. I'm more than ready to be her daughter again rather than her primary caregiver. And I realize now that making that possible means change is long overdue, and it has to start with my dad. While I channeled my grief into tending to Mama, he coped by avoiding the situation. But we've reached a point when pretending that's a solution doesn't benefit anyone.

If I want a chance at true happiness—making my sanctuary official one day and building a future with Walker—I have to take matters into my own hands. That means having the conversation with him that I've avoided since Mama's diagnosis.

I glance at Walker, who's watching me with calm reassurance.

"I've been thinking… once Mama's back home, my dad and I should talk. There's too much that's been left unsaid, and we can't avoid it any longer."

"I think that's the right call," he agrees, gently squeezing my hand. "I'll be here for whatever you need when the time comes. Whether you want me there for moral support or just to listen as you work through your thoughts."

I let out a soft sigh, resting my head against his chest. "Thank you, Walker. I mean it. I don't know what I would have done without you here today."

He brushes a soft kiss to my temple. "I'm exactly where I want to be, sweetheart."

It's then that I know whatever challenges lie ahead, I won't have to face them alone, and that makes all the difference.

CHAPTER 26

Guilty As Charged

Walker

BIRDIE AND I HAVE BEEN AT THE HOSPITAL SINCE HER MOM was admitted this morning. Aside from a quick trip to the cafeteria for lunch and stepping outside for a work call, the sheriff hasn't left his wife's side. It gives me hope that he's capable of changing and putting his family first, like he should have from the beginning.

The doctor came by early this afternoon to check on Elizabeth and confirmed that, as long as her pneumonia continues to respond well to treatment, she'll likely be discharged in a few days. The hospital staff has already given Birdie and her dad permission to stay overnight, so I'm heading to Birdie's place to grab her a change of clothes and feed the animals.

When I reach my truck, I hop into the cab and check my phone. Even though Birdie sent everyone an update this morning, I still have dozens of missed calls and texts from my family, checking in to see how things are going. I had turned it off earlier to avoid causing a distraction. I'm happy to provide them with an update on Birdie's mom, but I won't share her Parkinson's diagnosis. Birdie will have to share when she's ready.

First, I shoot a quick message to Ma letting her know everything's okay and that I'll call with more details later. Then I reply to Briar.

Briar: Please tell me Birdie's mom is all right.

Walker: The doctor said she should be able to go home within a few days if the pneumonia clears up.

Briar: That's a relief. I'll loop in Charlie and Wren.

Walker: Thanks. I'm sure Birdie will appreciate that.

Briar: How are you holding up?

Walker: I'm fine. Just here for whatever she needs.

Briar: She's lucky to have you.

Walker: I'm the lucky one.

I set my phone on the dash, start the engine, and pull out of the parking lot. No doubt when I get to Birdie's, I'll be greeted by a yard full of hangry animals eager to complain about having to wait all day for their next meal.

On my way, I replay the events of this morning. After Birdie overheard her dad and me talking, there was a gut-punching instant when I thought I'd lost her—just as a life together finally felt within reach.

Yet instead of the anger and frustration I expected, she met me with nothing but grace. In hindsight, I should've told her the truth sooner, her father's wishes be damned, but I can't change the past. All I can do is focus on the future. One where we're together and I earn back her trust.

Whatever comes next, Birdie will have me by her side through every high and low—celebrating her successes as if they were my own, wiping away her tears, and building a life together filled with laughter, joy, and endless happiness.

When I finally pull up to her house, I'm not expecting to find Heath's truck parked out front. He'd called earlier, and I planned to check in once I got the animals taken care of, but it appears he might have beat me to it.

He's sitting on the edge of the porch, attempting to feed Logan. The little menace is swatting the bottle away and hissing like Heath has personally offended him. Nugget stands close by, clucking in warning, clearly suspicious of the burly cowboy manhandling one of her babies. Meanwhile, Rory is draped over Heath's other thigh, fast asleep. Nothing fazes that one.

"Hey there, brother. The ranch not keeping you busy enough?" I smirk.

Heath *never* takes time away, not even when he's sick, so I'm beyond shocked to find him here.

He glances up, grunting as he adjusts the bottle in Logan's mouth. "Figured you and Birdie would be at the hospital all day and could use someone stopping by to take care of the animals. I've already made the rounds and am just finishing up by feeding this little troublemaker." He nods at Logan, who's finally settled down long enough to guzzle some milk.

I lower myself to the porch beside him. "How'd you get inside?"

Birdie locked up the house when we left and gave me the key before I left the hospital.

"Briar was tied up picking up Caleb from summer camp, so I

had to call and ask Charlie if there was a spare key hidden some-where. That stubborn woman wouldn't tell me where the damn thing was until I admitted that Peaches likes her more—which, obviously, isn't true," he mutters with a wry grimace.

"You've got to give Charlie credit—she got you good, con-sidering you went along with it," I taunt him.

Heath shoots me a playful glare. "Maybe, but she won't be so smug the next time she asks me for a favor, and I make her work for it."

Nugget waddles over, ruffling her feathers before settling beside me to bask in the sun. I run a hand over her back, and she closes an eye, clucking softly. Apparently, she's decided Heath can be trusted with the kittens without her supervision.

"Well, I appreciate you coming out to help. You didn't have to do that."

Heath raises a brow. "Hell yeah I did. Birdie's your woman, which makes her part of *our* family. That means taking care of her animals when you're tied up handling emergencies."

I gape at him. "Who are you and what have you done with my grumpy-ass brother?"

He rolls his eyes. "Don't be so melodramatic. It's not that big a deal."

"Heath, the only time you ever leave the ranch is for supplies or a late-night drink at the bar." I motion to Logan, who's back to swatting the bottle in his hand. "The last place I'd ever expect you to be is on Birdie's property cuddling with kittens, yet here we are."

"I don't mind the kittens." He nods to Logan. "I've just been thinking it's time for some changes around the ranch."

I reach over to rest my palm over his forehead. "Seriously, are you sick?"

He grumbles, and bats my hand away. "Will you cut that shit out? There's nothing wrong with me. I'm not doing anything drastic like retiring or shutting down the ranch. Just considering bringing on a foreman to handle things when I'm not around. With the business growing so fast and you splitting your time between the ranch and the sheriff's office, I could use the backup."

My mouth falls open in shock as I process what he's said before replying.

"*You* want to hire a foreman? I thought you hated the idea."

The last time I brought it up was two years ago, and Heath had flat-out refused, insisting we could handle the ranch on our own. After my conversation with Birdie, I planned to revisit the idea soon, but I never expected Heath to raise it himself.

"I changed my mind. After our talk the other day, I realized I've been too hard on you, especially when it comes to you being deputy," he admits, rubbing the back of his neck. "I won't lie, I was bitter when you first started volunteering. It felt like you abandoned your responsibilities, and I struggled to understand why it was important to you. However, I've seen the positive impact you've made over the years and how much you've enjoyed it."

"What makes you think that?"

He sets Logan on the porch, and he immediately bounds over to snuggle next to Nugget. Heath then turns his attention back to me.

"After every shift, you have the same contented expression I get after a long day in the fields—exhausted but proud of the work done. I'm bringing on a foreman so you have the freedom to choose your own future, whether that's becoming a full-time deputy or doing something else. You deserve the same choice that Dad gave me, and I'll support whatever decision you make."

I meet his sincere gaze. "You mean that?"

I may not have any concrete plans yet, but knowing he's in my corner no matter what I choose lifts a weight I've carried for years.

Heath claps me on the back, shooting me a pointed look. "Damn straight I do, but that doesn't mean you're off the hook for helping out on nights and weekends during the busy season."

I chuckle, shaking my head. "There's the Heath I know. Don't worry. I love the ranch, and even if I do change careers, I'll still pitch in whenever I can."

"Looks like I couldn't get rid of you even if I tried." He winks, his expression softening after a few seconds. "Now tell me, how's Birdie's mom holding up?"

"She should recover from the pneumonia, but she's been dealing with other health problems for over a decade."

"Damn, I'm sorry to hear that," Heath replies, giving my shoulder a squeeze. "I can't imagine what Birdie and her family have been going through, but whatever it is, I'm glad she's got you by her side to help her through."

"Yes, she does," I state. "There's something else I need to tell you, but it has to stay between us—especially from Ma. It would destroy her if she found out."

Heath cocks his head, sending me a sidelong glance. "Are you about to admit to committing highway robbery or pulling off a bank heist? Because I'm not prepared to hide a fugitive, even if it's my brother." He laughs lightly at the thought.

"It's nothing likely to land me on the wrong side of the law, unfortunately." *Unless we're counting tampering with evidence.* "Birdie and I were faking our relationship to start—well, she was. She'd never dated anyone before and asked me to teach her. I'd wanted her for so long that I suggested we tell everyone we were together so I could keep her close."

Heath lets out a low whistle. "Damn, I figured you'd make a move eventually but didn't think you had it in you to fake a whole damn relationship to pull it off. I'm impressed. You were clearly hooked when you kept going to the feed store every week, loading up on hundreds of dollars of supplies we didn't really need just so you could steal a few minutes alone with her."

"Guilty as charged—and I'd do it all again to end up here."

He studies me, amusement dancing in his eyes as he strokes Rory, who's just stirring awake.

"I take it that means your relationship is legit now?" he asks.

"Yep, Birdie's finally mine," I declare.

I can't stop grinning like a fool, thrilled to stake my claim openly. Nothing has ever felt so right. At this moment it hits me how deep my feelings for her run. I think a part of me has always loved her, and now she holds my whole heart and soul in the palm of her hand. More than ever, it's clear there's no future I want that doesn't include her at my side.

However, I keep my thoughts to myself for now, wanting Birdie to be the first to hear me say the three little words that convey everything I feel for her.

Heath leans back, smiling at me. "I'm really happy for you, Brother."

"Thanks, man. I appreciate it."

It's a relief knowing that I have Heath's full support in not only building a career for myself but, most importantly, a life with Birdie.

CHAPTER 27

Hearts Made Whole

Birdie

It's been a long day, but thankfully, Mama has settled into her hospital room and has spent most of her time sleeping. Dad and I have stayed close by, mostly in silence. We've agreed to wait until we're home to have any serious conversations. For now, I'm setting aside my frustrations and focusing entirely on Mama.

Dad stepped outside to take a call from one of his deputies, and Mama was craving a smoothie, so I ran down to the cafeteria to grab one for her. On my way back, I spot Walker in the hallway a few strides ahead of me. He has a bag slung over his shoulder and is carrying a stack of books in his arms. He'd left earlier to tend to the animals and run some errands, but he promised he'd be back later, and sure enough, here he is.

I don't call out to him. Instead, I slow my steps as he disappears into Mama's room. Once I reach the slightly open doorway, I look inside but keep mostly hidden, wanting to observe their interaction before I join them.

Walker takes a seat beside her hospital bed, setting the books on the chair next to him.

"My ma sent me with some romance books to help pass the time," he explains, leaning over to straighten Mama's blanket.

"Tell h-her thank you. That was v-very kind," she stammers, patting his hand.

We still haven't shared her Parkinson's diagnosis with anyone else yet. Our primary focus has been on getting her well enough to be sent home. Thankfully, the doctor recommended minimizing her interactions to reduce the risk of infection, so we didn't have to come up with another excuse for why she couldn't have visitors. Our friends have been incredibly understanding, though that hasn't stopped them from sending gifts, or in Julie's case, having Walker personally deliver books and a homemade dessert, judging by the see-through container of cookies sitting on the empty chair beside him.

I press myself farther against the wall, and peek my head into the room, hoping to go unnoticed for a little while longer.

"Let's see what we have here," Walker says to Mama, starting with the book on top of the pile. "*The Governess Who Tamed the Duke*. No surprise she included a historical romance—they're her favorites."

"What is i-it about?" Mama asks.

Walker flips the book over to read the blurb. "*When a spirited governess enters the quiet halls of Greyhaven Estate, the brooding Duke of Ashwood is unprepared for her wit and fiery independence. Their stolen moments in shadowed corridors and moonlit gardens defy what's expected of them and toss aside every high rule of society.*" He punctuates each word with a provocative lilt, carrying the same heat as his bedroom voice, but slower, and deliberately measured. "*But when whispers begin to circulate through the ton, they have to decide if being together is worth the price of scandal.*"

Now I see why Mama jumped at the chance to have Walker

read to her. It's far better than hearing it from me or one of her nurses.

When Walker glances up at her, she shakes her head, scrunching her nose. I bite my cheek to stifle a giggle at her unenthusiastic reaction.

"How about we check out what else we've got," he suggests, sliding the first book onto the rolling tray beside him and picking up another. "Next up is *Framed in Heat*, a contemporary romance by the looks of it."

The cover is a soft coral and slate gray, featuring a woman in a light blue blouse standing on a rooftop, her camera held out, facing the skyline, while a man watches beside her.

Walker rests back in his chair as he reads the description. *"Freelancer photographer Riley thought her biggest challenge when she lands a high-profile fashion shoot in Miami would be the scorching sun—not the infuriatingly arrogant designer, Ethan."* He slows his pace, drawing out the building tension. *"From heated arguments on set to unexpected rooftop encounters, sparks turn to desire. But can rivalry blossom into romance amid the chaos of fashion and fame?"*

Mama tilts her head, pinching her lips together.

Walker chuckles when he looks back at her. "Judging by that look, I'm putting this one straight in the no pile." He sets it on top of the last reject. "Why don't we see if there's something here that's more of a slow burn with higher stakes?"

"You k-know me well," Mama says, her hand shaking as she slides it over to give Walker's a squeeze, her eyes sparkling with affection.

His murmured reply is too quiet for me to hear, but it makes Mama laugh. He may have started helping her because of me, but it's obvious he's grown to genuinely care about her, and that means everything to me.

Walker thumbs through the remaining books, a spark of excitement in his eyes when he reaches the last one. "Ah, here we go," he exclaims triumphantly. "This bodyguard romance *Guarded Desire: A Love Story* looks promising," he notes, turning to look at the back.

"*Coleson Hayes built his reputation on discipline. Clients hire him because he doesn't make mistakes, won't cross lines, and never lets emotion interfere with the job. No attachments. No complications. Then he's assigned to Lina Jackson, a woman who tests his patience and whose beauty is as dangerous as her father's enemies. With every glance and brush of her hand, his restraint falters, and when he gives in to a single night of temptation, he's left—*"

I don't catch the rest of Walker's sentence, distracted by the sound of someone clearing their throat behind me. When I turn, I see Nurse Brown standing nearby with her tablet, likely finishing up her rounds before her shift ends.

"Good lord, that man's voice is ridiculously hot," she gushes in a whisper, nodding to Walker. "I could listen to that sultry drawl twenty-four seven and never get enough."

"He's taken," I blurt out.

I blink, heat rising to my cheeks as I realize how possessive I sound.

Nurse Brown flashes me a smirk. "Good for you, girl. He's a total dreamboat. I can see why you're so quick to claim him. If he ever retires the cowboy hat, he could absolutely be a narrator."

I laugh softly. "I'll make sure you're one of the first to know if he ever changes careers."

When my eyes return to Mama's room, I find her smiling at Walker as he opens *Guarded Desire: A Love Story* to the first page. A wave of peace washes over me, and I owe that all to him.

It's been five days since Mama was admitted to the hospital. I've barely left her side, afraid I might miss an update from the doctor.

Luckily, the pneumonia responded well to treatment, and she was finally discharged this morning.

We got back to my parents' house an hour ago, and she's already fast asleep. She was worn out when we arrived and seemed relieved to be back in her own bed.

Walker's working on the ranch today so he couldn't be here, but we're planning to meet up at my place once he's off work. As much as I've loved being with Mama, I'm excited to spend the night at home with him and to see the animals. I've missed them all so much.

I'm curled up in the rocking chair beside Mama's bed, keeping watch over her when my phone buzzes on the armrest.

Backroads & Bad Decisions Group Chat

Briar: Checking in to see how your mom is doing today.

Birdie: She's good. We got home an hour ago, and she's taking a nap now.

Briar: That's a relief. If you need anything, we're just a text away <3

Charlie: Yes! So glad she's settling in at home.

Wren: We sent flowers. They should arrive later today. Lottie insisted on adding a teddy bear because she says everyone needs a snuggle buddy when they're sick.

Birdie: Aw thank you so much. She's the sweetest.

Briar: When your mom's ready for visitors, let us know. Mama Julie's been asking when she can stop by.

Charlie: Especially if that means we can snuggle on the couch like old times and watch Gilmore Girls with her.

Birdie: We'd love to have you all over soon.

The girls have been incredibly supportive, and it's made me see how much I crave that strength and unity in every part of my life—especially as we navigate the later stages of Mama's Parkinson's. I don't want to hide it from them anymore.

I lean my head back and close my eyes. It's been an exhausting week since getting any rest in a hospital is nearly impossible. Thankfully, Walker's been my anchor through it all. He showed up before work every day with two fresh bouquets of wildflowers—one for Mama, and one for me—along with breakfast, Red Vines, and a variety of snacks. On top of all that, he and Heath have been taking care of the animals while I've been away.

In the evenings, he read to Mama while Dad and I got dinner in the cafeteria. I eavesdropped on at least a few chapters a night, and holy toledo, Nurse Brown was right—he makes the dullest sentence sound incredibly provocative, and his voice is downright sinful.

She must have spread the word about him moonlighting as a narrator because when Dad and I returned to her room last night, a group of nurses was huddled outside the door, listening to Walker read a steamy make-out scene. I could have sworn I saw one of them fanning herself.

My eyes flutter open at the sound of approaching footsteps, and I find Dad standing in the doorway, watching me with a somber expression.

"How's she doing?" he whispers, setting a prescription bag from the pharmacy on the dresser.

I stand and cross the room to join him. "She fell asleep pretty quickly. I think the trip back from the hospital left her exhausted."

Like me, he's barely left her side these past few days, except to check in with whichever deputy was covering for him. His entire team, including Walker, has handled everything so he could focus on taking care of his wife, which is what he should have been doing all along.

We have yet to address what I overheard at the hospital the morning Mama was admitted. Not only did he tell Walker about her diagnosis and ask for his help with maintaining the house but he also swore Walker to secrecy—even after he learned we were a couple. It doesn't matter that it started out as a fake relationship. He didn't know that. And while I understand how painful it's been for him to watch Mama's decline, he eventually has to take accountability for the decisions he's made along the way.

As if he can read my mind, Dad asks, "Can we talk?"

"Yeah, I think that's a good idea," I reply, managing a tentative smile.

He gives a small nod and heads down the hall. I linger long enough to check on Mama one more time before easing the door shut and following him into the living room. He settles on the end of the sofa beneath the bay window, sunlight spilling across the hardwood floors. I take a seat beside him, clasping my hands in my lap.

He clears his throat, sending me a cautious glance. "I owe you an apology, Birdie. I never should have asked Walker to keep our arrangement a secret. Hell, I shouldn't have dragged him into this at all. With everything piling up between work, your mother's care, and keeping the house in order, I turned to someone I could trust to help."

I shift to face him, pressing my hands into the couch cushion. "You're right. It was wrong of you to keep it from me. What hurt the most was how intent you were on keeping Mama's diagnosis a secret, yet you went behind my back and told someone I would have given anything to share it with. That decision left me feeling isolated and alone when it could have been used as a segue for us both to strengthen our circle of support."

I understand why he initially wanted to keep Mama's condition under wraps, given all the uncertainties, but having our friends there for us would have made things easier in the long run. Even Mama was eventually open to sharing it, but she respected Dad's wish for privacy.

He sighs, hanging his head in shame. "I'm sorry, kiddo. I haven't been the best husband or father, and there's no excuse. When I met Lizzy, she'd light up every room with that contagious smile of hers. God, she was so pretty, smart as a whip, and loved to dance. Every Friday night we'd drive to a honky-tonk that was an hour from Bluebell, and she'd move across the floor like she owned the place. It made me feel like the luckiest guy alive to have her in my arms." He looks back at me, his eyes glistening with unshed tears, and I scoot closer, taking his trembling hand in mine.

He's never opened up to me like this before. Mama is the sentimental one, constantly reminiscing about her favorite memories.

"When you were little, your mother would put on one of her favorite records, and the three of us would dance around the room for hours. Your laughter echoes like music of its own. We were so damn happy, and then our world came to a halt the week after her fortieth birthday when we were told she had young-onset Parkinson's." He falters as he releases a shaky breath. "I don't think I've ever told you, but we saw five different specialists early on, hoping someone would tell us it was a mistake. Yet every single one confirmed the original diagnosis, and we were left with the reality that she'd eventually lose her ability to dance... to live freely... and eventually be taken from us far too soon."

My chest tightens with a dull ache. "I'm so sorry, Dad."

We've never talked about what it was like for my parents in those early days or how they were told about Mama's diagnosis. I can't imagine how difficult it must have been to sit in a sterile doctor's office, only given a few fleeting moments to absorb life-changing news before I assume he went to see another patient.

"I convinced myself that if I pretended nothing was wrong, life would go on as it had before. But as Lizzy's health began to decline, I was forced to face the harsh reality that she wasn't going to get better, and I'd have to watch the love of my life, my best friend, fade away." He stares out the window, a muscle ticking in his jaw. "I'm not proud of it, but burying myself in work felt easier than facing it head-on. If I stayed busy, I could avoid the grief and fear that threatened to swallow me whole."

"I understand it was difficult, but you haven't been the only one watching someone you love slowly slip away, Dad. She's my best friend too," I say softly.

"If I could do it all over, I would. For starters, I'd make sure you never felt alone in any of this. Asking you to keep this from everyone was wrong," he admits, trying to steady the emotion creeping into his voice. "I thought that if fewer people knew about your mom, I'd be spared the constant questions and conversations that would force me to face it head-on. I was a selfish bastard. There's no other way to put it," he states solemnly. "You deserved your friends' support from day one, and I'm sorry I took that from you."

When navigating a rapidly progressing disease, there's no manual for how to grieve—no reset button for mistakes made, words misspoken, or moments when emotion overtakes reason. The only way to deal with the unimaginable is to lean on each other, offering compassion, patience, and unwavering love—and it begins with letting go of the hurt and resentment I've been holding on to.

I meet his apologetic gaze. "I forgive you, Dad."

A few months ago, I might not have been ready to see things from his perspective. But now, with Walker in my life, I can't fathom the pain of watching him—the person who's supposed to be by my side through it all—slowly fade, while being powerless to stop it. I understand now why Dad immersed himself in work—it was the only part of his life he still had control over. Sure, he could have done things differently, but he was put in an impossible situation with no easy choices. Regardless of what's happened in the past, what matters now is that we move forward together as a family.

"It's not too late to make new memories and treasure the time you have left with Mama," I add, echoing Walker's earlier advice.

Dad nods slowly. "I see that now, and I'm finished living with regret. These past few days, I've done a lot of thinking about how to fix things… and I've decided to retire."

I stare at him, stunned. "Wait… you're stepping down as sheriff?"

His job has been his identity for as long as I can remember, and the thought of him willingly walking away is hard to wrap my mind around.

"Yeah, I am." He shifts in his seat, swallowing hard. "I can't rewrite the past, but I can make sure I show up for your mother from now on. She deserves nothing less. Whatever time she has left will be filled with love, laughter, and dancing again." He shuts his eyes briefly, a wistful smile on his face. "I've drifted in a fog of grief for far too long, and I'm ready to live again—for your mother and for you."

Tears trickle down my cheeks, and I brush them away with the back of my hand. It seems Dad and I are both ready to let go of past regrets and disappointments, eager to start a new chapter. All I've ever wanted is for our family to find a way forward, free from the figurative distance that's kept us apart all these years, and I can hardly believe it's really happening.

I throw my arms around his neck, and he lets out a low grunt before returning the embrace.

"Thank you. Whatever comes next, I know we'll be alright because we have each other."

"We can get through anything as a family," he murmurs in agreement as he wipes away a stray tear from my face. "Though I reckon Walker will be relieved to have more time with you. That man has more than proved he's worthy of your heart."

I smile. "I couldn't be luckier."

Walker has become my North Star, constant and guiding when everything else has felt uncertain. He stood by me long before I knew the meaning of unwavering devotion. I've never been more certain that he's *my* person—the one I want to wake up next to every morning, drift asleep curled in his arms each night, and grow old and gray with.

I've fallen for him, utterly and completely, and I can't wait another day to tell him exactly what he means to me.

CHAPTER 28

Until I Found You

Walker

I'VE BEEN COUNTING DOWN THE HOURS UNTIL I CAN SEE Birdie again. Her mom was discharged from the hospital this afternoon, and though I offered to take the day off from the ranch to help out, she insisted they had it handled.

We planned to meet back at her place once I finished work, but I took off early so I could get here first, prep dinner, and feed the animals before she arrived. After spending a week caring for her mom, I wanted her to have a relaxing evening, being pampered and taken care of for a change.

I've just finished rounding up the geese and ducks into their coop for the night when I glance across the lawn and see Birdie striding toward me. Her hair is pulled into a messy braid, wisps escaping to frame her face, and the fading light skims across her features. God she's stunning.

"Howdy there, Birdie, baby," I call out.

She waves, her vivid blue eyes locking on me like nothing else exists. There's no better feeling in the world.

I lower the bucket of scratch grain to the grass and barely have time to straighten up before she reaches me, slipping her arms around my waist. I return her embrace, resting my hand on her back to draw her closer.

She tips her head to look up at me. "You were supposed to wait so I could help you with the animals."

"I wanted to finish before you got here so I could have you all to myself tonight. Can't say I feel too bad about it now that I have you in my arms." I cup the back of her neck, brushing my thumb just below her ear. "I missed you, baby."

Birdie gives me a quick kiss before pulling back slightly. "I missed you too."

"How's your mom holding up?"

"She's settled in for the evening and roped Dad into watching the first season of *Gilmore Girls*, so it should be a good night." She chuckles.

"What do you say we head inside? I picked up the ingredients for a veggie stir-fry and figured I'd handle dinner while you enjoyed a nice, long bubble bath. You deserve a night to unwind and relax."

"That sounds nice," she murmurs, although there's something in her tone that gives me pause.

Birdie nibbles her bottom lip, as if she has more to say, but doesn't elaborate. It's been a long day, and I don't want to push her, so I go with it.

"Perfect. I'll go get dinner started," I say, lowering my hands from her face.

I start across the lawn, stopping when I glance behind to see Birdie isn't following. She's rooted in place, fingers fiddling with the clasp of her necklace, her shoulders rising and falling with slow, measured breaths.

"I love you," she blurts out, her eyes widening the second the words leave her mouth. "These past few weeks have shown me that you're the one I want to share a future with, and you were right when you said none of this was pretend. What we have is real… more real than anything I've ever felt, and I'm completely, hopelessly yours."

My head spins, her declaration drifting through me like the last of the sunlight slipping through the trees, warm and fleeting. I'm not ready to let this moment go, desperate to confirm it's actually happening.

I step into her space, cradling her face in my palms. "Say it again."

Her mouth curves into a smile. "What we have is real, and I'm hopelessly yours."

"Now the first part," I urge.

Her eyes brighten with understanding, and she lets out a soft laugh. "I love you, Walker Halstead. I love you with everything that I am."

Never have I heard anything sweeter, and I'm so damn overjoyed it's like a dam has burst inside me.

Before I can respond, she rises to kiss me, threading her fingers through my hair. A low groan escapes me as her tongue claims mine. I shift my hands to her waist and hoist her into my arms, the taste of her overriding everything else.

Our lips remain locked as I stride across the lawn toward the house. Raw desire drives me as I carry her up the porch steps, the heat of her body pressed against mine. I swing open the front door and kick my boots off in the entryway as we move down the hall.

When we reach Birdie's room, we're both panting for air as I push her against the nearest wall, bracing my hands on her ass. She frantically tugs at the hem of her shirt, pulling it over her head and tossing it aside. I shift my hold, reaching behind to unclasp her bra and slide it off each shoulder, slowly letting it fall to the floor.

I trail my tongue along her neck, nipping along the curve of her jaw as a shiver runs through her. She digs her nails into my back as she presses herself against my rock-hard cock. With her full breasts on display, I bend down to suck a nipple in my mouth, my teeth grazing the soft flesh.

"Oh. My. Gosh," Birdie cries out as I breathe against her ear. "I need you inside me. Now."

Even now, in the heat of passion, she doesn't swear, and I love her fearless authenticity—how she's finally embracing herself fully, without apology. I love every damn inch of her, and it's past time I *show* her how I feel.

"Hold on, sweetheart," I say before carrying her across the room and setting her next to the bed.

Without prompting, she slides off her shorts and kicks them to the side. Next to go are her panties. She shimmies them past her hips, drawing my gaze to her pussy, already wet for me.

"Lie on the mattress for me," I rasp out.

She does as I ask, her chest heaving as she glances over, waiting for me to join her. I take a moment to appreciate what's in front of me, committing every detail to memory—the way her blonde hair spreads around her head like a halo, the soft curves of her waist.

It occurs to me that every time we've slept together until now has carried some sort of lesson, and I want tonight to be only about losing ourselves in each other, with no agenda or distractions.

Unable to stay away a second longer, I strip off my shirt, followed by my jeans and boxers, and toss them all to the ground. My rigid cock springs free, and Birdie's eyes are glued to mine as I get on the bed and crawl up her body, settling between her thighs.

I look down at her heaving chest, tracing her nipple, then trail my hand down her chest until I get to her stomach, mapping patterns with the pad of my finger. I draw lower, and her breath hitches when I reach the apex of her thighs and dip a finger inside her to discover she's dripping for me.

"Walker," she moans, arching her back.

"You need my cock to fill you up, don't you, baby?" I croon.

She nods as I run the head of my cock through her slit in teasing strokes, letting the shaft drag along her clit, eliciting sounds that leave me barely holding on. I keep my eyes on her as I line up at her entrance, working my hand up and down my shaft as I push in slowly. I lean my forehead against hers, fighting to steady my breath as the sensation of her tightening around me threatens my control.

Birdie gasps as I pull out, then push back in deeper.

"Relax for me. I'm almost all the way in." I lift my head to claim her mouth, relishing her soft sighs as I ease farther inside her.

Once fully seated, I intertwine our fingers and lift her arms above her head, focused on moving slowly, wanting to savor every second. It's the same position I had her in on the dock, but this time, there's only my hands anchoring her in place, fueled by a fierce need to *show* her how much she means to me.

Birdie's fingernails dig into my palms, sending sparks of heat shooting through me.

"I love being with you like this," she pants out, writhing beneath me.

I look her in the eyes. "What else do you love?"

"You," she murmurs. "I love *you*."

I brush back the hair sticking to her face, and she gazes back at me with those big blue eyes as I angle my hips in short, deep thrusts.

"I love you, Birdie."

Thrust.

"It's always been you."

Thrust.

"I've been yours from the start. I was just waiting for you to catch up."

My free hand moves to her clit, teasing it between my fingertips. Her body goes taut as she arches off the bed, squeezing my hand that's still holding hers above the bed, crying out as she tumbles into a free fall. She's never been more captivating, sending me barreling toward my own release. I capture her mouth with mine, craving to be connected in every possible way.

I love Birdie with all that I am. She's become the center of my universe, and I'll spend the rest of my life orbiting around her light, making sure her world shines just as brightly.

CHAPTER 29

Summoned By The Sheriff

Walker

T HE FOLLOWING MORNING, I GET A TEXT FROM SHERIFF Matterson asking me to swing by his office before my shift starts. When I arrive, the door is open, and he's at his desk, thumbing through a file. He glances up as I enter and take a seat.

"Halstead. Thanks for stopping by," he says, pushing his paperwork aside.

"Everything okay, sir?"

His stern features relax as he clears his throat. "There's something important I want to discuss with you, but first, I owe you an apology. I never should've put you in a position where you had to keep secrets from Birdie. That wasn't fair to either of you." He straightens in his chair. "I appreciate everything you've done for our family. I'll never be able to repay you, especially for reading to my wife. She's missed being able to do that on her own, and you've given her back a piece of herself she thought she'd lost for good."

"I'm happy I could do it, but you should know it was all for

Birdie," I answer honestly. "I'd do anything to give her peace of mind and remind her she's not facing this alone."

Sheriff Matterson's lips twitch into a rare, approving smile. "I'm glad she comes first for you. That's the way it should be." He pauses, lowering his gaze. "I'll be the first to admit I've been a lousy husband and father, and I'm committed to turning things around. That means making some big changes."

My brow creases in confusion. "Like what?"

He leans forward, resting his forearms on his desk. "I'm retiring, son. It's high time I prioritize my wife and take care of her the way I should have since her diagnosis—while also giving Birdie the space to reclaim a sense of normalcy. I can't do that if I continue to divide my attention between work and my family."

That's the last thing I expected him to say, but it's about damn time he put them above everything else.

"As much as you'll be missed, I think it's the right decision," I say, rubbing a hand over my stubble. "Have you told Birdie?"

He nods. "I broke the news to her yesterday, but asked her to wait before sharing the specifics. I wanted you to hear it from me first, and I'll tell the rest of the team next week."

Birdie mentioned she and her dad had finally talked, but we got a little sidetracked before getting into the specifics. Then this morning, I let her sleep in while I made her coffee and breakfast and fed the animals before heading here, so we didn't get the chance to discuss it then either. It was probably for the best so she didn't have to stress about keeping the details from me.

"What does this mean for the department?" He's been the sheriff for over thirty years, so it won't be an easy transition, no matter who takes his place.

The deputies who started with him retired years ago. I've been here the longest among the current team, and nothing this drastic has ever happened in all my time here. I wonder if he'll bring in a seasoned deputy from another city to take over. The problem is, there's a good chance they'll want to shake up how things are run, and adapting isn't exactly our strong suit.

"Halstead, are you listening?" I raise my head to look at Sheriff Matterson, who's staring at me with a concerned expression.

"Sorry, can you repeat that?"

A small chuckle rumbles from his chest. "I was asking how you'd feel about stepping in as sheriff."

I blink, pointing at myself. "Are… are you serious?"

"Sure am," he states. "You're the first person who came to mind when I made the decision to retire. You're my most senior deputy, and you care more about Bluebell and its residents than anyone else in the department or someone from out of town ever could."

I'm stunned speechless. I've considered a full-time deputy role, but *sheriff*? I've never considered it a possibility, so I haven't given it much thought. Still, the idea has a certain appeal. With the right processes in place and dependable deputies, it could be a career that lets me get home to Birdie at a decent hour while still helping Heath during the busy season at the ranch. It would also make it easier to keep an eye out for any local animals in need of rescue and prevent Birdie from going rogue to save them and getting herself in trouble again.

I love being a deputy—it gives me the chance to contribute to Bluebell and make a real difference in people's lives. Taking over as sheriff would allow me to have an even greater impact while staying connected to the work I enjoy. There's also reassurance in knowing that if I did take the job, I'd have Heath's full support, and that he'll soon have more help managing the ranch.

Sheriff Matterson studies me, drumming his fingers against his desk. "Don't hurt yourself thinking too hard, son."

I give an incredulous laugh, shaking my head. "You've given me a lot to think about."

"Is taking over as sheriff something you'd be interested in?"

"Yeah, I think I could be, but it's a big decision." I keep my response neutral. "I'll need time to think it over and discuss it with Birdie before I can give you a definitive answer. Right now, her happiness and goals come before mine. She's waited so long to make her animal sanctuary an official nonprofit, and I want to help her get it up and running as soon as possible. She does incredible work and deserves the space and funding to care for the animals without having to cover the costs herself."

I've explored every option to make her dream a reality, but so far, I haven't found a practical solution. One idea was to convert part of Silver Saddle Ranch into a rescue, but she's mentioned wanting space near her house so she doesn't have to relocate the animals already living there. Another idea was to build more sheds in her backyard, but that wouldn't solve the problem of the property being residential.

Hell, I'd buy her all the land she could ever want if I thought she'd let me. As it stands, I know she'd never accept it— not when our relationship is still so new, and she's been so determined to make this happen on her own terms.

Sheriff Matterson falls silent for a moment, tracing a finger along the edge of a photo of Birdie and her mom on his desk.

"I knew she went to great lengths to rescue animals in trouble, but I didn't realize how much she'd given up to do it—or that she planned to turn it into a nonprofit." He draws his hand back to his lap, guilt shadowing his expression. "Birdie's my daughter. I should've been more invested in the things that matter most to her and done more to help her achieve her goals."

A new idea sparks in my mind—one that might actually work if Sheriff Matterson agrees.

"You can still make a difference for her, sir. If Birdie had more land, she could expand her rescue efforts, get the nonprofit approved, and start accepting donations to keep operations running long-term. She thinks she has to make this happen on her own, but we can show her that she doesn't."

He tilts his head, studying me. "What did you have in mind?"

I lean forward, resting my arms on the desk. "Give me a few minutes, and I'll explain."

His gaze softens. "For Birdie, I have all the time in the world."

CHAPTER 30

Good Days Ahead

Birdie

WALKER PICKED ME UP FROM WORK AFTER HIS SHIFT at the sheriff's office, and we're headed to my place for a low-key evening with Nugget and the kittens. He intertwines his hand with mine when I lean my head back against the seat, his other hand resting on the steering wheel.

I break the silence with something that's been on my mind all day. "I want to tell the girls about how our relationship started. I think they deserve to know the truth."

Walker glances over, letting out a low hum. "I think that's a great idea."

"Really?" I ask, raising a brow.

He nods. "Yeah, of course. You know I told Heath, so if you think it's important for your friends to know too, you should absolutely tell them."

He told me about the recent conversation they had, and I'm grateful they had a long-overdue heart-to-heart. In many ways, it was just as important as the talk I had with my dad—finally addressing lingering conflict and long-standing hurt feelings—and I'm relieved they were able to resolve their differences.

"Although I don't think we should tell our parents. Ma may never forgive me for agreeing to our original arrangement," Walker adds, shooting me a wink.

I let out a relieved sigh, glad we're on the same page.

"I agree wholeheartedly," I say.

Before my nerves get the best of me, I pull out my phone and type a message in the group chat, exhaling sharply as I hit send. Maybe it would have been better to tell the girls in person, but this is the easiest way to get it out there, and I'll fill in the details when we're together.

Backroads & Bad Decisions Group Chat

Birdie: So I have something I need to confess…

Charlie: You raided my closest and took my vintage Levi's, didn't you?

Briar: Before you return them, I want a turn. They can be our version of the Sisterhood of the Traveling Pants.

Wren: Wait, are those the ones with the cute patchwork on the back pockets? If so, I call dibs after Briar.

Birdie: I guess I have two things to confess. Yes, I did *borrow* those for a date with Walker because they make my butt look great.

Birdie: But also, Walker and I actually pretended to date at the start because I sort of also asked him to give me bedroom lessons, but we're together for real now, and it's getting serious.

Birdie: Thanks in advance for understanding! K love you all, bye. *kiss face emoji

Charlie is starting a group call...

Call not answered.

Charlie: Birdie Mae Matterson, you will be spilling all the tea later.

Briar: Uh-oh, she used your full government name. You're in big trouble now, Birdie.

Briar: And for the record, I'm pretty sure Walker was never pretending.

Wren: So... does this mean half the group will be sisters eventually?

Briar: We could aim for three quarters. What do you think Charlie? *wink face emoji

Charlie: Never going to happen.

Briar: Never say never.

I glance up just as Walker drives past the turnoff to my place.

"Uh, my house is back there," I remind him, motioning behind us.

He gives me a sidelong glance before returning his focus to the road ahead. "Sorry, I must not have been paying attention. Looks like we're taking the scenic route today."

"I wouldn't exactly call another dirt road *scenic,* but sure," I tease as he takes the next left instead of turning around.

This route will loop us in a wide square before we end up back at my house. We pass by several open pastures and barbed wire fences stretching toward the mountains rising in the distance. The view is striking with the sun hanging low and the sky streaked with soft oranges and pale pinks.

I shift forward in my seat as we near Mr. Grady's property, my stomach dropping when I notice the For Sale signs that have long lined the front lawn are gone. I blink, disbelief tightening my chest, half convinced I'm hallucinating. Even knowing that owning the place was never a real possibility, the loss still stings. I can't help but wonder if another farmer bought it or if it went to an out-of-towner looking for a quiet country homestead.

I'm so wrapped up in my thoughts that I almost miss Walker pulling off the road and into the gravel area in front of the barn on Mr. Grady's property. I frown when I notice the sheriff's truck parked nearby.

I squint and spot my dad leaning against the driver's side with his arms crossed. "Why are we at Mr. Grady's? And what's my dad doing here? Is this about Peaches and Daisy?" I ask, panic creeping into my voice.

He cuts the engine and reaches for my hand, giving a gentle squeeze. "No, baby, it's nothing like that. Your dad wanted to show you something and asked me to bring you here to meet him."

"Oh. What is it?" I ask, catching my bottom lip between my teeth.

A mischievous grin spreads across Walker's face. "Only one way to find out." He gets out of the truck, circles to my side, and opens my door.

"Thanks," I say when he extends his hand and helps me down.

Dad pushes off his truck and walks over to join us. "Howdy there, you two. Appreciate you coming by."

"Of course," Walker replies, tipping his hat.

"Your mother wanted to be here, but she wasn't feeling up to a car ride. Tess is staying with her until I get home," Dad explains.

Now that he's retiring, we won't need nurses around the clock anymore, but the plan is for Tess to keep coming a few times a week, since she's Mama's favorite. It'll also help take some of the pressure off Dad. He's her husband above all, and I want to make sure he has the space to focus on spending quality time with Mama, and not just his role as her caregiver.

"I'm glad she's getting some rest," I reply, planting my hands on my hips. "Now are either of you going to tell me why we're on Mr. Grady's property?"

Dad shoots Walker a knowing glance before turning back to me. "It's not Mr. Grady's anymore, kiddo. It's yours now." He gestures to the surrounding pasture and barn. "Well, once the final papers are signed of course, but Mr. Grady and I shook on it, and he's a man of his word."

My mouth falls open, stunned. "Sorry... I don't understand."

"You've done so much for your mother and me over the years, and we wanted to do something to express our appreciation. We're both incredibly proud of you and everything you've accomplished." He straightens his shoulders, speaking with firm conviction. "When Walker told me how much you wanted this land for your animal rescue and to start a nonprofit, there was no question I had to make your dream come true."

I swore I wasn't going to cry again for a long while after Mama came home from the hospital yesterday, but tears spring in my eyes as I rush into his embrace, throwing my arms around his neck.

I'm utterly stunned by his grand gesture, and it means more than I could ever put into words. It's not just a gift—it's a symbol of a new beginning and a reminder that, despite our ups and downs, he's in my corner. That feeling is worth more than anything money could buy.

"Thank you, Dad," I choke out, lifting my head to meet his tender gaze. "Thank you so much."

He brushes a tear from my cheek. "There's nothing I wouldn't do for you or your mother. You know that, right?'

"I do," I whisper.

And for the first time since Mama's diagnosis upended our lives, I truly mean it.

"We can't wait to see what you do with the place, and whatever else you need along the way, we're here." He gives me another hug before pulling back and glancing at the setting sun. "I'd better head out before it gets dark. I promised your mother I'd swing by the Prickly Pear for that peach cobbler she loves."

"Thanks again, Dad. We'll stop by tomorrow," I say, motioning between Walker and me. "I'd like your input on some early ideas for the new sanctuary."

I've pictured this day for as long as I can remember, and I'm not about to waste a single moment turning it into reality.

"I'd like that," Dad answers with a smile. "See you both then."

"Have a good night," Walker replies with a tip of his head.

"You too, son." Dad gives him an approving nod before meeting my gaze. "You picked a good one, Birdie."

I let out a bubble of laughter, pride swelling in my chest. "I really did."

We watch him get into his car, and as he drives off, Walker winds his arms around me. I lean back against his chest, taking in the property stretching out before us.

"I can't believe this is really all mine," I say softly. "Thank you."

"It was all your Dad," Walker replies, gently rubbing my back.

He may not admit it, but I know he played a big part in making all this possible. From the beginning, he's been the driving force behind turning my hopes and dreams into reality and reminding me that the best parts of life are shared with the people who matter most. He's also shown, by example that the right person will help carry your burdens, not out of obligation but out of love and devotion.

Walker leans down to press a kiss to my hair. "This place is going to be incredible once the renovations are done and it's filled with rescue animals," he says, nodding to the barn.

I tilt my head to glance back at him. "I'm going to need a strong man to help with all the manual labor. You in? A shirt is optional," I tease with a wink.

"With a proposition like that, how could I refuse? Though if I take your dad up on his offer, I'll have to put in nights and weekends around here."

I ease out of his arms, spinning around to face him. "What offer?"

"He asked me to take over as sheriff," Walker explains, his tone measured.

"That's great news," I exclaim, clapping my hands.

He rubs his palm over his jaw. "I told him I'd have to think about it."

I shift back slightly, frowning. "Why?"

It's a once-in-a-lifetime opportunity, one that he'd handle brilliantly, if it's what he wants.

Walker swallows hard, slowly meeting my gaze. "I had to talk with you first. We're a package deal now, and any major decisions I make should be made together."

"I think it's an incredible opportunity to expand your career. You've accomplished so much as a deputy, and this would let you make an even bigger impact in the community. The real question is, do you *want* to be sheriff?"

He stares off in the distance, his expression unreadable as he thinks it over.

The offer must have caught him off guard, given that my dad gave no indication of retiring until this week. Still, there's no denying he's the right man for the job. Walker's been clear that he wants to stop dividing his time between the ranch and the sheriff's office, and this might be the change he's been waiting for. Now that he's talked to Heath, I hope it brought him some clarity as he weighs his next step, especially knowing his brother stands behind him no matter what he decides. More than anything, I want him to be fulfilled and find meaning in whatever he chooses next.

When he finally speaks, he bridges the distance between us. "I do want to be sheriff. It's an unexpected change, but with time, I'd like to think I could grow into the role." He cradles my face in his hands. "But my career's no longer the center of my world. I have something far more important now."

I place a hand on his chest, holding his gaze. "Oh? And what's that?"

He leans close, his lips brushing mine. "You." My breath catches, my fingers tangling in the fabric of his collar. "Plus, someone's got to make sure you stay out of trouble, and what better way to do that than by being sheriff?" he taunts playfully.

I smirk. "And here I was hoping for the chance to add another mug shot to my collection."

A teasing glint lights up his eyes. "I can think of a few ways you could do that and still skip the handcuffs and paperwork."

"I wouldn't mind the handcuffs, *Sheriff*," I murmur, brushing my mouth against his.

"Fuck me," he breathes out. "That title sounds so sexy when you say it."

"I love you, *Sheriff* Halstead. I love you very much."

"I love you too, Birdie, baby," he whispers.

CHAPTER 31

The Beginning Of Forever

Birdie

One Week Later

"**M**AMA, DID YOU WANT MORE SOUP?" I ASK, NODDING to her empty bowl.

She shakes her head, slowly moving her hand to her stomach. "I c-couldn't eat another thing. I'm stuffed."

"Does that mean you're going to pass on the chocolate pudding Julie made for dessert?" I tease, the corners of my mouth lifting.

Her eyes flicker toward the kitchen, her resolve faltering. "I s-suppose a few bites wouldn't hurt."

My smile widens. "I had a feeling you might say that."

"That better mean you're bringing pudding for me too," Charlie pipes up from the recliner. She's moved it several feet from the bed to keep her distance from Logan and Rory, who are curled up asleep on Mama's lap. "Between trying to keep my allergies from flaring and bingeing *Scandal,* I've earned a sweet treat, don't you think?"

A few days ago, I told Walker's family and our friends about Mama's Parkinson's diagnosis. I gave them the chance to ask questions so they had a better picture of what we've been managing on our own, and they wasted no time offering to step up and lend a hand however they can.

Like today, Charlie kept her shop closed so she could be here to introduce Mama to her favorite TV show. In her view, *Gilmore Girls* was far too tame compared to the books Mama reads, and she wanted to be the one to expand her horizons.

"Fine, but only because if you have to get it yourself, you'll complain about missing a scene." I motion to the screen where Olivia Pope has just entered the Oval Office, her gaze fixed on Fitz.

"Thanks. You're a lifesaver," Charlie calls out as I leave the room.

I carry Mama's tray down the hall to the kitchen, where ABBA plays softly on the portable radio Julie brought. She's bustling about, preparing her fourth freezer meal of the day. Meanwhile, Briar and Caleb hover over the kitchen table, folding paper into origami animals they're going to hang in Mama's room. Wren has called me every day to check in and has promised to come visit soon. I've been so amazed at how they've all rallied around me and my parents.

The whole town knows what's going on with Mama now and has responded with genuine concern and kindness. We've received an outpouring of additional meals, flowers, and offers to help in any way we need. Even Mrs. Bixby stopped by with one of her famous veggie lasagnas and a heartfelt apology for opposing my animal sanctuary. Although she seemed relieved to hear that I've acquired more land to expand.

It still feels like a pinch-me moment. I've gone over to Mr. Grady's old property every day since I found out it was mine, and when Heath, Jensen, and Walker removed the fence between the two lots yesterday, that's when the reality started to sink in that it really belongs to me.

"Sweetie, do you think your mom would like some premade strawberry-banana smoothies if I whipped up a few?" Julie asks from the sink.

I place the tray on the nearby counter. "I'm sure she'd enjoy them, but you've already done so much. Between everything you've made and what the neighbors have dropped off, I don't know if we can fit anything else in the freezer."

At this rate, Dad's going to have to invest in a second one just to store it all.

Julie dismisses my concerns with a wave. "Nonsense, I want to do it. And don't worry, I'll make space."

"Best to let her be," Briar adds with a chuckle. "She doesn't know how to take no for an answer."

"Very true," Julie agrees as she rinses a bunch of spinach and pats it dry. She tosses it into a blender already filled with strawberries and bananas.

The front door swinging open cuts our conversation short, and moments later, Walker steps into the kitchen. He's in a pair of Wranglers and a white T-shirt smudged with paint.

"How are my favorite ladies and my favorite nephew doing?" he drawls.

He slides off his work gloves, and tucks them into his back pocket, then strides over to stand beside me. He drapes an arm over my shoulders and kisses my temple.

Mama Julie swats him with a hand towel on her way over to the fridge. "No shoes inside next time." She points at his boots. "I just vacuumed, and I want the Mattersons' house to stay clean for more than five minutes."

Walker ducks his head, a blush creeping up his neck. "Sorry, Ma."

"Uncle Walker, you're silly," Caleb pipes up from the table.

Walker glances over with a raised brow. "How's that, buddy?"

"You said I was your favorite nephew, but I'm your *only* one!" Caleb exclaims, dropping his work-in-progress origami frog and planting his hands on his hips.

Walker smirks. "All the more reason you're my favorite."

Caleb bursts into giggles.

"How are things going outside? I hope no one's trying to outdo each other with their power tools," Briar teases Walker.

Heath, Jensen, and our dads are helping build a ramp out front so it'll be easier for my parents to go on walks around the neighborhood. Mama's been limited to the house and the back-yard for so long and is excited to be able to explore outside in-stead of looking at the same four walls every day. We're not letting a moment go to waste, and moving forward, we will fill her days creating as many new memories as possible while she's still feel-ing up for it.

Walker rolls his eyes, chuckling. "Heath and Jensen were rac-ing to see who could sink the most screws in sixty seconds. Jensen might have been the underdog, but he's shockingly fast when brag-ging rights are on the line."

"He's got a competitive streak, that's for sure," Briar remarks with a smirk.

Caleb tugs at her sleeve, and when she bends down to check on him, he holds out his origami frog and asks her to fix it. With Briar distracted and Julie busy rummaging through the fridge, I take the opportunity to tell Walker what's on my mind before he heads back outside.

I rise on my toes, resting a hand on his shoulder.

"Thank you," I whisper.

He gazes down at me. "For what, sweetheart?"

"For reminding me that I have a whole community behind me, and that I'm not on my own anymore."

He cups my cheek. "You'll never be alone again, baby."

This is the life I've always wanted—surrounded by family and friends, sharing laughter in peaceful moments, and offering strength and courage through every challenge. Whatever the future holds, I know with certainty that I'll have a support system to lean on, and Walker Halstead is at the center of it.

What started as a simple request for some lessons fueled by a few shots of tequila, quickly blossomed into a storybook romance I never saw coming. Little did I know that he believed we belonged together long before I even realized it was a possibility—and that he was prepared to do whatever it took to lasso my heart.

CHAPTER 32

A Lesson In Edging

Walker

"WALKER, PLEASE LET ME COME," BIRDIE CRIES OUT.

She's bent over a tool chest, her arms tied above her head to a metal ring bolted to the closest wooden support beam. Her hair clings to her damp forehead and sweat glistens along the curve of her neck. Her pear-shaped ass is lifted in the air as I fuck her from behind.

"Patience, woman." I give her a light spank on the left cheek. "You're forgetting who's in charge right now, and that to-day's lesson is one hundred and four: edging. It's about control, not instant gratification."

"Not sure that I'm a fan," she mumbles.

God, I love when she's fiery.

I slowly push my cock back inside her, my jaw tightening as I force myself to keep an unhurried pace. She might think the past hour of edging has been torture, but it's been just as brutal on my self-restraint. It's not easy resisting when her pussy is dripping, and she lets out throaty moans whenever I enter her.

We came to the ranch to visit Peaches and Daisy, but I couldn't resist pulling Birdie into the nearest barn and tying her up so she's completely at my mercy. Not when I found the perfect coil of rope to bind her with.

I slide a hand down her front, bringing my fingers to her clit, circling it with just enough pressure to make her shiver under my touch. The rope slightly tugs on her wrists as she leans into me. My pulse races as I revel in her sweet surrender.

She tips her head back, gazing up at me with parted lips.

"You're doing so well, baby," I croon as I continue working her clit between my fingers. "Be my good girl and tell me who's in control."

A wicked glint sparks in her eyes. "You are, *sir*."

Holy fuck. My cock twitches inside her, the title making my blood hot. A reminder that I'm not immune to the burning agony I'm inflicting. Birdie's deliberately taunting me, knowing exactly which buttons to push to make me lose control, and it's close to working.

I wait until she's just on the verge of coming undone before I pull my hand away from her clit.

"Walker. No," Birdie whimpers. "I was so close."

"If you want to come, tell me what I want to hear."

"I'm all yours, Walker, and you're the one calling the shots tonight." She licks her lips, looking at me with wide eyes. "Now *please* let me come."

It's the pleading and the way she calls herself mine that does me in. When I pick up my pace, her slick walls grip me, and my balls tighten as her inner muscles flex around me. Every groan falling from her mouth has me thrusting harder, urgency taking the reins. I'm driven by the obsession to make her addicted to the way I fill her up, unable to think of anything but being stuffed full of my cock.

"Don't stop. Please don't stop," she cries out.

"Not this time," I vow.

Birdie gasps for air as I slam into her—harder, faster—with each pulse pulling us closer, until I can't tell where she ends and I begin. I'm powerless against this woman and bask in the satisfaction that I get to claim her like this for the rest of our days.

She lets out a low, desperate whimper, meeting me thrust for thrust as I adjust my angle, telling me I've hit her most sensitive spot. I drop my head to her shoulder, my brow damp from the exertion. She shudders, her hips jerking involuntarily, but this time, I don't let up.

"Scream my name when you come," I grunt out.

I move my hand back to her clit, rubbing it between my thumb and forefinger, and soon, we're both barreling toward release. Birdie shatters with a force so fierce that another cry tears free, and my name falls from her lips. My own pleasure hits me, and I tense above her, my throat raw and vision blurry.

While her body still hums with euphoria, I untie the rope around her wrists. As it slackens, Birdie falls back into my arms, and I lift her, settling onto the blanket covering the tool chest I'd laid out before we started playing.

"How do you feel?" I ask as I examine her wrists. There are faint marks where the rope pressed into her skin. "We should head back to the loft and clean you up."

Birdie leans against my chest with a contented smile. "I'm fine, I promise. And before you try to tell me otherwise, we're definitely doing that again. I love when you tie me up."

I run a hand along her jawline before kissing her softly. "Whatever you want, Birdie, baby."

I can't bring myself to deny her, and I don't want to. As long as she's happy and safe, I'll give her whatever her heart desires.

She's my sun, brightening every corner of my life, and I'll never take that for granted. That's why I'm already plotting how to make her mine in every way—including legally. I want her to have my last name, leaving no doubt who she belongs to.

EPILOGUE

Our Happily Ever After

Birdie

6 MONTHS LATER

I LEAN BACK IN MY CHAIR, STARING AT THE RING ON MY finger, the pear-shaped diamond catching the last golden rays of light shining through the window.

"I can't b-believe our little girl is getting married tomorrow," Mama says, leaning over to give my hand a squeeze.

"Neither can I," Dad adds from across the table, taking a sip of his whiskey. "We're so happy for you, kiddo."

A smile spreads across my face as I look between them. "Thank you. Having you both there to celebrate with me tomorrow makes it all the more meaningful."

More than words could ever convey.

I glance over at Walker, who's pulling a casserole dish out of the oven. Tonight, he's in dark-wash Wranglers and a crisp white button-down, looking ruggedly handsome. He moved in with me shortly after he became sheriff, and it's been wonderful sharing our lives. Still, there are moments like now, when I can't believe he's mine—and that I'm really his fiancée, at least until tomorrow.

He proposed last month at the lake. I thought we were there for one of our regular picnics, but I was caught by surprise when he dropped to one knee and asked me to be his wife. It was the easiest "yes" I've ever said.

We agreed on a small ceremony at the ranch and had our rehearsal this afternoon with both our families. Some might say we're moving too quickly, but neither of us saw the point in waiting. I've never been more certain that he is my future.

It was also an easy decision, knowing we didn't want to risk Mama missing it. Her health has been holding steady, but it could change at any time, and Walker and I both want her there, fully present, to share our special day. That's why we decided to keep things simple with dinner at our place with my parents tonight. We wanted to add another memory to our ever-growing collection that we can always remember fondly. Thankfully, the Halsteads were supportive about not being here, and Julie even insisted on making the meal so we just had to reheat everything.

"Dinner is served," Walker announces as he crosses the room.

He sets down the dish of vegetable Wellington next to the wild mushroom risotto and the basket of homemade rolls.

"Everything s-smells so good," Mama says.

"I'll fix you a plate," Dad chimes in.

He stands and moves to her side, leaning down to press a gentle kiss on her forehead. Mama gazes up at him, blushing like a schoolgirl, and my heart feels full seeing them so happy.

Dad's retirement was a big adjustment, but he quickly settled into the slower pace. It's been heartwarming to see Mama and his relationship blossom again—watching them laugh at an inside joke or finding them in the living room with Dad cradling her in his arms as he sways to a Frank Sinatra record. On days when Mama is feeling up for it, they take a trip into town and stop by the Prickly Pear for lunch.

They still have neighbors who bring them meals, and the love and support surrounding them has been constant, showing no signs of stopping anytime soon. It's a reminder for Dad that relying on others can be a good thing, especially during hard times.

Walker slides into the seat next to me, scooting my chair closer to his, and he slings his arm around my shoulders.

"Tomorrow i-is going to be wonderful," Mama exclaims, slowly clasping her hands together. "Though I'll b-be sad when it's over."

"My ma said the same thing this afternoon," Walker replies, taking a roll for each of us before handing the bowl to my dad. "I didn't realize you both had so much fun planning the wedding."

"We g-got married at the courthouse," Mama replies, gesturing between her and Dad. "So it was e-exciting putting together a full ceremony with all the little touches."

When I mentioned we wanted to have a small ceremony in the Halsteads' backyard, I was thrilled when both our moms jumped in to help. Julie has spent countless hours at my parents' place over the past few weeks with Mama, planning everything. I've only had to share my preferences for the overall look and feel, but truthfully, I'll be happy with anything they decide.

When we look back on photos of our special day, it will be even more memorable knowing the two women who love Walker and me the most poured their hearts into every detail.

Walker leans in and nuzzles his nose along my ear. "Ready for tomorrow, Mrs. Halstead?" he whispers.

I brush my fingers along his cheek, meeting his gaze. "I've never felt more ready for anything."

I couldn't be more grateful for the life Walker and I have built together, and in less than twenty-four hours, I get to marry him surrounded by everyone we love most. It doesn't get any better than this.

If you loved *Lassoed Love,* be sure to keep reading for an excerpt from my single dad/nanny, age gap, grumpy/sunshine, small town romance: *If You Give a Single Dad a Nanny.*

CHAPTER 1

Dylan

"DADDY, I'M HUNGRY AND BORED," LOLA COMPLAINS. She flits into the kitchen, wearing a rainbow-colored tutu paired with a fuchsia shirt adorned with a unicorn on the front. Her long blonde hair, pulled back into a half pony-tail and accessorized with a sparkly red bow, sways as she spins to the rhythm of the classical music playing in the background.

I chuckle at her dramatics. "I left a bowl of carrot sticks and blueberries on your craft table." I nod to the other side of the room. "You can eat those while you wait for dinner."

It's no easy feat keeping a highly energetic five-year-old entertained.

"I love blueberries," she declares.

"I know you do."

She goes off in search of her snacks, and I turn my focus back to preparing her lunch for school tomorrow. I carefully assemble her lunchbox, filling it with cherry tomatoes, carrot sticks, blueberries, cheddar cheese cubes, hummus, and pita bread cut into the shape of a unicorn. The final touch is a pink sticky note with *have a magical day* written on it.

After putting the packed lunch in the fridge, I gather the ingredients required to make chicken noodle soup for dinner. The life of a single parent requires juggling a never-ending schedule and a list of to-dos, but I wouldn't trade my world for anything. I place the carrots and celery on the counter just as Lola's infectious laughter fills the air. I look up to find her with her face pressed against the sliding glass door, her eyes sparkling with excitement as she surveys the backyard.

"Ladybug, what are you doing? I thought you were hungry."

"I am, but there's a dog rolling around in the snow. He's so cute and fluffy," she exclaims. "Can I go play with him? Pretty please?" She clasps her hands together.

Aside from her unwavering love for unicorns and rainbows, Lola's newfound fixation is *Bluey*, a cartoon dog. While she's been asking for a dog for the past few months, the addition of an imaginary one in our backyard is a recent development.

"Maybe later." I take a knife out to chop the vegetables when I hear the unmistakable sound of barking from outside. I step over to the bay window overlooking our backyard, and lo and behold, there's a medium-sized dog rolling around in the snow with its tongue hanging out.

What the hell is a dog doing in our backyard?

"Isn't he the cutest dog in the whole wide world?" Lola squeals. "He really wants to play with me." She's practically bouncing on her feet with uncontainable anticipation.

"Ladybug, I need you to stay inside. It could be dangerous."

The dog could have rabies. Its erratic behavior definitely seems abnormal.

"He doesn't look dangerous," she states matter-of-factly.

"We're not taking any chances. Stay inside," I instruct in a gentle tone as I put on my shoes.

She folds her arms across her chest, pouting as I open the sliding glass door and step outside.

I stride across the deck, and the dog stops its playful antics, turning my way when it hears me. I note its unique combination of one brown and one blue eye and a distinctive tri-colored coat in white, black, and tan. Despite sharing several characteristics of an Australian Shepherd, this dog is smaller and has a long torso, short legs, and ears that are comically large for its body.

As I approach, a woman's voice grabs my attention.

"Waffles, get back here," the stranger whisper-shouts. "You can't go into other people's yards without an invitation. You're going to get us into trouble."

"What the…" I trail off as I spot a woman with long blonde hair in two fishtail braids, straddling the wooden fence running the perimeter of the left side of my property. I can see the top rung of a ladder on the other side that she must have used to climb over.

Her outfit is vibrant and colorful—a bright pink puffer coat, faded floral overalls, and silver sneakers with ribbon laces. She's most certainly not dressed for a winter in Maine.

"Hi there, new neighbor." She waves at me with a broad smile, losing her balance in the process.

Shit. She's going to fall.

I run down the steps of the deck and race toward her just as her hand slips. I open my arms to catch her, but the force of her falling sends me sprawling backward. The impact knocks the wind out of me, and I grunt when I make contact with the ground.

"Oh, no," the woman cries out as she falls awkwardly on my chest with a thud.

Once I've regained control of my breathing, I prop myself up on my elbow and give her a once-over to make sure she's okay. The last thing I need is for a stranger to complain that they got hurt in my backyard.

Relief washes over me when she finally lifts her head, and I draw in a deep breath as her gaze meets mine. I'm greeted with a captivating combination of one blue and one green eye. She has a pert nose, full, inviting lips and her cheeks are flushed as she looks down at me. I'm struck by the thought that I've never met someone this uniquely beautiful.

"Thanks for catching me." The woman lets out a melodic laugh as she pushes against my chest and stands up.

She has a smudge of yellow paint on her cheek, and I suppress the urge to wipe it off with my thumb. I'm so lost in my admiration that I'm caught off guard when the dog suddenly darts across the yard, heading for the house.

I scramble off the ground and sprint in the same direction. When I get to the backdoor, I find Lola on the ground, giggling uncontrollably while the dog playfully licks her face. I kick my shoes off before going inside and pulling the dog off Lola. She shoots me a disapproving scowl.

Feet slapping against the floor has me turning to find the woman from the backyard has followed me inside, trailing snow and dirt along with her. This is why I've stood my ground when Lola begs me to get a dog. They're messy, unpredictable, and high-maintenance—all things I like to avoid.

I prefer things to be organized and predictable, which is why I thrive when I have a routine and a structured environment. It's especially challenging to adjust to unexpected changes.

"Oh gosh, Waffles, what have you gotten yourself into now?" The woman puts her hands on her hips like she's scolding a child.

"Your dog scared my daughter," I say with concern, gesturing to the furry culprit.

"No, he didn't, Daddy," Lola chimes in. "Waffles was just giving me kisses, weren't you, boy?" She rewards the mutt with a good scratch behind the ear, and he thumps his tail, reveling in the attention.

I wince at the obscene amount of hair now on Lola's clothes. This is great. She's already calling the dog by its name. Next thing I know, she's going to invite him over for a playdate.

I pinch the bridge of my nose, praying for patience. Dealing with a pair of intruders before dinner wasn't on tonight's schedule.

"Waffles is completely harmless," the stranger says. "He was just eager to meet his new neighbors."

"Who are you?" I tilt my head at her.

This woman might be attractive, but her lack of manners

and careless attitude are bothersome. She's making herself right at home, without considering the possible intrusion she's caused by coming into someone's house uninvited.

"Oh, sorry, I forgot to introduce myself. I'm Marlow Taylor," she says with a smile, her eyes bright. "We moved into the pink house next door a couple of days ago. It was a last-minute decision," she rambles, "but as soon as I saw it posted online, I knew we had to live there."

I stare at her outstretched hand, reluctant to accept the gesture. Despite my irritation, her presence sparks an unfamiliar fluttering in my stomach.

"Tell me, Marlow, is trespassing on other people's property and coming into their homes uninvited a regular pastime for you and Waffles?" My tone is mildly sarcastic as I glance back at her.

A flush of embarrassment spreads across her cheeks, and her eyes dim like a flickering candle as she pulls her hand back to her side. Something unpleasant gnaws at me, and a pang of regret creeps in, but I push it aside.

"You're absolutely right," she acknowledges. "I apologize for Waffles' unruly behavior. I let him out to play in the snow while I unpacked and when I went to check on him, he was gone. He must have escaped through a hole in the fence. I figured I could get him out before you noticed, but that didn't work out so well."

"I hadn't noticed." I deadpan. "How exactly did you plan on getting back to your yard? I saw that you used a ladder to climb over, so I'm assuming it would be tricky to get you and a dog back over the fence without it."

"Honestly, I hadn't thought that far ahead," she admits.

"That's what I thought," I mutter under my breath.

"It's just that Waffles can be quite the handful." She chews her lower lip. "I was worried what kind of trouble he might get into if I left him unsupervised for too long. He's not great at following directions."

That's the understatement of the century.

"He's a dog. He's literally trained to take orders."

"Um… not Waffles," Marlow corrects me hesitantly.

"What does that mean?"

"He's a rescue. I got him from a shelter in Los Angeles and haven't started training him yet." She looks down at the ground, shifting her feet side to side. "He's overly energetic, that's all."

As if he can sense that we're talking about him, Waffles yips while running around Lola. Unfortunately, she finds his antics thoroughly amusing.

"Well, I'd appreciate it if you'd make sure he stays in your yard from now on," I say through gritted teeth. "It's not safe to have an untrained dog around my daughter."

"Obviously," Marlow replies flatly as she watches Waffles and Lola play like they're the best of friends. "Come on Waffles. We've clearly overstayed our welcome."

He ignores her in favor of chasing his tail, while Lola claps her hands. Marlow is unfazed, taking a leash out of her coat pocket and clipping it to Waffles' collar.

I direct them to the front door as Marlow practically drags Waffles out, oblivious to the water, dirt, and dog hair being tracked through my house.

Before they can step outside, Lola darts past me, dropping to the floor to hug Waffles, her arms encircling his neck. "I'm going to miss you." She looks up at Marlow with pleading eyes. "Can I play with Waffles again soon?"

I'm stunned speechless when Marlow crouches down in front of Lola and tucks a piece of stray hair behind her ear. "Of course, you can." She shoots me a glare, daring me to say otherwise. "Besides, I don't think I could keep him away now that he's met you."

"Yay," Lola cheers, bouncing up and down in excitement. "Hey, Marlow?"

"Yeah?"

"Why do you and Waffles have eyes that don't match?"

"Lola, remember our talk about not asking strangers personal questions?" I ask.

"Oh, it's fine." Marlow offers a friendly grin to my curious daughter, before her gaze darts to me. "We're not strangers, *neighbor*. It's called heterochromia," Marlow replies without missing a beat. "We were born with it. When I found Waffles at the shelter, I knew he was special, so I took him home with me."

"I think you're really pretty," Lola whispers.

My daughter's not wrong. Marlow *is* gorgeous, and despite her overly cheerful disposition and blatant disregard for other people's property I can't help but be drawn to her.

Marlow puts her hand over her heart in response to Lola's comment. "And I think you're beautiful." She lightly taps Lola on the nose. "I love your skirt. Rainbows are my favorite," she says in a low voice, like she's sharing a secret.

Lola's eyes widen in disbelief. "Mine too." She beams with pride. "Hey, Marlow, how come you have a flower sticking out of your shirt?"

Sure enough, a single daffodil is poking out of the front pocket of Marlow's overalls. How it survived her climb over the fence, I'll never know.

"I like to paint flowers, and I keep a fresh bouquet of them at home," she explains. "When a certain flower inspires me, I study it before I paint, and I tend to forget that I'm carrying it around." She plucks the flower from her pocket and hands it to Lola. "Would you like this one? It's a daffodil. It represents new beginnings, which I think is fitting for our situation."

"Yes, please." Lola carefully takes the flower from Marlow's hand.

"It might be thirsty, so make sure you keep it in water so it doesn't wilt."

Lola looks up at me. "Daddy, will you get my flower a drink?"

"Sure, ladybug, but let's see Marlow and Waffles out first."

The sooner our uninvited guests leave, the sooner I can get this mess cleaned up and finish getting dinner ready.

"It was such a pleasure to meet you, Lola," Marlow says.

When she stands up, she leans toward me so only I can hear. "I'm not sure I can say the same for you, but thanks for the tour, regardless." She winks. "You shouldn't frown so much or someday your face could get stuck that way." Her tone is teasing.

I raise a brow. "Did you consider I might have one less reason to frown if you and your dog didn't show up unannounced?"

The fluttering sensation is back in my stomach accompanied by a rush of remorse that proves more difficult to stifle than before.

She places her hands on her hips. "Did I not apologize for the intrusion, and promise you it won't happen again?"

"You did," I say, but I have a sneaking suspicion this won't be the last time Waffles and Marlow drop by for an unexpected visit.

Marlow tilts her head as she studies me, and an indecipherable expression crosses her face as if she's trying to read me. I school my expression, a carefully crafted wall firmly in place.

I clear my throat and pointedly glance at the door, hoping she'll take the hint and make her exit. I'm relieved when she finally steps onto the porch, leash in hand.

"Come on, Waffles. Let's go home and get you a treat." He barks with gusto, eagerly following her.

The unconventional duo strolls down the sidewalk as if they don't have a care in the world.

I glance over at the pink house next door and can't help but think that the color of the exterior matches the personality of the woman who now lives in it—obnoxious, quirky and eccentric, yet undeniably intriguing and charismatic.

Surveying the hallway, I notice the trail of melted snow and dirt left behind. It's a visible reminder of the disorder and chaos accompanying someone like Marlow wherever she goes. She leaves her mark, without recognizing the aftermath of her actions. What scares me most is the feeling that she could alter the carefully constructed life I've built for Lola and me if I let my guard down.

"Daddy?" Lola tugs on my pant leg.

"Yes, ladybug?"

"My flower is really thirsty." She holds out her daffodil.

"We can fix that."

She follows me into the kitchen and climbs onto the closest barstool.

I fill a glass halfway with water and set it on the counter for Lola. She triumphantly gives her flower a drink.

"Thanks, Daddy. I hope Waffles comes to visit tomorrow. I miss him already." She sighs.

We'd be much better off if we steered clear of Marlow and her over energetic dog. Although something tells me Lola won't stop asking until she sees her four-legged friend again—and soon.

Read the rest of Dylan & Marlow's story HERE:
https://geni.us/AENanny

Want more Walker & Birdie? Grab the bonus scene for *Lassoed Love* and join Birdie and her friends for a bachelorette night that quickly turns into an impromptu animal rescue. Type this link into the browser to read it:
https://dl.bookfunnel.com/zelghg6u2k

Thanks again for reading *Lassoed Love*. If you enjoyed it, please consider leaving a review on your preferred platform(s) of choice. It's the best compliment I can receive as an author, and it makes it easier for other readers to find my books.

OTHER BOOKS BY ANN EINERSON

All Books Available in Kindle Unlimited

SILVER SADDLE RANCH SERIES

Wrangled Love (Jensen & Briar)
Tension quickly turns to temptation in Bluebell, Montana, between a single dad and his nanny in this steamy age gap, best friend's brother, small-town cowboy romance.

ASPEN GROVE SERIES

If You Give a Single Dad a Nanny (Dylan & Marlow)
A swoon worthy, single dad/nanny, age gap, he's grumpy, she's sunshine, banter-filled spicy small-town romance

If You Give a Billionaire a Bride (Cash & Everly)
A marriage of convenience that starts with a Vegas wedding between a reformed playboy and his best friend's sister in a banter-filled spicy billionaire romance.

If You Give a CEO a Chance (Harrison & Fallon)
An enemies-to-lovers, second-chance love story between a retired hockey player and his new live-in private chef, in a banter-filled spicy romance.

HOLIDAY NOVELLAS

Dreaming of a Cowboy Christmas (Shep & Noelle)
*A spicy, age gap holiday romance between a sunshine girl and a
grumpy cowboy who uses toys as teammates.*

If You Give a Grump a Holiday Wishlist (Presley & Jack)
*A small town, fake dating, one bed,
spicy workplace holiday romance.*

The Holiday Claus (Brooks & Lila)
*A holiday romance where a grumpy billionaire falls for his best
friend's sunshine sister, wrapped in an age gap,
only one bed spicy novella.*

STANDALONES

When You Give a Lawyer a Kiss (Dawson & Reese)
*A workplace romance between a grumpy billionaire and his new
assistant in an age gap, banter-filled, spicy love story.*

The Spotlight (Conway & Sienna)
*A best friend's brother, opposites attract, dating in secret,
spicy rockstar romance.*

ACKNOWLEDGMENTS

So many people made this book possible, and I can't thank you all enough for your love, kindness, and support. *Lassoed Love* wouldn't have been possible without each and every one of you.

To Bryanna—For being my ride-or-die through this wild publishing journey. Part dev editor, part therapist, and full-time work-wife—you've stuck with me through every plot twist, late-night call, and looming deadline. This book exists because you never let me quit and believe in me, even when I didn't always believe in myself.

To KP and Becca—Your feedback is invaluable, and I can't thank you enough for always cheering me on from the sidelines.

To Jess—For being my creative partner from day one. Your talent for bringing each story to life with stunning graphics and videos never fails to inspire me. I'm incredibly lucky to have you on my team.

To Kayla, Madison, Logan, and Chasity—I can't thank you enough for the time, care, and heart you poured into helping bring these characters to life. I'm so grateful for your patience with all my DMs, questions, and concerns. Forever grateful for you both!

To Britt, Jenny, and Virginia—I couldn't have asked for a better editing team. I'm grateful for your expertise and for pushing me to write a story worth reading.

To Ceilidh, Wren, Kat, Charley, Sarah, Hunter, Page, Danie, Nicole, Gabrielle, Tracey, Charlie—Thanks for reading *Lassoed Love* early and providing the honest critique that challenged me to raise the bar and deliver my best work.

To Madison and Chelsea—For creating the most amazing cover. It was love at first sight, and it makes my heart so happy that my readers love it as much as I do.

To my ARC/Content Teams—Thank you for all your

thoughtful messages, posts, stories, reviews, and comments. Your endless love and support never cease to amaze me.

Most importantly, thank **YOU**. There are so many incredible books to choose from and I'm honored you took a chance on Walker & Birdie's story. None of this would be possible without you! Every single tag, share, and DM means the world and motivates me to keep writing on the days I think this might be for nothing. I hope you enjoyed your time in Bluebell, Montana!

ABOUT THE AUTHOR

Ann Einerson is the author of enchanting contemporary romance novels that will keep you hooked until the very last page, complete with heroes who fall hard and the heroines who keep them on their toes. She believes sometimes the best family is the one we find, curiosity is good for the soul, and a good book isn't complete without banter.

You can find Ann surrounded by her ample supply of sticky notes ready for inspiration and ideas. When she's not writing, Ann enjoys spoiling her chatty pet chickens, listening to her dysfunctional playlists, and going for late-night treadmill runs. She lives in Michigan with her husband.

KEEP IN TOUCH WITH ANN EINERSON

Website
www.anneinerson.com

Newsletter
www.anneinerson.com/newsletter-signup

Instagram
www.instagram.com/authoranneinerson

TikTok
www.tiktok.com/@anneinersonbooks

Amazon
www.amazon.com/author/anneinerson

Goodreads
www.goodreads.com/author/show/29752171.Ann_Einerson

www.ingramcontent.com/pod-product-compliance
Lightning Source LLC
Chambersburg PA
CBHW020904060726
47591CB00004B/1082